COLD AS MARBLE

ALSO BY ZOE AARSEN

Light as a Feather

COLD AS MARBLE

BY ZOE AARSEN

SIMON PULSE

NEW YORK LONDON TORONTO SYDNEY NEW DELHI

SIMON PULSE

An imprint of Simon & Schuster Children's Publishing Division
1230 Avenue of the Americas, New York, New York 10020
First Simon Pulse edition October 2019
Text copyright © 2019 by Zoe Aarsen
The author is represented by Wattpad.
Cover illustration copyright © 2019 by Avery Muether
All rights reserved, including the right of reproduction in whole or in part in any form.
SIMON PULSE and colophon are registered trademarks of Simon & Schuster, Inc.
For information about special discounts for bulk purchases, please contact
Simon & Schuster Special Sales at 1-866-506-1949 or business@simonandschuster.com.
The Simon & Schuster Speakers Bureau can bring authors to your live event.
For more information or to book an event contact the Simon & Schuster Speakers Bureau
at 1-866-248-3049 or visit our website at www.simonspeakers.com.
Cover designed by Laura Eckes
Interior designed by Mike Rosamilia
The text of this book was set in Adobe Garamond Pro.
Manufactured in the United States of America
2 4 6 8 10 9 7 5 3 1
Library of Congress Cataloging-in-Publication Data
Names: Aarsen, Zoe, author.
Title: Cold as marble / by Zoe Aarsen.
Description: First Simon Pulse paperback edition. | New York : Simon Pulse, 2019. |
Series: [Light as a feather ; 2]
Identifiers: LCCN 2019020411 (print) | LCCN 2019021939 (eBook) |
ISBN 9781534444317 (hardcover) | ISBN 9781534444300 (paperback) |
ISBN 9781534444324 (eBook)
Classification: LCC PZ7.1.A145 (eBook) | LCC PZ7.1.A145 Col 2019 (print) |
DDC [Fic]—dc23
LC record available at https://lccn.loc.gov/2019020411

FOR CAMRYN C.

CHAPTER 1

STEAM FILLED THE WINDOWS OF MISCHA'S PARKED car as we sat in the parking lot of Tallmadge Park on Christmas Eve, discussing the deadly predicament we were in.

"We have to consider the possibility that we might have been wrong." I chose my words carefully, not wanting to set Mischa's temper ablaze. Once she was upset about something, calming her down was quite a task, and we didn't have any time to spare. Or, more accurately, *she* didn't have any time to spare. "I don't think the locket was connecting Violet to the curse. You might actually . . ." I trailed off, earnestly wishing I didn't have to say the words that followed. "Still be next."

We were the only people at the park, which had been dusted with snow that morning before the temperature dropped into the single digits. Although I'd been back in Willow from my boarding school for two days already, it had taken some effort to convince my mom to allow me to leave the house with a friend. To be fair, my mom's concern that I was going to get myself in more trouble while home for the holidays from the Sheridan School for Girls was a valid one.

In fact, it was a pretty safe assumption that trouble was once again on the horizon ever since Mischa had sent me a letter at school—e-mail was not allowed at Sheridan—in which she'd mentioned that she'd heard Violet was giving kids tarot card readings and was telling them how they were going to die . . . similar to a game of Light as a Feather, Stiff as a Board.

And that game was how this nightmare had started in the first place. At the beginning of the school year, Violet had predicted the deaths of our friends Olivia and Candace with such eerie accuracy that we'd concluded she'd actually *caused* their deaths with her predictions. I'd gotten myself expelled from Willow High School with my attempt to prevent Violet from ever killing anyone else using the same method. I was only back in town for winter break and had been planning on spending my time at home trying to mend my relationship with my mom. Now it seemed like every second that I didn't dedicate to figuring out how and why Violet had killed my friends—and was rumored to still be predicting deaths—increased the probability that Mischa could die at any second.

We had just eight days to stop Violet, and that was *if* Mischa lived past the next new moon.

Mischa stared straight ahead through the windshield for a long moment. "Impossible. It had to be the locket, McKenna. Everything feels normal now. You guys broke the curse. It's over." She hesitated before adding, "Besides, I'm still alive. That has to mean something, right?"

I could understand why Mischa was eager to believe that the curse had been broken. She was supposed to die after Candace, according to the order in which we'd all taken turns playing the game at Olivia's birthday party. Back in September, Violet had just moved to town, and we'd thought we were being nice by inviting the shy new girl to hang out with us. We'd had no idea that we'd welcomed a killer into our social circle.

"Maybe it was never the locket," I mumbled. "And maybe there isn't even an object connecting her to the curse. We could have been wrong about all of it. It's not like Trey and I are experts in ghost stuff or anything."

Desperate to prevent Mischa from dying after Candace drowned in Hawaii in October, my boyfriend Trey and I had researched curses and tried to piece together clues we'd gathered from communicating with spirits using a Ouija board. We'd tried—and mostly failed—to understand messages from the spirit that had been haunting my bedroom since September, which we assumed to be that of my friend Olivia. Olivia had been Violet's first victim in our town, killed in a grisly car crash the night of a big football game. Her visits had grown increasingly violent as she attempted to help us prevent Candace's death. Curiously, she hadn't seemed to follow me to Sheridan, for which I was grateful. It would have been awkward to explain to my roommate the urgency of my need to decipher clues from a vengeful ghost, even though she was a self-professed fan of horror movies and claimed to know a lot about witchcraft. I had assumed Olivia's ghost had abruptly left me alone when I'd left home because we'd broken the curse. But now that I realized Violet had tricked us, I was afraid that Olivia was just fed up by my failure.

"But didn't Father Fahey tell you that an object connected her to the 'other side'?" Mischa asked in a high-pitched voice that suggested she was getting herself worked up. "Why would a priest lie?"

3

I thought back to the day when Trey and I had gone to St. Monica's parish to seek out help from Father Fahey, the priest who had baptized both of us. He'd been reluctant to help us, claiming that he didn't want to involve himself in anything dangerous for fear of jeopardizing the safety of the other priests who lived above the rectory. "He may have just been speculating."

Father Fahey had convinced Trey and me that Violet had acquired her power to issue death sentences from something in the spirit world, and that a tangible object was the conduit of power between the spirits and her. We'd both gotten ourselves into a ton of legal trouble when we stole her locket and led local police on a wild car chase across central Wisconsin. It turns out that parents on school boards don't like when moody guys known for mouthing off to teachers and daughters of women who are considered to be town eccentrics threaten pretty girls on the pom squad.

However, since arriving back at home in Willow, I had two plausible reasons to believe that Trey and I had failed to completely break the curse. The first was that someone had anonymously sent me a mysterious lunar calendar with the dates of Olivia and Candace's deaths circled on it to suggest a pattern, along with obituaries of kids from Lake Forest, Violet's hometown. I would never have guessed that the moon had anything to do with my friends' deaths, but if I was right about the logic suggested by the dates circled on the calendar, Mischa should have died exactly as Violet had predicted: before the most recent new moon.

The second reason I doubted that we'd actually broken Violet's curse had been provided by Mischa, herself. Although Mischa's parents had transferred her out of Willow High School and enrolled her at St. Patrick's in Ortonville to put distance between her and Violet, her boyfriend, Matt, was still at Willow. He was the one who'd told her about the tarot readings that Violet gave in study hall. "I mean, if we really broke the curse, then why is she still making kids play games with her?"

Mischa demanded, "Let me see that moon thing again." I handed her the piece of paper that I'd been carrying around, folded in my back pocket, for the last two days. She squinted at the five columns organized by phases of the moon, and the dates circled in red pen. "This just looks like a bunch of moon shapes and circled dates. Who did you say sent this to you?"

I shrugged. "I don't know. Someone just put it in my mailbox addressed to me the day I got home. There wasn't even any postage on the envelope. But if you look at the dates they circled, it's like they're trying to suggest someone Violet's predicted a death for dies during each moon cycle, between one new moon and the next."

Mischa frowned and raised one eyebrow at me. "No offense, but I think you might be reading too much into this. This just looks like someone's trying to track down a werewolf."

There was another reason why the lunar calendar had me on high alert about Violet's continued game-playing while I'd been away. Students at my boarding school weren't allowed to have cell phones. So from the second my mom had given me back my phone for the duration of my time in Willow, I'd been voraciously research-ing the connection between the moon and witchcraft, as well as paranormal powers. Most practitioners of witchcraft believe that the phases of the moon play a significant role in the success of casting spells. Furthermore, I read that some people who believe in psychic or mystic abilities think that anyone born under a full moon has a greater likelihood of developing those kinds of strengths.

There had been a full moon the night before my twin sister, Jennie, and I were born.

And Olivia's ghost had chosen to haunt *my* bedroom, or perhaps had only been successful in catching *my* attention.

"It's simple," I said, annoyed by Mischa's insistence that I was turning the lunar calendar into a bigger deal than it was. "One death for every cycle of the moon."

"Look, sorry to disrupt your astrological theory, but according to this, I should have died before the new moon on November twenty-sixth. But I was at school that day. In fact, I had to bring a stupid sweet potato casserole for a Thanksgiving potluck lunch. The curse has to be broken. How else could I still be alive unless it skipped me or something?" She wiped her nose on a crumpled tissue from the pocket of her winter jacket and turned the car's engine back on so that she could run the heater.

"Maybe something prevented the curse from reaching you before November twenty-sixth—you know, like some kind of spiritual force field," I suggested. "Think back to last month. Were you doing any-thing to, like, protect yourself?"

Mischa rolled her eyes at me. "You mean like bathing in holy water and wearing garlic around my neck? No. Of course not! I wasn't doing *anything* because I thought I was safe. Besides, I've been kind of busy acclimating to my new life. You're not the only one who got carted off to a new school, remember?"

"I know, I know," I replied, aware that Mischa probably couldn't fathom how much worse my new educational environment was than hers. It wasn't fair of me to even expect her to try. "But seriously, maybe being at St. Patrick's every day is a form of protection. You're basically, like, surrounded by nuns there, right?"

She fell silent for a moment, thinking hard about what might have been safeguarding her life since early November. "The principal, who's a nun, had me come in for an interview before I was allowed to register. She'd heard about both Olivia and Candace dying and wondered if my transferring had something to do with all that. So I told her the truth—I mean, not the whole truth, but that they were my friends, and that I thought one of my classmates in Willow was responsible."

"You told her about the game?" I asked, surprised. Trey and I had been very careful about which adults we'd confided in about our suspicion that Violet had killed my friends. Poor Candace had run her mouth all over town and had been shipped off to the psychiatric ward for treatment before Violet's prediction for her came true in Hawaii. I was very aware that I'd sound like a lunatic too if I went around blabbing about a girl who could dictate exactly how someone would die simply by telling a story.

"I didn't tell her any details!" Mischa insisted. "I actually wanted to get *admitted* to that school, not be banned for life. I just said that we might have unintentionally dabbled in some evil stuff with bad repercussions. She didn't ask any questions. But she did make me go to a special mass before I was allowed to enroll in classes. Kind of extreme, right? Making a Jewish girl attend a Catholic church service?"

"What kind of church service?"

Mischa exclaimed, "I have no idea! Are there different kinds?"

It was just as well that Mischa didn't know what type of mass she was asked to attend since my mom and I had stopped regularly going to church when my twin sister had died eight years earlier. I was hardly an expert in Catholic votive services. "Maybe that was enough to protect you from the curse for the last few weeks. Do you think?"

"No, I don't think!" Mischa snapped. Her lower lip was trembling and tears were forming in the corners of her eyes. "I don't want to think anything's been protecting me! I want to think that you and Trey saved me from whatever Violet did, and it's done. It's over."

Snow flurries blew around Mischa's car as if they were dancing on the bitter winter wind. Telling her how afraid I was that she would die within the next twenty-four hours wasn't going to bring her any comfort, although the thought of my failing to save her chilled me to the bone. Olivia's death had been a surprise, and Candace's had been a sickening confirmation of a hunch. But if Mischa died, it would be due to my inability to outsmart Violet. I had known Mischa since preschool, and we were bound together in this hellish game. If I lost her, I'd be the only person remaining who had been at Olivia's party with Violet the night this all began. The burden of that memory combined with the grief of losing all three of the childhood friends with whom I'd shared that experience would just be too much to bear.

I couldn't explain to Mischa why I was so sure that we'd failed to stop Violet. But now that I was back in Willow, geographically closer to where we'd played the game at the Richmonds' house (as well as closer to Violet), I was positive: Mischa's death was still imminent. It was almost as I if I could smell the doom encircling her, rotten and acrid.

"It's not over. I'm really so sorry, Mischa. Trey and I tried, but it's not. And we don't have a lot of time to end it for real before I go back to school," I said softly.

"What am I supposed to do if we don't figure out how she did this to me—and why—before you leave again?" Fat tears rolled down Mischa's cheeks, and she didn't bother wiping them away. Her voice dropped into a hoarse whisper. "I don't wanna die. Not the way she said I would. Turning blue, with blood vessels bursting in my eyes? And my heart feeling like it's exploding inside my rib cage while I choke?"

I shivered. I remembered that Violet had predicted Mischa would choke, but I hadn't been paying attention to the details when it was Mischa's turn to play dead during the game.

"We're going to figure it out. I promise. We're going to do everything we possibly can in the next eight days to ruin that bitch."

"How?" Mischa asked in between sobs. "She's smarter than us. Look what she's already done. We don't stand a chance against her."

I didn't want Mischa to know that I had my doubts about whether or not we'd be able to take Violet down. Even though she had every right to be terrified about death closing in on her, I needed her to get motivated to fight. Just as important, I was going to need her to drive me to downtown Chicago, since my license had been revoked by Judge Roberts in Shawano County. "Look, here's my plan. We need to figure out how and why Violet predicts deaths for people. If we know that, then we'll have a better shot at making her stop. But now we also need to find out what kept you from dying last month. Maybe someone else died instead of you."

"This is a small town. If someone else in Willow had died in November, I would have heard about it."

"Okay," I said, trying to stay on track. "Then there had to be another reason it skipped you. If someone can help us figure out what that was, then we'll just keep doing it to buy ourselves more time."

Mischa stared straight ahead out the windshield at the snow flurries. "How are we going to do all of that in eight days? We wasted so much time in the fall, all for nothing."

I tried to sound positive. "I said I have a plan, didn't I? There's a bookstore on the North Side of Chicago that specializes in witch-craft stuff."

"I don't have time to read a book!" She waved the lunar calendar at me and crumpled it into a ball. "This says there's another new moon tomorrow! That means I might die *tonight*. Whatever the nuns were doing to protect me back in November, I'm sure they stopped doing it as soon as they let us out for winter break on Friday."

There *was* the issue of the new moon expected to rise in about thirty-six hours, a day and a half. I hadn't mentioned that horrid deadline out of fear that it would freak Mischa out even more than the fact that I was headed back to Sheridan on January first, but I should have known she'd figure that out for herself the instant she looked at the lunar calendar.

"We're not gonna read books, okay? We're going to ask someone who knows a lot more about this kind of stuff than we do for their advice," I said, feeling a strange but familiar tingling sensation spread across my scalp. "My roommate at Sheridan told me about this place, and I looked it up on Yelp. The lady who owns it is supposed to be legit."

I handed my phone to Mischa so that she could read some of the store's reviews from shoppers. I didn't mention to her that saving her life wasn't the only reason I'd been looking for experts in occult practices and paranormal phenomena. I'd been experiencing weird stuff the entire time I'd been at Sheridan, and had been mystified by why new strange things were happening even though Olivia's ghost had completely abandoned me. My roommate at Sheridan claimed to practice Santeria. Alecia had ended up at Sheridan because she'd beaten her stepmother to a pulp, so I kept a safe distance from her, but she'd told me about the store in Chicago when I'd politely asked how she became interested in dark magic (which she spelled in her doodles as "magick").

It was eleven in the morning, and Trey had told me during our most recent phone call that he would be arriving home in Willow that day. My heart fluttered at the possibility of being reunited with him in a matter of hours—an irrepressible burst of joy at an otherwise morbid moment. The last time I'd seen him had been at the Shawano County courthouse, when we'd hastily said good-bye before being sent off to our respective boarding schools. We hadn't even had a chance to kiss before courtroom security guards pulled us apart. Without having my phone with me at Sheridan, I hadn't even been able to look at pictures of him while I was away to keep the details of his face sharp in my mind.

I'd told my mom that Mischa and I were going out for coffee, which wasn't a lie; we just hadn't sat at the coffee shop as I'd maybe allowed Mom to believe we would. While we were there, the coffee shop owner had side-eyed me while the barista, who was a sopho-more at Willow High School, had made our lattes. I hadn't realized how much of a local celebrity I'd become, although I shouldn't have been surprised. The chase on which Trey and I had led police up to White Ridge Lake back in November had been front-page news in the *Willow Gazette*.

"Look, I wish we could just drive to Chicago right now and get started, but I need to get home because I told my mom I wouldn't be gone long. But the store's open until six today," I said, hoping Mischa would understand the speed with which we were going to have to move if we stood any chance of making progress before the next new moon passed through the sky in our region of Wisconsin.

Mischa asked, "Is your mom going to let you leave the house again?"

"Not sure," I said honestly. My mom and her insistence on keeping me on the right side of the law may very well have been just as big an obstacle in us saving Mischa's life as Violet's secrets were. "I'm going to tell her that I need to go Christmas shopping to buy her a gift. I don't know if she'll fall for it, but it's all I've got."

I had to convince my mom to let me out of the house. There was little chance that Sticks & Stones, the occult bookshop that would be our destination later in the day, or any bookshop for that matter, was going to be open on Christmas Day. There was also pretty much no way Mom was going to let me run wild with a friend when she'd already told me she'd invited her boyfriend over for Christmas dinner. Mom had started dating our dog's veterinarian, Glenn, in the weeks I'd been gone. Although she hadn't wanted to talk much about it, it seemed like it had gotten kind of serious, fast.

We were both quiet as Mischa drove me home. She was most

likely wondering if Violet's prediction that she'd choke would come true before December 26.

On State Street, we lingered at the intersection by the shopping center as three consecutive police cars raced past.

"Geez. Has there been a crime wave on Christmas Eve?" I joked. There was practically no crime in Willow, and it was odd to ever see more than one police car at a time except in the parking lot at either the police station or the donut shop managed by Matt Galanis's mom.

"Stephani deMilo ran away from home," Mischa informed me. "At least that's what everyone's been saying. She went out for a run yesterday morning and never came back."

The police cars cleared the intersection, and Mischa gently eased on the gas. "That's weird," I replied. "Stephani doesn't seem like the kind of person who'd run away."

"Yeah, well, I bet it had to do with the whole Shannon-and-Nick thing," Mischa said, confusing me.

"Stephani liked Nick Maxwell?" I guessed. "I thought she'd been going out with Michael Walton's brother since they were in junior high."

"No! God! Have you been living under a rock? Stephani and Shannon were hooking up for, like, a year! It's not like it was some big secret. But then I guess Stephani just found out that Shannon's also been hooking up with Nick, and she went ballistic."

"Stephani deMilo's bi?" I asked in surprise.

Mischa rolled her eyes at me. "Yes, um, *hello*. Did you seriously not know that?"

I didn't remind her that before September, I hadn't ever sat with

13

the popular girls in the cafeteria before, and I knew precious little about Stephani deMilo's life. Before Olivia had welcomed me into her circle, I'd been as out of the loop on the details of the lives of Willow High School's hipster crowd as Principal Nylander probably was. Stephani's family owned one of the biggest commercial farms in the county, and she drove a powder-blue Mini Cooper convertible to school every day. She dyed the tips of her long dark hair royal blue. "I had no idea."

Something about the police searching for Stephani troubled me, even though I had bigger things to worry about than a rich senior with a broken heart.

The sun would be setting in less than six hours. But only the tiniest sliver of a moon would appear in the night sky because tomorrow night there would be a new moon. Everything I'd learned about Violet up until that point led me to believe that Mischa would choke before the sun came up again. Violet didn't like to cut it close with deadlines.

Back in November, when I'd been sent away from Willow, I never would have thought I'd find myself back in this awful situation of racing against time to figure out what Violet had done to my friends—and how. But now it was more urgent than ever to figure it all out, because if I wasn't able to save Mischa's life, I'd feel partially responsible for her death.

CHAPTER 2

I F YOU'RE SERIOUS ABOUT GOING TO THIS SATANIC cult store today, we need to leave Willow by one o'clock. It'll take us over three hours to drive down to Chicago, and it's pointless to go all the way there and not have enough time to ask questions before they close," Mischa warned me as she pulled into our driveway. "Plus, it's supposed to snow more later on."

"Fine. Pick me up at one. And it's not *satanic*," I grumbled. Only as I was about to close the passenger-side door of her car did I happen to notice something strange next door on the front lawn at Trey's house: a FOR SALE sign.

"What the . . ."

Trey hadn't mentioned anything about his parents' intention to sell their house on our phone calls, which made me wonder if he was even aware that his house had been put on the market.

"Is Trey's family moving?" Mischa asked from behind the wheel of her idling car.

"Don't know," I replied as if in a daze. It shouldn't have mattered if the Emorys were moving. Trey was a senior, and I was a junior; under different circumstances, if we were finishing out our high school careers in Willow instead of at boarding schools, we'd both be making plans to leave this neighborhood anyway. But Trey's family had lived next door to my house since we had moved in when I was eight. I couldn't imagine any other family occupying that house, or looking out my bedroom window and seeing someone other than Trey staring back at me from across the yard.

"Very weird," Mischa said. She sounded far away. "My mom always knows about every house for sale in Willow, and she didn't mention that Trey's family was selling."

I mumbled to Mischa that she should come back to pick me up at one. Numbly, I walked across my yard and up the steps to the front door of my house, unable to tear my eyes away from that FOR SALE sign. As I reached into the pocket of my jeans for my key, a strange sensation that had become familiar in the last few weeks came over me. My scalp tingled as if I'd just used peppermint shampoo, and I waited, listening, already knowing what would shortly follow. These creepy but comforting vibes were some of the weird things that had started happening at Sheridan that were making me wonder if I was either going insane, or in need of the advice of an expert in paranormal phenomena.

A soft chorus of harmonic voices chanting, *letter, letter,* rose in volume from a hiss of whispers to a rhythmic cheer inside my head. My eyes drifted toward the metal mailbox mounted on the wall next to the Emorys' front door, and before I even knew what was happening, my feet began moving back down the steps and in that direction. Mail had already been delivered on our block, and I could see envelopes peeking up through the top slot on the mailbox.

One of them must have been what the voices wanted me to see.

As I crossed the patch of grass between our houses, I didn't have to look up and down Martha Road to know that there weren't any people around making the sound I was hearing. The voices had surfaced as soon as I'd arrived at the Sheridan School for Girls in mid-November. At first they'd been as soft as a whisper, so quiet and unintelligible that they kept me awake and staring at the ceiling some nights, wondering if I was totally losing it.

Over the course of the last few weeks, the voices had grown louder, and their messages had been clarified. I didn't know who the voices belonged to or why I was hearing them. However, once they'd risen in volume enough for me to understand them, they seemed to consistently warn me about dangerous situations. My third weekend at Sheridan, I heard the voices caution me against eating the corn bread served in the dining hall, which struck me as odd guidance since that was typically the only edible food at dinnertime. The following Monday morning when I reported for my turn at kitchen duty, I realized why they'd encouraged me to avoid it: There were maggots in the cornmeal.

From that point onward, despite my being a little concerned about my sanity, my ears sought out the comforting guidance of the voices above the din of my school's hallways and classrooms. Even though I was the only one who could hear them, I was convinced they were real, coming from *somewhere*, as real as the crunching of my boots on the frozen grass. However, I hadn't told anyone else about this. I had a sickening hunch that the voices had waited until that year—the year I'd entered into some kind of death game with Violet Simmons—because maybe I had something in common with her.

Something evil. Or at least something dangerous.

As I ascended the front steps to the Emorys' porch and lifted the top of their mailbox, I hoped none of our neighbors on Martha Road happened to be peeking out their windows at that very moment to notice me riffling through my neighbors' mail. There were two Christmas cards, both in bright red envelopes, but neither of them caused a spike in the level of tingling across my scalp. A cable bill, a coupon flyer from the grocery store . . . still, no additional tingling. And then an official-looking letter with a computer-generated address label on stationery from Ekdahl, West & Strohmann, attorneys-at-law.

With that envelope against my fingertips and my eyes focused on the return address, the volume of the voices increased—*the letter, the letter*—and the skin across the top of my head prickled. This was it, what they wanted me to see, but—

I heard a car turn the corner at the end of our block and shoved all of the Emorys' mail except for the letter from the law firm back into the mailbox. As I folded the letter from Ekdahl, West & Strohmann in half and slid it down the back pocket of my jeans, I turned to see Mr. Emory's Hyundai Sonata approaching. It pulled into the Emorys' driveway, and I saw Trey's familiar profile in the back seat.

My heart leapt in my chest when he waved at me. It took every ounce of restraint in my body to keep myself from dashing down the steps to intercept Trey before his dad's car disappeared into the Emorys' garage. As the garage door automatically raised, Trey hopped out of the back seat and trotted over to me, ignoring his mother when she also got out of the car and shouted, "Trey!"

Assuming it would only be a matter of seconds before our respective parents interrupted us, I ran down the cement stairs, and leapt into Trey's arms. He hugged me so tightly it felt as if he might break one of my ribs.

"Hi!" I whispered, feeling my eyes flood with tears of joy.

His warm lips pressed against my mouth, and we kissed as if the world were ending around us, even though his mom was still hollering from the driveway for him to get inside the house.

"I missed you so much," he said, his lips buried in my hair. I leaned back to take a good look at him. As impossible as it may sound, I'd kind of forgotten just how hot he was. His hair, which used to be long enough to tuck behind his ears, had been shaved off, which only served to make his aquamarine eyes look larger and bluer. His face looked leaner, and his jaw was better defined, as if he'd matured into more of a man in the six short weeks he'd been away.

"Same," I managed to say.

"It's, like, amazing to see you. I can't believe we're both here, together again."

Not only had we not seen each other in six weeks, but our phone calls had been monitored by our respective schools, and neither of us had access to e-mail. We'd never had a chance to discuss what we'd done the day we'd stolen Violet's locket because staff members listened in on our conversations on both ends (supposedly to report any mentions of self-harm, but I suspected primarily just to keep tabs on us since we were both considered to be violent). We'd been too shy to express our true feelings for each other over the phone when we knew we had a captive audience. There had been many nights when I'd lain in my bed at Sheridan trying to block out my roommate's snoring, wondering if I'd ever see Trey again.

It was so good to see him that I didn't even want to blink for fear he'd be gone when my eyes reopened.

"Trey! Come on. Inside," Mrs. Emory demanded from where she stood in the driveway. Mr. Emory had already driven the car into the garage, and he and Trey's brother, Eddie, both slammed their respective car doors.

"Just a second, Mom," Trey yelled over his shoulder without tearing his eyes away from mine.

Suddenly unable to bear the thought of spending the afternoon in Chicago with Mischa and without Trey now that he was right in front of me, I blurted, "Try to meet me out here at one o'clock. We have to go somewhere with Mischa."

Mrs. Emory put her hands on her hips and shouted, "Trey, *now!*"

He raised an eyebrow in confusion at me and asked, "Go where? Is this, like, a Christmas thing?"

I shook my head from side to side, frowning. "No. It's, like, a Violet thing."

The brightness in Trey's eyes seemed to dim as the meaning of what I'd just said sunk in. His smile faded.

"What do you—"

"Just go," I urged him as his mother walked toward us. "Don't make your mom mad. But try to meet me out here at one."

Thin, weary-looking Mrs. Emory reached us and pointed toward the open garage door. "McKenna, your mother and I are in agreement that you and Trey will not be spending any time together this week. It's just too soon after the court proceedings to risk the two of you violating the terms of your punishments," she told me.

Trey rolled his eyes. "Seriously, Mary Jane? We just wanted to say hello."

"Need I remind you that you'll be eighteen in seven months? Do you want to be transferred from your school to a prison, Trey? Why don't you give the Simmons family more of a reason to consider a civil suit against our family and see how that turns out?" she snapped at Trey. "Let's go. In the house."

Trey trudged over the lawn to the garage door behind her, and nodded at me over his shoulder, which I understood to mean that he'd do his best to somehow get out of the house at one. I was going to have to find a way to tell him that we hadn't beaten Violet's game and that I was pretty sure the curse on Mischa was still in place. He'd probably driven home with his family that morning from Northern Reserve Academy thinking that if we were lucky, we'd get to spend a few hours in privacy at some point over the next week.

In actuality, we'd be lucky if neither we nor Mischa died before New Year's.

Considering the amount of trouble we'd managed to get into less than two months earlier, our parents were probably wise to try to keep us separated. I'd been charged with failure to observe a traffic signal, exceeding speed limits, resisting arrest, and disorderly conduct. Quite an impressive record for a girl who'd previously never even served a detention in her entire sixteen years of life. I'd been very lucky that Mrs. Emory hadn't added vehicular theft to the list, since technically she had loaned her Honda Civic to Trey and not to me on that fateful day when he and I had sped off to White Ridge Lake to hurl Violet's locket over the side of a bridge.

Behind me, my mom had opened the front door and stood in

the doorway. "Come inside. I've got Christmas carols on and sugar cookies in the oven." She'd been in a turbocharged parenting mood since picking me up from Sheridan. I usually spent lengthy stretches of the summer with my dad and his wife, Rhonda, in Florida, so the weeks that I'd been in boarding school weren't the longest amount of time I'd ever been away from home. But this separation had been particularly hard on both of us because it had been so abrupt, so unexpected. She'd saved trimming the tree for my arrival, and I'd tried to seem excited for her benefit.

In our foyer, I kicked off my boots, buzzing with excitement now that Trey was just a hundred feet away from me inside his own house.

"Mary Jane and I have been speaking, and we think it's best that you and Trey not spend so much time together while you're home for the break. Maybe this summer we'll feel differently. But for now . . ." She drifted off, cutting right to the heart of what she'd been vaguely suggesting for the last two days.

My mom was no dummy. She was still—underneath all of her Christmas spirit—very cross with me for not confiding in her the reason why Trey and I had gotten into so much trouble in November. To anyone who didn't know the details, it seemed like we were just bullying Violet, the new girl who had joined the junior class after moving to our town from the suburbs outside Chicago. It appeared as if for no good reason at all, I had attacked her in the school hallway during the basketball game against Angelica High School, chased her all over school property, knocked her to the ground, and stolen the beloved heirloom locket she'd inherited from her grandmother.

"I know, Mom," I told her gently. "I'm not looking for trouble. I just wanted to say hello. That's all. *Hello.*"

The reaction Candace had gotten from people she'd told about the game we'd played with Violet had served as a warning to me; school administrators had panicked about her mental health, and her mom admitted her to the psychiatric ward of the hospital. Even though my mom took me seriously, no adult was going to believe me that Violet had manifested Olivia's and Candace's deaths.

My mother's mouth remained in a firm, disapproving line. "Well, that's just how things are. I figured you were out there catching your death in the hopes of welcoming him home."

My death already caught me. According to Violet, I'm already dead, I thought grimly.

"I was thinking it might be fun to bake all afternoon. Then you could take some treats back to school with you," Mom said, sounding so enthusiastic about spending the day with me that my stomach soured. Under any other circumstances, I would have loved staying home that afternoon. Baking would have been a perfect way to get her to ease up on letting me see Trey; she never would have denied me a chance to walk next door with a tin of cookies for the Emorys. But the trip to the bookstore couldn't wait another day, and lying to her made me feel lousy.

"Actually," I replied, "would you mind if I go shopping with Mischa this afternoon? I really wanted to get you a better Christmas gift than the crappy pot holder I made for you at school."

Mom playfully mussed with my hair. "Funny, a crappy pot holder is exactly what I wanted for Christmas."

"Mom."

"McKenna, you don't have to get me a gift. My gift is having you home this week."

She was giving me no choice but to take my lie to the next level. It wasn't surprising that she was gently turning down my request, but I had to insist. "Mom, come *on*. After everything I put you through this year, you deserve something better." Then I pulled out my hat trick, since I knew if there was one thing Mom couldn't stand, it was wasting money. "Besides, I didn't want to tell you this, but Mischa helped me order something in advance with her credit card, and we have to pick it up at the store because obviously I couldn't have it shipped to school."

My mom protested, saying that I really shouldn't have gotten her anything, but ultimately said that I could go. Already expecting that we'd be driving home through heavy snow, I didn't mention that it was unlikely I'd get home before nine or ten o'clock that night. She'd be disappointed, I'd be burdened with guilt, and there was simply no avoiding any of it. So instead of trying to prepare her for her inevitable anger with me later that evening, I promised her we'd drive carefully and keep a safe distance from Willow students.

At five minutes before one o'clock, I was surprised to see a Mercedes pull into our driveway instead of the tiny silver GTI that Mischa shared with her older sister. Behind me, in the kitchen, Mom was reminding me for the millionth time to stay out of trouble and wear a hat to avoid getting sick, but I wasn't listening. My heart was beating a little wildly because Mischa was sitting in the passenger seat of the Mercedes . . .

. . . and behind the wheel was Henry Richmond.

Henry, Olivia's hot tennis star of an older brother. Henry, who would have been my date to the Fall Fling if Olivia hadn't died in a horrifying car accident the night of the big football game against

Kenosha. As a ninth grader, I'd watched him move through the hall-ways as if he were the star of a soap opera. He was adored by teachers, admired by other guys, and pursued by girls from every social circle. In September, when he'd asked me if I wanted to go to the Fall Fling with him, it had been just about the most exciting thing that had ever happened to me in my entire life.

I hadn't seen him since Winnebago Days, when I'd been too shy to even say hi because we'd never tied up loose ends about our plans to go to the dance together. It wasn't as if we'd ever hooked up; he'd asked me to the dance as a favor to Olivia, and I'd gotten a little car-ried away in romantic hopefulness before . . . well, before everything terrible had started happening.

Since all of that had happened, I'd fallen in love with Trey.

"Okay, Mom, love you!" I called over my shoulder as I hurried out the front door.

The surprise of seeing the Richmonds' Mercedes in my driveway made me momentarily forget that I'd instructed Trey to try to meet me outside. I climbed into the back seat with my nerves on edge, eager to get away from my house before my mother looked out the window and spotted Mr. Richmond's car. One of the downsides to living in a small town was that my mom knew every kid from the public school system around the same age as me, and their parents. If she saw me and Mischa with Henry, she'd know instantly that we intended to do something related to Violet Simmons that afternoon, which was exactly what Judge Roberts had forbidden me from doing.

"Um, hi," I said, appreciating the warmth inside the car. I'd been in the back seat of that Mercedes before when Henry's dad had hired me to do yard work at the Richmonds' house during the rake sale fund-raiser I'd planned in the fall. The event had been organized to raise money for the junior class ski trip that Violet had promised in her Student Government campaign speech. "Wow. Henry. I was definitely not expecting to see you today."

I overcame my nervousness about seeing my former crush the second I realized that Mischa must have clued him in to all of the suspicious-sounding stuff we'd been up to in order to manifest him being there, in my driveway, that afternoon. She'd probably told him about the game we played with Violet, possibly about the curse, the ghost of his dead sister haunting my bedroom, and a whole bunch of other things that were so creepy and weird that I didn't want the guy I'd lusted after from sixth grade until mid-September to know I'd been doing.

In an affected tone to let her know I was kind of annoyed, I asked, "What's going on, Mischa?"

Mischa replied matter-of-factly with a hint of cheerfulness in her voice, "Look, Henry wants to help, okay? And since we have no idea what we're doing, I figured having one more brain on our team couldn't hurt."

I steadied my temper and asked calmly, "Would you mind driving down the block a little bit so my mom doesn't see your car in the driveway, and then pulling over?"

"Um, sure," Henry said, and put the car into reverse. We drove halfway down Martha Road before he came to a stop along the side of the road and idled.

"Are you *mad*?" Mischa asked, turning to face me over the back seat.

"No," I lied. "Just—how much does Henry know about where we're going today and why we're going there?"

Mischa replied, "I told him everything. Well, everything that I can remember, that is. And only what *I* know, obviously, since you know more than I do."

Henry spoke up. "I hope you're not angry, McKenna. Whatever you guys are doing, I want to help. My parents and I don't know what really happened back in September. All we know for sure is that Olivia's dead, and I heard that before Candace died, she was telling everyone who would listen that the new girl, Violet, had something to do with Olivia's accident. Maybe some people in town didn't take Candace seriously, but my parents did."

"It's cool if you want to help," I said, even though I didn't consider it cool at all. I wasn't sure why I felt so strongly against Henry getting involved. Part of it was an aversion to introducing anyone new to what was an extremely high-stakes situation. The other part of it had something to do with the way Henry's green eyes made my head spin a little as he watched me in the rearview mirror. I guess it wasn't realistic to think I'd stop having a crush on Henry even though I was completely infatuated with Trey. "It's just . . . This is dangerous. I know it all probably sounds ridiculous. But it's very, very real, and your mom and dad already lost one kid."

My attention was caught by the sound of a car approaching us from behind, and I noticed as it passed us that it was Mr. Emory's Hyundai. Although I could see people in the car, I couldn't tell who they were or if the entire family had just left the house. I wondered for a second about whether or not Trey had remembered to try to meet outside at one, but I was pretty sure his mom hadn't given him his phone back as soon as he'd gotten home. I had no way of getting in touch with him and didn't want him to think I'd blown him off if he'd been a few minutes late in trying to escape from his house.

Either Henry wasn't taking me seriously or he was so intent on involving himself in our mission that he wasn't intimidated by the risk. "I have a pretty good idea of what I'm getting myself into. I mean, that moon thing really freaked me out, but I figured if anyone knew what it meant, it would be you."

It took a second for me to realize what he was implying. "You're the one who left that lunar calendar in my mailbox!"

"Yeah, well, I didn't want to leave it with your mom in case she opened it. It's kind of shady-looking, right? I wouldn't want her to think you were into witchcraft or anything." His green eyes opened a little wider, and he waved his hand from Mischa to me and added apologetically, "I mean, unless you *are*—into witchcraft, that is— which would be totally fine, considering our destination today—"

I was about to try to dissuade him when the back door on the other side of the car opened and Trey slid into the seat next to me. "Thanks for waiting," he said, sounding out of breath.

"Oh hey, man," Henry said, not sounding especially happy to see Trey. "Didn't know you'd be joining us today."

"Yeah, neither did I, to be honest," Trey said. Before Henry had graduated, he'd been the kind of overconfident jock who poked fun at moody guys like Trey, who didn't quit fit into the social grid of American high school life. I couldn't recall Henry ever having directly bullied Trey, but the energy inside of the Mercedes definitely changed now that Trey was among us. This was likely because Henry knew that Trey had been driving the car in which Olivia had died, and I doubted either of them felt comfortable about that fact. The

Richmonds hadn't taken legal action against Trey since the accident had occurred during a freak hailstorm, and it had probably been less Trey's fault and more the fault of the truck driver who'd hit Trey's Corolla head-on.

But still, the explanation Trey had given me for why he'd been at the mall in Green Bay, so very far from home, the night he'd offered Olivia the ride home that had resulted in her death had never made sense to me. He'd said he had been looking for spark plugs for Coach Stirling's Cadillac, which he'd been working on with the guys in his shop class, but there were plenty of automotive stores closer to Willow than Green Bay. Being reminded of that again drove a sharp jabbing pain across my rib cage. I couldn't believe that Trey would ever lie to me or intentionally hurt another person, but I would have been hugely relieved if he'd just been able to answer that question. As much as I was desperate to better understand how he'd gotten himself mixed up in Violet's prediction for Olivia's death that night, we were both home from our schools for such a short amount of time that I didn't want to pick a fight with him and risk having to return to Sheridan on bad terms.

"You made it!" I exclaimed. I reached across the back seat and squeezed his hand, simultaneously peeved with Mischa for inviting Henry and delighted that I would get to spend an entire afternoon with Trey.

"My mom is volunteering at the soup kitchen at St. Monica's with my brother's Boy Scout troop," he announced as he fastened his seat belt. "And my dad's supposed to be keeping me on lockdown. But a water pipe just burst at my grandmother's house, and she can't find a plumber who will come over because of the holiday, so my dad's driving up to Keshena to deal with it. Lucky break for me." He grinned at me. "So, where are we going?"

"Sticks & Stones Bookstore in Chicago," Mischa replied. "McKenna thinks we can find out more about how Violet acquired her power to kill people, and if we can figure that out, then we'll have a better shot at breaking the curse."

Trey turned to look at me in confusion. "But the curse is broken."

I shook my head slowly at him. "We're pretty sure it's not."

CHAPTER 3

"GOOD OLD EVANSTON," HENRY MUTTERED AS we passed the exit to the university he had been attending earlier in the fall until Olivia died. It was strange to speculate how different Henry's life would have been by then if Olivia *hadn't* died. He'd have been in a frat, probably going to parties all the time. Maybe he and I would have ended up dating after the Fall Fling, but it was more likely that he would have found a girlfriend on campus.

That didn't matter anymore, though—none of what any of us were *supposed* to be doing with our lives mattered.

The wide streets of the North Side of Chicago were slippery with snow as we drove south on Clark Street in search of Sticks & Stones. Mischa was reading aloud Yelp reviews of the store from self-professed witches insisting that the store's merchandise was hands down the best in the city for casting spells and warding off evil. "If Morgan F. says it has the most mystical vibes in town, then it *must* be legit," she joked.

I was overly alert—jumpy, even—on the drive to Chicago. I suspected we were getting close to our destination when there was a noticeable increase in the number of hipster bars and coffee shops we passed. The windows of overpriced boutiques and bookstores were all decorated for Christmas, and last-minute shoppers hurried along the sidewalks among snow flurries, carrying bags.

"It's got to be right around here," Mischa said, referencing the map on her phone.

Trey tapped on his window and pointed. "That must be it," he said as we passed a store with a display of candles, skulls, and cobwebs in its window. "Unless witchcraft is a booming business in Wrigleyville and they've got competition."

I tapped his palm with my fingertips, kind of wishing we could be alone for a few minutes since we hadn't had a chance to catch up. Mischa and I had filled Trey in on what Violet had been up to since we'd left town in November, but I was dying to ask him what Northern Reserve was like since he'd probably been lying to me on the phone about the conditions there. I was also eager to confide in him about the strange sensations I'd been experiencing since my arrival at Sheridan. Although I definitely didn't want Mischa and Henry to know I'd been hearing inexplicable sounds, Trey had been present a few times when Olivia's ghost had created disturbances in my bedroom, so he'd be less likely to think I'd gone crazy. If my roommate from Sheridan was right and the staff at this store really could answer our questions, I was going to have to find a way to shake off Henry and Mischa so that I could ask someone knowledgeable what was happening to me.

Henry grumbled, "I have no idea where I'm going to be able to park around here."

I thought about asking him to just drop Trey and me off at the store before looking for a spot, but decided that would be rude.

Henry had volunteered to drive, after all. The situation was awkward enough already, with my not knowing whether or not Mischa had told Henry that Trey and I were together. I didn't want it to seem like I was trying to sneak away from him and Mischa, even though I was desperate to get a few minutes alone with a clerk at the bookstore.

Luckily, we found a public parking garage a few blocks away and didn't have to backtrack too far in the bitter cold. We pulled our hats down over our ears and rewrapped our scarves more tightly around our necks. The snow was starting to stick, and we had to trudge through a few inches over sidewalks that had not been cleared because so many stores had already closed for the holiday.

When we reached the small storefront of Sticks & Stones, we stood outside gathering our courage instead of entering. On display in the window was an arrangement of a very commercial-looking hardcover book of spells entitled *Everyday Witchcraft*. A hand-lettered poster was also hung in the window, advertising a mid-winter sale—25 percent off all herbs and candles. Despite all of the paranormal activity I'd been involved with over the last few months, I was intimidated by having to interact with real, live people who claimed to know how to deal with ghosts and evil. It felt like crossing the threshold into the store signified that we were entering into a new phase of this battle with Violet—one that might permanently change our lives.

"So, what's the deal? Did your roommate mention if there's one employee here who specializes in how to deal with bitches who put curses on people? Or can we just ask anyone?" Mischa asked.

I rolled my eyes at her. She was acting so flippant since Henry had entered the scene that she was challenging me to not be resentful that we were far from home in the freezing cold to save her life. "I guess we can ask anyone."

A chime sounded as we opened the creaky front door of the store, and I felt a little more at ease about entering into a store specializing in weird horror items as soon as I heard a song by the Cure playing on the store's sound system. The store was surprisingly busy for Christmas Eve, when I would have thought most people might lay off the witchcraft. A few shoppers were poking around in the herbs and dried goods section at the back, and a woman with frizzy hair was examining a display of polished rocks sorted by color and arranged in heaps atop small plates. She lifted rocks one at a time, whispering something to each and holding it up to her ear as if she was expecting a reply before putting it back onto its respective dish.

"I don't think a rock has ever spoken to me before," Trey whispered to me sarcastically. "Have I been doing something wrong my whole life? I want to know what's up in the world of rocks too. Do you think they gossip?"

"Shh!" I scolded him playfully.

On my left, Mischa seemed to shrink inside her puffy winter jacket. "This place gives me the willies," she said quietly, eyeballing what appeared to be a human skull for sale on a bookshelf.

Once again, I wondered what the heck was wrong with me because although I could understand why the store creeped Mischa out, I was fascinated by everything I saw. Never before in my life had I visited a place like that, which was both cozy and intimidating at the same time. Religious iconography—statues of Buddha, posters of Hindu deities, Tibetan prayer flags, and posters of pentagrams—decorated the space to the extent that it felt cluttered and smaller than it actually was. It smelled of an intoxicating blend of burning sage and sweet incense, and for the first time since arriving home from Sheridan I felt as if it weren't Christmastime at all. There was something strangely familiar about it, kind of like when I'd gone to the top of the John Hancock building as an eighth grader on a class trip after not having been there since first grade.

Henry, who was as wholesome as whipped cream on top of a mug of hot cocoa, with his broad shoulders, dimples, and short auburn hair, wandered along the bookshelves, taking in the titles of books. If he was freaked out, he was doing a good job of hiding it. I never would have expected to find myself in a place selling custom voodoo dolls alongside former tennis star Henry Richmond, but there we were, on Christmas Eve. It was kind of adorable, actually, how effectively he was keeping up the appearance that this was all normal for him. I wondered how long his chill demeanor would last if he were to receive a visit from a ghost.

The young female sales clerk behind the counter greeted us without a smile. She appeared to be the only staff member on duty. "Can I help you?" she asked. She had shoulder-length hair dyed bright red, and wore black cat-eye glasses with little rhinestones on them. Even though she was probably the same age as Henry, she seemed displeased to have a bunch of teenagers who didn't appear to be typical Wiccans milling about her store.

"We were hoping to ask you some questions about curses," Mischa announced, walking right up to the counter confidently as if she were a regular customer. "Like, say, for example, someone put a nasty spell on you, and you wanted to flip it around and put it back on them. How would someone go about putting a curse on another person that was strong enough to kill them?" Mischa asked, casually placing her elbows on the counter and resting her head on her hands.

The sales clerk rolled up the sleeves of her yellow cardigan to reveal colorful tattoos. She raised an eyebrow at Mischa and replied in a bored voice, "We only advise on spell casting for people who know what they're doing. This is serious stuff, and we don't just send amateurs home with powerful magic."

I turned my back to my friends and stepped up to the display of rocks and crystals where the whispering woman had just been standing. On the drive down from Willow, I'd thought my scalp would start tingling as soon as we got close to the store. I had been expecting some kind of corporeal sensation that would confirm we'd find answers here, or that the voices would chime in to encourage me. But even though I felt comfortable in the store, I didn't feel anything special or different at all now that we were here.

However, it felt as if there was something magnetic in one of the piles of rocks drawing me toward the table, so I reached for one of the rocks—a white one, selenite, as identified by a label on the dish. I held it between my fingers and took in its smooth, marbled surface, vaguely aware of the sales clerk asking Mischa to wait a moment while she rang up a customer's purchase.

"What's wrong?" Trey asked me, noticing that I'd stepped away from him and the others.

I shrugged. "Nothing's wrong, it's just . . . nothing's right, either. I thought I'd feel something when we got here, you know? But this—"

"Hey. Step away from the crystals, please." Trey and I both turned in surprise to find that the sales clerk was pointing at us even though her customer was still standing at the counter, fumbling with his wallet.

"I was just looking," I said apologetically. Carefully, I set the piece of selenite in my hand back down on the pile of other white rocks. Almost instantly, I missed the sensation of holding it, as if simply by touching it I'd established a bond with it that now felt as if it was pulling my hand back toward it.

"Nope. No way." The sales clerk, sounding inordinately cross about someone simply touching a rock, stepped out from around the counter and walked briskly toward us. Suddenly, I was terrified that Trey and I had unintentionally done something that was going to get us in even more trouble with the law. "You're draining all of them! You guys are gonna have to leave."

I looked to Mischa and Henry for assistance, and they both looked baffled. "I'm sorry, I don't understand. I wasn't trying to drain them. I wouldn't even know how to drain them if I tried. I'll buy the one I was touching if you want." This was a bluff on my part, since I really didn't want to spend a penny of what little money I had on a shiny, polished rock.

The sales clerk put her hands on her hips. "I don't want you to buy anything, and I don't want you to touch *anything else*. Didn't you see the sign on the door when you came in? Arcanists *not welcome*."

Trey laughed in surprised amusement. "We're not arcanists!" He turned to me to explain with a wicked grin. "'Arcanist' is, like, a Dungeons and Dragons term, or an old-timey word for a magician who recklessly fools around with magic, causing chaos wherever he or she goes."

I wondered what had given the sales clerk the impression that we had anything at all to do with magic. Her assumption was kind of flattering because I thought we just looked like a bunch of teenagers from the suburbs, sticking out on the stylish North Side of Chicago. Mischa wasn't even wearing her fake septum ring.

Henry stepped forward, intending to play the role of peacemaker. He was, after all, supposed to be majoring in political science with a focus on conflict resolution at Northwestern instead of seeking answers to questions at occult bookstores with us. "I think there may be a misunderstanding here. We'd like to ask for your help with a problem we're having, and you might be our only hope."

The sales clerk narrowed her eyes at me as if trying to determine if I was a good witch or a bad witch. I bit my lower lip and tried to smile innocently at her, still not having any idea why she thought I was trying to manipulate the crystals. "It's a matter of life and death," I added, hoping that the urgency of our situation would hold some appeal. Without meaning to, I looked over at Mischa, who leaned against the counter with her arms crossed over her chest.

The sales clerk followed my gaze over to Mischa and then frowned at me. She bit her lower lip, which was coated in maroon matte lipstick, and studied me for a long moment as if I were an optical illusion and she was trying to see more than one shape in my design. "Stay here and don't touch anything. I mean it."

We all dutifully remained where we were, and Mischa joined us as the sales clerk finished processing her customer's transaction. She then leaned forward over the counter and in a raised voice announced, "We're closing in five minutes, everyone. Closing early because of the snow."

After checking out the last two customers who wished to make purchases and shooing them out the door, the sales clerk flipped the OPEN sign hanging in the door to CLOSED and twisted the dead-bolt lock. She didn't look the least bit pleased that we were still standing there when she turned to face us. "Tell me why you're here and don't lie. I'll know if you're lying."

"Do you know the game Light as a Feather, Stiff as a Board?" I asked, cutting to the chase. "Where a storyteller predicts your death, and everyone chants—"

"And a demon lifts the body of whoever's death was just predicted? Yeah, I am familiar with that game. It's really old, dating back to the plague epidemic in seventeenth-century Europe, and probably all the way back to the original plague infestation that killed almost half the population on the continent. Were you stupid enough to play that game?" the sales clerk asked me in a condescending tone.

A demon. I hadn't thought about *demons* as a possibility for what we were dealing with.

"Yeah," Mischa snapped back at her. "We were."

The sales clerk cast an accusatory glance at Henry, who smiled crookedly to exonerate himself.

"Not him," Mischa clarified.

"Not the boys," I added. "A bunch of girls, including myself and my friend here. In the last four months, two of our friends have actually died exactly as someone predicted they would in that game. So we're hoping you might be able to tell us how the girl who told the stories when we played the game was able to make our friends die just like she said they would, and how to stop it from happening again."

The sales clerk look at me dubiously. "You played the game, and people actually *died*?"

39

"The first one to die was my sister," Henry said. His admission surprised the sales clerk, and her eyes revealed a new appreciation for us.

"Geez," she said finally. "That really sucks." She turned back to Mischa. "You said *two* of your friends died after playing the game."

"Yeah, our friend Candace drowned in Hawaii about a month after Olivia, and the way she died also matched her prediction, like, *exactly*," Mischa said.

"We thought we'd ended the game because the girl who was the storyteller always wore this locket, and we had this theory that somehow the locket connected her to her dead grandmother as, like, a channel for communication between the real world and the spirit world. We thought maybe the dead grandmother was the spirit who had given this girl, Violet, the ideas for the death stories that she told during the game," I continued. "But now we're pretty sure we were wrong. Violet's still trying to get people at school to play similar games."

The sales clerk sighed. "I'm not the best person to help you. My boss is in London for the holiday, and she's the real expert around here."

This made me a little disappointed; we needed an expert, not an apprentice. But we didn't have time to be choosy. "Anything you could tell us would help," I begged.

She continued, "Look. At least eighty percent of the people who come in here are just poseurs buying stuff to take home to try to get someone in their office to fall in love with them. It's sad, really. But you guys have a legit paranormal problem on your hands. I'll do what I can to help you. Let's go in the back."

She led us toward the rear of the store, which was lined with shelves of herbs. There were chairs arranged around one of the tables displaying books, and she sat down in one before motioning at us to also take seats.

"I'm Kirsten, by the way," she said, introducing herself. We provided her with our names.

"Henry," she repeated after Henry introduced himself. I was kind of getting the sense that Kirsten was flirting with him. I had also noticed that she kept looking at Mischa, or rather, *around* her, as if Mischa had a spare head growing out of her shoulders.

Kirsten took a deep breath before speaking. "So, you probably already know this, but the original way that kids used to play Light as a Feather, Stiff as a Board was not so different from today. There's historical evidence of the game being played all across Europe in a variety of languages. One kid would lie on the floor, everyone else would place a finger under the body, the story about how that kid would die was told, and everyone would chant."

Mischa interjected, "Yeah, except when we played the game, the person telling the death stories actually saw fire when it was McKenna's turn, which is freaky because—"

I tried to silence her with a frown, but she rolled her eyes at me. Ever coming to my defense, Trey was the one who said sharply, "Don't."

"Come on!" Mischa insisted. "If she's going to help us, she needs to know everything!" I felt my cheeks get hot and looked at my feet, not really wanting to be present while Henry heard the full nerdish details of what we'd done in his family's basement the night of Olivia's birthday party. "It's freaky because McKenna's sister died in a house

41

fire when we were in second grade. It was like Violet saw Jennie's death when she was trying to predict McKenna's. That should have been our first clue that something about Violet was majorly effed up. She'd just moved to our town, and there was no way she could have known that McKenna's house had burned down."

Kirsten's eyes brightened and fixed on me. "Wait a second. Your sister who died—was she a twin?" I nodded. "Identical?" she asked. I nodded again.

"They were super close," Trey added. "They were the kind of twins who made up secret languages and stuff."

She clapped her hands together in glee. "This is amazing. Stay here for a second." She got up from the table and returned to the counter. With a key she wore on a chain around her neck, she unlocked the glass display case of jewelry and withdrew something from it. From underneath the counter, she dug into her handbag and removed what looked like a cigarette lighter. With a small adjustment on the light dimmer, she lowered the lights in the store to create a cozier atmosphere. She then took a small bunch of sage off of the herb shelf at the very back of the store. Returning to the table, she looked directly at me. "Do me a favor and just hold this in your hand."

Into my palm she dropped a cold brass necklace with an oblong rose-colored stone pendant on it. It was heavier than it looked like it would be. "What should I do with it?" I asked.

"Just hold it. Don't worry, it's only a pendulum. Wiccans often use pendulums to pose questions to the spirit world, or the earth goddess, or whatever you believe in. I just want it to pick up some of your energy," Kirsten said as she lit one end of the sage smudge stick on fire and shook it to calm the flame. All of this was making me uncomfortable, as if she was about to ask me if I ever heard voices, as if she knew that I had shown up at Sticks & Stones on a different mission from the others.

I held the chain between two fingers and let the pendant dangle. Smoke curled up from the sage, filling the store with a powerful odor that smelled like fancy pizza with a lot of basil on it. Henry pointed upward at a smoke detector on the ceiling, and asked, "Is that going to be a problem?"

"Oh, that? No, we don't keep batteries in it . . . for this reason," Kirsten said. She stood up and moved the sage in a circular motion in my general direction while quickly whispering unintelligible words under her breath. I was officially starting to get very creeped out.

"If you don't mind my asking, what are you doing?" Mischa asked on my behalf.

Kirsten finished the prayer before replying to her. "Whenever I use a pendulum or perform even the most minor Wiccan task, I just like to cleanse the room and put up a little spiritual safety screen. Nothing too crazy, but, you know. Safety first." Funny she should mention safety, I thought, since she'd just admitted that the store's smoke detector was a decoy.

"When should I stop?" I asked, feeling self-conscious about sitting there holding the pendulum.

"Just let it hang," Kirsten instructed me. "Sometimes—not always, but sometimes—there's a psychic bond between twins that transcends the line between the material and spiritual worlds."

Trey, next to me on the left, rested his hand on my knee and gave it a little squeeze, knowing that I didn't like discussing Jennie with other people.

"She wouldn't want me to say this, but the ghost of our friend has been haunting her bedroom," Mischa told Kirsten. I narrowed my eyes at Mischa and shook my head. I didn't mind so much that she'd told Kirsten, but really wished she had given some thought to the fact that Henry was sitting right there beside her. I didn't know if she'd told Henry about the bedroom hauntings before they picked me up that afternoon, but if my dead sister were haunting one of my friends and they didn't tell me about it, I would probably be pretty angry about that. "They weren't even really that close before Olivia died, but for whatever reason—"

Henry sat up straighter in his chair. "Wait a minute. Olivia's been haunting your bedroom?" he asked, confirming that Mischa must have left that part of the story out earlier that afternoon. He sounded hurt, which was understandable. I even felt a little guilty for not having told him about it in the fall, but it would have been extremely weird to have reached out to him with that news under the circumstances of everything that had happened.

"I thought you said you told Henry everything before you picked me up!" I snapped at Mischa.

Henry blinked twice without moving any other muscles in his body before saying, "My dead sister has been haunting your house?"

Kirsten's eyes danced as if she kind of wished she'd made popcorn for this. "What sorts of things does this Olivia do when she visits you?"

The pendulum in my hand was starting to swing ever so slightly, but I attributed that to the fact that I was moving around a little, anxious about with the direction this adventure had taken. I'd thought we were coming here for answers about Violet, and now I felt as if I was the one being investigated. "Little things, really," I insisted so as to try to downplay the haunting for Henry's benefit. "Like knocking stuff off shelves, turning my music boxes on at night." I didn't want Henry to get the idea that Olivia was roaming around the afterlife in agony, even though my impression was that until I'd left for Sheridan, she'd been plenty pissed off about what Violet had done to her.

"Then how do you know it's Olivia?" Henry asked. "And not just a draft?"

"Oh, she does bigger things, too," Trey said, sounding for a second kind of like he was bragging. "She writes messages on mirrors with lipstick, tries to flip the bed over."

Again trying to downplay Olivia's hostility, I said, "I think mostly she was trying to give me clues about what was going to happen to Candace. Only, it took me too long to figure it out, and I couldn't save her."

Henry looked as if I'd stabbed him right in the gut. "Why your house and not mine? If her spirit isn't at peace, then why didn't she come home?"

I looked to Trey for help, and he shrugged, encouraging me to just tell Henry everything. "She probably wouldn't want you involved in this," I speculated. "That's why I didn't tell you about it sooner. I mean, it sounds crazy, right? And I don't think Olivia would want you getting anywhere near Violet."

"I have a different theory," Kirsten announced. She sat down on her chair again and smiled at me, clasping her hands excitedly. "But first you have to establish rules with the pendulum. Ask it to show you what *yes* looks like."

I looked dubiously at all of my friends, suddenly afraid of what might happen once I started interacting with the object in my hand. "It's all right," Kirsten assured me. "This is a safe store. If we get weird vibes from anyone coming in here, we don't sell to them. My boss is a good witch. We spiritually cleanse this space every day before we open and every night when we close. You're much safer here right now than you were when you played Light as a Feather, Stiff as a Board. Trust me."

I took a deep breath, reaching out to Jennie in my thoughts for protection just in case I was about to get myself into even more seriously deep trouble with the spirit world. "What does *yes* look like?" I asked aloud, feeling like a total weirdo.

Without any movement from my hand to inspire the pendulum to begin swinging, it slowly began rotating in a clockwise motion. "Oh my God." I winced. It gained momentum and broadened the diameter of the circle in which it swung.

"This is crazy!" Kirsten gasped, shaking her head, quite happy with how the pendulum was reacting in my hand. "You're a medium, did you know that? I've never seen a pendulum move like that for anyone before!"

There was fear in Henry and Mischa's eyes, and I suddenly wished I hadn't insisted that we come to the store that day.

CHAPTER 4

M CKENNA'S A *MEDIUM*?" HENRY ASKED. "WHAT does that mean?"

"It just means that for one reason or another, she's more receptive to energy and messages from the spirit world than other people," Kirsten explained. "I think that's why she's the one who received visits from Olivia's ghost. More accurately, Olivia may have tried to connect with all of you, but McKenna was the one who was easiest for her to communicate with."

I don't want to be a medium. I don't want messages from the spirit world, I thought. Henry was staring at me as if I were a monster.

"It's not a bad thing," Kirsten told me, interpreting the look of fright on my face. "It may very likely have something to do with the fact that you have a twin on the other side. It sounds like she managed to establish contact with you when you played that game, which just made the wall between your world and hers a little more transparent. You know? Like, that first contact kind of made a little path for the others to follow, and the more often spirits reach out to you, the wider and clearer that path becomes."

"Can I make it stop?" I asked impulsively, not wanting to be the only one among my friends who carried the burden of communicating with dead people.

"Stop? Why?! Damn. I'd trade places with you in a heartbeat, you know that? I take classes to try to develop my communication powers, and you just have them naturally. *So* not fair."

"What should she do next? This is freaking me out," Mischa said, watching the pendulum continue to swing from my fingers.

"Try it out," Kirsten instructed me. "Ask it a question with a yes-or-no answer."

Nervously, I looked at Trey for direction. "Ask it if Violet knew she was killing Olivia and Candace when she predicted their deaths during the game."

I licked my dry lips and queried in my hoarse voice, "When we played Light as a Feather at Olivia's house, did Violet know that Olivia and Candace were going to die exactly how she said they would?"

The pendulum had slowed its speed, but picked up again, continuing in a clockwise direction. *Yes.* A chill ran up my spine. I'd suspected that all along, but the confirmation stunned me anyhow. Violet was a murderer. Olivia and Candace's deaths were not accidents.

"Jesus," Kirsten said, sucking in her breath in a way that made a *whoosh*ing sound. "This is heavy."

"Ask it if it skipped me because I'm safe," Mischa urged.

I hesitated, not sure I really wanted to know the answer. "I don't think that's—"

"God, Mischa! Why would you think that?" Henry exclaimed. "Did she predict your death too?"

Mischa nodded, her eyes enormous. It was starting to seem like

Mischa hadn't told Henry very much at all before arriving at my house that day. "I can't believe this," Henry muttered.

Before I could pose the question to the pendulum, Kirsten held her arm out toward me to suggest I stop. "Don't ask it that. It can only answer based on what it knows right now at this second. Our actions can still change the future, and it's important to remember that we have some control over what happens to us." I was grateful for her explanation, even if I wasn't sure if I believed her.

Like the tenacious pit bull she often was, Mischa wouldn't drop the issue. "Then why did it skip me? There has to be a reason or none of the rest of this makes sense."

"Not too many things can block a powerful spell," Kirsten told her. "A counterspell would do it. But no offense, it doesn't seem like you guys know your asses from your elbows well enough to cast anything. The prayers of a saint—"

"Wait a second," Mischa said, holding up her hand. "What if a bunch of nuns were praying for me every day? Because they were. The nuns at my new school."

"Maybe," Kirsten said hopefully. "Nuns often pray the rosary with beads that have roses inside of them. Sometimes they have a set of beads that were blessed by the Pope, or even more rarely, they have beads with roses inside of them that were blessed by actual saints. Any chance the nuns at your school might have that kind of swag?"

Mischa looked dumbfounded for a second and then turned to me. "Ask that thing."

"Right," I said. I looked down at the dangling hunk of rose quartz and asked, "Pendulum. Did Violet's curse skip Mischa because the nuns at St. Patrick's were praying for her?"

Again, clockwise, swift and certain.

"Are they still praying for her?" I asked. The pendulum's trajectory grew wobbly and then slowed down. It then began moving in the opposite direction, reestablishing its orbit around my hand in a counterclockwise movement. "I'm guessing that's a no," I said, looking to Kirsten for confirmation.

She nodded.

"Those bitches!" Mischa hissed. "Why are they slacking on their prayers just because it's Christmas break?"

"Maybe it's not the best idea to refer to nuns as bitches right now," Trey suggested.

"Well, where can I get some magic rosary beads? I need to start praying, like, right now!" Mischa said.

"You're in the wrong store," Kirsten informed her.

I dropped the pendulum into my left hand. "I think I've seen enough. This is kind of scaring me. What we really need to know is how Violet's able to do what she does, and what we have to do to save Mischa's life. And that's way too complicated to ask in yes-or-no questions."

Kirsten looked around at all of us, drumming her fingertips on the tabletop. "I don't suppose you have anything of hers here with you," she murmured. "This would be a lot easier if we actually had one of her possessions."

Trey frowned at me. "We never should have thrown that damn locket over the bridge at White Ridge Lake."

He was right. The only possession of Violet's I'd ever held in my hands even for a short while was the locket we'd torn off her neck, and now it sat at the bottom of a lake, irretrievable. It was pretty ironic that we probably could have both spared ourselves the court-room drama and banishment from our hometown if we'd not gone to such extremes to keep Violet from ever getting it back.

"What about a picture?" Henry asked hopefully. "I have a picture on my phone."

Kirsten reached for the phone. "Not ideal, but we could try."

Henry swiped through his photos until he found one of the five of us posing around Olivia's red Prius in the Richmonds' driveway the morning of her sixteenth birthday. I had forgotten that Olivia's parents had asked us to pose together in our pajamas so that Henry could snap a pic. Mischa and I both indulged in a moment of quiet reflection examining the picture. In it, we all looked so young. Even though it was only a few months ago, so much had happened since that morning, when my friends had already been doomed but just didn't know it yet. It had been weeks since I'd seen a picture of Candace's face, weeks since I'd thought about how funny her scratchy voice and endless flirting had been. It had been even longer since I'd seen a picture of Olivia, since I didn't have access to social media at Sheridan, and I'd forgotten just how pretty she'd been. And there, next to Olivia, smiling coyly, was Violet, the architect of their untimely deaths.

"That's my sister, the blond one," Henry said, flipping his phone around so that Kirsten could see the picture. He rested his finger on Olivia's face. "And that's Candace, the second girl who died. And right here, with the dark hair? That's Violet."

Kirsten bit her lip as she studied the picture for a second, then said, "All right. I have a crazy idea. I need to get some stuff to make this work." She got up from the table and hurried to the front of the store.

In Kirsten's absence, I apologized to Henry. "I'm sorry, Henry. We should have warned you about how messed up all of this is. Maybe you should go back to the car and wait for us."

Henry didn't move a muscle. "She was my sister. I have to know what happened."

With a slight edge in his voice, Trey said, "He's a big boy. He can make his own decisions."

Just as I began wondering if Trey was trying to start something with Henry, Kirsten returned to the table with a tall, thick white candle and two circular mirrors that looked like ordinary, medium-size cosmetic mirrors. She positioned the white candle at the bottom of Henry's phone and lit its wick. Next, she picked up the sage smudge stick from the dish where she'd left it, and waved it in the air around the white candle.

"Actually, is there something *more* you could do to keep us safe?" I asked. "What we're dealing with is, like . . . no joke." If whatever was helping Violet had the power to make an eighteen-wheeler crash head-on into Trey's Corolla—or, hell, had the power to conjure up a hailstorm—I doubted sage was going to do much to protect us.

"You mean a spirit other than Olivia's?" Kirsten asked.

"Uh, yeah," I admitted. "There may have been some others we contacted when using a Ouija board. And Violet told us that when she tells stories for people, something shows her what to say. That could only be spirits, right?" Kirsten had mentioned demons playing a role in the game, and I hadn't forgotten about that.

Kirsten's shoulders heaved. "It most *likely* means spirits. But it could mean a demon's possessing her, or a hellhound is on her tail.

There are a lot of different kinds of demons, all of which need to be dealt with differently."

Mischa and I both gasped in unison. It felt as if the temperature in the store had dropped by twenty degrees, even though the overhead light still filled the store with a cozy glow. "That all sounds . . . really bad," Mischa managed to reply.

"Yeah, well. Let's try to figure out what exactly it is and *hope* it's just a bad ghost or two. Spirits would be the easiest of the mix to deal with because they're pretty limited in what they can do to us on their own. I can give you a book about their abilities to take with you," Kirsten offered. "But if it makes you guys feel any better . . ."

Taking a stick of chalk from a pile on the herb shelves, she bent over and awkwardly made her way around the table at which we sat to draw a large pentagram on the floor. She dropped to her hands and knees to crawl underneath the table as she drew the star on the inside of the circle. "Scoot in," she ordered Mischa so that her chair fit within the outline. Now that a literal border had been drawn around our safety zone, I checked the legs of my chair to make sure I was entirely within it. I had a suspicion this was not the first time a pentagram had been drawn on the floor around this table, nor would it be the last.

"Whew," Kirsten said, sitting back down in her seat. "That'll have to do, since it would be impossible to get a shaman over here on such short notice."

The top of the white candle had started to melt, and a slim bead of melted wax rolled down its side. Kirsten handed one of the mirrors to Mischa and asked her to hold it at shoulder height.

"Like this?" Mischa asked, raising the mirror so that it faced Kirsten. Then, with her left hand, Kirsten held the second mirror up to the flame so that we could see ourselves in it, and she took her time angling it until she could see its reflection in the mirror that Mischa held.

"What are we trying to do here, exactly?" Trey asked.

Kirsten replied matter-of-factly, "This is a truth spell, to help us see the truth about this girl Violet's past. You guys said you wanted to know how she came to have the power to predict deaths, right? So, if it works, just . . . watch the mirror, I guess." She tapped Henry's phone on the tabletop to activate its screen again, returning the photo of all of us posing in the Richmonds' driveway back into view.

Holding her mirror steadily, Kirsten closed her eyes and said in a firm voice, "To see the truth, to know her way, I command of thee, her truth display." Kirsten then blew out the candle slowly, releasing a surprising amount of smoke from its wick. Directly into the smoke she said sternly, "Violet."

Trey, Mischa, Henry, and I all leaned forward to look more closely in the mirror in Kirsten's hand. As the smoke from the candle cleared, all four of us gasped and Trey coughed into his hand. In the mirror, we saw a blurry shape form into the image of a girl around our age with short dark hair. She seemed to be looking in our direction, as if she knew we were there but couldn't quite see us past the boundary of the mirror.

"That's Rebecca Shermer!" Mischa exclaimed. "I recognize her from Facebook. She died in Violet's old town last year!"

"Shh!" Kirsten commanded, and Mischa fell quiet.

Rebecca appeared to fall backward, out of view, and another girl rose into the mirror. This one had fiery red hair to her shoulders. She, too, blinked around in wonderment before falling backward, just as Rebecca had. Her image was replaced by that of a teenage boy who looked a little younger than us, thin and gawky. The blurry shape of a fourth person emerged, and it looked as if she could see us too, which was startling. She blinked a few times and appeared to lean closer toward the mirror to see us better as the features of her blurry face became sharper.

And then there she was . . .

. . . Olivia in the mirror, looking right at us. She looked like she was wearing the same baby-pink leather jacket she'd had on the last time I'd seen her as she had walked away from me down the hall at school, on her way to the mall in Green Bay. She seemed to be looking directly at Henry, her eyes huge and filled with urgency, moving her lips and gesticulating as if she was trying to tell him something. But her image in the mirror was too blurry and unsteady for any of us to determine what she was saying.

"What is it, Olivia? I can't hear you," Henry said to the mirror. He looked up at Kirsten and asked in desperation, "Can she see us?"

Kirsten answered apologetically, "I don't know."

But then Olivia fell backward, just as the others had. Next was Candace, who looked surprised to see us, and blinked a few times as if she couldn't believe her eyes before she fell backward.

And what happened next made all of us jump—Violet's mother appeared to rise into the mirror from the space into which the other bodies had fallen. Unlike the kids whose deaths Violet had predicted, Vanessa Simmons didn't seem to be aware of us watching her at all. As her image lingered, it grew clearer, and then we saw what looked like a store appear in the background of her reflection. It looked as if she was at the grocery store in Willow, and we were watching her shop.

"Is that . . . Violet's mother, like, right now?" Mischa asked.

"It looks like it," Henry said. "It looks like that's her, doing whatever she's doing at this very moment."

Kirsten shook her head and said, "That doesn't make sense. We asked for the truth about Violet, not her mother."

The image in the mirror held by Kirsten faded to black, and when nothing else appeared after a few seconds, she put the mirror down. "What could that possibly mean?"

"Maybe the truth about Violet is actually the truth about her mother," Mischa suggested. "I mean, does this truth spell ever lie?"

"Maybe," I proposed, taking to heart what Mischa had just said, "we've been thinking all along that Violet has been predicting people's death for some blatantly evil purpose. But what if . . . Violet's doing what she does to save someone else? Like her mom?"

Trey raised an eyebrow and leaned forward. "Wait a minute. What's that quote about the most powerful villains always believing their intentions are good?"

We all looked around with blank faces, having no clue what he was talking about. Kirsten brightened and pointed at him, catching his drift. "Yeah," she agreed. "Like how in the Superman comics, Lex Luthor is a super genius, and he really thinks that if he can kill Superman and rule the planet, he'll be able to advance humanity forward with his technological knowledge?"

Again, blank stares. "Um, if you guys say so," Henry said, sounding doubtful.

"Okay," Trey said, shaking his head, a little annoyed with our ignorance of comic-book story lines. "Just follow me, here. What McKenna said makes sense. What if Violet knows that killing people is wrong, but she has to? Like, she believes ultimately it's a good thing because by killing other people, she's keeping her mom alive? Or protecting her from something?"

We all fell quiet, thinking this over. Before Olivia had died, Violet had never struck me as greedy, selfish, or evil. When we'd accused her of intentionally killing Olivia and Candace, she had tried to convince us that what had happened wasn't her fault—that she hadn't had any control over it. Maybe that hadn't been a total lie. She'd only started acting like a selfish scene-stealer after Olivia had passed away and she'd settled into the role of the most popular girl in the junior class.

"You recognized all those people in the mirror?" Kirsten asked us.

"Not all of them. But enough to assume they're all the kids who Violet has killed so far," I said glumly.

"You wanna know what I think?" Kirsten asked with a proud grin.

"We drove all the way down here in a snowstorm to find out what you think," Henry teased.

Kirsten eased back in her chair, crossed her legs, and folded her hands on her knee. "I think you're dealing with some kind of a sacrifice curse. The way Violet's mom appeared in the mirror was the reversal of how the other people left the mirror. That makes me suspect that she—and everything she's doing right now—is the flip side of the others dying. Get it? Her life is the result of their deaths."

Sacrifice. One sacrifice for each cycle of the moon.

Henry looked at me as if seeking permission before asking, "Is there any significance to making a monthly sacrifice that coincides with the phases of the moon?"

Kirsten looked blank-faced at Henry for a long moment before breaking into hysterical laughter. "You're kidding, right?" She continued howling, rocking back in her chair before recovering. "You just described pretty much every natural phenomenon on planet Earth and the basis of Wiccan practice! The lunar calendar influences everything from our sleep patterns to the tide. I mean, hello, menstruation—if that's not a metaphor for a monthly sacrifice, I don't know what is."

"Right," Henry said, turning red.

"But seriously," Kirsten continued as she calmed herself down. "Yes, there's a connection between casting spells and the moon. A lot of spells can only be effectively cast during full moons or new moons. I guess the same is probably true for curses, which is essentially just a bad-intentioned spell."

Trey cleared his throat and bobbed his head in the direction of the store's front windows. "It's starting to really come down." The snow had picked up and was falling in larger flakes. I glanced at my phone and noticed that it was almost six o'clock. Even under ideal driving circumstances, it would take us more than three hours to get home.

"We should get going," I said.

"Wait! What about breaking the curse?" Mischa demanded. "So Violet sacrifices someone every month—how do we *stop* that?"

Kirsten held up her hands in defeat. "I'd need more time to figure that out. This is way over my head. If you guys don't mind, I want to contact my boss in London and ask if she has any advice for you. You should give me your contact info so that I can get in touch with you. Are you from around here?"

"We're from Wisconsin," Henry said.

"Oh, that's a shame," Kirsten said, and this time I was sure she was flirting with Henry. I felt my lips twist into a little bit of a frown. It shouldn't have bothered me at all for a girl to show interest in him. My own boyfriend was sitting right next to me, and Henry looked like a dreamy movie star. Girls probably flirted with him all the time.

But it still struck me as kind of inappropriate considering that we'd just summoned the ghost of his dead sister into a pocket mirror.

At the front of the store, we traded e-mail addresses and phone numbers with Kirsten so that she could pass along messages from her boss. I had an annoying hunch that Henry was going to hear from her first. Trey passed Kirsten's phone to Mischa when it reached him, announcing to no one in particular, "I'm pretty much unreachable these days."

Kirsten threw one pointed finger in the air and said, "Before I forget!" From one of the bookshelves, she pulled a paperback and handed it to me. *Understanding the Spirit World* was printed across its cover, and its pages were yellowed as if it had been on the shelf for decades. "Read this and you'll have a better idea of what the forces aiding this girl Violet can and can't do to you."

I examined the book in my hands skeptically. It looked like it had been printed in the seventies, and when I flipped open the cover and checked out the copyright, my assumption was confirmed. "So you think they're spirits and not demons, after all?"

"That would be my assumption, yes," Kirsten said. "I don't think the spell would have shown us anything if your friend were being controlled by a demon. Demons have a will of their own. They don't submit to influence."

I realized that I was still holding the pendulum, and offered to return it to Kirsten. However, she refused it. "You should keep it. It works well with your energy, and now that you've used it, it won't ever work quite right for anyone else."

"I've only got twenty bucks," I blurted, not really wanting to take anything intended for communicating with spirits home to my mother's house. I wasn't lying about the money; I wasn't allowed to carry cash at Sheridan and wasn't exactly allowed to have a part-time job while enrolled there.

"I'll buy it," Henry offered. "It could be really helpful. We should keep it around, just in case."

I felt the weight of the pendulum in my coat pocket as Henry gave Kirsten his credit card to pay for it, and as he signed the receipt, he said, "I'll go get the car and come back to pick you guys up. There's no point in all of us walking to the garage in the cold."

Mischa was lingering near the front window texting someone on her phone when Kirsten called her over to the counter. "Mischa, is it? Come here. I want to give you something."

She pulled one of the rainbow-striped candles in a jar off of a shelf and set it down on the counter. "I want you to have this. It's a gift."

Mischa sniffed the top of it and wrinkled her nose. "I thought it would smell good."

"It's not scented," Kirsten clarified. "It's a seven-day candle. See? There are seven colors. Tonight, before you go to bed, sit on the floor and light the wick. Put your hands on both sides of the glass, like this, and as you watch the flame burn, just think about your life, and your future. And survival. Do that for at least ten minutes. Then, don't blow the candle out, but put it somewhere in your room where there aren't any drafts and where it's not likely to get knocked over. Let it burn for seven days straight."

"Seven days! Are you serious?" Mischa asked. "If I leave a candle burning in my room for a week, my mom will flip out!"

"Just . . . trust," Kirsten said kindly, smiling sadly at Mischa.

Outside, Henry pulled up in his dad's Mercedes and honked the horn. Mischa thanked Kirsten for her help and for the candle and left, but I lingered. My feet felt like cement blocks. I had more questions for Kirsten now than I'd had when we'd first arrived, and this might have been my only chance to ask them. Trey held the door open for me, waiting.

Kirsten asked, "McKenna, can I talk to you for a second?" It was as if she had heard my thoughts about needing to speak to her privately before I left.

For a second, it looked like Trey was about to reply on my behalf, but I said, "I'll just be a minute." He pulled the door closed behind him and followed Mischa to the car.

"Your whole thing as a medium," she said, smiling bashfully, "it's real. You can take classes to learn how to develop it, you know. You've probably experienced weird things and weren't sure what was causing them, right?"

"Why is this happening to me?" I asked, cutting right to the chase. "My whole life, up until a few months ago, I never heard weird stuff or had inexplicable things happen to me. And now it's like there's more and more of it. I don't know how to turn it off." In September, I'd thought my life was going to change for the better because people at school started treating me differently. Suddenly, I was no longer the shy girl whose sister had died in a house fire and who everyone wanted to avoid. But receiving messages from the spirit world was pulling me back, away from the normal life I wanted. I was already worried that my getting sent away to boarding school was going to wreck my future. Ongoing communication with dead people wasn't the kind of future I wanted either.

Kirsten smiled encouragingly at me. "That's just how it is for some people. There was probably one event, one little tiny crack in the wall between our world and the spirit world, and that was the beginning."

I thought of the moment on the night of Olivia's party when Violet had announced that she could think only of fire when she touched my temples. That may very well have been the beginning, even before the first time Olivia's ghost had ever visited me.

"Once your body knows how to interpret those vibrations, it's impossible to ignore them, you know what I mean? So it's less like you're experiencing it more often, and more like you're just aware of it now."

Kirsten handed me a few sticks of palo santo, which she said was a kind of sacred wood I could burn at home prior to using my pendulum to cleanse the space. She then tore off a tab from a flyer taped to the wall promoting classes for learning how to have out-of-body experiences. "The guy who teaches this class, Brian, could probably really help you develop your gift, if you were interested in that. I mean, he does this out-of-body stuff just to make some money because people are always curious about dabbling in paranormal abilities, but that's kind of, like, child's play. I think he'd be psyched to meet you."

I thanked her and put the bit of paper she handed to me in my pocket alongside the pendulum.

"And Mischa," Kirsten said, looking at me with pity. "She's next, isn't she?"

I didn't know how to answer. We'd mentioned to Kirsten that Violet had told a prediction for Mischa, but none of us had specifically said that Mischa's turn was next.

"I can read auras," Kirsten said, shrugging. "It's the only paranormal thing I've really been able to master. Yours is this zany purple color, really saturated. I've never seen anything like it before."

"Does that mean anything?"

Kirsten shrugged. "Indigo is supposed to be associated with higher spiritual awakening, like if your third eye is open. It's the color associated with the crown chakra. It means—and I hope this doesn't scare you—that someone's here for a higher purpose than other people, but it also usually means that the person has to overcome some kind of obstacle to achieve it."

"What does Mischa's look like?" I dared to ask.

"She doesn't have one. That's how I know she'll be the next to die. She's doomed."

I swallowed hard, feeling as if I was about to cry. The sun had set while we were in the store, and my mom had already texted me once to ask what time I was coming home. It was easy to imagine having to attend Mischa's funeral within the next few days, and having to endure the rest of my life knowing that I'd failed to save one of the most important people in my life. Since September, I'd come to think of Mischa and me as being in this nightmare together. I couldn't fathom going back to Sheridan and moving on if she were to die. Even the promise of a future with Trey might not have been enough to lighten the weight of grief I'd carry around in my heart if I couldn't break the curse in time to save her. There must be a point at which a heart exceeds its capacity for sadness, and I had to be close to reaching it.

"She has to burn that candle like I told her," Kirsten insisted. "And one last thing." She took a step toward me and placed her fingertips gently on my shoulders. "That guy? Your boyfriend?"

"Henry's not my boyfriend," I corrected her, feeling a blush creep into my cheeks.

"Oh, I know that. I meant the other one. Sexy danger with the ice-blue eyes."

Trey.

"What about him?" I asked, terrified of the answer.

"You can't trust him. I don't know what his connection to this whole thing is, but when I blew out the candle earlier after saying Violet's name? The smoke drifted directly toward him. That usually means something . . . and something not good."

CHAPTER 5

WE WERE ALL IN A MOODY STATE OF heightened sensitivity, and our conversation was tense as we rode home, each of us processing all we'd learned from our short visit to Sticks & Stones. Mischa was jumpy and irritable in the front passenger seat—understandably so, since we hadn't gotten a definitive answer about how to prevent her from dying within the next twenty-four hours.

"What'd that girl want to talk to you about alone?" Mischa asked as if already suspicious that I'd lagged behind to discuss her impending death.

I considered telling her what Kirsten had said about her lack of an aura in the hope that she would take to heart the need for her to burn the candle Kirsten had given her. There was no way I was going to divulge Kirsten's suggestion that I take lessons to further develop my ability to receive messages from the spirit world. My friends had already heard her talk more about my paranormal abilities than I would have preferred. I was especially edgy about giving Trey any more reasons to think that I had special abilities to communicate with ghosts after Kirsten had cautioned me against trusting him. So instead of telling the truth, I told a lie that slightly twisted my heart. "She wanted to know if Henry has a girlfriend and what his deal is."

"Oooh," Mischa teased. "I could *totally* see Henry with a hot hipster witch."

Henry replied, "We've got to break this curse on you before I'll have any time for wedding planning."

I got the sense that even though I hadn't told Mischa about Kirsten guessing her death was imminent, the candle she had been given had heightened her awareness of the fact that her prediction was due to come true within hours. As we sat, frustrated, in jams caused by fender benders, she asked Henry if he'd mind if she lit the candle from Kirsten in the car.

"Driving on these bad roads with an open flame in the car while we're all wearing highly flammable polyester coats is a really bad idea, Mischa," he said. She didn't ask a second time.

The falling snow had made a mess of the toll road, and just before crossing over from Illinois into Wisconsin, we witnessed an accident involving a plow and a minivan.

"Side streets it is," Henry announced as we took the next exit.

Henry navigated state highways through forests and small towns as I fired off text responses to my mom's increasing concern that Mischa and I were out screwing around in dangerous weather.

One of the main roads we could potentially take through Ortonville over to Willow had not yet been plowed, so we had to drive about thirty miles north out of our way and then backtrack south toward our town. Henry was about to make a right turn onto South Marx Road, which would take us most of the way home, when suddenly my scalp began tingling so much that I impulsively scratched at it.

"No! Go straight. Let's take Route 32," I suggested, surprising myself. I hadn't been thinking about potential travel routes, but out of nowhere it just seemed imperative that we take that street home and no other.

Henry lingered at an intersection with his right signal clicking. "Are you sure about that?" Luckily, ours was the only car on the road.

"Yes," I said. "I don't know why. It just seems right."

"Okay," Henry agreed, sounding surprisingly open to it. "If the medium in the car feels strongly about the path home, listen to her." He winked at me in the rearview mirror, and Trey snorted quietly next to me.

Route 32 was a wide-lined rural state highway that had mysteriously already been plowed. As we passed the part of the highway that was heavily dotted with gas stations and convenience markets and entered into the section that cut through the Brillion Wildlife Area, thick with trees on both sides of the road, it began to feel like it was a lot later than ten thirty at night.

"Could we turn on some music?" Mischa asked Henry. We'd been listening to the weather and traffic report for the last twenty minutes due to Henry's paranoia about impassable roadways. "It's starting to feel like we're Hansel and Gretel, leaving crumbs to find our way back out of the forest."

"We'll be home in an hour and fifteen minutes," Henry assured all of us. To appease Mischa, he switched the satellite radio station to hip-hop.

Knowing I'd be home soon didn't make me feel any better, even though the tingling across the top of my head had settled down again. Kirsten's parting words at the store had rattled me. Trey was the only person I'd trusted completely since all of this began, and now I had reason to believe that my paranoia about his explanation for being in Green Bay at the mall the night of Olivia's accident was justified. Although we were holding hands in the back seat of the Mercedes, my fingers were numb to his touch. More than once I'd sensed him looking over at me in the hope of catching my eye, and I refused to meet his gaze. What I'd wanted most in the world that morning when I'd gotten up was to see him again, but now I wondered if he even knew what his connection to Violet was, or that he posed a threat to me.

There was also still the possibility—although I didn't want to believe this because I'd known him my whole life—that he was intentionally allowing me to get closer to the danger, and had even aided me in confronting Violet back in November because he *wanted* me to get in trouble and be removed as an obstacle from her mission. It seemed far-fetched that he'd go to such an extreme in order to ensure Violet could continue killing people, but I would be naïve to rule out the possibility that he was working as her accomplice, whether he was aware or not.

"So what do you guys think the moon has to do with Violet exactly?" Henry asked. "Like maybe once every thirty days, she has to make a sacrifice, so her power to predict one death is renewed—"

·Although Henry had fessed up to leaving the lunar calendar at my house, it suddenly struck me as odd that he'd done so days before Mischa had told him anything about what we'd been up to for the last few weeks. "Wait a second. I thought the moon theory was yours?" I asked. "You said you were the one who left the calendar and the obituaries in my mailbox?"

Henry clarified, "Oh, it's not my theory. Someone sent that calendar to my house anonymously. No return address, but it had a Lake Forest postal—"

"Henry, stop the car." Mischa's voice was a low growl.

"What do you mean? Are you going to be sick?"

"Just stop. Right now."

Henry rolled to a stop, and the tires crunched on the half inch of snow that had collected since the plows had come through. I leaned forward over the back of the front seat to peer through the windshield in the space between Henry and Mischa, and my heart stopped beating when I saw what Mischa had seen first.

Our headlights were shining on the back of a slim girl with long dark hair walking barefoot in the snow about one hundred feet ahead of our car. She wore a silky pastel dress with a floral pattern on it, and a pink cardigan. In her right hand, she carried a pair of eggshell-colored ankle-strap pumps.

They looked like exactly the kind of shoes that Olivia had been shopping for the night she died, shoes that would match her homecoming dress.

The girl's bare feet weren't leaving footprints in the snow that had collected on the asphalt. Henry noticed this at the same time I did and he muttered in a barely audible voice, "What . . . the . . . hell."

My blood ran ice-cold. I was certain, more certain than I'd ever been about anything, that we were looking at a ghost.

"Jesus," Trey whispered next to me.

"We shouldn't be driving down this road when it's snowing! That's Bloody Heather, don't you get it? Just like in the story," Mischa rambled. Her voice was more high-pitched than usual, as if she were about to break into tears. "Turn around! We can't drive past her!"

Suddenly understanding why my scalp had been tingling and what it meant I had to do, I unbuckled my seat belt. "Wait for me," I ordered Henry.

"What are you doing?" Trey asked, grabbing my arm as I opened the car door.

"If Mischa's right, and that's a ghost, then maybe she can help us. We still don't know how to break Violet's curse. Maybe she can tell us," I said. It seemed logical that another entity from the spirit world might be able to explain why the spirits working with Violet wanted a sacrifice from her every month. And even though I was so afraid that my fingers were trembling as I pulled on my gloves, it seemed obvious to me that I was the only person in our car who stood any chance of getting an answer. "Just wait for me."

"Oh my God, oh my God, oh my God," Mischa chanted. She had pulled her knees up to her chest and wrapped her arms around them, tightening her entire body into a ball.

Henry hesitated for a moment, his eyes fixed on the back of the girl walking through the snow in the beam of his headlights, before shaking his head and mumbling, "No. Don't get out of the car. This is just too—"

"Henry," I said firmly. "I have to." I slowly climbed out of the back seat and left the car door opened by a crack behind me, fearful that a loud slam might make the specter ahead of me vanish—or worse, turn around to take me by surprise with a shockingly grue-some face.

Not knowing how to best establish contact with her, I fell into lockstep behind her, walking far enough to step outside of the bright safety of Henry's high beams. I relied on the local legend of Bloody Heather to ask as if scripted, "Do you need a ride?"

The girl stopped walking as if she had been expecting me.

Fear decelerated my perception of time. My heart felt like it had slowed to a dangerously low speed. I could hear my own blood pumping through my ears, hot with fright. *Thump. Thump. Thump.* My breath was raspy, and I tried to focus to prevent myself from hyperventilating. Even though she must have sensed me behind her, she didn't turn her head to look at me.

On legs so numb with fear I could barely feel them, I took a few steps forward to stand next to the girl. Nausea overwhelmed me. Behind me, I heard the Mercedes advance by a few feet. Only then did I dare to tilt my head slightly to the right to take a look at the ghost in profile. Her long dark hair hung in her face, obscuring her features, but even still I gasped, making a sound that sounded like, "Ha!"

She looked exactly like me.

Or, rather—I could only guess—exactly like what Jennie would have looked like if she were still alive at the age of sixteen, like me. My entire body went rigid with horror; I felt the muscles of my face distort involuntarily, and the bones of my fingers locked into position inside my gloves. The temperature outside felt as if it had dropped about thirty degrees since I'd stepped up alongside the ghost, who finally turned to face me, twisting her neck stiffly as if it were painful for her to move that way. Just as I expected from her profile, her full face was astonishingly familiar. It had been so very long since I'd looked at someone else who shared my appearance that for a second,

I was convinced I was looking at my *real* twin. An emotion I'd never experienced before swelled in my throat, something halfway between the relief you feel when you find something you thought you'd lost forever and the simple but pure joy of climbing into your own familiar bed after spending time away from home.

With a trembling voice, I asked her, "Where are you headed?" Even if the ghost—*Jennie*—looked exactly like me, I was afraid she would disappear if I deviated from the Bloody Heather story line. She wasn't transparent, as ghosts sometimes are in movies. But she was distinctly not flesh and blood, either.

"Ten Martha Road," she replied in a monotone, slurring voice. This was how the legend went; the ghost requested an address where she wanted to be dropped off.

My heart skipped a beat. I bit into my lower lip so hard that I tasted blood. She'd given me my old address, the address of our house that had burned down on what was now the empty lot on my corner.

"Okay," I said, choosing my next words carefully so as not to deviate too far from the dialogue that Bloody Heather was rumored to always have with the people to whom she appeared in the legend. "I know where that house is. I used to live there. My name's McKenna. Do you know me?" Although the ghost had angled her face toward me, a white sheen covered her eyes kind of like cataracts, and they were fixed on a place behind my head as if she was looking past me. Just like Violet's victims that we'd seen in Kirsten's mirror back at the store, it was as if Jennie were aware of my presence but a layer of tissue or fabric in between us prevented her from actually seeing me even though I could see her.

"You're my sister," the ghost replied.

I could hear the staccato beat of blood coursing through my ears and wished I hadn't insisted on confronting the ghost alone. Wished I weren't close enough to smell the scent of blood wafting off her. The only voice I was able to squeeze out was barely audible. "Who are you?"

"I'm Jennifer Laura Brady," she replied.

I hadn't had a chance to even skim through the book Kirsten had given me about the behavior of spirits, but after having been tricked into believing that destroying Violet's locket would break the curse, I knew that spirits—or ghosts—were perfectly capable of deceiving people, of tapping into their desires for their own purposes. "Prove it," I whispered.

"How?" she asked.

"Tell me a story that only Jennie would know." Now I was really straying from the Bloody Heather story, but I had to know if this spirit was really that of my twin before I could trust anything she told me. My heart felt as if it had paused in between beats, and I didn't want to allow myself to feel the full rush of happiness that was building up inside of me for having been reconnected with Jennie until I was absolutely sure that it was her.

Staring straight ahead rather than looking at me, the ghost hesitated as if it was difficult for her to make her lips force out words before replying, "You left me in the tree."

My heart resumed beating, flooding my body with a torrent of glee. I felt the urge to both cry and laugh, as if someone had stabbed me beneath the ribs and tickled me simultaneously. It was a ridiculous detail that only someone who'd grown up on Martha Road with us would know, which made me confident that the spirit standing next to me was definitely Jennie's. One summer, Trey had taught Jennie and me how to climb the tall pine tree that used to stand in his front yard. When we'd reached the top branches, Jennie had been too afraid to climb down. After panicking for a while, Trey and I had run inside my house for help. My mother had called the fire department, and they'd sent a truck, sirens blaring. One of the firefighters had climbed a tall ladder to retrieve Jennie, who kicked and howled all the way down.

Then, the very next day, we'd climbed back up into the tree and Mom had had to call the fire department again.

"Yes, I did," I agreed. I hadn't thought about that tree in ages. Dad had cut it down after our second climb to the top. A tear escaped from my eye, and I wiped it away, grateful for the memory even though my whole body ached at the realization that that had been our last summer together, the summer before Jennie died. "Sorry about that."

The ghost took another step forward and resumed her slow-paced walking, as did I. I heard the Mercedes behind us rolling along on the snow.

I knew we didn't have much time left to save Mischa, but if this was my one and only chance to reconnect with my deceased twin— to fill her in on eight long years of regret, guilt, and heartbreaking grief—I couldn't waste the opportunity. I had to tell her how much Mom missed her, how she used to sit on the porch swing after the house fire and stare hopelessly toward the end of the street. I wanted her to know that Dad was so saddened by how much Mom missed her that he left us because it was easier for him to start a new life in Florida than deal with the grief that filled the walls of our house. I wanted to tell her how terrible it had been to go back to school and be the only Brady girl, when everyone in our small town knew that once upon a time, we'd been a pair. So I blurted, "Mom misses you so much. I mean, Dad does too, but Mom really . . . and I'm so sorry that I couldn't—"

"There isn't much time," Jennie said, sounding as if she hadn't even heard me. Without my even steering the conversation toward Mischa's impending death, Jennie seemed to know exactly what we had driven out there to discuss with her. I wondered if this stretch of Route 32 was particularly easy for spirits to access, which was why the Bloody Heather legend had developed here, or if there was truth to Kirsten's theory about paths accessed by spirits becoming wider and clearer with use. If that was the case, then Jennie had infiltrated the path often used by the real ghost of Bloody Heather specifically to connect with me. "There are two in line to die. The third is crossing over as we speak."

Terrified that the car was going to frighten Jennie away, I whirled around and gestured wildly at Henry not to come any closer. I could barely see the car as I peered directly into the headlights, but I could see Mischa in the front seat, her eyes enormous with horror.

"Is Mischa one of them? Is she the one who's dying now?"

"Next," Jennie said ominously. "She will always be next until she's dead."

"Who else is in line to die?" I asked, wondering how many times Violet had read tarot cards for kids while I'd been away at Sheridan. "What are their names?"

Jennie coughed, startling me. "I don't remember their names. It's been so long." She coughed again, this time her face wrinkling as if she were in distress. "I only see their shapes."

According to the Bloody Heather legend, eventually the ghost would dissolve into a bloody mess in the back seat if she was offered a ride home to the destination she provided to the driver. Sensing that my time with Jennie was running out, I asked, "What's causing all of this?"

"When the grandmother died, they surrounded Violet. She transfers souls at their command, one for each moon." She grasped desperately at her throat again before sputtering, "She tried to transfer you, so I showed her my death to confuse her."

I gasped in surprise and felt hot tears roll down my cheeks before I even sensed them welling up in my eyes. I had been wondering why Violet hadn't been able to predict my death, and if Jennie had stepped forward to prevent her from dooming me. Even though it had seemed ridiculous, I'd been right. Jennie had saved me. I flinched when I noticed blood oozing between her teeth as she formed words.

"Is that why Violet said I was already dead?" I asked.

But instead of answering me, Jennie set me back on task. "To save Mischa, you have to stop them all."

It felt as if the night went completely silent. For a few seconds, I wasn't even aware of the crunching noise of my feet on the snow. Out on the track at school, when Violet had insisted there was nothing she could do to change the outcome of the game we'd played at Olivia's party, she'd said, *They don't take requests. They just arrive, show me stuff, and leave.* The way Jennie was referring to the spirits giving Violet her powers as "them" matched the way in which Violet had referred to them. There was more than one. We didn't know what we were up against.

Jennie began coughing again, this time more violently. Her

hands clutched her throat, and dark blood, black as ink, rocketed from her mouth in droplets. Even though I knew I wasn't observing her actual death—she was already dead—but was instead seeing part of the routine that the Bloody Heather ghost went through each time she appeared to a witness, Jennie still seemed like she was in agonizing pain. I'd watched her die for real when I was eight years old, and I'd had nightmares about watching flames swallow her for the eight years that followed. There was nothing I could do to save her the night of the fire, and there was nothing I could do tonight either. An awful rotting smell blossomed in the night air around us.

I was vaguely aware of Sven's ahead of us on the road, an old dive bar with a fluorescent COORS sign hanging in the window, which was usually mentioned at one point or another during retellings of the Bloody Heather legend. Its parking lot was pretty full despite the unrelated facts that it was snowing and it was Christmas Eve.

I asked, "Who are you talking about? Who are 'they'? How many are there?"

Jennie's raucous cough continued. More blood flew from her mouth, staining the snow ahead of her on the ground. Some of it sprayed onto me, sprinkling across my right cheek and the front of my jacket in a mist, but I tried to ignore it. The skin around her eyes began to darken.

"Five," she sputtered. "There are five! Five sisters!" Her lips were growing darker. "Her dead sisters are her strength too."

We'd put at least thirty feet between us and the Mercedes, and I heard it creeping up on us again but didn't dare take my eyes off of Jennie. Through the falling snow, I saw the headlights in the distance of another car on the road coming our way. This was bad;

outsiders posed a threat, whether they were other drivers who might pull over and see me with Jennie, or drunk bar patrons stumbling out of Sven's. I sensed that I was going to lose Jennie in a matter of seconds. There were so many things I still needed to tell her—most important, how sorry I was that I'd abandoned her in our house as it burned to the ground—but I knew the information I received from her in these last remaining moments was our only chance at preventing Mischa from choking.

So I asked, "How do we stop them and save Mischa's life?"

Jennie's eyes bulged, and she gasped for air, clawing at her throat. Dark blood seeped from her eyes and nostrils.

"You must break the connection between Violet and the others," Jennie whispered in between gagging coughs.

"How? How do we do that?"

Dark blood spilled out from between her lips as she replied, "The curse won't be broken until they see Violet in their own realm."

Barely able to believe what she was suggesting, I asked, "Do I have to kill Violet in order for Mischa to live?"

Jennie launched into a coughing fit so violent that I was afraid she wouldn't be able to recover to answer. The other car on the road was about fifty feet ahead of us, close enough for me to observe that it was a station wagon. "Light as a feather." She coughed. "Cold as marble."

I shuddered. "What does that mean? Do we have to play the game with Violet again?"

The station wagon was passing me, and I sensed the driver behind its wheel craning his neck at me. I couldn't tell if he could see Jennie or not, but he could definitely see me and was probably wondering why I was walking alone in a snowstorm with a Mercedes full of kids trailing behind me.

"Play the game and I'll show you her death. It's the only way."

HONK!

I whirled around and saw that behind me, Henry had slightly swerved into the left lane and narrowly missed hitting the station wagon. He slammed on the brakes and slid right off the pavement and onto the gravel shoulder. The station wagon also slammed on its brakes, its back wheels skidding on the fresh snow.

I stole a glance over my shoulder and saw that Jennie was gone, but a dark puddle of blood remained on the snow where she'd just been standing. As if someone had just punched me in the solar plexus and knocked the wind out of me, I doubled over in pain. She'd vanished without my having had a chance to tell her so many things I'd kept bottled up since second grade, and ask her if there was any message she wanted me to give to Mom on her behalf. And I'd failed to ask the most important question of all: How would I get in touch with her again?

The Mercedes rolled about forty feet behind where I stood on the road, finally coming to a stop right in front of Sven's.

The driver of the station wagon had gotten out of his car and left it idling to walk across the snowy road toward me. He was middle-aged with a beard, wearing a heavy winter jacket unzipped to reveal a hideous holiday sweater. There were other people in the station wagon—probably his wife and kids.

When he got within a few feet of me, he asked, "Are you okay? What are you doing out here so late at night?"

"I'm okay," I insisted, but my entire body was violently shaking from both the cold and the emotional intensity of what I'd just experienced. With my gloves, I wiped tears from my cheeks and knew that it must have looked very suspicious that I was clutching my stomach and crying on the side of the road while my friends watched from behind me in a warm car.

"Are those kids bothering you?" he asked, nodding his head in the direction of the Mercedes. Henry had gotten out of the car and was standing there with the door wide open, as if preparing to dash over and rescue me if necessary.

"No, no," I assured him. "Those are my friends." I wiped away snowflakes that had collected on my eyelashes, suddenly fully aware of how sinister it must have looked that I was walking along the highway with a car following so closely behind me.

"Then why aren't you in the car with them? It's freezing out here," he said, sounding angry with me for not needing his help.

"McKenna," Henry called. "Let's go."

To the driver of the station wagon, I lied: "Everything's fine. It was just a game." Then I trotted off across the snow toward the Mercedes, and Trey leaned across the back seat to push the door I'd left open more widely so that I could climb inside.

"You kids had better be on your way home. The storm's coming in strong," the station wagon driver called after me.

"Thanks!" I shouted.

Henry didn't even wait for me to buckle my seat belt before laying on the gas despite the slippery snow. We drove for a few minutes in silence, allowing me to gaze out my window at the silent highway surrounded by the peacefulness of falling snowflakes. I wished Henry would turn on the radio so that my friends wouldn't be able to hear my stifled sobs. Losing Jennie a second time around would be even worse than when she'd died because now there was hope in my heart that I might be able to reestablish communication with her, although nothing she'd told me hinted that might be possible.

The blood spilling from Jennie's mouth had deeply disturbed me. Even though I assured myself that it was just part of the Bloody Heather legend and I wasn't even sure if ghosts could experience physical pain, the gore—the stench of it, the heat rising off the dark liquid—had been the most realistic part of her presence. It was unbearable to imagine Jennie suffering like that on a constant basis in the afterlife, and I fervently hoped that her having to experience such a disgusting ordeal was just a required part of taking advantage of the snowy night on Route 32 in order to meet with me. The blood had also served as a reminder of the prediction that Violet had given Mischa. Choking, gasping, unable to breathe. The new moon would be rising in about twenty-four hours, and Jennie had just told me that someone was already in the process of dying.

Yearning to see traces of Jennie among the stars, I looked up at the sky, but my view of the fluffy clouds overhead was obscured by lacy falling snowflakes. I felt a sensation inside my heart that I could only liken to the blooming of a flower. It was like an artery that had been closed off since I was eight years old had suddenly opened, and a torrent of hot blood had rushed in, carrying in its current a buzz of happiness that I'd forgotten existed.

Jennie had been expecting me. She'd been holding on to her love for me just as long as I'd been missing her, watching out for me. But I had failed to even ask her if she'd been suffering during the brief time we'd had together. The familiar darkness of knowing that I was the twin who had escaped death—not only once, but twice, since Jennie had prevented Violet from condemning me—crept back into my heart. I was a selfish monster; I couldn't even remember if I'd thanked her when she'd told me about showing Violet her own death to protect me.

It hadn't occurred to me to ask her if there was any way that I could make it up to her for surviving the fire that had killed her.

"That was . . . insane," Henry finally mumbled, interrupting my tearful reverie.

"So, what's the deal?" Mischa asked. "Am I gonna die tonight or what?"

Trey reached across the back seat and took my hand in his. Jennie had confirmed our fear that Mischa was still *next*, whatever that meant. She hadn't specifically said that Mischa wasn't the one of Violet's three current sacrifices who was dying at that very moment.

I took a deep breath and pushed aside the pain in my heart to inform my friends of everything Jennie had told me on our ride back to Willow.

CHAPTER 6

FROM THE FRONT SEAT, MISCHA BELLOWED, "HOW the hell are we going to get Violet to play the game again with us? McKenna and Trey aren't even allowed within one hundred feet of her." This was true. Violet's parents had been granted a restraining order against both of us back in November, which was a little overkill since we'd both been sent to schools far from Willow as well.

Henry looked hopeful. "We can figure this out, you guys. Not tonight—I mean, it's Christmas Eve. We're not going to lure her anywhere tonight. But we have the answer now!"

He had a point. We had a lot more answers now than we did when I'd left my house earlier in the day. It was hard to get excited when there was still so very much left to do before I went back to Sheridan, but we'd accomplished more in a day than I'd expected. Seeing Jennie in such agony before she vanished made it easy to overlook that she'd told me exactly what we needed to do, as impossible as it sounded like it would be to accomplish.

"What was that bit about the five sisters? Who has five sisters? I thought Violet was an only child," Mischa said.

"She made it sound like Violet has five *dead* sisters," I said, trying to remember exactly what Jennie had said about them being a source of Violet's power, presumably just as Jennie was a source of mine, although I'd yet to figure out exactly what my "power" was. "That sounds pretty dark, though, right? Five dead sisters?"

"Doesn't matter," Trey said. "We just have to play the game and predict Violet's death, and then we're done with this."

"You guys? Don't hate me, but I told my mom I was out shopping for her Christmas gift with Mischa all day and it's gonna look really bad if I show up at home empty-handed," I said. I hadn't thought about it until that very moment, but my mom was going to be extra suspicious and possibly angry if I made it so obvious that I'd lied about my reason for being away from home all day.

"Would your mom like a Mercedes S-Class?" Henry joked. "Because I'm not sure I ever want to see this car again after tonight." We all smiled, grateful for a moment of humor. "If I explain to my dad that I trailed a ghost down Route 32, I think he'll understand."

"Seriously," I insisted. "Can we drop Mischa off so she can burn her candle, but then stop at Hennessey's so that I can get a bottle of perfume or something?"

For the rest of our drive back to Willow, the comforting voice of Bing Crosby singing, "Silver bells, silver bells. It's Christmastime in the city. . . ." filled the car. We drove through the security checkpoint at Mischa's gated community, which was decorated with holiday lights. Henry let the guard scan his driver's license, and he let Mischa out at the curb in front of her house.

"Call me or text me in an hour so I know you're okay," I requested.

She dashed off with her candle in her hands, hopefully to follow Kirsten's instructions exactly.

Henry idled as we watched her enter her house through the front door. I was wondering if I'd seen the last of Mischa alive, but if I'd interpreted what Jennie had just told us correctly, someone else was in the process of dying that night instead of Mischa. It was rotten that this brought me relief, because I didn't know who that other person was, but still . . . I was confident that I'd hear from Mischa an hour later.

The parking lot at our town's drugstore was crowded despite it being Christmas Eve and getting late. There weren't too many stores open in our town past eight o'clock at night on any weeknight, but Hennessey's had a twenty-four-hour pharmacy.

"I'm staying in the car," Trey announced as Henry parked. "I don't need gossip making its way back to my mom that I was out shopping when I was supposed to be under lock and key at home."

Henry accompanied me inside under the pretense of wanting to pick up orange juice for his mom, but I suspected his real motivation was wanting to avoid alone time with Trey in the car. Henry had been kind enough not to make a point of it throughout the day, but he probably had just as many questions for Trey about the night Olivia died as I did.

We split up once we were inside and I ventured over to the cosmetics aisle, having no idea what to bring home for my mom. Mom wasn't really into makeup; she considered unscented skin moisturizer to be an indulgence. A set of memory foam leg pillows caught my eye. Just as I was reaching for them to check the price, I recognized a female voice farther down the aisle over the Christmas carol playing on the store's overhead audio system, and I flinched.

"Yeah, we were supposed to fly out yesterday, but my mom was admitted to the hospital, so we rescheduled it for February." She paused before continuing. "She's already doing much better. It was just the flu, but my dad wanted her to stay in the hospital because our house is so drafty. Anyway, it sucks that we had to delay our trip, but St. Barts will always be there. The good news is that my parents are going into the city for New Year's. Yep. Mandarin Oriental, every year. So you know what that means. . . ."

Ever so slowly, I turned my head in the direction of the voice, and even though I knew it belonged to Violet Simmons, my stomach still turned when I saw her standing in front of the nail polish display, phone pressed to her ear. Looking as deceptively angelic as ever, Violet wore a scarlet wool coat and an ivory beret, her dark hair cropped just below her jaw in a new trendy lob haircut. She was completely oblivious to my presence, and kept chatting away.

"Yeah. You know it," she continued, mindlessly lifting up a bottle of ballet pink and examining it. I couldn't help but notice that her fingernails looked as if they'd been chewed down below the quick, with bloody scabs on both sides of the nail on her thumb. Violet had always had perfectly manicured nails at the beginning of the school year; I didn't have a single memory of seeing her biting her nails when we were still in classes together. "You have to hurry up and get well so that you can be there next week! Pete's brother just turned twenty-one, so he thinks he can get a keg. It's gonna be bomb." She paused, listening, before adding, "Well, I'm sure she'll turn up. I mean, first-world problems, right? It's one thing to be sad that you got dumped, but a little much to have the entire police force looking for you on Christmas Eve."

I was caught between desperately wanting to hear more of her conversation and needing to slip away unseen. Technically, even though it wasn't my fault, I was violating the restraining order I'd been issued by Judge Roberts. Despite the danger of her spotting me, I couldn't resist listening for just another second, so very much more curious about her after my encounter with Jennie's ghost. Five sisters . . . What could that have meant? If Violet had sisters, why hadn't she ever mentioned them? And why hadn't I seen traces of them when I was at her house?

As I carefully placed the leg pillows back on the shelf with the intention of sneaking away to find Henry, I noticed him appear at the other end of the aisle, no doubt looking for me. I shook my head at him in warning, but it was too late.

Violet had noticed him, and she followed his line of sight over to where I stood.

"Tracy, let me call you back," Violet said, and tapped her phone to end her call. Ignoring me, she waved at Henry and said to both of us, "Well, this is unexpected. Merry Christmas, I guess. Are you guys, like, together now?"

Henry replied, "We're just friends."

I turned to walk away, knowing nothing good would come from engaging with her, especially not in public. We were going to somehow have to get her alone to play Light as a Feather, Cold as Marble with us, and having a showdown at the pharmacy on Christmas Eve was not going to make arranging that any easier.

But she said calmly to Henry, "I'm really sorry for your loss. I didn't get a chance to tell you at Olivia's wake, but she was a wonderful person. She was very welcoming to me when I first moved to Willow."

Henry's green eyes darkened as he processed Violet's words. She obviously didn't realize that Henry knew she was responsible for Olivia's death, and that he was just as intent on getting justice as I was on preventing Violet from killing more people. She really had some nerve, making such a kind gesture toward him right in front of me when back in the fall she'd practically confessed to me what she'd done. I hoped Henry would have the sense not to rip into her, but when I saw him furrow his brow as he struggled to form a response, I stepped past her and grabbed him by the arm to lead him toward the checkout area.

"That's very kind of you to say, Violet," I said, trying my best to sound sincere. To Henry, I commanded, "Let's go."

He glared angrily at Violet over his shoulder as he followed me down the aisle until he lifted the leg pillows he'd seen me holding off the shelf. "Did you want to get these?" he asked me, remembering that we'd come to the store in the first place to pick up a gift for my mom.

I was nodding in reply, my back to Violet, when I heard her ask, "How's Mischa?" There was no bitterness in her voice insinuating that Mischa should have been dead by then, even though I knew that was why she was asking. She sounded just as polite and sweet as she had at the beginning of the school year, as if she actually cared about Mischa's well-being.

"She's just great, actually," I answered cheerfully, not wanting to let on that Mischa was probably lighting her seven-day candle at home at that very moment and not even allowing herself to drink water for fear of choking.

We stepped into line, and as the clerk gave me change from my twenty-dollar bill, I noticed Violet walking toward the checkout area with her father.

The voices in my head stirred, and I commanded them to stop. I managed to successfully keep them at a low murmur as I thanked the clerk. *The eyes, the eyes,* they seemed to be saying. Although I knew whatever they were trying to convey was probably important, I just didn't want to hear them at that moment. And yet I involuntarily turned to look once again at Mr. Simmons over my shoulder.

When he and Violet's mother had sat in on all of my court hearings in the fall, I'd noticed that he was exceptionally handsome, just like Mrs. Simmons was remarkably beautiful. Neither of them looked like the other parents in town, which wasn't to say that everyone else's parents were unattractive. Mischa's mom did Pilates and had a forehead frozen by Botox. Candace's mom always had a flawless spray tan and wore skinny jeans.

But Violet's parents looked like movie stars. Her father had broad shoulders, a square jaw, and just a hint of silver at his temples to make him look sophisticated, and was slim enough to suggest that he could probably compete in a triathlon if he felt like it. In his charcoal-colored wool-and-cashmere coat, with his leather driving gloves folded in one hand, he presented himself more like the prime minister of a foreign country than as a suburban dad in Wisconsin stepping into line at the pharmacy to buy a roll of wrapping paper and bottle of mouthwash.

For a split second, Mr. Simmons's eyes met mine. He recognized me—how could he not? But if he was angry to see me at Hennessey's, his expression didn't suggest so.

"Come on," Henry said, leading me toward the store's exit. The

Simmonses *did* have a restraining order against me, and I was definitely within one hundred feet of Violet inside that store. "Nice and easy. Let's just leave."

When we returned to the car in the lot, it felt strange to climb into the back with Trey and leave Henry alone in the front as if he were our chauffeur, so I took the front passenger seat.

"You saw who went in there, right?" Trey asked us.

"The princess of death and her father?" Henry said as he started the car's engine.

"I wish I had a phone so I could have warned you guys," Trey said. "I was a little afraid things were gonna get rough in there."

As we backed out of our spot, Mr. Simmons and Violet exited the store. I watched them walk across the parking lot in the side-view mirror as Henry navigated us back onto State Street, and wondered how Violet could sleep at night knowing what she'd done, and continued to do, to innocent people. The day Trey, Mischa, and I had confronted her on the track about killing Olivia and Candace, she had seemed overwhelmed with emotion, insisting that the deaths weren't her fault while admitting that spirits guided her on what to do. Now she was acting completely oblivious about the tragedies, practically daring me to correct her in her apology to Henry. What had changed? Had she convinced herself of her innocence? Did she think perhaps I'd forgotten she'd confessed her involvement?

I thought once again of her ragged fingernails and wondered if Violet's new cavalier attitude was actually a cover. Maybe she was putting on a brave face to convince herself that she was strong enough to do what was required even though she was just as afraid of her actions as we were. I wondered if anyone in Lake Forest had ever gotten as close to figuring out what she was doing as we were getting, which made me curious once again about who had sent the lunar calendar to the Richmonds. Violet wasn't as good at covering her tracks as she believed herself to be, and maybe she wasn't the heartless villain her dilemma required her to be either.

"Check it out," I told Henry and Trey. "I overheard her talking to Tracy Hartford on the phone. I guess her parents are going to be in Chicago on New Year's, so Violet's going to throw a huge party at her house."

"The perfect opportunity to predict more deaths," Trey grumbled.

"Yeah, but then she said something that I think was about Stephani deMilo. You guys know she's missing, right?" I asked just as Henry hit the brakes. Two police cars raced through the intersection of State Street and Wisconsin Avenue, cutting him off. Their sirens were roaring and lights were swirling. Just then, my scalp began tingling again, which was kind of infuriating. Why hadn't it tingled at Hennessey's to make me aware of Violet's presence? Kirsten hadn't given me an explanation for the purpose of the voices and the tingling, at all. The police cars were headed in the direction of the deMilos' family farm, and suddenly everything clicked into place.

Everything.

"Stephani deMilo? Isn't she that senior who's on pom squad with Violet?" Trey asked from the back seat. But his voice was a blur as my eyes followed the police cars. Yes, Stephani and Violet were friends. It made perfect sense that Violet knew Mischa wasn't dead yet because if Mischa was next, according to Jennie, and would always technically still be next in the order to die as long as the curse kept skipping her every month, then Violet would have had to make a different sacrifice that month.

She hadn't sounded the least bit concerned that Stephani had gone missing when she'd been on the phone with Tracy. Honestly, I'd kind of forgotten about Stephani's disappearance since Mischa had mentioned it that morning because I didn't know Stephani too well. But it was definitely odd for any kid in our town to vanish for more than a day, and now that I had seen police heading toward Stephani's family's property and my scalp was tingling, I got a bad hunch that Stephani wasn't missing.

Stephani was probably dead.

"You guys?" I said. "Hear me out. What if the curse skipped Mischa last month because the nuns were praying the rosary for her, and Violet didn't make a sacrifice because she thought Mischa was a done deal? And because she didn't make a sacrifice . . ." My scalp kept tingling, burning as if it were hot to the touch. The elements of the story all arranged themselves like a constellation in my head, dots forming a shape. Even Violet's ragged fingernails—had she started chewing them because she was freaked out? "Her mom started getting sick—sick enough that her family had to cancel their holiday trip to St. Barts? So then she told a prediction for Stephani, and now Stephani's missing?"

Henry turned left onto Maple Road and smiled at me. "I'd say it sounds like a very detailed theory. Maybe too detailed. I mean, it's been a long afternoon. We should be careful not to overreact."

In the back seat, Trey scoffed at Henry. "Um, were you not just with us a few hours ago when McKenna interrogated a ghost? She's not someone who overreacts."

I slid lower in the front seat, mashing my lips together, kind of wishing I hadn't shared my theory. It all lined up for me. My heart was racing. I practically wanted to type it all into a note on my phone so that I wouldn't forget how the pieces all worked together. It frustrated me that Henry and Trey weren't as excited as I was.

After a minute of contemplative driving, Henry added, "What you're proposing sounds logical." Henry looked over in my direction and asked, "Are you okay?"

Truthfully, I felt like I was overheating, about to break into a sweat. This was the most intense case of the tingles I'd had yet, which convinced me that I was onto something.

Although Trey was taking my side, his tone bothered me a little. If Henry was going to be pitching in on our mission, animosity toward him from Trey was going to slow us down. We turned onto Martha Road, and I realized that we hadn't made plans for next steps.

Our street looked magically beautiful in that calm, safe way residential streets seem to during the holidays. Glowing plastic figurines of Santa, Rudolph, and Frosty the Snowman decorated snowy rooftops, and the Blumenthal family across the street had put an enormous plywood dreidel and plastic menorah in their yard. Trees heavily wrapped in lights and garland watched stoically in front windows.

"So, what do we do next?" I asked, wondering just how serious Henry was about seeing this through.

"Regroup the day after tomorrow and figure out how, where, and when we can get Violet to play the game," Henry said.

In the back seat, Trey quipped sarcastically, "Right." He was making fun of Henry's delivery, as if the four of us convincing Violet to do *anything* were going to be easy. Trey got out of the back seat of the car, and I unfastened my seat belt.

"Thanks for coming with us today," I told Henry. "And for driving, you know. But mostly for coming with. I can't even imagine what you're thinking right now, after the day we've had."

"I'm thinking," Henry said, and paused before continuing, "that my sister was really lucky to have a friend like you. I mean, anyone would be. I don't think I've ever known anyone as brave as you before."

I was highly aware of Trey waiting for me just outside the car, but I didn't want to rush this moment with Henry. "I don't know if I'm *brave*," I said. "Maybe *desperate*."

"Nah. You're brave. I have something for you, from my parents. I hope it's not weird for you that they got you a gift." He reached past me and opened the glove compartment, withdrawing from it a small box wrapped in sparkling gold paper with a fat gossamer bow tied around it.

I was so flustered that the Richmonds had bought me a gift that I didn't know how to respond. "You didn't have to bring me anything! That was really nice of you." It would have never crossed my mind to buy a gift for him. I'd assumed after Olivia died that I'd probably never interact with Henry again. Although his parents had sat in on my hearings with the judge back in November, Henry hadn't accompanied them to Shawano County Court.

"I did. *We* did," Henry corrected himself. "It's something that my mom got for Olivia every Christmas. One of her favorite things."

"That's really . . . Wow. I don't know what to say." Through my window, I'd noticed that Trey had taken a few steps away from the car and was now pacing impatiently in the snow. The kitchen light was the only one that was on at his house, which meant that no one else was home yet.

Henry took a deep breath and blinked away tears that were forming in his eyes. "My parents have to believe *something*, because it's too hard for them to believe that Olivia died in a random accident, and that just a few weeks later, Candace also ended up dead. So whatever it was that you and Trey were doing in November, my parents believe that you were trying to avenge Olivia's death. They're grateful, I guess." He looked out through the windshield at my house as if he was a little embarrassed before adding with more confidence, "Yeah. *We're* grateful."

I never would have imagined that Olivia's parents, who were well-respected pillars of our community, were supportive of what Trey and I had been trying to accomplish. Henry's opinion shouldn't have mattered to me. Whatever romantic possibilities had ever existed between us were ancient history now. But still, even if it was simply because I had admired Olivia when she was alive, her brother's opinion of me *did* matter. "What do *you* think?"

"I think . . . you should rest up because we've got a game to play," Henry told me.

When I stepped out of the car, I saw a flash of motion in the living room window of my house. It was my mom, waving at me. Luckily, Trey had predicted that the longer the Mercedes idled in our driveway, the more chance that she'd look outside. He'd inched up to our garage door, where he'd be out of her view.

Henry backed out of the driveway, and my mom vanished from the window, probably assuming I'd enter the house in a matter of seconds. Instead, I trotted toward Trey, and he pulled me close. "Am I going to get to see you at all while we're home?" he asked, wrapping his arms tightly around my torso as if he didn't want to let me go. Even though my heart was urging me to melt into him, Kirsten's warning had driven an ice pick into my stomach. I was as wary as if a hornet were circling my head, and paranoid that he would notice how tense I was under his touch.

"I'm sorry," I whispered. "I thought all of this was over. I thought we'd be able to spend these few days making plans for . . ." My words drifted off. The fantasies I'd had at Sheridan about the two of us finding a way to be together after he turned eighteen and was released from Northern Reserve that summer now seemed naïve. I'd imagined us both moving down to Florida closer to my dad, where I could finish high school in Tampa and Trey could get a job fixing cars. Now I was relieved that I'd never shared such notions with him, even if only because our phone calls had been monitored. If he *was* intentionally deceiving me, revealing my blind trust in him like that would have confirmed what a good job he was doing.

However, even though the smoke had curled toward Trey when Kirsten had blown out her candle, Jennie hadn't instructed me to be cautious about him, and the story she'd brought up about the tree in our yard had involved him. I pressed my nose against his neck to inhale his smell, truly not knowing what to believe. It was out of the question to simply ask him why Kirsten had urged me not to trust him and if there was something he wasn't telling me. If there was anything he hated, it was when people misjudged him. He'd been mouthing off to teachers since elementary school, and there was no changing his mind once he became convinced that someone was his enemy. I didn't know which would have been worse: finding out that Trey was actually working with Violet to safeguard her murderous practice, or wrongly accusing him and having him turn on me. "I was really hoping we would get to be alone together today," he said, his voice weighted with longing. "There are, like, a million things I need to tell you." We kissed, and as soon as I felt his mouth on mine I knew there was a risk of us getting carried away and my mom catching us. I needed to get in the house before she stepped outside to find out what was taking me so long. Whatever danger he posed to me, while he was kissing me, I didn't care. The whole time I'd been away at Sheridan, suffering through commands barked by cruel guards and nasty comments from other students, my hope for being reunited with Trey was all that had kept me going. This was the peak of the danger I was in if he was lying to me, and I knew it. Whenever he reminded me that I, alone, was special, I was willing to cast aside my doubts about his intentions.

I pushed him away gently, sensing that at least a minute or two had passed since Henry had backed out of our driveway. "I have to go," I reminded him. "Or my mom will totally know you're out here with me."

"I know," he said, pressing his fingertip against the cupid's bow of my upper lip. "Tomorrow, somehow."

"Tomorrow," I agreed, although I had absolutely no idea how either of us was going to slip away from our punitive home situations to connect.

I reached the path which led to my front steps, and heard Trey call out behind me, "McKenna." He was still standing where I'd left him. "If you're right, and Stephani deMilo dies tonight, then Violet's still a month behind. Unless she killed some random stranger in another town or something."

He had a valid point, and I was still thinking about it when I entered the house and unlaced my snow boots. Jennie had said there were three, and one was crossing over. Violet had been talking to Tracy Hartford when I'd overheard her on the phone, and had said something about wanting Tracy to feel better in time to attend her New Year's party. That meant Tracy was sick, which was a far cry from her being close to death, but still . . . Could Violet be desperate or evil enough to kill off her closest friends?

"I hope you had a fun day," Mom said, standing in the doorway to the kitchen and looking cross with me. A Christmas movie was on TV; my mother's puppy, Maude, was curled up on the couch; and Mom had turned on the lights on the tree, which were softly blinking.

I held the bag from Hennessey's behind my back while wiggling out of my coat. "I did, although the snow really messed up our plans. Mischa was trying to find a lip gloss kit for her sister, and it was sold out everywhere, so we had to go to three different malls." The lies just rolled off my tongue, which made me feel awful. I never used to lie to my mother before that year. "Then it was a mess getting home because so many roads haven't been plowed yet."

I hurried down the hall to toss my purchase into my bedroom, and then joined Mom in the kitchen, grateful to discover that she'd saved me a plate. She'd prepared a small feast of my favorite dishes: roasted chicken with garlic mashed potatoes, split-top dinner rolls, and baked carrots. We didn't typically have a special meal on Christmas Eve, so I felt guilty that she'd gone to all this trouble for my benefit, although the sight and smell of so much food was making me nauseous after what I'd witnessed just two hours earlier.

"Thank you for this." I kissed her on the cheek, something I hadn't done in longer than I could remember. My desire to tell her about finding Jennie on Route 32 was making me feel like a balloon about to pop, but I couldn't drop a bomb like that on her without upsetting her in addition to giving her good cause to send me to a sanitarium. "I'm starving."

"That looked like Randy Richmond's Mercedes in the driveway just now," Mom said as she sat down across from me at the table.

There was no point in lying about Henry; she'd seen the car with her own eyes. "Yeah. Henry drove us. Mischa didn't tell me that she'd invited him."

She lifted an eyebrow ever so slightly without saying a word, but implying that there was a reason other than holiday shopping why Henry had accompanied us. "It's not like that, Mom," I corrected her. "He just misses his sister and wanted to hang out. That's all."

"If you say so," Mom said, but I could see the ends of her lips curling into a smile. "It wouldn't be the worst problem to have if he had a crush on you, would it? I mean, he is totally hot."

"*Mom*," I groaned.

After having seen the grisly spectacle of Jennie's ghost bleeding all over the highway, I didn't have much of an appetite. But I did my best to push aside everything Kirsten had told me and the lingering visuals in my head of Jennie spattering blood onto the snow to focus on our conversation. Before that year, I had been very close with my mom, and seeing Jennie earlier that night had made reestablishing my bond with her a top priority. She shared with me a little bit more about her relationship with Glenn than she had previously, and told me that they'd met years ago when he had been a visiting professor at the University of Wisconsin–Sheboygan before his divorce. It broke my heart that I couldn't tell Mom about reconnecting with Jennie, because it would have meant so much to her that Jennie was keeping watch over us from the afterlife. Even though I couldn't share that with her, I kept Jennie close in my thoughts, hoping that her spirit could channel some of the rare happy moments in our household.

It had turned out to be an oddly wonderful Christmas Eve, only just as Mom handed me a bowl of ice cream to take into the living room so that we could watch a holiday movie together before bed, the voices began to murmur in the back of my head.

At first I thought they had resumed their chorus of *the eyes, the eyes*. But as they grew louder, it sounded more like they were saying, *the ice, the ice*. Although our living room was toasty, I began shivering, and after thirty more minutes of mental torment I announced to my mom that I was turning in for the night. She made a joke about Santa already knowing that I had been naughty that year, but I was too distracted to react.

In my room, I typed as much as I could remember of what Jennie had told me into a memo on my phone, just in case a long night's sleep made me forget some of it. By the time I'd gotten to the part about the five sisters, I was so cold that my teeth were chattering, and I wondered if I had caught a cold that day by meandering around in the snow. I tapped to close the memo I'd created and placed the pendulum Henry had purchased in the drawer of my nightstand. I plucked the tab from the flyer about spiritual training that Kirsten had given me out of my wallet and analyzed it. I put that in my drawer too, for future consideration. *The ice, the ice.* It was impossible to think straight with the voices demanding my attention. I decided to save the gift from the Richmonds for the morning.

As I tugged off my jeans, something fell out of my back pocket and hit the floor. It was the envelope that I had pulled out of the Emorys' mailbox earlier that day. I had completely forgotten about it all day long, and now sank onto my bed, studying it.

It was addressed to Mrs. M. J. Emory. The envelope was a creamy, heavy paper stock, the kind of sophisticated stationery that meant official business. I ran my fingertips over the label, and then the embossed return address in the top left corner: Ekdahl, West & Strohmann. The law firm's address was in Green Bay. I feared that not even Trey would be understanding if I were to ever get caught spying on his mother. Opening someone else's mail was a federal offense, not to mention a serious invasion of privacy.

But I had to know why Kirsten had warned me about Trey. If there was any possibility that he was endangering our chances of saving Mischa or shutting down Violet's murderous game, I had to know. So I slid my finger beneath the flap of the envelope and held my breath as I raised it, trying very hard not to tear it just in case I might try to glue it shut later and return it to the Emorys' mailbox.

Inside of the envelope was a single sheet of heavy paper, the same eggshell color as the envelope. My eyes had to scan it multiple times before the words forming the letter began to make sense to me. It mentioned that Mary Jane Svensson Emory, Trey's mom, had violated terms of a contract she had signed eighteen years earlier. She had received payment for compliance with that contract, and now an unnamed client of the law firm was suing her for damages, with interest. This letter was a second notice. Mrs. Emory would be summoned to appear in court if she failed to contact the law firm to make payment arrangements by the first of January.

My hands trembled so violently that the letter shook as I reread it for the fifth time. The Emorys must have been selling their house because presumably Mrs. Emory needed money. And the amount of money that was owed to the firm's client was so astronomical that the value of an unremarkable three-bedroom house in Willow, Wisconsin, was barely going to make a difference.

What could Trey's mother have possibly done eighteen years ago to have gotten herself into so much legal trouble? And then it hit me. Trey would be turning eighteen in July.

The eyes, the eyes. Of course. Mr. Simmons's aquamarine eyes, the very same that Violet had inherited, were the same hue and shape as Trey's. Now that I was thinking about the resemblance between Trey and Violet's father, their relationship was so absurdly obvious that it seemed outrageous that Mr. Simmons had sat in on Trey's courtroom hearings back in November without everyone in attendance realizing instantly that Trey was his son.

Violet's father was Trey's father, or at the very least, his uncle. What kind of contract could Trey's mother have possibly violated eighteen years earlier, when she was probably just a college student? Was it possible that Violet's father was the client of Ekdahl, West & Strohmann seeking payment from Trey's mom?

Violet and Trey were half siblings, which definitely seemed like a good enough reason for Kirsten to have warned me about Trey . . . only did Trey *know* who his real father was? He and Walter weren't close, but I had never suspected growing up that Walter wasn't Trey's biological father. Walter's boringness matched Mary Jane's; they had always seemed to me like a typical Willow couple who were perfectly content to drive used cars and live in the old, inexpensive part of town. Now I realized how completely ignorant I'd been my whole life. Trey looked nothing like heavyset, grumpy Walter. Walter liked to watch Packers games and true-crime television shows, and Trey read books about the design of space shuttle engines.

Trey was tall, with long limbs, elegant features, and a pale complexion, like Violet. He had an enormous appetite for knowledge on topics of interest to him. Everything about him suggested that he would have thrived in the Simmonses' world if he'd been told growing up that he had the same potential as Violet—one of opportunities for higher education, world travel, and a chance to have a remarkable career outside of our tiny town. And if he knew that was where he rightfully belonged, then even though I didn't know all of the details, somehow getting himself on good terms with his biological sister and father seemed like ample reason for him to be assisting them instead of me.

From where I lay in bed, through the horizontal slits in between the blinds on my window, I could see the light on in Trey's room. I wondered if he was thinking about me, and drifted off to sleep annoyed with myself for still hoping that he loved me and wasn't lying to me despite the abundant reasons I'd been given that day to believe that I should be highly suspicious of him.

CHAPTER 7

I SLEPT TERRIBLY THAT NIGHT, TOSSING AND turning, cold no matter how tightly I pulled my blankets around me. My dreams weren't about anything in particular, but rather clouded with a powerful sense of loss. I wanted to find Jennie again. Reconnecting with her once had made me desperate to communicate with her at least once more. I doubted driving up and down Route 32 the next time it snowed would produce her a second time, and the distress of not knowing where she'd gone woke me up throughout the night.

I was surprised, since Stephani was missing, that Olivia's ghost hadn't been making a racket in my bedroom. In the past, she'd done a thorough job of making sure I knew whenever I'd failed to prevent Violet from killing again. Maybe Stephani hadn't actually played any games with Violet, and she really had just run away from home. But still, my ears listened for stirrings from within my closet, where my music boxes were packed away, and it made me uneasy to instead hear the sound of snowflakes drifting against my windowpane, with sirens (real or imagined) in the distance.

When the sound of the doorbell woke me up shortly after

dawn, I was shivering beneath my blankets. I wandered into the living room to see who had stopped by and found Mom standing in the open front doorway with her robe wrapped tightly around her. It was Christmas morning, and although we were expecting Glenn over for dinner later, she hadn't mentioned expecting any guests so early in the day. "Who's here?" I asked. She stepped aside, and I saw Trey standing there in his winter coat, shoulders slumped, head hung.

Now that I'd had the epiphany that he was a blood relative of Violet's, reminders of her face hung on every minute detail of his. The same blue eyes fringed with jet-black lashes. The same full lower lip, slightly upturned nose.

"Hey," he said, looking past my mom. "I can't stay long because we're about to drive up to my grandparents' house. But we were just at church and Father Fahey dedicated the service to Stephani deMilo."

I opened my mouth, but no sound came out.

"Her body was found early this morning in the pond behind her house. She fell through the ice and it froze over her."

The ice, the ice.

Surprisingly, Mom didn't intervene when I invited Trey inside and led him down to my bedroom so that we could talk privately. Although I intended to ask him for details about Stephani, it occurred to me that I might not have another moment of privacy with him while we were both home for the holidays to find out how much he knew about his connection to Mr. Simmons. Whether or not he was aware of his biological father's identity and his feelings about being related to Violet might make it clearer to me whose side he was on. Asking simply couldn't wait.

Once I closed the door, the first words that popped out of my mouth were, "Why didn't you tell me about your father?"

Trey looked confused. "What about him?"

"Not Walter," I said. "Your *real* father."

He knew instantly what I was talking about, and didn't even try to deny it. He slowly shook his head at me, and his shoulders slumped as if he were apologizing to me for having done something wrong. In fact, he seemed afraid that I was angry at him. But he didn't turn away; he looked me right in the eye. "I would have told you, but honestly, I don't really have anything to do with the guy. My relationship to him feels more like paperwork than DNA."

And now, seeing that he seemed ashamed about the topic, I asked more tenderly, "How long have you known?"

"A long time. I mean, I knew *about* him, but I didn't think about it much until they moved to Willow. I didn't tell you because I didn't think it mattered," he said. He looked up at the ceiling and inhaled so deeply that his shoulders heaved. "I mean, I don't think of him as my father. I don't really think about him at all. He's never been a part of my life. But now, I guess, all of that does matter."

"I wish you'd told me sooner," I said. *They don't have a story for him,* Violet had said when we'd suggested playing the game again. It was all I could do not to scream at him because Violet must have known all along. Even the afternoon of Olivia's birthday party, when his name had been suggested as a possible date to the Fall Fling for her, she'd pretended not to know who we were talking about. And she'd completely duped me with her little act. I'd even been jealous that my friends had suggested he'd be a better match for her than for me, which was obviously nonsense now that I knew the truth:

Violet was Trey's half sister. In the way that I thought about siblings because I was a twin, this made her bond with him much stronger than mine.

"Does he know about you? Mr. Simmons?" I asked. My parents had known the Emorys since moving to Martha Road. It was entirely possible that Trey's mom hadn't told Walter Emory whose baby she was carrying; I was pretty sure his parents had gotten married before Trey was born.

Trey replied, "He knows." He paused. "There's more, a lot more, but I don't have time to tell you all of it now." Seeing that I was upset, he reached for me and kissed me. "Honestly, I would have told you. But I've never even had a conversation with the guy. You saw him. He sat in the courtroom back in November and just, like, frowned at me the whole time. My mom thinks he may have even paid off that judge in Shawano County to send me as far away from Willow as possible to keep me out of his life."

This rang true; Trey's punishment had been more severe than mine. The school to which he'd been sent was a medium-security military-style academy. A lot of girls at my school had committed crimes, but from what I'd seen on the website, Trey's school was surrounded by a high fence topped with razor wire like an actual prison. It was a three-hour drive from Willow—far enough that Trey's mom had only driven out once to see him for weekend visitation.

In light of the letter that I'd stolen from the Emorys' mailbox, it didn't seem outrageous to think that Mr. Simmons had paid off a judge to get Trey out of town at all. I wanted to believe Trey that he really hadn't thought that the secret he'd been keeping from me about his paternity was a big deal. But I had to ask, "Did you know about Violet? What she does?"

He shook his head and looked directly into my eyes. "No. I didn't even know she existed until the week before school started, when my mom sat me down for an important talk and told me I should stay away from the new girl at school."

I asked, "Why would she want you to stay away from your own half sister? It's only fair that you'd be curious."

A car honked outside. "I've gotta go. I'll try to come by tonight to explain more, but tomorrow's a better possibility," he said. He kissed me again and promised, "I swear I didn't know what Violet could do."

Expressing enthusiasm for my Christmas gifts was a challenge that morning, given that every thought running through my head was laced with doom. Stephani was dead. Somehow, I'd known all along that her death would involve ice. I'd failed to ask Jennie where the voices that only I could hear were coming from, and if I could trust them. I wanted to believe that Trey hadn't told me about his relationship to the Simmons family because he thought it wasn't important, but it still struck me as deceitful that he'd withheld that personal information from me. It was all I could do to muster up a little bit of holiday cheer for my mom's benefit despite my heavy heart.

"Oh, Mom. You shouldn't have. It's *so* nice."

I held a brand-new black tote bag in my hands, and I examined every zippered pocket and pouch inside of it.

"Glenn helped pick it out. He knows more about the cool styles than I do," she said, blushing a little. It was a generous gift, especially after a year when I had been a hell of a lot naughtier than nice. "He said this was the brand all his nieces wanted for Christmas. I told him you had never seemed very interested in brands, but he said . . ."

Her voice faded out as I drowned in my thoughts. Stephani deMilo and I hadn't ever been friends. But the news about her accidental death was like the sun passing in front of the moon during an eclipse; it was blocking out all of the light. Under different circumstances, my mother probably would have been more sensitive toward me about the death of another classmate. That morning, however, she was completely focused on trying to maintain her holiday cheer.

Although Mischa had texted me after we'd dropped her off at home the night before, I was eager to slink off to my room to text her again and make sure she was still okay. I'd left my phone recharging down the hall, knowing how much Mom hated when I texted and scrolled through Instagram if we were spending time together. I was now desperate to know exactly what Violet had been up to since I'd left for Sheridan. I couldn't shake Trey's suggestion from the night before that even with Stephani's death, Violet was still a month behind in her sacrifices. And according to Jennie, in addition to Mischa and Stephani, there was still one more person in line to die.

"You may have to leave it here while you're back at school, but you can use it next year," Mom said hopefully, nodding at the tote bag.

Judge Roberts had said my case could be up for review after school let out for summer if I stayed out of trouble at Sheridan. I had little hope that I'd be allowed to return to my old school for my senior year; presumably Violet would still be in attendance there and I'd never be able walk the same halls as her again. But instead of reminding Mom about that, I nodded enthusiastically and thought about how this beautiful bag would sit in my closet for a long time before I'd be able to carry it. Once upon a time, before Violet Simmons had entered my life, I'd considered studying veterinary science in college, but that fantasy now seemed pretty impossible. Admission was going to be pretty challenging because of my record, and the tuition at the Sheridan School for Girls was no doubt draining the meager college fund my parents had set up.

"Sorry, Mom. I know it's kind of weird," I apologized as she opened the gift I'd bought from Hennessey's and examined the leg pillows as if uncertain about their purpose. "But I know how you like to put your feet up at night when you watch TV, and these are supposed to improve circulation."

"These are great. I'll use them," she told me. I wished I were in a position to give her diamond earrings or a sophisticated wool coat to replace the unfashionable stuffed winter puffer she'd been wearing since I was in elementary school.

I opened the rest of my gifts in a rushed daze. Dad and Rhonda had shipped me a new bathing suit, probably because they'd assumed just like my mom that I'd be relocating to Florida that summer. The gift that Henry had given me contained a bottle of Olivia's favorite perfume. Simply lifting the cap and catching a whiff of it made my throat tighten as if I was about to cry.

An hour later, when I was helping Mom make pancakes, Mischa dropped by unannounced. My mom wasn't thrilled to see her, as she associated Mischa with my expulsion from Willow High.

I informed my mom that we were taking Maude outside, and we stepped out onto our deck. We brushed snow off of our deck furniture and sat down as Maude played in the snow.

What I'd discovered about Trey's paternity was on the tip of my tongue, but telling Mischa about his connection to Violet was out of the question because of her tendency to overreact. Luckily, she'd come over specifically to tell me everything she'd heard about Stephani.

"They're calling it a suicide," Mischa told me, her words laced with disgust. "At least they're using that kind of delicate language, you know? Like how it's so tragic that Stephani just went through a breakup and hadn't told her parents that she's bi, and she didn't have anyone to confide in. It's ridiculous. Who kills themselves by wandering out onto thin ice in the dead of winter?"

"The police just found her body this morning. How have you already heard gossip about how she died?" I asked.

"Matt's mom had to keep the donut shop open overnight because the cops were searching the pond on the deMilos' farm." Matt's mom, Mrs. Galanis, managed the strip-mall donut shop next door to our town's one and only Laundromat. "Matt and his brothers had to get up early this morning and go help her. He told me they think she fell through the ice on Monday when she took her dog out for a walk and didn't come home. Her body was almost frozen solid. They're trying to figure out if her cause of death was drowning or hypothermia, although I guess it doesn't matter. If they're right about her falling in on Monday, then she was in the water almost forty-eight hours. If you ask me, I think her dog probably ran out onto the ice and she was trying to save him. Even if that was part of Violet's story, most people would try to save their dog, right?"

Her theory about Stephani venturing out onto the ice after her dog gave me a chill. Maude had scratched a heart shape into the dirt in my yard earlier that fall, leading me incorrectly to believe that the object that gave Violet her powers was a locket she wore. I was reminded of the book Kirsten had given me, and vowed to read it that afternoon. My own experience definitely suggested that ghosts or spirits were able to manipulate animals with ease. I shuddered again, imagining what that moment must have been like for Stephani, having to decide within seconds whether to risk her life despite what Violet may have told her, or watch her dog die.

"What happened to the dog?" I dared to ask, not sure if I wanted to know the answer.

"He turned up back at the house on Monday. Stephani had his leash wrapped around her arm when they found her, so they think maybe she took him for a walk, saw the ice, decided to jump in, and let him run home." Mischa shook her head.

I asked, "What made them decide to search the pond if they originally thought she ran away from home?"

"I guess her car was in her parents' driveway the whole time, and yesterday her dad noticed there was a patch of ice out on the pond that looked different from the rest, like there was a hole in it that had frozen over again."

"Is your candle burning at home?" I asked her.

"God. Yes—in my closet with the door cracked just a bit so it doesn't run out of oxygen. Although if my mom finds an open flame in my bedroom while I'm out of the house, she'll strangle me before

I have a chance to choke the way Violet said I would," Mischa said.

I explained Trey's theory to her that Violet was still one sacrifice behind, and that it matched up with what Jennie had told me about there being three in line to die. As of that morning, there were two remaining: Mischa and someone whose identity we didn't know.

Mischa mulled this over for a long time before replying. She looked out over the backyard and watched my dog toss a stick around in the air. Finally, when she spoke, she said solemnly, "You know, when you describe it all that way, it's kind of like I killed Stephani by not dying when it was my turn."

"No," I insisted. "Don't even say that. None of this is anyone's fault except Violet's."

Her lower lip quivered, and I hoped she wouldn't start crying. I knew my mom was probably keeping an eye on us from the kitchen, and emotional outbursts were going to make it very clear for her what we were discussing.

"My whole life, all I really cared about was being the best at gymnastics. I'm supposed to compete in the state championships in Wisconsin Rapids this spring, and then the Pan Am Games in June. Did you know that? My coach thinks I might really have a shot at making the Olympic team."

I hadn't known that. Sometimes it was easy to forget that Mischa spent every morning and almost every night at the gym. It was part of why Olivia and Candace had been closer friends with each other than with her; Mischa had always had a completely separate life outside of school.

"Now? It's like none of that matters at all. Even this morning at practice, I barely had any energy for it. All I want to do is walk around outside and smell the air. Lie in my bed and enjoy how warm it is. I've missed out on so much of what everybody else gets to do with their lives, all so that one day I might get to win an Olympic medal. And now the only way I get to keep living long enough to try is if other people die in my place."

"Not if we break the curse," I told her. "We know what we have to do now, and if we can figure out who, other than you, is still in line, then maybe we can save them, too."

"And you think that third person might be Tracy," Mischa said doubtfully after listening to my hypothesis.

"It's all I've got," I admitted. "Unless Violet drives to other towns and reads tarot cards to strangers."

"No way. Tracy follows Violet around like an obedient puppy dog. Dracula wouldn't kill Igor, if you know what I mean," Mischa said, and I snickered, because her analogy of how Tracy had sucked up to Violet after Olivia's death was so accurate.

I had my doubts too, but added, "It can't hurt to find out just how sick Tracy is. Did Matt mention her being absent from school before the break started?"

Mischa snorted. "Matt does *not* keep tabs on sniveling windbags like Tracy Hartford."

I had a terrible idea, one that made me feel guilty before I even spoke it aloud. "I could ask Cheryl if Tracy's really sick. They're cousins. I'm sure they're scheduled to see each other at some kind of family event today."

"Cheryl Guthries! Isn't she that girl in band who kind of looks like a turtle?"

"You mean that girl in *color guard* who's the president of the

French National Honor Society and on the yearbook staff? *That* Cheryl Guthries," I corrected Mischa. Earlier in the school year, when I was desperate for Olivia and my new popular friends to like me, I probably wouldn't have dared to defend my old friend Cheryl. I didn't feel much better about defending Cheryl's reputation now, though, since I was suggesting that we pull her into Violet's dangerous game. Despite the terrible way I'd treated her in the fall when I'd suddenly found myself hanging out with popular girls like Olivia, Cheryl had written me letters consistently while I'd been away at Sheridan.

Mischa dramatically sighed. "Okay. Yes. *That* Cheryl Guthries."

"Like it or not, Mischa, your fate might rest in the hands of a girl who doesn't even have Snapchat," I teased. "Honestly, Cheryl is awesome."

Mischa rolled her eyes at me. "Fine. I'm sorry I called her a turtle. If you're going to ask her about Tracy, you might as well ask her if she's heard anything about Violet's New Year's party. I was thinking about it, and a house party might be a perfect setting for us to force Violet into playing a game."

I whistled at Maude for her to follow us inside. "A wake at a funeral parlor might work well too. Did you hear anything about what Stephani's family has planned?"

"The ground's frozen solid," Mischa replied. "No one's getting buried in central Wisconsin until spring. As far as any kind of memorial service? I don't know. They probably haven't had time to process yet."

Mischa left without staying too long, explaining that her family's Christmas Day tradition was to catch a movie in Ortonville and go out for Chinese food. In my bedroom, I unplugged my phone and noticed that I had over one hundred missed calls.

"Geez," I grumbled. Who'd been trying to call me so often? No one who had my phone number besides Mischa and Henry even knew my mom had let me have my phone back for the holiday break. I tapped into the list of missed calls and was stunned by what I saw.

I'd gotten one hundred and twelve phone calls the night before, while my phone was on silent mode. One every few minutes.

They were all from 000-000-0000. ID Unknown.

Anyone else would have assumed this was the work of a robot caller, an automated service just calling phone after phone, programmed to launch into a recording about how I'd won a free stay at a hotel chain if I answered. But I knew better. These calls were probably how Olivia had been trying to express her anger at me for not saving Stephani in time. I'd been wondering if Olivia's ghost had lost track of my whereabouts while I was away at Sheridan, and if I was right, these phone calls were proof that she had. Maybe Olivia only knew how to reach me in the same ways she had while she was alive: at my house or on my phone.

And just like that, the phone rang in my hands. I almost dropped it from sheer fright. It rang only once before the call ended. When my heart rate returned to normal, I put my phone back into silent mode so that future phone calls—and I suspected there would be more—wouldn't nearly cause me to go into cardiac arrest.

Cheryl answered on the second ring when I called. "Hey! You got your phone back!"

If I were a good friend, I would have called her sooner after arriving back in Willow, but there was a part of me that wanted to keep Cheryl away from everything having to do with Violet for her own safety.

"Yes," I said. "Technically only for emergencies, but I guess this kind of counts."

"A Christmas emergency?" Cheryl asked.

"Kind of. You're cousins with Tracy Hartford, right? Is there any chance you're going to see her at some point today?"

"The whole family will be at my grandmother's in an hour," Cheryl said, but then added, "But I don't think Tracy's coming. She had to go to the ER on Saturday, and they admitted her. She has bacterial meningitis."

"Um, I'm not a doctor, but that sounds really bad," I said. Bacterial meningitis was serious enough to imply that Tracy may very well have been one of Violet's three slated sacrifices.

"Yeah, I guess it is. She fell asleep during history class on Friday, and Mr. Dean yelled at her, but it turns out she's genuinely sick. It's super contagious. They might even delay the reopening of school because they need to send in cleaning crews to wipe down anything she might have touched last week."

"Well, it must be a cold day in hell if they're actually cleaning Willow High School," I joked in an attempt to cover up how thoroughly freaked out I was. "There's gum on the bottom of some of the desks that's probably been there since our parents were students." *Meningitis.* Tracy must have already been in the hospital when I'd heard Violet talking to her on the phone the night before.

"Bacterial meningitis is serious. It can be lethal."

"You're right," I said. "That wasn't funny. I'm sorry."

Well, of course it could be lethal. I could have guessed that much. As much as I disliked Tracy in high school for her cattiness and tendency to be a busybody, because I'd known her since preschool, I still felt protective of her. I couldn't just relax with the suspicion that she was doomed without at least *trying* to save her life.

"Is she at St. Matthew's?" I asked, already anxious about what I had in mind. Cheryl confirmed that she was. "Any chance she's allowed to have visitors?"

"She's been on antibiotics for a few days, so she's allowed to have visitors now. I'm supposed to go with my mom tomorrow," Cheryl said, not sounding enthusiastic about it at all. "I kind of don't want to, though. Just because we're cousins doesn't mean we're friends."

Crashing Tracy's hospital room with Mischa, Henry, and possibly Trey in tow was going to result in disaster. There would be too many of us, Tracy would freak out, and we wouldn't accomplish anything. If I were going to attempt to save Tracy from being Violet's next sacrifice, I was going to have to handle it on my own. "Any chance I could go with you? I kind of want to apologize for getting her caught up in all the stuff with Violet in the fall. Would that be weird?"

"I mean, other than the fact that Tracy hates you," Cheryl teased, and I could tell that she was smiling on the other end of the phone. "But I don't think my mom knows that."

We made plans for her to pick me up the next morning around ten, and my mom responded with surprise that I cared enough (or claimed to) about Tracy Hartford to give up a few hours of my time away from Sheridan to visit her. "Meningitis is serious, Mom," I said to reinforce that I really wanted to go.

That afternoon, I dove into my copy of *Understanding the Spirit World* because I had burdened myself with the task of finding a way to safeguard Tracy's life without having access to nuns, fancy rosaries, or an extra seven-day candle (which was out of the question anyway, since I was sure nurses weren't going to overlook a burning candle in a hospital room). Everything that the book explained about the behavior of ghosts or spirits—both good and evil—matched up with my experiences.

Spirits were able to manipulate energy with the most ease. This is what made their meddling with electricity so common. Lights flickering, turning television screens to static, causing computer glitches: These kinds of things required little effort. It took a great deal more power for spirits to impact matter—in other words, to make objects move. Only super-motivated spirits, or those that had been kicking around long enough to have had a lot of practice, were able to achieve this. And even still, because it was so difficult for them to interact with material objects in the living world, they tended to focus on movements that would capture the attention of the living.

In other words, a person might not necessarily notice that a heavy chair had been moved a few feet across a room unless they witnessed it in motion. But if a spirit were to instead wind up the crank of a small music box, for example, the end result would be much more attention-grabbing and instantaneous, similar to the relatively small amount of effort a spirit might put into twisting the knob on a gas stove instead of moving a chair, which would result in an open flame that would probably catch someone's eye and cause panic.

The book claimed that some spirits were able to alter the temperature of their surroundings, more often with cold than with warmth. The most dangerous and rare thing that spirits could do was implant an idea in someone's head, which they could do by either leaving "clues" using the tactics above, or by strongly influencing a person's senses. This was particularly hard for them to sustain for more than a few seconds because of the amount of effort it took, and the author of the book emphasized strongly that this was very different from spirits being able to impact a human's will, which they could not do.

Toward the end of the book, it went into specifics around clairvoyance and clairaudience, which were powers that some mediums had that made them particularly sensitive to spirits' attempts at communications.

Clairaudience, I repeated in my head. That was what I had: the ability to hear spirits' messages. By the time Glenn arrived for the glorious Christmas meal that Mom had prepared, my head was spinning. "Your mom tells me you have plans to study veterinary science," Glenn said, trying to make polite conversation with me while we ate.

"Yes. That would be cool. But I don't know. A lot's up in the air right now," I answered, not really wanting to get into a conversation about my dicey academic standing that night. After dinner, I noticed that Glenn knew exactly where to put dishes away as we cleaned up. He was pretty familiar with everything in our house, from how our ancient television remote control worked to where Mom kept her favorite chamomile tea bags in the cabinet next to the sink. I wondered if perhaps his relationship with Mom was a little more serious than she'd let on. That wouldn't have bothered me; I wanted Mom to have a cool boyfriend and to be happy. It just hurt my feelings a little that she hadn't been entirely honest with me.

That night in my room, I researched online extensively in the hope of finding a method to protect Tracy from Violet's prediction the same way in which Kirsten was protecting Mischa with the candle. The most promising possibility I came up with was similar to Kirsten's explanation for why the nuns' rosary beads had protected Mischa after she transferred to Catholic school. A blessed object given to the cursed person specifically for the purpose of protection might do the trick, although I was positive without even looking that there weren't any religious artifacts lying around our house that had been blessed by any saints or the Pope.

It was already eleven o'clock at night, and there was little chance I was going to talk my mom into driving me to a church gift shop at the crack of dawn. Suddenly, I had a burst of inspiration. I opened the drawer on my nightstand and pulled out the pendulum. I was about to ask it to reiterate what *yes* looked like when I remembered Kirsten's emphasis on safety first. I found matches in the kitchen and then returned to my room, praying that burning the palo santo given to me by Kirsten wouldn't set off the smoke alarm in the hallway. I raised my window, removed the screen, lit one end of the stick of smooth wood, and held it outside my room by a few inches, waving just a bit of the smoke back inside in a very rudimentary attempt to cleanse the space.

Only after blowing the flame out and closing my window, I dangled the pendulum from its chain with my right hand and asked it once again to show me what *yes* looked like. It swung in a clockwise circular motion just like it had in the store, which was all the encouragement I needed to keep going.

"Pendulum, is it possible for an object to offer protection to someone who has been cursed?"

Yes, it continued swinging.

"Would that object need to have some kind of blessing on it?"

Still . . . yes.

Deciding to get a lot more specific, I asked, "If I were to give Tracy Hartford something that belonged to my sister to protect her, would that be enough to keep her from dying before the next new moon?"

The pendulum slowed down considerably. Its trajectory grew wobbly, as if it wasn't completely sure it wanted to commit to an answer. And yet it remained moving in a clockwise motion.

That was a good enough answer for me.

CHAPTER 8

SINCE JENNIE HAD DIED AT THE AGE OF EIGHT and almost everything we owned at the time of her death had burned up, not many of her belongings still remained. Even the photos of us as kids that hung in our living room were reproductions of prints that my mom had given to our grandmother before our house fire. The only physical objects that I knew of that had once belonged to or been handled by Jennie were stored in airtight plastic containers in the garage. They were a tragic assemblage of oddities: drawings, crayons, a pair of scissors and an art smock left behind in Jennie's desk in our second-grade classroom, a spring windbreaker and a small stuffed giraffe that had been in my mom's car in our garage the night of the fire (which had not burned down completely), and a pair of size-six children's jeans that had been in the dryer the night of the fire. The dryer had been reduced to a charred cube, but amazingly enough, the clothes inside of it hadn't burned.

One denim belt loop from those jeans was what I carried with me to St. Matthew's Hospital the next morning when Cheryl and her mom picked me up in their station wagon. If there was one remarkable thing about the Guthries family, it was that they were always in a good mood. Even despite the icy roads, Mrs. Guthries was letting Cheryl drive for the practice, and we drove all the way to Suamico with the Holly channel blaring on satellite radio.

Once we reached St. Matthew's, we roamed every floor of the crowded visitors parking structure in search of a spot. It was odd to think that business went on at hospitals as usual in spite of holidays. As Cheryl set the parking brake, Mrs. Guthries told us both calmly, "I think it would be best if we didn't mention the news about Stephani deMilo to Tracy this morning."

Cheryl and I followed her mom into the lobby, waddling in our snow boots. The visitors' center was nothing at all like an emergency room. Cutout Santa Claus images and tinsel from the recently passed holiday still decorated the area. A fake pine tree had been erected in one corner of the lobby, under which similarly fake wrapped gifts had been placed. There was a sign near the tree announcing that the ornaments on its branches contained the Christmas wishes of terminally ill children at the hospital. It made me a little sad that it was December twenty-sixth, and unclaimed ornaments still hung from branches on the tree.

The nurse at the front desk informed Mrs. Guthries that Tracy was on the fourth floor, which was reserved for children. We would have to wear masks while visiting her, but they were for her protection instead of ours, since she'd already been on antibiotics since Saturday and was no longer contagious. I looked around as Mrs. Guthries wrote our names in marker on our visitor badges, growing uneasy. It felt sinister to be there, intending to visit someone who was probably not going to be pleased to see me. This was the hospital where I'd been taken after our house burned down. This was the building where I'd been given soup and pudding while my parents' burns were treated, where they'd learned that it was me who'd survived the fire and not Jennie.

It was also the hospital where Trey had been taken after the accident in which Olivia had died.

"Do you guys mind if I stop by the gift shop?" I asked on the way to the elevators. I couldn't very well hand Tracy a scrap of fabric from my dead sister's jeans and expect her to hold on to it for a few weeks.

From a display of stuffed animals, I chose a plush dog that would be perfect for my plan and paid for it with the twenty dollars my mom had zipped inside one of the inner pockets of the handbag she'd given me for Christmas. Mrs. Guthries bought a small arrangement of peach roses for Tracy, and Cheryl bought herself a bag of plain M&M's before we headed up to the fourth floor.

Once we stepped off the elevator and found Tracy's room, I excused myself to use the bathroom and said I'd be right back. In the bathroom down the hall, I used a small sewing kit that I'd brought from home in my coat pocket to cut a hole along a seam in the plush dog's neck. Into it, I tucked the piece of denim from Jennie's jeans, and I sewed the hole up as best I could. There was no way Tracy was going to want protection from a curse, even if I explained to her in detail why she needed it, which I'd never have an opportunity to do with her mom, Cheryl's mom, and Cheryl hanging around. As I stepped out of the stall in which I had been conducting this covert operation, I smiled at another visitor, who was washing her hands, and thought to myself that I had never felt creepier in my whole life.

As I walked back down to Tracy's room, the nurse behind the

kiosk smiled at me without interest. Colorful GET WELL balloons bobbed up and down, waiting to be delivered, and the ward buzzed with weekday morning activity. I peered into rooms with opened doors and noticed listless children lying in beds watching cartoons on televisions mounted to ceilings. Eight years ago a room like one of these had been mine.

I arrived at room 418 and was about to cross the threshold when I heard Mrs. Hartford's familiar voice. "Well, dear, we've been through this. Even if you're no longer contagious, there's no way I want you staying up all night doing God knows what less than a week from now," Mrs. Hartford was saying.

I took a deep breath and entered, wondering if Cheryl and her mom had already informed Tracy that I'd come along for the visit that morning, or if I'd be making a surprise entrance.

As usual, Mrs. Hartford looked like the ultimate Midwestern mom, wearing a red holiday sweatshirt with a reindeer appliquéd onto it and a festive gold headband. Her face stretched into a wide, fake grin when she saw me.

"Well, there she is. McKenna Brady! How kind of you to pay Tracy a visit," she gushed in a phony voice.

"I heard that Tracy was really sick and wanted to come in person and apologize for the way I acted in the fall," I lied. I smiled at Cheryl, who sat in the corner, as if relying on her to back me up, but my eyes fell upon Tracy lying in bed. She looked downright awful. Her overall pallor was a sickening shade of greenish yellow, like a bruise that had faded. A tube ran from a bag of saline hanging on a rack next to her bed into an IV on the inside of her elbow. Skin pulled tautly over her cheekbones, and her eyes sank into her face.

Cheryl had said she'd only gotten sick the previous week, but she looked as if she'd been ill for a long time. Her lips were colorless, and her hair was greasy and limp. While Tracy had never been an especially gorgeous girl, she'd also never been ugly, either, and now she just looked *ghoulish*.

She replied in a flat, tired voice, "I find that hard to believe. What do you want?" She tilted her head in the direction of her mother and said, "She's the one who attacked Violet and stole that car, Mom." As if Mrs. Hartford didn't already know what I'd done in November. Mrs. Hartford had her finger on the pulse of every rumor and secret in town. My temper flared.

"No, really, Tracy," Mrs. Guthries insisted. She sat in the chair next to the bed. "McKenna fell in with a bit of a bad crowd at the start of the school year. She feels very bad about everything she did that may have hurt other people."

I bit my tongue. I'd never said anything of the sort to Cheryl or to Mrs. Guthries, and in fact, I wasn't sorry about anything I'd done in the fall except for playing Light as a Feather with Violet in the first place. But it didn't benefit my cause to contradict Cheryl's mom. I needed Tracy to accept my peace offering and keep it close to her. So I added, "I think my paranoia got the better of me after Candace died, and I did some very stupid stuff. I mean, I barely know Violet. But I've known you since we were little, so I feel especially bad if I hurt your feelings."

Tracy snorted at my attempt at an apology. "Do you think I'm dying or something? Is that why you're here begging for forgiveness?"

Her question was so on the nose that it stumped me for a second before I realized that she was joking around. Maybe she wouldn't have cracked that joke if someone had informed her about Stephani, especially if she'd been present when Violet had predicted how Stephani would die. "Because if I'm dying, it's from boredom. Not from meningitis. They don't even have HBO here."

Cheryl shifted uncomfortably. "God, Tracy. She's just trying to make amends."

"I know you're not dying," I managed to say, pitying Tracy because it was overwhelmingly clear to me that she was, in fact, dying. I wondered exactly how Violet had said she'd pass away, and if a brief stint in a local hospital was part of the story. "But I brought this for you, anyway." I handed her the stuffed white dog, hoping she wouldn't roll her eyes or wave it away.

It was a relief when she reached for it and tucked it under her left arm. "Cute. Thanks. You know, you really kind of missed out on getting to know Violet. She's awesome. She's worked so hard on planning the ski trip for the entire junior class. She even negotiated a discounted rate at a really awesome hotel with a . . ." Tracy faded away, pausing for a moment to catch her breath.

The ski trip. At the mere mention of it, my scalp began to tingle. Violet had promised it during her campaign speech when she'd run for class president without even asking for permission from any school administrators, and I'd organized and managed the fundraiser that had made it possible. It had never occurred to me before to be suspicious about why Violet would have proposed something so outrageous during the election, except that now I had to question what would have been appealing to her about having the entire junior class assembled at the base of a mountain in the middle of winter. There were a wide variety of other preposterous campaign promises that probably could have gotten her elected, like arranging for Federico's pizza to be available in the cafeteria or convincing the principal's office to ease up on the dress code, which forbids shorts, even in sweltering temperatures.

But a lot of bad things could happen at a ski lodge.

The tingling suggested there was something important about the ski trip for me to discover. This was probably the only chance I was going to get to pose questions to someone who was close with Violet, so I said to Tracy, "Wow. I'd forgotten about the ski trip. It's really happening?" I looked over at Cheryl for confirmation, knowing that Tracy would cut her off if she attempted to reply.

As Cheryl nodded and her lips parted, Tracy interjected, "Totally happening. We booked luxury tour buses to drive us up there on January twenty-third. It's gonna be so—so . . ." She fell quiet again, her eyes blinking slowly. This much socialization and excitement was obviously tiring her out.

Cheryl cut in with, "It's actually not going to be terrible. They're letting us sign up for snowboarding or ski lessons in advance.

Tracy attempted to sit up a little taller on her bed because she had something more to add, but she couldn't find the strength to prop herself up. Mrs. Hartford rose to her feet and set her magazine down on the table next to her chair. "Tracy's still in very fragile condition. She's probably not quite ready for so many visitors yet."

"Yes," Tracy agreed, finding her voice. "I need to rest so that I can get out of here this weekend."

Mrs. Hartford shot Tracy an annoyed frown. "Enough of that already, Tracy. We discussed this. Even if your doctors think you're well enough to be released, you're not going to any parties."

She must have been referring to the party at Violet's house the following week. If there was any teenager in all of Willow who cared so much about social status that she was willing to tell her mom that she wanted to go to an all-night rager where there was sure to be tons of alcohol, drugs, and kids hooking up, Tracy was the one. And Mrs. Hartford was probably the only parent in town who wouldn't want her daughter to miss out on such debauchery under normal circumstances.

"Right, Mom. Like that's fair. I'll be the only kid in the entire junior class who isn't there that night," Tracy sarcastically whined.

Cheryl grinned at me and interjected, "Except me, since I'm not even invited."

Mrs. Hartford gestured at Cheryl. "See? Your cousin isn't going."

"She doesn't go anywhere except band practice."

"You'll be lucky if you're well enough to go on the ski trip in a few weeks," Mrs. Hartford warned her. I didn't know who Mrs. Hartford thought she was kidding; Tracy didn't look like she'd have the strength to go skiing for another couple of *months*.

"Listen to your mother, Tracy. You wouldn't want to miss that, would you?" Mrs. Guthries asked Tracy. It struck me as fascinating how different Mrs. Guthries was from her sister. Cheryl's mom taught religion class on weekends and volunteered at the community shelter in Green Bay. Tracy's mom hosted a Real Housewives cocktail night at her house every week. Maybe having such drastically different mothers was how Cheryl and Tracy had ended up nothing alike.

"There's no way I'm missing that," Tracy replied, sounding winded.

We all turned our heads toward the doorway when a light knock interrupted our conversation, and I saw Violet Simmons standing there holding a dozen pink roses. Before I had a chance to panic about violating my restraining order, she smiled with sickening sweetness at everyone in the room. "No one told me there was a party going on in here," she gushed.

Mrs. Hartford rushed toward her, beaming, arms outstretched. "Well, hello, dear. It was *so lovely* of you drop by!" She patted Violet on the shoulder and took the roses from her. "Look, Tracy. Aren't they beautiful?"

"So beautiful," Tracy agreed.

My heart started beating erratically. What were the odds of running into Violet again less than twenty-four hours from when I'd seen her at Hennessey's? Beads of sweat were forming on my forehead. It was suddenly sweltering in Tracy's room, and I wished I'd taken off my winter coat sooner. I was overwhelmed with dread at the thought of Tracy mentioning to Violet that I'd brought her a gift, and Violet knowing immediately why I'd done so.

"Well, I'm actually here to visit my mom, but I couldn't very well drive all the way out here and not at least say hi to my best friend," Violet gushed.

Tracy frowned with genuine concern. "Did your mom get worse the other night after we talked?"

"We thought it was just the flu when she got sick on Sunday, but her fever spiked yesterday morning, so my dad brought her to the emergency room. They thought it would be best to admit her and get her on fluids." She turned her head ever so slightly toward me and side-eyed me before adding, "But she's already improved so much that they're talking about releasing her this afternoon."

As Violet yammered on about how Pete had asked her to pass along his wishes for a speedy recovery, I shot a desperate look at Cheryl in the hope that she'd sense my discomfort and suggest we leave.

Catching my unspoken drift, Cheryl discreetly elbowed her mother, who caught on instantly. "We should be going," Mrs. Guthries said, standing and swinging her tote bag over her shoulder.

We said quick good-byes, and I encouraged Tracy to get well soon while avoiding eye contact with Violet. I nearly passed out from relief when we stepped back out into the hallway, grateful for what felt like cooler air. The tingling eased up immediately. "That was a little tense," Cheryl quipped as we walked toward the elevator bank.

"Yeah. Geez," I said, realizing that Cheryl was referring to the entire experience, not just the part after Violet crashed our visit. "I feel like I could use a nap, and it's not even noon yet."

"McKenna."

I stopped in my tracks and turned to see Violet standing behind me, her lips curled into a smile. "Can I speak to you for a second?"

Mindful of Cheryl and her mom, I replied, "I think that would probably be a bad idea, considering the restraining order and everything."

"It's okay," she insisted. "It'll be fast."

With my scalp tingling as if needles were being pressed into my head, I took a few steps forward. "We'll wait for you downstairs in the lobby," Mrs. Guthries told me before she and Cheryl continued down the hall.

Violet's smile vanished, and the sparkle in her blue eyes was replaced with a stone-cold fury. "I'm only going to tell you this once. Stay away from Tracy."

For a moment I panicked about the stuffed dog I'd left behind, terrified that Violet might have guessed what I'd done and taken away the only form of protection Tracy had working in her favor. But I forbade myself to even think about it, as if there was a chance she could read my mind. "I was just visiting," I said innocently. "You might not remember this, since you're new in town, but the rest of us have known one another since preschool."

Violet took another step closer to me, balling her fists at her sides and squinting her eyes into slits. "I know exactly what you're up to, and if you're successful, you're going to be very, very sorry that you messed with me."

I was grateful for my heavy winter coat, which covered the full-body chill that rippled through me. My first impulse was to panic about the safety of my mom and Maude at home, but then I remembered what the book I'd read had defined as the limitations of spirits' power. I had no reason to believe that Violet could do anything to my loved ones unless she somehow convinced them to play her game, and my mom was most certainly not the game-playing type.

Somehow I found the courage to lie straight to her face. "I don't know what you're talking about. I know better than to mess with you, Violet."

I turned and continued toward the elevator, sensing the hatred she was directing at me boring into my back like a laser beam until I rounded the corner and disappeared from her sight. In the elevator, I trembled all the way down to the ground floor. Perhaps Violet wouldn't have an easy time causing harm to my mom. But she could easily find a way to doom more people our age, especially with the big party at her house coming up and then the ski trip.

The question I longed to ask the pendulum burned at my nerves as we walked through the cold parking structure to the Guthries' car. I couldn't wait to ask it about the theory we'd come up with regarding the link between Violet's predictions and protecting someone she cared about. Was it a coincidence that her mother had made a miraculous recovery? When Cheryl suggested that we go out for lunch in Ortonville before driving back to Willow, I was tempted to lie and say I didn't feel well, but then reminded myself of how poorly I had treated her back in September. I politely smiled for another hour as her mom treated us to Olive Garden, even though I was already rehearsing questions to ask the pendulum in my head.

As we turned onto my street, my phone began blowing up with Instagram messages from Mischa, who tended to contact me across several different social media apps depending on whichever she had been using at the moment when she decided to reach out. I think I figured out the five sisters! Call me asap!

"It was very nice to see you, McKenna," Mrs. Guthries said as we pulled into my driveway.

"I got a gift certificate to go to the ceramics place in Suamico from my grandparents for Christmas," Cheryl told me as I unbuckled my seat belt in the back. "We should go before you go back to school!"

Before even replying, I knew I wasn't going to have time to paint ceramics with Cheryl in Suamico while I was at home in Willow. "That would be awesome," I said, already dreading how I'd have to make excuses to avoid plans. Trey was scheduled to go back to

Northern Reserve on Sunday. It was already Thursday, and I'd barely seen him—plus, I still had no idea how we were going to convince Violet to play a game with us before we all went our separate ways.

"How's Tracy doing?" Mom called from the kitchen as soon as I stepped through the front door.

"Fine!" I fibbed before slipping into my bedroom and closing the door behind me. I wanted to ask the pendulum my questions before speaking with Mischa, but she called the instant I took it out of my drawer.

"Okay. So check this out." Mischa hadn't even said hello, she'd just started talking as soon as I tapped my phone to answer. "I went to one of those family tree websites and created an account as if I were Violet."

"Don't you need to know, like, personal stuff, like birth dates and maiden names, to do that?" I asked.

"Yep. Violet's birthday is April fourth. That's on her Facebook profile, easy enough to find."

"Wow. Violet's still on Facebook?" I marveled.

"Her profile is super old, and it doesn't look like she posts anymore, but yeah. Besides, I probably could have found it in old Insta comments or whatever. Stalking people online is one of my superpowers."

"So . . . what's the deal with the sisters?" I asked, now genuinely curious about what Mischa had discovered. My attention was caught by a very light tapping on my window, and my heart leapt with hope that it might be Trey standing outside. I raised my blinds and was confused to see nothing there at all but snow on the ground. Across the yard, I didn't even see any activity in Trey's room. His shade was pulled down.

"You're not gonna believe this." I could tell she was excited. If there was anything Mischa loved, it was telling a scary story. "Four years before Violet was born, a baby girl was born at Northwestern Memorial Hospital in Chicago, Illinois, to Vanessa and Michael Simmons. She was named Christina Ann Simmons. Born on September ninth, died on September ninth."

As Mischa spoke, I became aware of something strange happening in the steam that had collected on my windowpane. It was as if someone was drawing a picture in it with their fingertip. An outline of a circle appeared first, followed by the crooked shape of a stick-figure body. The lower half of the body was a triangle, which meant *girl*.

"Holy . . . ," I murmured. I replayed the words that Mischa had just said in my head, realizing that the baby had died the same day it was born. "Now you're freaking me out." I didn't tell her what was happening on the window because I wasn't sure what I was supposed to infer from it yet.

"Oh, that's not all," Mischa continued, delighted by my reaction.

Another circle was drawn in the steam on my window, next to the first stick figure, as if Olivia's ghost (I assumed) was drawing girls standing next to each other.

"A little over a year later? Another daughter, *this* one named Ann Elizabeth Simmons, was born on January third, and died on January third. And then *another*, Elizabeth Jane. Born and died on the same day the following November."

I had goose bumps up and down my arms. "How did they have three daughters in a row who died on the same day they were born?" Legs were added to the third stick figure of a girl drawn on my window. Whatever Olivia was doing, it was as if she could hear Mischa.

"My friend Megan, whose mom works at St. Matthew's? I asked her and she said that birth and death certificates are issued for still-born babies. And on this website, you can actually see the certificates scanned in from hospital records. The time of birth is the same as the time of death." Mischa was breathless with excitement.

"Mischa, I feel really, really weird about this," I said.

"I do too. Like, super creepy," she admitted.

The drawing on my window had stopped, I thought, but then I realized a fourth circle was being drawn a few inches away from the third as if to leave a gap in between the third and fourth stick figures.

"That brings us up to the year when Violet was born. Her birth certificate is there too. On this website, it shows that Michael and Vanessa Simmons were married in the Cook County clerk's office the year before the first baby was born. By the time she had Violet, Mrs. Simmons was almost forty years old. They must have really wanted to have a baby by the time they had her."

Jennie had said there were five sisters. "That's only three sisters," I commented.

Mischa said, "There was *another* baby," she continued. "Another girl. Jane Victoria Simmons, born on June sixth, three years after Violet was born. She lived a day. The death certificate gives her date of death as June seventh."

"That's only four sisters, not five," I pointed out.

"You said Jennie told you they had something to do with it, right? We have to figure out why Violet was the one who lived. Like maybe the ones who died are pissed off that she survived, so they control her from beyond. Or maybe"—her voice became raspy, as if she was falling more in love with the idea of her narrative—"the dead sisters all take turns controlling her body. Like a new one takes over with each cycle of the moon!"

A fifth and final stick figure had been drawn on my window, leaving a row of three, then a gap, and then two more. The gap must have been where Violet belonged. There was something to this that I was missing, I was sure of it, and I suspected it had something to do with Trey. He was, after all, their brother. He would have been born about four months before the third daughter, Elizabeth Jane.

Of course, I couldn't tell Mischa that, even though I was dying to tell *someone*. There was no way of knowing how she'd react if I informed her that Trey was Violet's blood relative, but it was a safe bet that she'd tell Henry. And if Henry believed for a second that Trey was in cahoots with Violet, and that he had intentionally gotten into the accident in which Olivia had died, there was a chance that Henry might really hurt Trey. No matter what, sharing that information was going to make it impossible to confront Violet before the next new moon.

We only stood a chance against her if we worked together.

"We might be overthinking this," I told Mischa. "Violet might not even know about the dead sisters, you know? At least not the ones who died before she was born. She's never referred to the spirits that tell her how people are going to die as sisters."

"Well, the dead sisters are real. That part of what Jennie told you pans out. There was probably another, you know? The fifth? Maybe a miscarriage or something, and a birth certificate wasn't issued. So what Jennie told you about breaking the curse by playing the game again must be true. We have to play Light as a Feather, Cold as Marble and predict her death so that they see her with them." Mischa was really wound up. I couldn't remember ever actually talking on the phone with her before I'd gone off to Sheridan. All of my communication with friends was conducted primarily with one- and two-word text messages and emojis, so it was strange to hear so much zeal in her voice. It sounded like she was pacing on her end of the conversation.

"I know, I know. I went with Cheryl this morning to visit Tracy in the hospital, and she mentioned that New Year's party. I think that might be our best shot at cornering Violet," I said.

Waiting until New Year's Eve was risky. I was scheduled to drive back up to Sheridan the next morning. But we knew exactly where Violet would be that night, and there wouldn't be any parents around. Plus, if kids were drinking, it was a lot less likely that anyone would dare to call the cops if I showed up uninvited. I told Mischa how awful Tracy looked and how I was willing to bet that she'd played a game with Violet, but I didn't mention that Violet had made a surprise appearance at the hospital.

"I'll float it past Henry," Mischa announced.

"Keep that candle burning," I urged her.

I ended the call and immediately reached for the pendulum, not bothering to cleanse the space because I had just burned palo santo the night before. "Pendulum, did the ghost of Olivia just draw these stick figures on my window?"

Counterclockwise. *No.* "Was it Jennie?" I asked. The pendulum slowed down and started up again in the other direction. *Yes.*

Jennie! Joy surged in my heart. Kirsten had said that the more often I communicated with spirits, the easier it would be for me to receive messages from them. I dared to hope that interacting with Jennie the other day on Route 32 had strengthened the channel between us. It seemed like she was invested in making sure I followed her advice. "Was it Jennie who kept calling my phone last night?" The pendulum wobbled and then rotated in reverse, counterclockwise. "Was it Olivia?" Clockwise. So Olivia's ghost seemed to only get in touch with me to express anger when another one of Violet's victims was about to die.

"Pendulum, does Violet have a fifth dead sister?" I asked. The pendulum continued swinging in a clockwise motion, not slowing down in the slightest.

"Did Violet's mother get sick because no one who Violet predicted a death for actually died in November?" It picked up momentum. Clockwise.

Yes.

Our theory was correct; Violet was sacrificing souls to keep her mother alive. It was perhaps a strange thing to take pride in, but we were slowly setting the pieces of the puzzle into place.

CHAPTER 9

WE WERE IN WAY OVER OUR HEADS—MORE than even back in November.

It was starting to feel like I'd tumbled down a well and just kept falling without ever hitting bottom. I'd come home from Sheridan expecting a relaxing visit with my mom, during which I had hoped to repair our badly damaged relationship. I'd thought Trey and I would find a way to see each other, and that I'd possibly even lose my virginity to him before heading back to Sheridan since it had been on my mind the whole time we'd been separated. Stupid me. Now, Stephani was dead, Tracy was dying, and worst of all, Violet was onto us.

That afternoon, the snow started up again, and this time the flakes were much heavier than the ones that had fallen on Christmas Eve. Through our living room front window, I noticed Trey outside shoveling. I was in agony not having had a chance to ask him more questions about his relationship to the Simmons family, and I was going to have to take a risk to get some answers. I couldn't stand the idea of him going back to Northern Reserve on Sunday morning without my having disproven Kirsten about him being dangerous.

The snow continued to fall after it was dark outside. By the time I let Maude outside for her last outdoor romp of the day, there was over a foot of snow on the ground. Mom turned in for bed early, claiming that she had to drive to campus in the morning. She'd been reviewing research theses since I'd gotten back from Sheridan and wanted to log her notes into the system from her office at the University of Wisconsin–Sheboygan because she'd been too lazy to learn how to use their Virtual Private Network to log onto their intranet securely from home. Even though the weather report suggested it was going to snow all night, making a drive to Sheboygan pretty treacherous by morning, I didn't mention that to her. Instead, I listened for the *click* of the lamp on her bedside table turning off, waited an hour, and then climbed out of my window.

Knowing that I was leaving behind a telltale trail of footprints from my bedroom window to Trey's, I walked along the side of my house to the fence that encircled our backyard, and then walked next to that until it met the fence around Trey's house. Then I crept along the side of his house, below the windows of his kitchen and his brother's room, to make my trajectory a little less obvious. Once I reached Trey's window, I threw a loose handful of snow at it. Almost a minute passed before the shade lifted and I saw Trey standing there in a T-shirt and sweatpants, smiling. He raised the window a few inches and asked, "Can I help you, miss?"

"Help me up! It's freezing out here!" I whispered. Trey's brother's bedroom was next to his, so I had to be quiet to avoid waking him.

Trey raised his window as high as it would go and removed the screen. I hoisted myself onto the ledge and rather ungracefully contorted my legs to make my way inside. As quietly as possible, Trey lowered the window again and popped the screen back into place. "My mom sets her alarm to come in here every hour to make sure I haven't snuck out," he whispered.

"Is it safe?" I asked, shaking with cold. I'd slept over in Trey's bedroom once before, but that was long before my mother and his parents had started watching us like hawks.

"Take off your boots and coat."

He placed my boots behind his dresser and pushed my puffy coat under his bed, and then tossed a sweatshirt onto the floor to cover the clumps of snow I'd carried in with me. He then lifted the blankets on his bed and pointed for me to slide in, which I did.

"All she ever does is open the door and make sure I'm still in bed," he whispered as he crawled in beside me and pulled the comforter up to our chins. "So you could probably stay all night as long as you stay hidden under the covers."

"Very tempting, but I have to get home while the snow is still falling," I said, being completely honest about how much I wanted to just stay with him. It had been so long since I'd been this physically close to him, warmed by his body heat. I wrapped my arms around him and was surprised to feel his ribs so prominently beneath his T-shirt; he really had lost quite a bit of weight. "Footprints."

"Ah," he said, instantly understanding. "Good point. I guess that *would* be pretty incriminating. We should have rigged up a zip line a long time ago."

I giggled, imagining the two of us gliding back and forth between our windows in the middle of the night. "You're crazy."

"That's what they keep telling me at Northern Reserve," he said. "The psychiatrist there just can't wrap his head around why

I'd steal my own mother's car and swipe a necklace from a girl I barely know."

"Oh, Trey. I'm sorry. I really am," I said, cradling his head and rubbing my thumbs over the stubble on his scalp, which was all that remained of his dark hair. Everything that had happened in November must have sounded outrageous to other people. My mother's attorney had suggested that I consider using the defense that stealing Violet's locket and driving to White Ridge Lake had been Trey's idea, which, naturally, I had flat-out refused to do. "Is it awful there?"

I could tell by the way he waited a second before replying that he was deciding whether or not to give me the unedited lowdown. "I'm sure it's not much worse than yours. You know. Line up in the morning, line up before bed. The hardest part is keeping to myself," he told me, and added sarcastically, "since I'm such a social butterfly." He'd encouraged me before I'd left for Sheridan to avoid trying to make friends and to keep a low profile, and I'd realized the value in that advice during my first twenty-four hours away from home.

"What's up with your parents putting the house up for sale?" I asked.

As he stared into my eyes, he ran his finger down the bridge of my nose, down its tip, and traced the curves of my lips. "They think it's best for my brother, you know? He got bullied pretty bad at school during all that court stuff." His answer was so sensible that I wondered if he had any idea his mom was in financial trouble.

"That sucks. I didn't think what we did would have any impact on Eddie," I admitted. Truthfully, we hadn't put much thought into how our predicament with Violet would have affected any of our family members. Now, especially when our parents were paying for both of us to attend expensive boarding schools, that seemed like an obvious oversight.

"I know. I feel really bad about it."

"It's gonna be weird when you don't live next door anymore."

"It won't matter. Nothing's ever gonna be the same as it was before." He sounded so sad that I hated myself for ever wondering if he'd been collaborating with Violet. But still . . . I couldn't fight the urge to press him for the full truth. I wanted so much for Kirsten to be wrong.

"I visited Tracy Hartford in the hospital today, and she—"

Trey raised an eyebrow at me. "Tracy's in the hospital?"

"Yeah. Turns out she has bacterial meningitis, the super-dangerous kind."

He exhaled in disgust and shook his head. "Why am I not surprised?"

"I know, I know. I can't believe Violet would do that to her most devoted worshipper, but no one's safe," I said. "Anyway, Tracy said that Violet's throwing a big New Year's party. Mischa and I think it might be the only opportunity we'll have to try to get Violet to play the game with us."

Trey was silent for a moment, thinking this over. "That's Tuesday. I'll already be back at school by then."

"We might not get another chance. I'm supposed to go back on January first," I reminded him. The timeline was so tight it was dizzying; I was due back at Sheridan twelve hours after the stroke of midnight, when I hoped to be at Violet's house, breaking the curse.

Trey shook his head. "It's a bad idea to confront her on her own property. She knows the layout of that house, and you've only been there, like, once. The more I think about this notion of playing the game again, the more it seems like this isn't the right time. I know you're worried about Mischa, but there has to be a way we can keep protecting her until we have a better plan. We're not going to get more than one chance. If we blow it, then she'll know what we're trying to do, and we could end up in so much more trouble."

Despite the coziness of our embrace, I felt my limbs turning cold. Everything he was saying suggested he didn't want to even try to break the curse, which certainly seemed like evidence that Kirsten had been right about him. "But even if Mischa isn't the person who dies, *someone* dies with each cycle of the moon," I argued. "We're the only ones who can do anything to stop this."

"That's not true, though," Trey said. "The kids in Lake Forest could have done something about her, but they didn't. It's not fair that we have to. You and I can't afford to lose any more than we already have. I mean, for you, college is on the line. The rest of your life is at stake."

I felt my throat closing up as if I was going to cry. It sounded like he was backing out on helping me, Mischa, and Henry. I was starting to wish that I hadn't walked over, even though if Kirsten was correct about Trey, I had to know. "I'll understand if you don't want to help us. I know your situation at school is worse than mine. But I have to see this through. I can't even explain why—it has to do with Jennie dying in the fire instead of me. Like maybe some kind of survivors' guilt. But I just can't quit. Every time someone else dies, it feels like I'm responsible for letting it happen."

Trey stroked the side of my face and gazed into my eyes before saying, "McKenna, you're all I think about at school. I mean, all of this stuff with Violet and everyone dying is just . . . Who could have guessed that this would happen to us? But I believe, I *have* to believe, that you and I will leave all of this behind and be together. That's all I want. For this to be over and for us to be together, away from here."

"I want that too," I assured him, meaning it. I missed the feeling of our fingers interwoven on long walks to school. I missed his breath on my neck in the middle of the night, and the comfort in knowing he was just a few inches away if I woke up in the dark. I missed the cool blue pools of his eyes, and how I felt when he looked at me like I was the only person in the world who really *saw* him, and how he was the only person who really saw me, too.

"Then please don't do anything that will make it impossible for us to be together," he pleaded. "If she found a way to do something bad to you, I don't know what I'd do."

I knew he was expressing genuine concern for me, but I couldn't get rid of the lump in my throat. He was holding something back from me—I sensed it, and I might never have a chance to demand answers from him if I didn't work up the courage right there and then. "Trey? What were you doing in Green Bay at the mall the day Olivia died?" I'd asked him that question once before we'd been sent away, but his explanation about being out in Ortonville to buy spark plugs just didn't seem right. "Please don't say it had something to do with Coach Stirling's car."

As I feared he would, he looked up at the ceiling so that I couldn't see what was going on behind his eyes. Trey shut out the world when he felt like someone was incriminating him. It was how he had landed in such poor favor with so many teachers at school even before the chase with the cops in the fall. "I'm not accusing you of anything," I clarified. "But it's starting to seem like maybe you know how we could end all of this right now, and for some reason you aren't telling me."

"There's a lot you don't know about me. I don't know even where to start."

My heart sank like an anchor. So there *was* more. Trey and I had lived on the same street our whole lives, and Violet had grown up in another state. How could there possibly be elements of his life that were unknown to me? If he'd been working with Violet all along, or had known how the curse functioned but had neglected to tell me, then all of the nights we'd spent together in my room, all of the effort he'd put into researching ghosts, had been . . . for what?

To impress me?

Or to keep Violet's ruse going a little longer by throwing me off course?

"Just . . . start at the beginning." I needed to hear it all.

He chose his words carefully, speaking slowly and in a whisper. "Sometimes I have dreams, and parts of them come true. It's always been like that, as long as I can remember. The dreams aren't like the predictions Violet has," he explained. "They usually don't make any sense. Only sometimes they're a little more real than other times, and right before Olivia died, I had a dream that she went to the mall and a storm was coming. I saw her stranded in a car that wouldn't start . . . and it seemed like something bad was, like, coming to claim her—which is a weird way to put it, I guess. I didn't really think anything was going to happen, but I followed her to the mall that day out of curiosity. That's it. Honestly. Paranoia. And then she was there, in the parking lot, and her car wouldn't start, exactly like in my dream. I thought I was doing her a favor by offering her a safe ride home. I thought I was saving her, as stupid as that sounds now."

After carefully considering how much I wanted to confide in Trey about the progress Mischa had made, I told him, "Mischa found out that Violet's mother had stillborn daughters before and after Violet was born. There were five sisters—or, well, four that we know of for sure—just like Jennie said. I personally think the spirits of those sisters are who provide Violet with the predictions she gives people. Do you think your dreams might come from them too?" I intentionally didn't phrase my last question the way it had formed in my head, with an addendum about those spirits being Trey's half sisters.

He mulled this over, clearly uncomfortable discussing it. "Yeah," he finally admitted. "That day out on the track when we confronted her? The way she described how the things that show her people's deaths are, like, spirits, or ghosts? How they tell her things without her really hearing voices? That's how my dreams are."

The expression on my face must have told him exactly what I was thinking: There had to be a connection between his experiences and Violet's. So he added, "But if you think I know anything about how Violet does what she does, you're wrong. Like I said, before my mom told me I might see her at school in September, I didn't even know she existed."

"What other kinds of dreams have you had?" I asked. "Ones that weren't about Olivia?"

"Just really dark stuff." He seemed a little bashful about sharing details. "Mostly dreams about how *I* would die. They always start off kind of innocent, like I'll be walking along the side of a road for a while and then come across a bridge, and I'll dream that I climb over the side. Even though I won't want to jump into the water, I'll feel the sensation of falling, my arms and legs flailing around in the air, and then just as I hit the water, I wake up. And I can sense them suggesting what I should do. Like chanting, but more like pushing my thoughts, egging me on."

Voices. I decided to take a risk and tell him about the phenomena I'd been experiencing since leaving home. "I'm going to tell you something, but please don't ever tell Mischa or Henry."

He rolled over onto his side and propped himself up on one arm. "I'm listening."

"Since I arrived at Sheridan, I've been hearing weird things. It's not really an *audible* kind of hearing, more like this sensation of a chorus inside my head. It doesn't happen very often, only when I'm supposed to notice something or pay attention to details for my own safety. And then other times I feel this weird prickling across the top and sides of my head," I whispered. "I think it only happens when something bad is about to go down, like if a fight's about to break out and I should keep my head down."

He tapped the tip of my nose. "And this has only been happening since you got to Sheridan? Why do you think it only happens there?"

I didn't tell him that it had also been happening since I got back to Willow, because then I'd have to tell him about the letter I pilfered from his mailbox, and I wasn't sure how he'd react. Instead, I replied, "I suspect it has less to do with Sheridan and more to do with maybe some kind of door being opened between me and the spirit world when Jennie saved my life at Olivia's party. That girl at the bookstore told me that sometimes it's just one event that makes you know better what to listen for. Like, maybe everyone can technically receive those kinds of messages, but after you're aware of it the first time, you're more aware of it afterward."

"Wow." He smiled at me. "You really *are* a medium. Maybe you could get your own show on cable, reconnecting people with their dead loved ones."

"Pass," I joked. "But I bet that's what it is for you. You have a door open to those spirits too. And sometimes they climb through and inspire your dreams."

Trey rolled over onto his back. "I really don't like the sound of how you just put it, like they can crawl in and out of my head."

I was reminded of the old wives' tale about dying in real life if you die in your dreams. "Geez. Do you still have dreams like that?" I asked.

"The one about Olivia was the first I'd had in probably a year. And it was weird, because it was about her death and not mine. I was freaked out about it because I'd thought I was done with the dreams, you know? And then to have that dream out of nowhere, so vividly . . ."

Our conversation was making my chest hurt. Violet's spirits visited her to supply her with visions of other people's deaths. It was sounding like her spirits had come to Trey to try to coerce him toward his own. "Trey, that's . . . just awful."

"It is, but I always thought it was just me, you know? That I was messed up to be having such weird dreams. Until Olivia died. Then I realized that they're part of something bigger."

We both froze when we heard footsteps in the hallway outside his doorway, and I slid lower beneath the blankets, hoping that his lumpy comforter would effectively conceal the shape of my body next to his. I heard the metallic *click* of the doorknob twisting and then a creak as the door opened inward. As Trey pretended to be asleep, his breathing grew heavier. I held as still as I could until I heard the door creak again and then softly clap shut.

For another minute or so we remained still, listening as Trey's mother walked back down the hallway. Then I pushed the blankets off my head and whispered, "She *really* checks on you every hour?"

"All night long," he confirmed. "Not to freak you out or anything, but I think she realized I was going over to your house every night. I don't know whether or not she said anything to your mom."

The heat of shame crept up to my face. I chose to believe my mom didn't know anything about Trey keeping me company at night because she hadn't said anything to me. It would have been much more like her to corner me into an awkward conversation about safe sex at her earliest convenience. But the amount of effort that our moms were putting into keeping us separated over the break made me wonder if perhaps my mom *did* know and had just thought better of saying anything to me.

To change the topic, I said softly, "I'm really curious about the five dead daughters. Why do you think Violet was the only baby that survived?"

"I don't know," he mumbled. "But her father must have been plenty annoyed that my mother had me without any problems while his wife was going through all that at the same time."

I hadn't thought about the timing of it all too much. What had been going on in the Simmonses' marriage that Mr. Simmons had cheated on his wife while she was struggling with fertility issues? "Do you know how your mom met him?"

Trey shook his head. "She didn't give me details. And honestly, I don't want to know. She was in college and dropped out. After her freshman year at the University of Chicago, she ended up back in Willow with a newborn. Exactly where she didn't want to be. That's all I know about it, other than she married Walter before I was born." He fell quiet for a moment and then asked, "Did you tell Mischa and Olivia's brother? About me and the Simmons family?"

"No," I assured him. "I don't want them to think you were, like, working with Violet."

He stared into my eyes for a long moment before saying, "I hope that's not what *you* think. I mean, I'm doing time in a military school because of her—and I'd do it all again—but, McKenna, I would never, ever do anything to hurt you. You have to believe me."

I wanted to believe him. But it was getting late, my eyelids were growing heavy, and I needed to get back to my own room before I fell asleep and before it stopped snowing, since I was counting on snow covering up the tracks I'd left. As I climbed back outside through his window frame, he said again, "I don't think crashing Violet's New Year's party is a good idea. Please promise me you won't try to do that without me."

"I won't. I swear," I told him, hating that I was heading back out into the cold, hating that I couldn't spend the whole night in his arms, and hating myself for becoming a habitual liar. Despite the fact that I believed everything he had just told me about his dreams, it didn't seem advantageous for him to know that I still had every intention of confronting Violet at her party. Lying to him, or more specifically, my reason for lying to him, tied my intestines into knots as I crept through the snow along the fence to try to obscure my footprints once again.

The next new moon would fall on January twenty-fourth. I would be far from Willow, back at Sheridan with no phone privileges, no Internet privileges other than heavily monitored browsing usage for classwork, and no possible chance of talking my way into a few days of leave. The entire junior class would be on its ski trip in Michigan. Mischa, Henry, and I were going to have to find a way to play the game again with Violet on the night of her big party, or we were going to miss our chance.

Back in my own bedroom, I crawled into bed with my phone, knowing I wouldn't get any sleep until I had been able to determine the connection between Trey's mother and Violet's father to better understand what had happened between them. I Googled "Michael Simmons," "Wisconsin," and the word "banker." His professional portfolio on the website of Tall Trees Finance, the investment bank for which he worked, popped up as the top result.

There it was—the answer I was looking for. In Helvetica font. It had been there all along, if only I'd been looking for it. Michael Simmons had received his MBA from the University of Chicago three years before Trey was born. His professional experience indicated that he'd been an adjunct professor in the University of Chicago's Booth School of Business the year Trey's mother would have been a freshman in the undergraduate program. At the time, he was also working as a junior associate at a small investment bank.

My discovery proved nothing other than that they were both in Chicago, on the same campus, at the same time. But it also connected the dots. They could have met any number of ways; Trey's mom had been pretty, and Michael Simmons must have been even more handsome eighteen years ago as a young professor than he was now as a middle-aged businessman. Out of curiosity, I looked at Vanessa Simmons's LinkedIn profile, which stated that the year Trey was born, she was a staff attorney at a law firm in Chicago that specialized in tax law.

As I drifted off to sleep, it occurred to me that I hadn't told Trey that I'd tried to protect Tracy Hartford's life with advice from the pendulum, or that his mother had violated the terms of a contract she'd signed shortly before his birth, which he may not have known about. I also hadn't told him or Mischa about how Violet had threatened me at the hospital. Keeping straight which information I was sharing and withholding from everyone was already becoming a heavy burden. Even though I was back in my own town surrounded by my closest friends, I felt more alone than ever before.

Violet's words to me at the hospital . . . *If you're successful, you're going to be very, very sorry that you messed with me.*

The last thought I had before I drifted off to sleep was how infuriatingly ironic it would be for the secrets I was keeping to somehow give Violet an advantage over me.

CHAPTER 10

*H*ER LIPS TURNED BLUE AS SHE DESPERATELY *tried to breathe—even just enough to cough. But she couldn't get any air into her lungs. Blood vessels burst in her eyeballs and on her eyelids, making her look like a monster. She dropped her phone as she collapsed, knowing as soon as she hit the floor that she had already taken her last breath. Still, she ferociously clung to hope even as her soul left her body, and she lay on the floor. . . .*

That night I dreamed about Mischa choking. She ran up and down the hallways of Willow High School as her face turned blue, with kids ignoring her even after she fell to the floor and writhed there, her hands clamped around her neck. I woke up terrified that Mischa had let the candle burn out, and panicked for a full hour after texting her while I waited for her response. She didn't reply until after her morning practice session at the gym, at which time I had already contemplated calling her landline to ask her mother if she was okay.

It's burning! she texted back with a flame emoji. *But it's melted a lot after just two days. I don't think it's going to last a whole week.*

The snow had continued falling steadily after I'd gotten home from Trey's house, all through the night and well into the morning. Mom greeted me in the kitchen with the announcement that she wasn't going to drive to Sheboygan, after all. Everything in our area of Wisconsin was coated with a thin sheet of ice, making the roads extremely dangerous.

Although I did want to spend time with her, it was already Friday, and Violet's New Year's party was in four days. Having Mom around all day put a serious damper on contacting Mischa and Henry about exactly how we were going to infiltrate the Simmonses' mansion to carry out our mission to play the game again. Being trapped at home all day made me impatient and eager. There was still so much to do, so many preparations to be made, that I felt completely vulnerable and ineffective.

At Henry's suggestion, I did my best to draw a map of the inside of the Simmonses' enormous house from what I could remember. The house was set quite far back from the road at the end of a long private drive. The property was encircled by a tall brick wall, and it was at least a mile in every direction from any other houses in the area, so there was little chance of an annoyed neighbor calling the cops to make a noise complaint even if Violet's party raged until the break of dawn. From what little of the house I'd seen, I suspected most of the party activity would be held in the huge front parlor under the intimidating oil painting of Grandmother Simmons hanging on the wall. But I remembered that a set of stairs led from the hallway near the kitchen down to the basement, and it was entirely possible that Violet had a basement like the one at the Richmonds' house: fully renovated for entertaining guests.

Over text messages, Henry, Mischa, and I made plans to regroup in person later that afternoon, after some of the ice was supposed to have melted, using the excuse of going to the movies to see a holiday comedy to convince my mom to let me out of the house. Just in case my mom was suspicious, I researched movie times and told her, "We're seeing the twelve fifteen showing at the Ortonville Mall, so I should be home by three."

"This makes me very uncomfortable, McKenna," Mom said. "You're technically still in a lot of trouble, and I don't like the idea of you gallivanting around."

"I know, but Mom! I won't be able to leave school again until April for spring break, and I'll be in Florida then. This is my only chance to hang out with my friends before the summer," I argued, trying very hard to not sound like I was whining. My mother hated whining as much as she hated dishonesty.

She looked up from her laptop to frown at me. "Just remember what it was like to sit in that courtroom and have everyone look down on you," she said. "And I'd *better* not find out that Trey Emory is meeting up with you at any point today."

It took every ounce of control I had to resist rolling my eyes at her.

Mischa and Henry gave their parents the same details about our outing just in case my mom got proactive about confirming my whereabouts. Exactly an hour before the movie was scheduled to start, they picked me up in Mr. Richmond's Mercedes. From where I stood in the living room watching out the front window, I hoped that Trey didn't happen to be keeping an eye on our driveway. It probably would not have thrilled him that I was spending more time with Henry, but as it turned out, including Henry in our effort to overpower Violet had some advantages that I couldn't have predicted. He was friends with Pete Nicholson's older brother, the person Violet had recruited to supply booze for the party.

"I could ask him what he's up to for New Year's," Henry suggested on the way to Ortonville. "I'm not best friends with the guy, but that wouldn't be weird. I mean, his brother went out with Olivia for, like, as long as I can remember. He knows I'm back in town."

"Yeah, but is he actually *going* to the party, or just buying the alcohol? I mean, Justin Nicholson *must* have better things to do on New Year's than to hang out with a bunch of high school kids," Mischa said. "I mean, he's old enough to go to an actual *bar*."

"A bar around *here*?" I asked sarcastically. "If the weather's bad and he can't drive to Green Bay, I doubt he'd want to ring in the New Year at the Carousel." The Carousel was our town's one and only bar, typically open and rumored to be busy at six a.m., when workers at the oil refinery in between our town and Ortonville changed shifts. It was not exactly a hot scene.

"It can't hurt to ask," Henry insisted. "Then, at least, I can get inside the house and find a back door or something to let you guys in."

Gaining access to the house was going to be the first big challenge we faced in trying to get Violet to play the game again the night of her New Year's party. I suggested that Mischa's boyfriend, Matt, tag along with some of his friends from the wrestling team and text us once inside, but Mischa was dead set against involving him in any way. Besides which, she said, "I've told him everything that bitch has done, and especially now, since Stephani? I don't think he could be around Violet for even one minute without attacking her."

It took us a while to find parking at the mall, which was packed despite the previous night's inclement weather, since every store was promoting sales that suggested prices had dropped by over 50 percent in the last three days. We walked past the nail salon that was managed by Candace's mom, which reinforced our purpose for strategizing that day. The last time I'd seen her had been at Candace's wake, when she'd been out of her mind with grief.

By the time we found an available table at the food court and settled in for a conversation, Justin Nicholson had texted Henry back and confirmed that he was, indeed, going to be hanging out at Violet's house on New Year's Eve. "What'd I tell you? It's the party of the year," I muttered. I withheld comment as Mischa tore into a large order of french fries, the disturbing memory of Violet's prediction for her still fresh in my mind.

With no time to waste, we got down to serious business. Under different circumstances, Violet might not have considered it strange for Henry Richmond to show up at her party, but she'd just spotted me at Hennessey's with him. She was likely to be suspicious if Justin mentioned that Henry planned to attend. We agreed that it would be best for Henry to tell Justin he was going to play it by ear, and then commit to plans an hour or two before the party started. Mischa and I would drive over together, but we'd have to figure out some means of getting through the security gate, a small but important detail that I recalled from the time I'd gone over to Violet's house after school. There was video security, and guests had to either punch the secret code into the touch pad on the gate or into a mobile app, or buzz the house to request that the gate be opened.

"Text Matt and ask if anyone knows anything about the security gate," I commanded Mischa. She whipped out her phone and fired off a message. He wrote back quickly, informing us that everything about the party had been disseminated via word of mouth. Violet had asked everyone at school to avoid mentioning the party on social media to keep it off the radar of parents in town. Matt's wrestling team buddies hadn't mentioned anything about security at the house; people had just been told to come around nine or ten.

"She can't just stand next to the video monitor reviewing who's arriving all night," Mischa speculated, and then added with sarcasm, "I mean, she's the host. She's going to be busy sentencing people to death."

"Maybe you could just idle outside the house and follow somebody else in when the gate's open," Henry proposed.

I thought about this, and how my mom would be planning on waking me up early the next morning for the long drive to Sheridan. We couldn't leave a single detail to chance. "We need to lock this down," I said. "She might not even let Henry in if he shows up alone."

"We're probably overthinking this," Mischa said. "The wall around her property isn't that high. I bet it's not even over my head. We could drive around the back of her house and climb over it with my mom's kitchen step stool and bypass the security stuff completely."

Henry pointed at Mischa. "Yes. We should go over to her house and make sure that'll work."

"No. That would be too weird," Mischa said. "What if she sees you? We have to be super careful." She turned to me and asked, "Can't you just ask that necklace you bought at the bookstore whether or not we can climb over the wall?"

It hadn't even occurred to me to bring the pendulum with me, although my initial reaction was that it wouldn't have been helpful anyway. Even though I'd only used it twice at home so far, asking it questions felt like performing a ritual, one that was profoundly personal, not one to be undertaken at a food court, twenty feet away from a Cinnabon. "Kirsten said that the pendulum can only tell us what's true right now. It wouldn't necessarily know in advance if Violet will find out about us crashing her party, or predict how she'd react."

We couldn't very well go around snooping along the perimeter of the Simmonses' property, since I was sure they had some kind of private security firm. So we decided that Henry would drive over alone later that afternoon in his dad's car instead of in his pickup truck and use a tape measure to confirm the height of the wall around the property. He'd also snap a few pictures over the wall from Fenmore Lane, the residential street that ran along the back of the property, to give us a better sense of the distance we'd have to cover to reach the house in the dark.

"Okay," Mischa said, gesticulating as she often did when she was excited. "Assuming we make it over the wall and through the garden, we'll need Henry to let us in. You said there was a back door near the kitchen?"

"Yes, there's, like, a sunroom," I said, trying my best to remember. An indoor porch, bright and sunny, ran along the back of the house next to the kitchen where I'd baked cupcakes with Violet for her Student Government campaign. She'd shown me the room quickly on the tour of the house she'd given me, and I vaguely remembered seeing a door that led out to the garden.

"Once we're inside, people will obviously notice us, but hopefully we'll find Violet before someone tells her we're there," Mischa said.

Getting ourselves into Violet's party somehow was going to be our first major challenge of the evening, but once inside, I had no idea how we were going to make Violet agree to let me predict her death. Jennie hadn't specified how she was going to help me once I got to that point, even though she'd said she'd show me what to say. "So . . . we need some kind of leverage to make her play the game again," I said. "She's going to know why we're there, and if we tell her I want to predict her death, there's a good chance she'll know why. Anyone have any ideas on how to bully her into cooperating with us?"

Mischa folded her hands and set them on the tabletop. She said enthusiastically, "I'm not suggesting that we go in this direction, but . . . my dad owns a gun."

Henry shrugged at me as if this was worth consideration, but I shook my head. "Bad idea."

Mischa leaned back and rolled her eyes in annoyance with me. "Why? We're not going to *shoot* her. It doesn't even have to be *loaded*. But it would make getting her into a room away from everyone else a lot easier."

"I don't like the idea either, but think about it," Henry said. "We're only going to get one chance."

Mischa was known for her wild suggestions—like breaking Candace's legs to prevent her from going to Hawaii—but Henry's consideration of the idea surprised me. "No guns. We have to find a way to do this without a weapon." Showing up at the Simmonses' with a gun greatly increased the likelihood of someone getting *killed*. I'd just lied to Trey about confronting Violet at her party because he was worried about me getting into more legal trouble, which would keep us apart longer. That was making me feel guilty enough. Getting tossed in jail for attempted murder—or worse, getting shot—was definitely not how I wanted to end my holiday break at home in Willow. . . .

Especially because in either of those scenarios, Violet would remain free to keep doing whatever she wanted.

"What if . . . ," I speculated, "she's already planning on playing some form of the game with all the kids who show up at the party, and we barge in and push her to play the game *our* way? Maybe we use some kind of trick from Kirsten to create a cool ghostly spectacle to blow everyone's minds, and we, like, peer pressure her into letting me predict her death in front of everyone?"

"No way," Mischa said. "*That* sounds dangerous to me. The fewer witnesses, the better. We may have to pin her down or restrain her, you know? Imagine if people take videos of that. It would be really bad for all of us if people were, like, Instagramming a live assault."

A middle-aged mom sitting at the table next two us with her two toddlers must have been eavesdropping, because she looked at all three of us as if we were crazy before clearing their table and evacuating the food court.

"That's just great," Henry grumbled. "Why do I have a feeling that lady is going to be interviewed when someone produces a Netflix true crime documentary about us?"

Another hour passed and we couldn't come to an agreement on the best way to initiate the game. If anyone at the party thought we were there to start trouble with Violet, it was impossible to guess whether they'd try to stop us or call the police (even though Mischa insisted no one would call the cops to a house party on New Year's Eve if just about everyone present was drinking underage). There were just too many unknowns to put together a game plan. As much as I really did not like the idea of showing up at the party unrehearsed and unprepared, it was seeming like being nimble and focused on our goal was the only way we were going to get the task done that night. Kidnapping Violet from her own home—at gunpoint or otherwise—was just too dramatic. Too many things could go wrong, and we'd be dooming ourselves if we took that path and weren't successful in breaking the curse.

"You guys realize that it would probably be easier to plan a bank robbery than to get Violet to lie down on the floor so that we can form a circle around her, right?" Mischa joked. But she was right. It would have been a lot less weird, too.

We trudged out of the mall frustrated and scared. It was colder than it had been when we'd arrived, and the day's slow drizzle had added to the slippery ice coating the blacktop of the parking lot. As we carefully wandered through lanes of parked cars, I found myself wishing Trey were there with us. I felt much more certain about our purpose and better about our chances of success when he was involved. Mischa and Henry walked ahead of me, discussing videos they could watch on YouTube to learn Krav Maga holds they might use on Violet the night of the party, but I was lost in thoughts about how I might admit our plan to Trey so that I could get his input. But then—

All of us were brought to attention by an awful crunching noise.

I saw a flash of movement about twenty feet ahead of us over the tops of cars, and Henry said, "Oh, shit!"

Following his lead, we broke into a trot toward his dad's Mercedes and saw instantly that the windshield was completely destroyed. It looked as if an asteroid had smashed directly into its center, radiating a web of shattered glass outward from the point of impact. As we got closer, it became more obvious what had happened: An enormous icicle had fallen off a branch of the tree under which we'd parked.

"How did this happen?" he asked. I looked up at the branches at the other icicles, and they were all barely five inches in length. Henry carefully opened the driver's-side door, and we all peered into the car at the icicle that had punctured the windshield. Its pointy tip had smashed into the gearshift between the driver's seat and the front passenger seat. The icicle itself was a monstrosity—almost three feet long and probably four inches wide at its thickest point.

"Oh my God, oh my God." Mischa began rambling. "This wasn't an accident. They know we're here! They know what we're planning!"

Henry took out his phone and tapped its screen. "Let's stay calm, okay? It's not a big deal. My dad has Triple-A, and I'm gonna call for a tow. It's just an icicle. This kind of stuff happens in Wisconsin. It's perfectly normal."

But I was just as shaken as Mischa. I didn't remember noticing an icicle that large hanging off any of the branches when we'd gotten out of the car. My pulse was racing, and I felt just as sure as Mischa that this was a warning, although from what I'd read about spirits' capabilities in the book Kirsten had given me, it seemed like an extraordinary amount of energy must have been assembled by Violet's spirits to move such an enormous object.

Henry paced as he spoke to the AAA operator, and I wrapped my arms around Mischa to console her, squeezing her over her puffy winter coat. A bitter wind blew, rattling all of the icicles hanging from tree branches throughout the parking lot. "Look at this as a good thing," I whispered into her hair as she squeezed me back. "It means we're getting closer to breaking the curse."

She squeezed her eyes as tears rolled down her cheeks. "Did you see the size of that icicle? All it means is that they can kill us whenever they want to. What if that had fallen a few seconds later, after we were already in the car?"

"But it didn't. I don't think they can move solid objects with that much precision or control over timing," I assured her. "The point is, we're fine."

"No!" Mischa exclaimed. "The point is, I'm going to die no matter what we do!"

She was on the brink of hysteria the entire time we waited for a tow truck, and all the way home as we rode in an Uber back to Willow. "I don't want to play the game again," she kept saying. "I don't want to go to her house. You guys are gonna have to do it without me. It's too dangerous."

I kept quiet. The idea of finding a way to play the game with Violet by myself was petrifying, and with Trey scheduled to be back at Northern Reserve and now Mischa flipping out, it was becoming a distinct possibility I'd find myself in exactly that situation.

Henry made the executive decision to drop Mischa off first because she was babbling about evil spirits and dying, convinced something terrible was going to happen to us on our way back to Willow (which was surely freaking our driver out). We left her at the guard station of her subdivision because she insisted she preferred walking home the last two blocks of the journey to spending another minute in the car.

"I'm worried. Do you think she's going to pull it together?" Henry asked me after our driver pulled back out onto State Street. "Because if we're going to do this on Tuesday night, we all need to be one hundred percent focused."

"I don't know," I admitted. "I don't want to criticize her for being high-strung because it's understandable in her situation. But I'm worried about whether or not she's gonna be cool once we're at Violet's house. It could be really, really bad if she loses it that night."

We turned the corner onto my street, and my heart stopped when I saw a police car pull into my driveway farther ahead. My first panic-inducing assumption was that Violet had called the police about my violation of her restraining order against me at the hospital the day before, but then the car parked and Mom got out of the back seat. I gasped in surprise. "Oh my God," I said, unfastening my seat belt.

"I'll get out here," Henry told our Uber driver. "You can skip the third stop."

The driver pulled over so that we could get out, and I sprinted toward my house over our neighbors' lawn as my mother walked up our front steps carrying her enormous purse and a paper bag from the grocery store. Two uniformed cops in heavy winter jackets trailed a few feet behind her.

"Mom!" I called. "What's going on?"

She turned and noticed both Henry and me approaching as she dug through her bag. She seemed jittery and unable to find whatever it was she was looking for in her bag as she said in a shaky voice, "Just a little drama down at the grocery store. Not a big deal. It's nice to see you, Henry."

Of course my mother would have recognized Henry Richmond, even though she probably hadn't spoken to him directly in eight years, because our town was small enough that she'd shared Classroom Mom responsibilities with Mrs. Richmond at one point or another. Everyone in Willow knew everyone else's kids, even long after friendships began and ended.

"Hi, Dr. Brady," Henry greeted her. Mentally, I gave him points for remembering that my mom had a PhD. "Happy holidays."

"Why are the police here? Were you in an accident?" I asked.

She finally found her house keys in her bag and with an unsteady hand managed to twist open the two locks on our front door to step inside. She grabbed Maude by the collar before motioning for the police to follow her in. I recognized the officer who wore glasses as one of the arresting officers who had apprehended me and Trey back in November. *Great.* With even less enthusiasm, I realized that the name on the tag pinned to the outside of his coat was MARSHALL. I guessed I had always known that Dan Marshall, the kid whose locker had been next to mine when I'd still attended normal high school, was the son of a cop, but had forgotten that even though Dan was dating Cheryl.

Mom ignored my question and instead replied in an exhausted voice, "Come on, everyone in and we'll get this squared away. Don't all let the heat outside."

In an almost frantic state, I entered the house behind the cops and motioned for Henry to come along. The police, who seemed like giants taking up too much space in our cozy living room, wobbled into the center of the room, leaving clumps of snow on our carpeting.

"Where's the car?" I asked her.

"Everything's fine," Officer Marshall told me as he took out a small notebook. "We just brought your mom home to make sure she's doing okay."

"Why wouldn't you be doing okay, Mom? What's going on?"

My mother took her coat off and hung it on the rack just inside our front door. "Please, have a seat," she told the officers, motioning to the couch. It seemed to me like she was moving kind of slowly, like she was a little stunned. Maude ran back and forth from the police officers as they sat down to Henry standing behind me, sniffing around with her tail wagging, ecstatic to have such an abundance of new smells to investigate.

After kicking off her snow boots and setting down her grocery bag, Mom perched on the edge of our recliner. "I was just in a small mishap at the shopping center. I still, for the life of me, don't understand exactly what happened." She was wringing her hands as if she was still very shaken up by whatever she'd just experienced.

I felt Henry place a hand on my shoulder to steady me. A sense of despair grew in the pit of my stomach.

"Ma'am, you said that when you tried to hit the brakes, they failed to work," Officer Morris said, referencing his notebook.

"Yes, yes," Mom agreed, remembering. "I started the car and pulled out of my parking spot. Drove to the edge of the lot as if I were going to turn left back out onto State Street, and then my oil light began flashing out of nowhere. I looked at it for just a fraction of a second, and then when I tried to brake at the stop sign, my brake pedal just didn't do anything. It just wasn't . . ." Mom shrugged. "The car just didn't stop."

Just then, my cell phone buzzed with a text from Mischa.

MISCHA 3:06 P.M.
WTF! Call me right now!

"And have you ever had any previous problems with your brakes?" Officer Marshall asked my mom. She was already shaking her head to indicate that she had not before he even finished asking the question. "Seems like a relatively new car."

"I bought it last year. I've never had any problems with it before. The only mileage on it is from my driving to and from the University of Wisconsin in Sheboygan a few days a week," Mom said. Her voice was still trembling. I couldn't recall ever having seen her so distraught before, not even in the days right after our house fire.

"Mom, did you hit someone?" I asked, aware that my voice came out of my body a lot more loudly than I had intended for it to.

"Another car hit me."

Officer Marshall interjected. "Your mother's car was struck on the driver's side. She's very lucky to be sitting here right now. If the other car had hit hers even a second sooner, things could have been very, very ugly."

My phone buzzed again.

MISCHA 3:07 P.M.
Is your mom OK?

I tried to ignore the text for a moment even though I was wondering how Mischa already seemed to know something had happened to my mother.

"I don't know what happened exactly," Mom murmured. "I thought the oil light came on as I was hitting the brakes, but then the car just plowed right out of the parking lot and into oncoming traffic. The brakes didn't do a thing."

"Oh my God, Mom," I said. My body felt freezing cold.

"I'm so lucky to be sitting here without a scratch on me," my mom said. "But I feel so bad for Elena. She must have thought I was asleep at the wheel."

It took a second for the full meaning of my mom's words to hit me. *Elena!* She had been the other driver whose car had struck my mom's. There was only one Elena in town I knew of—

Elena Portnoy.

I wasn't sure if Henry had made the connection as quickly as I had, so I looked over my shoulder at him and quietly told him, "That's Mischa's mom."

Was it a coincidence that my mother and Mischa's mother would be involved in a freak accident in which they could have both been seriously injured or killed—within an hour of an icicle impaling Henry's windshield?

I excused myself as the cops asked my mom if she was sure she didn't want them to give her a lift to the hospital to be checked out. Henry followed me into the kitchen, and I immediately called Mischa.

"What the hell?" I barked.

"I know," Mischa said, sounding out of breath. She had picked up before the first ring of the phone. "You said that spirits couldn't make things happen in our world. But they caused your mom's brakes to fail! This is it. They're really coming after us. They're warning us not to start anything with Violet at the party."

I didn't bother explaining to her my theory that Violet's spirit helpers hadn't done anything to my mom's brakes. It was far more likely that they'd manipulated my mom's thoughts for a few seconds by making her oil light flash to distract her. If I was right, this would have been an example of what the author of *Understanding the Spirit World* had described as one of the psychological tricks that spirits could play on humans.

Henry stood close to me as if trying to hear what Mischa was saying over the phone. As usual, his temperament was calm and reasonable. "It's a small town. It could have just been an innocent accident. People get in car crashes all the time."

"My mom said your mom was, like, completely surprised. Like, the brakes just failed at the very last second," Mischa said. She was talking in a low voice, presumably in her bedroom. She fell silent for a long moment and then said, "We have to stop. If they do something bad to my mom, then I won't even want to be alive anymore. I really won't, McKenna. None of this would be worthwhile."

"I know! I feel the same way. I would never forgive myself if something bad happened to my mom. But, Mischa," I cautioned, "you know what happens if we stop."

"I know," she croaked, her voice breaking with a sob. "But I was the one who stupidly played that game with Violet. I deserve to die. My mom didn't do anything. If something bad happens to her, it'll be my fault. I don't want that. I'd rather just get what's coming to me."

I didn't want to prolong the conversation and listen to Mischa get herself wound up. I needed her to calm down within the next three days and tap back into the anger she'd had for Violet in the fall so that she could be a helpful participant in her own salvation. I reminded her to make sure her candle was still burning and told her I'd call her later.

We heard the police leave, and Henry summoned another Uber to take him home. He assured me that in spite of the icicle at the mall and the car accident between my mom and Mischa's, he was still going to drive over to Violet's house in his mom's car to measure the wall. "We can't give up. That's all they want, for us to give up, because they know we can end this if we try. Promise me you won't change your mind about Tuesday night." His green eyes were solemn, and I was struck again by how different he was in reality from the impression I'd had of him when he was a star athlete in high school. Before graduating, he'd seemed like someone who'd never had a serious problem in his whole life, which had led me to believe he was probably a little shallow. But now he was volunteering to trespass on private property and complete outrageous tasks in freezing cold weather. He recognized the risks involved with avenging his sister's death and was eager to take them anyway.

I hesitated because Henry was asking me to commit to doing exactly what I'd assured Trey I wouldn't do the night before. Even though I knew I had no choice but to confront Violet at her party, his asking me to promise felt like a huge betrayal of trust. "I won't if you won't," I replied. As I watched him climb into the back seat of his Uber in our driveway, it struck me as ironic that only three days after learning the truth about what Violet had done to Olivia, Henry seemed much more eager than Trey to assist me in saving Mischa's life, and Trey had known about what we'd done at the party since shortly after Olivia had died. Maybe Henry's willingness was actually recklessness, but I wished Trey were as sensitive as Henry was to the urgency in our mission.

Henry remained true to his word, and later that afternoon he texted me photos he'd taken around the rear of the Simmonses' property. The wall surrounding their land stood exactly fifty-six inches high, which would make it easy enough to climb over with a three-step ladder. Unless we experienced a freak heat wave in the next four days, the fall on the other side of the wall would be softened by snow. By his best estimate, the distance from the fence across the Simmonses' expansive garden to the back of the house was around the size of our high school's football field. There was a chance we'd be spotted if Violet's family had heavy surveillance on their garden, but the distance wasn't so unreasonable that we might freeze to death before making our way to the house.

In other words, this was manageable. Scaling the fence was going to be a much more straightforward way to gain entrance to the party than trying to slip through the security gates. However, my scalp began tingling as I tapped and zoomed in on the photos he'd taken of the back of the Simmonses' house. I couldn't tell if it was because we were taking all the right steps to ensure success, or if there was something I was supposed to be considering more cautiously about the back entrance to the house. I'd seen the vast garden behind Violet's house before, through the kitchen and sunroom windows, but never from the other side. If there was something in the garden that I was supposed to notice, it would have been pretty hard to tell from Henry's photo what it was. All of the rosebushes and plants were covered in snow.

This is happening, he texted me, reiterating his commitment to our plan for Tuesday night.

Maybe Henry was only interested in helping me break the curse out of a powerful need for revenge. It made my heart flutter that Trey was reluctant to confront Violet out of fear that either of us getting into more trouble might prevent us from being together. But I felt a lot more confident about our chances for success on New Year's knowing that Henry was in it for the long haul with me.

CHAPTER 11

THAT NIGHT, I BURNED JUST A LITTLE BIT OF PALO santo in my bedroom and set about asking the pendulum questions.

"Pendulum, are the answers that you give me provided by Jennie?"

It swung around clumsily, not really clockwise or counterclockwise, as if it was uncertain about how to answer. I was a little disappointed and unsure of what to make of that response, but I'd never assumed that it was Jennie who was communicating directly with me through the pendulum. "Is Violet's mother still in the hospital?" I asked. Now the pendulum swung in a counterclockwise pattern. To confirm its response, I set it down on my nightstand, called St. Matthew's in Suamico, introduced myself as Vanessa Simmons's daughter and asked to be put through to her room.

"Vanessa Simmons was discharged yesterday," an exhausted nurse told me on the other end of the call. It was almost one in the morning. "I'm sorry, I don't have any additional information about her."

I tapped my phone to end the call. Simply having the hospital staff acknowledge that Mrs. Simmons had gone home, and that the pendulum could be trusted, was all I needed to know. Stephani had died, so Mrs. Simmons was recovering. But for how long? Violet was still one sacrifice behind. I guessed it didn't matter; what was important right then was that if Mrs. Simmons wasn't in the hospital, then Violet's parents had no reason to cancel their plans to go to the city for New Year's.

Just to make absolutely sure, I looked up the phone number for the Mandarin Oriental on Lake Shore Drive and called claiming to be Mrs. Vanessa Simmons. "I just wanted to confirm our reservation for New Year's Eve," I told the concierge who answered.

"Checking in on the thirty-first and checking out on the second," the concierge said after typing some buttons on his keyboard.

"Yes," I replied, very pleased with myself for gathering so much information of value.

Satisfied with my sleuthing for the night, I flipped my light switch and immediately noticed a pulsating light flashing in through my blinds. When I raised my blinds to see what was going on, I saw the light in Trey's bedroom turning on and off like a strobe effect. After about fifteen seconds of this, he noticed me standing there watching, and walked over to his window to wave at me. While he had my attention, he pointed to the back of his house and then raised a sheet of paper so that I could see it. On it was written: 9 A.M.

In the morning, I poured coffee into a thermos and took Maude into the yard. The sun was shining for the first time in a while, which meant the yard was a slushy, dripping pool of mush as the snow melted. A few minutes after nine, the sliding door on the Emorys' patio opened, and Trey stepped outside wearing his winter coat and carrying an ax. He waved at me and descended the steps from his patio into his yard, and walked around the side of his house toward me to speak to me over the fence.

"An ax? That's a dramatic prop," I teased.

"We have mice," he announced. "Walter wants me to chop all the wood stacked against the house and restack it at the back of the yard because he thinks they started nesting in there before it snowed, and now they've found a way into the house."

We were both smiling, similarly pleased to have a reason—any reason—to see each other. "There are sexier circumstances under which we might have gotten to hang out, but I guess I'll take what I can get," I said.

He looked back at his house over his shoulder to make sure neither of his parents were watching us through the kitchen window. "There's no one there," I assured him, since I could see the window clearly from where I stood. "It's safe."

"I needed to see you before I leave tomorrow. I found something."

I pulled the letter I'd stolen from his family's mailbox out of my coat pocket and handed it to him. "I did too. Well, sort of. I honestly don't know why I did this, but I took this out of your mailbox and opened it before you got back from school," I admitted. Not telling him about what I'd done had been nagging at my conscience, and I was grateful for the chance to confess in person, even though there was a possibility he was going to be very angry with me.

He took the envelope from me and looked it over, front and back.

Coming completely clean, I added, "I read it too. I'm sorry. I know, I totally invaded your mom's privacy, but it seemed like it might be related to everything somehow."

"This law firm has sent letters before. Actually, my mom gets stuff from them all the time," he said, not sounding upset that I'd read the letter.

"It says your mom violated some kind of contract eighteen years ago and now she owes their client money, plus damages and interest," I told him. "I don't want to stick my nose in your mom's business, but if the contract they're referring to had something to do with Michael Simmons, then it's kind of all of our business. Can you think of anything she would have negotiated the year you were born?" Trey's mom had only been around nineteen years old when she'd had him. I couldn't think of many legal agreements common for nineteen-year-olds to enter into unless they were basketball players being drafted into the NBA or rappers being given record deals.

Trey's bright blue eyes sparkled. "That has to do with what I found yesterday. My mom kept a diary when she was a teenager. She kept it all the way through high school and her freshman year of college."

"Wait, what?" I asked, in disbelief that we could be so lucky as to have discovered a recap of what his mom had been doing the year she met Violet's father. "Did it mention anything about Michael Simmons?"

"Yeah. Well, kind of. I just skipped to the end because I didn't really have time to read it all. But check it out. There's something in it toward the end about how he asked her to meet with his lawyers after she found out she was pregnant. They literally offered her money to terminate her pregnancy because he was worried about paternity issues down the line. She wrote all this stuff about how he tried to spin it like she was too young for such an enormous responsibility and would be throwing away all of her potential, but she saw right through that. Well, not really, actually. At first she was really angry and offended by their offer to pay her, but then she wrote all this lovesick gibberish about how she knew he'd change his mind after I was born."

I wished there weren't a fence between us so that I could reach for his hand. "That's so sad. It sounds like she was really in love with him and he broke her heart. God, what a creep."

"Yeah, that's the thing—not only did he refuse to ditch his wife for my mom, but he told her that his wife had just lost a baby and it would be too cruel to leave her while she was still grieving," Trey scoffed.

Trey's mom had always been so thin, so nervous, like someone afraid of her own shadow. I never thought of her as being ten years younger than my mom because she seemed just as old and disappointed by life. Everything Trey was telling me made my heart ache for her; she must have been devastated that the man she loved thought so little of her that he was willing to pay her to not have their baby. "God. I feel so bad for your mom," I said. And although I didn't say so, I felt bad for Trey, too. It couldn't have been pleasant to learn such awful things about your own biological parent.

"Don't feel too bad for her," he said with amusement. "The last couple of pages I skimmed were pure rage. Like real, psychotic, messed-up stuff. She was totally out for—"

We both startled as the Emorys' sliding door opened and Mr. Emory stepped onto the deck. "Trey. Are you gonna chop that wood or are you gonna stand around running your mouth all morning?"

With his back to Mr. Emory, Trey grimaced at me and rolled his eyes. "I'll get it chopped."

"Hi, Mr. Emory," I said and waved, wondering just how many details Walter Emory knew about his wife's life, how and why he'd agreed to marry her when she'd returned to Willow several months pregnant and let everyone in town believe that Trey was his biological son. Either he really loved his wife, or there was something else going on.

"Glad to hear it," Mr. Emory told him, ignoring my greeting, before going back inside.

Unable to suppress my excitement, I asked Trey, "Where is this diary? I want to read every word of it."

He shifted his weight from one foot to the other and replied, "Uh, that probably can't happen. If my mom knew I found it in the basement with all her other crap from my grandparents' house, she would kill me. I feel bad for even poking around down there, but I was curious to see if there were any pictures of them together. I would have just given it to you, but I don't know if she goes down there and looks at it often or what."

Still thinking about the law firm's threat against Trey's mom and the FOR SALE sign on his lawn, I asked, "Do you think your mom accepted money from Violet's dad to have an abortion, and then changed her mind?"

Trey thought this over. "Maybe. But it's not like we live in Sherwood Hills or anything," he reasoned. Sherwood Hills was the high-priced subdivision on the other side of town where the Portnoys lived and where Candace had lived. "As far as I know, my mom doesn't have a secret bank account somewhere. We're not poor, but you know. Walter drives a Hyundai."

He hadn't yet read the letter folded inside the envelope, so I gave him a bit of a spoiler for its content. "That letter says your mom owes that law firm's client almost two million dollars."

Trey blinked in surprise, and his lips cupped to form an O shape. "Dang. Two million dollars! He must have *really* not wanted his wife to find out about me."

"Yeah, but think about that. Your parents are selling your house. If your mom had two million dollars when she was not much older than us, then where did it go?"

Our conversation was interrupted again by Mr. Emory, who'd once more opened the screen door to shout, "Trey!"

"Okay, okay," Trey called. He smiled at me apologetically and lowered his voice. "Look, we can try to keep talking while I chop wood, but it's not going to be easy. So just in case I don't see you again before I leave, I wanted to give you this."

He handed me a small wooden box with hinges and a capital *M* burned into the top of the lid. "It's not a big deal. I just have to take wood shop at Northern Reserve, so I made this. I wasn't going to give it to you, but it's all I was able to get for Christm—"

I stood on my toes to lean over the fence and reached for his face. I pulled him close enough to kiss his lips and said, "Trey, I love it."

He turned pink, which was a rare sight, and looked cuter than ever. "It's the second one I made. The first one didn't turn out so well, and I wanted it to be perfect."

"I really love it," I insisted. Having something handmade by him was far more precious to me than anything he could have bought for me in a store, even if I knew I wasn't going to be permitted to bring it with me to Sheridan. "Listen," I said, not wanting him to go back to school with any lies remaining between us. "I think we're going to try to play the game again at Violet's party. I've been thinking about it, and there's just no other way. The next new moon is at the end of January, and Mischa will be here by herself."

Trey nodded and looked down at his feet. "I know. I knew when we talked about it the other night that you were going to at least try. Just . . . be smart. And if anything happens and you need to get in touch with me, you might be able to call my school and say that you're my aunt Nancy. She's an Emory, on Walter's side. They might ask you for a pass code, and I don't know what it is, but my mom set it, so it's probably the word 'turquoise,' since that's her favorite color and she uses it as her password for basically everything."

"Got it," I assured him. I leaned over the fence and we kissed again, more desperately this time because we both knew this was probably the last time our lips would touch for a very long time.

Just as we both suspected, our parents did not grant us another chance to say good-bye before Sunday morning, when I heard the Emorys' automatic garage door rise before I was even out of bed. I threw back the blankets and sprinted into the living room just in time to pull back the curtains, and I saw the back of Mr. Emory's car slowing down at the corner. Watching the distance grow between Trey and me as the car vanished from view made it feel as if my blood were draining out of my body. My chest was hollow. I didn't know when I'd ever see him again, or, depending on how things went on New Year's Eve, *if* I'd ever see him again.

And then, just as I heard Maude stirring down the hall in my mom's bedroom, my scalp began tingling, and I suspected I knew exactly why. I needed to see Trey's mom's diary, and I had a perfect opportunity to try to find it while his family was away for the day taking him back to school. As soon as I had the impulse to sneak into Trey's house, I tried to fight it. He had specifically told me he hadn't let me check out the diary firsthand because it was probably precious to his mom and she might notice if it were missing. Going inside his house to find it was not only illegal but a violation of his judgment.

But the tingling wouldn't stop. I was meant to see that diary; there was something in it of great importance. It wasn't quite seven o'clock yet, and I could assume since it was a Sunday that Mom would stay in bed another hour or so before getting up. I dressed quickly and pulled on my boots. Seething with self-hatred, I slipped out our back door, descended the stairs from our deck to the grass, unlocked our gate, let myself into Trey's yard, and found his house's sliding door unlocked, as I knew it would be.

The last time I'd been in the Emorys' kitchen had been the night Trey and I had taken my Ouija board down to the basement to give it an inaugural whirl, but everything was exactly the same as I remembered. The cuckoo clock that Jennie and I used to sit and watch turn hours still hung on the wall next to the fridge. Mrs. Emory still had a Snoopy cookie jar on the counter. I lifted its lid and took a peek inside to see that, yes, it still contained Oreos. Feeling sinister to be moving through someone else's house when I wasn't supposed to be there, I didn't linger.

Their basement, like ours, smelled like mildew. Everything that the Emorys had outgrown was boxed and stored there. There were utility shelves on which boxes containing everything from old Halloween costumes to previous years' taxes were stacked. I was sure Trey had said that the diary was in the basement somewhere along with other things his mother had brought home from her parents' house to store, but he hadn't mentioned where. I looked over all of the boxes on the shelves and even rifled through a few that weren't labeled, but none contained items that looked like they'd belonged to Mrs. Emory when she was young.

Then I noticed the cedar chest near the sofa, which was used as a coffee table. It had marks all over it from us leaving cups and plates on it without coasters or place mats since we were little. I'd sat on the couch many times without ever thinking too much about the fact that wooden chests, like the box that Trey had made for me, opened with hinged lids. A surge of tingling made me suspect I was on the right track. I knelt down in front of the chest, unfastened the latches, lifted the lid, and found myself looking at what appeared to be every object Trey's mom had probably ever owned as a young woman. There were folded notes and T-shirts from charitable events that had been held at Willow High School twenty years ago, stuffed animals, photo albums, yearbooks, and then . . . tucked down along one side of the chest, a leather-bound diary.

I checked the time on my phone. It would be hours before the Emorys got home, but my mom would probably wander out to our kitchen to make coffee within the next twenty minutes. So I flipped through pages to the year Trey was born, reading passages here and there. . . .

> *October 15*
>   *. . . ordered a double espresso, which was so sophis-*
> *ticated, and we talked about the implications of the*
> *Multilateral Agreement on Investment on foreign*

markets. I was so flattered that he thought I knew enough about international business to dive into those topics with me, and as we were leaving he asked if I had plans on Friday after class.

From the entries early in the autumn, I gathered that Michael Simmons had taught one of Mrs. Emory's introductory business classes. By Christmastime, they were sleeping together and she was head over heels in love with him. She'd gone back to Willow for her holiday break fantasizing about him and the life they'd have together because he'd told her he loved her and hinted that one day he might leave his controlling, superficial wife to be with her. Once she returned to campus at the end of January, she realized she was pregnant and was excited to tell him. Skipping ahead by quite a bit, I found the entry Trey had told me about, in which she described meeting with Michael Simmons's lawyers at their office in Chicago. He had urged Trey's mom to end her pregnancy for the reasons Trey had shared with me, but the lawyers informed her that there was also a matter of inheritance.

The Simmons family was very, very wealthy, and Mr. Simmons's attorneys' primary concern was making sure that Mary Jane Svensson understood her illegitimate child would never have a claim to any of that fortune. As a consolation, they were offering her 1,450,000 dollars to terminate her pregnancy and never contact Michael Simmons again. At that point in the diary, the entries became erratic, with Trey's mom acknowledging that she wasn't ready to be a parent and that the money would allow her a chance to study abroad, then becoming furious that the child he'd fathered with her was so hateful that he was willing to pay her to erase what he'd done. The name Vanessa began to appear more frequently on subsequent pages, as Trey's mom aimed her jealousy and fury toward her.

As I turned a page, a loose sheet of lined paper fell out of the diary, folded in half. When I unfolded it, I thought at first what was written on it was a poem, but then realized it was a *spell*.

By the light of the full moon
Light a black candle
Dig a hole in the earth
Pour vinegar into it and allow the earth to absorb
 the bitterness
Set a bare-root perennial plant in the hole
As the plant grows, so will your revenge
Nourished by bitterness
With each cycle of the moon, year by year
As your plant blooms, your enemies will suffer.

I gasped. What on earth did Trey's mom know about witch-craft? Although I knew relatively little about the topic, this spell seemed extremely dark, and I wondered if perhaps all along we'd been wrong for assuming Violet's family was to blame for the curse Violet wielded. . . .

Maybe someone else had put the curse on *her*.

Maybe that someone else had been Trey's mom?

I took a picture of the sheet of paper on which the spell was written and texted it to Kirsten, asking for her input on it and telling her where I'd found it. Then I tucked it back into the diary, returned everything to where I'd found it, and ran to my house feeling sick to my stomach.

Hours later, as I was trying to catch up on math homework from my Willow textbook since I'd already learned the advanced algebra my class was being taught at Sheridan, Kirsten texted me back and asked if it was okay to call.

"Sorry it took me so long to get back to you," she apologized. "I went a little too hard on the pinot last night."

"That's okay," I said, grateful that she'd replied at all.

"So, what you sent me looks like some dangerous-ass stuff. You didn't actually cast that spell, did you?"

"No. I wouldn't try to cast anything. I don't know what I'm doing," I admitted. I filled her in on the backstory of how Trey's mom had met Violet's dad, and she guessed correctly that Mr. Simmons was Trey's biological father.

She went on to explain that casting any kind of spell for revenge or putting hardship on someone else was strictly prohibited in witchcraft. Casting a spell for your own selfish purposes like that would bring the rule of three into effect, which essentially meant that three times the hardship you had inflicted on someone else would be reflected back at *you*.

"But do you think the spell that Trey's mom cast for revenge might have somehow backfired in a way that makes Violet have to sacrifice another person every month?" I asked. It seemed like the spells were related somehow, especially in the language around the revenge growing with each cycle of the moon. However, it didn't really make sense that Violet having to reap sacrifices somehow counted as a form of revenge that benefited Trey's mother. It was a terrible obligation that Violet had to fulfill, but it was also a malevolent form of power.

Even Kirsten was stumped. "I'll have to do some research. Honestly, this seems to me kind of like spell interaction."

I asked her to elaborate on what that meant.

"Like a spell that someone casts that doesn't mix well with a spell that someone *else* cast. Maybe your boyfriend's mom put a spell on her lover's wife, not realizing that there may have already been a spell on the lover's wife."

Two spells. That seemed unlikely. "What are the odds that two people who knew Violet's mom both cast spells?" I wondered aloud doubtfully.

Kirsten laughed. "Oh, you'd be surprised. Enough people are interested in casting spells for us to comfortably be able to pay rent on our storefront in Wicker Park. People turn to witchcraft when they're desperate for something. And a lot of people feel that way."

As we hung up the phone, it occurred to me that after having three stillborn daughters, Vanessa Simmons might have felt desperate too.

CHAPTER 12

HAVE FUN TONIGHT," MOM TOLD ME AS I unfastened my seat belt. She was dropping me off at Cheryl's house, where I'd told her I was spending the night on New Year's Eve. I didn't feel great about lying to my mom or to Cheryl, but sleeping over at the Guthrieses' seemed like the most credible and benign way to escape from my house the night of Violet's party.

I climbed out of the car with my overnight bag and said, "We will."

"And don't stay up too late. I'll be here at eight sharp. We need to be on the road by nine thirty to make it up to Sheridan by noon," she reminded me.

"I know, I know," I grumbled. The long drive back up to my boarding school was the least of my concerns that evening. Little did my mom know that with all I intended to accomplish that night, there was a very good chance I'd never be going back to Sheridan. I'd even taken a long, nostalgic look around my bedroom before leaving the house, wondering if I'd ever set foot in it again. "Get home safely," I told her. If it wouldn't have put my mom on red alert about my activities, I would have also warned her about using electrical appliances, knives, and walking with scissors that night, out of my concern for her. But I left my precautions at driving and waved wistfully as she backed out of the Guthrieses' driveway, with my heart twisting into a knot, hoping that this wouldn't be the last time I'd see her.

Cheryl greeted me at the front door beaming from ear to ear. "Yay! I'm so glad you're here!" she said as I stepped inside her house, which always smelled like potpourri. "We're going to have so much fun tonight!"

I felt like the most sinister person in the world as we microwaved popcorn and settled into her living room to watch movies rented from iTunes with her mom, dad, and younger brother. I'd called Cheryl on Friday to express regret that we hadn't had a chance to hang out at any other point during the break, which had been my way of gently manipulating her into extending an invitation to me to spend the holiday at her house. The entire time I sat quietly with her family, I could hear my phone buzzing with incoming texts from Mischa and Henry, making anxiety build like a Jenga tower in my chest.

I hadn't filled Cheryl in on my full agenda for the night when I'd excitedly accepted her invitation. But after we ordered pizza and watched a second movie, I knew I had to act quickly if I was going to make it outside to meet Mischa at ten fifteen, when she was scheduled to pick me up. When I'd left my house with mom, Mischa was still leaning toward avoiding the party. It was only through my persistent reminders that her seven-day candle had reached its seventh day, and she could no longer assume she was safe, that she'd agreed to drive over to Cheryl's to fetch me. Her predicament that night was a classic case of damned if you do, damned if you don't. She was either going to have to summon the courage to venture over to Violet's with me, or risk choking at any given moment.

I followed Cheryl down the hall to her bedroom when she announced she was going to change into pajamas and closed the door so that I could ask her for a favor without her parents overhearing.

"Cheryl, I'm the worst. Really, the worst person of all time. But I have to ask a huge favor of you," I said.

Her face fell a little bit, and my stomach ached. I could tell how much this night had meant to her, and now of course there was a hitch because I was a terrible, selfish, untrustworthy person. Worst of all, I wasn't even going to be honest with her about why I was sneaking out of her house. If she knew I was headed over to Violet's party, she might tell her parents out of genuine concern for my well-being. Instead, I aimed to appeal to her sense of romanticism. "I haven't had a chance to see Trey this whole week, and I have to go back to my boarding school tomorrow." She didn't know that Trey was already up north, spending New Year's Eve in his dorm room, lights out at ten o'clock, or that he'd be distraught knowing exactly what I was up to at that moment.

Something shifted in her eyes, something I hoped was a form of empathy, so I kept going. "We've been kind of hoping to, you know, be alone for at least a few hours during this break, and our parents have been totally against it."

"So, I don't understand," she said, the hurt evident in her voice. "You want to leave?"

"Just for two or three hours," I said, trying to make it sound less terrible than I knew it was. "I'll be back before two in the morning. I swear. There's no way we can spend the whole night together because his parents will be home at one, and then I'll come straight back here."

She looked conflicted, and even though I had anticipated that she wouldn't be pleased about any of this, she was reacting more emotionally than I'd been expecting. "You could get me in a lot of trouble, McKenna. If you're not back by morning, or if my parents catch you sneaking back in, they're not like your mom. They'll call the police and report you missing, or—I don't even know what they'll do."

I chose to overlook her comment suggesting that my mom was a lenient parent. "I won't. I swear, Cheryl, I won't. This is just my last chance to see him probably until July, and maybe not even then because I'll be in Florida for the summer and there's no guarantee he'll be released from his school when he turns eighteen."

She sat down on her bed, shoulders slumped, and surprised me by asking, "Are you sure you aren't just going to Violet's party and lying to me? I mean, I'm not an idiot. I know why you wanted to come with us to visit Tracy in the hospital."

If there's a worse feeling than being caught in a lie, I couldn't have named it that night, the way Cheryl was looking at me. It was already ten o'clock. There wasn't much point in insisting that I was going run off and be with Trey. I could tell that she wasn't going to believe me. "I never told you everything about Olivia and Candace," I said solemnly. "Everything that Candace said at school about the game that we played at Olivia's house and how Violet predicted their deaths? It was true. I know it sounds crazy. But it was all true."

Cheryl nodded, never taking her eyes off me. "And what about Tracy? Did she predict a death for Tracy?"

I frowned. "I don't know. I think so, because I heard she was reading people's tarot cards at school. But I don't know for sure."

Surprising me completely, Cheryl seemed more certain than I was. "Because Tracy got so much better after we went to see her on Thursday that she was sent home on Saturday, and I overheard my aunt Joyce telling my mom that Tracy was asking her doctors if there was any chance she was going to have a heart attack. Like, if the meningitis was going to increase the odds of her having a heart attack while she was still in high school. Why would a seventeen-year-old think they're going to have a heart attack?"

I didn't know how to respond. If I didn't make it to Violet's party that night and force her into playing Light as a Feather, Cold as Marble, then someone—quite possibly Tracy, despite her miraculous recovery—was going to die before the end of January. "Okay. I'm going to Violet's party," I admitted, deciding to risk everything because I was desperate for Cheryl to cooperate. "Mischa Portnoy is picking me up in fifteen minutes outside. We have a plan to go inside Violet's house, be there for about fifteen minutes, and then leave. That's it. We're not going there to start a fight, or steal anything, just to finish what Violet started and hopefully save Mischa's life. And Tracy's."

Cheryl's lips pressed into a firm line, and she stood up. "Look, I'll go tell my parents right now that I don't feel well and we're going to sleep early so that you can wake up on time for your mom to pick you up in the morning. But only if you let me come with you tonight and help."

Those were the last words I expected to hear Cheryl say, and the condition she'd proposed was certainly not one I had ever considered entertaining. With the clock ticking away, I wasn't in a position to tell her she couldn't come with, even though I tried to dissuade her. "It's going to be dangerous. Not necessarily in a way that might get us in trouble with police. But more like in a way that could get us dead."

My not-so-subtle warning did nothing to lessen Cheryl's interest in joining me. We both walked back down to the living room and announced that we were hitting the hay for the night. Her parents suspected nothing and wished us sweet dreams. Ten minutes later, with her bedroom door locked from the inside, we scrambled out her bedroom window and down the sloping roof of the garage, from which we dropped off the side onto her front yard and ran to Mischa's Volkswagen GTI.

"No way," Mischa said as I climbed into the front passenger seat and Cheryl hopped into the back. "A third wheel was not part of the plan."

I shivered inside my coat, shaking off the bitter cold. I was wearing a hoodie with a knit hat pulled down under the hood to obscure my face once we got to the party, but I was glad to have chosen to wear such warm clothes that night. "She's part of the plan now," I said, hoping Mischa wouldn't be difficult about this. Kids were probably already arriving at Violet's house. Henry had texted me to tell me that he was getting a ride with guys he knew from his own graduating class rather than with Justin, and they were picking him up at ten thirty. Our mission was on a countdown now, and we didn't have time to argue over who was coming with and who was staying home.

"Well, if anything happens to her, that's on you," Mischa snapped at me. "I've already got one death on my conscience."

Our drive across town was silent and tense. We passed the big green sign on the outskirts of town on which was printed: WELCOME TO WILLOW. POPULATION 4,832. That number couldn't possibly have been accurate anymore, at least not to reflect how much the population had been reduced since Violet had moved to town.

Almost forty minutes after leaving Cheryl's, when we reached the front entrance to Violet's property on Deerfield Road, there was no indication that anything out of the ordinary was happening behind the massive front gate. However, when Mischa slowed down so I could peer past the gate into the darkness surrounding the Simmons property, I saw a swarm of red taillights in the distance as cars parked along the private drive leading to Violet's house. "Wow," I said, impressed. I couldn't even guess how many cars were there, but there were more than I'd ever thought I'd see at any high school party. "There's definitely a party going on here tonight."

People in a car behind us honked at us to get out of their way, and Mischa accelerated and then pulled over so that we could watch in her rearview mirror how the guests were gaining access to the party. The kids in the car behind us pressed a button on the gate's touch pad and then waited for someone inside the house to open the gate remotely. As unlikely as it seemed, Violet actually had someone inside the house monitoring the gate over the video security system to control who could drive onto the property and who couldn't.

"Glad we didn't try to come up with a strategy to get into the house that way," Mischa said. "Because one of us—probably me—

would have ended up riding in the trunk like being smuggled across a border." She wasn't wrong; that tactic had crossed my mind.

We drove to the next stoplight on Deerfield Road and hung a right, and then made another right turn onto Fenmore Lane, following the perimeter of the Simmons property. "Is there a back entrance?" Cheryl dared to ask from where she was being very quiet in the back.

"Sort of," I answered. There wasn't much traffic on Fenmore Lane, which was heavily wooded, so no one witnessed us parking along the gravel shoulder of the road. Without exchanging words, Mischa and I got out of the car and Cheryl followed, and we walked around to the hatchback door to take out the small folding stepladder that Mischa had brought from home. My phone buzzed in my back pocket, and I checked it to see a text from Henry.

HENRY 11:02 P.M.
Here

"It's only three steps, but Henry thought it would be high enough," Mischa said.

"Well, we're about to find out." I carried the stepladder over to the wall with my pulse racing. Even though there was no one around, I wanted to get this part over with quickly, before anyone drove past and spotted us.

Cheryl followed us over to the whitewashed brick wall, where I opened the stepladder and set it down in the snow. There was over two feet of snow on the ground, and I did my best to make sure the ladder had been set down in a place where it was even and its base wasn't resting on any rocks. The first rung of the ladder was mostly beneath the snow, making it seem all the more absurd that we were trying to sneak onto the Simmonses' land this way in the dead of winter.

"Are you guys serious?" Cheryl asked.

"Totally serious," Mischa said as she climbed to the third rung and brushed snow off of the top of the wall with her glove. "Problem," she announced. "There's something along the top of the wall here that's . . ." She took out her phone and tapped it to use it as a light for a better look. "It's like pieces of crushed glass smashed into the cement."

Of course. Something sharp that would cut anyone who tried to climb over the same way we were, but without the aesthetically displeasing appearance of razor wire. "Do you have anything in your car we could put down?" I asked. "Like a blanket or a heavier coat?"

Mischa's eyes lit up. She had two heavy wool yoga blankets in her the back of her hatchback, and after climbing back down the stepladder to fetch them, she set them atop the wall side by side to prevent us from cutting our hands or clothes when we swung our legs over the top to get to the other side. Mischa was the first over, and we heard her announce, "It's not that bad," after she dropped into the snowbank on the Simmonses' side of the wall.

I looked at Cheryl. "Do you still want to come with? Or do you want to wait in the car?" She hesitated for a moment before saying, "I'm coming with," and climbed up the stepladder.

The drop from the top of the wall was more intimidating than I'd thought it would be. I was grateful that Mischa had so much athletic junk in her car and that we were all wearing heavy winter gloves, or the glass on top of the wall would have been a serious problem. Even still, Mischa was a gymnast who did backflips and handsprings every single day as part of her floor routines, so a drop into a snowdrift wasn't as big a deal for her as it was for me. I closed my eyes, counted to three, and pushed myself toward the ground.

Once all three of us were over the wall, we looked back at the yoga blankets, and I realized we weren't going to be able to get back to the car this way later on. We'd have to walk all the way around the perimeter of the property—*miles*—or get someone to drive us back to Fenmore Lane. I hadn't put much thought into anything that might happen after we forced Violet into playing the game, and I tried not to stress about that. I had enough things to figure out related to how we were going to find her in the crowd and separate her from her friends. Even from where we stood, on the far side of a wooded patch of land that gave way to wide-open space and then rows of rosebushes covered in a blanket of snow, we could hear the bass pumping from inside the house. The party had definitely started, and it was time for us to accomplish what we'd been planning for the last week.

As much as the snow had worked to our advantage in some ways, I wished we weren't attempting all of this in the middle of winter as we trudged across the Simmonses' property. It was downright freezing, so cold outside that my toes were going numb inside my boots. I jabbed at my phone with gloved fingers to check a series of text messages from Henry, telling me that the whole house was packed. The party wasn't confined to just the parlor or just the basement—there were kids everywhere, and not just from Willow. He'd be waiting for us in the sunroom off the kitchen like we'd discussed, but he warned me that there were kids in there smoking weed.

Our arrival would definitely be noticed.

I decided not to share this with Mischa and Cheryl as we pressed on. By the time we reached the rosebushes farthest from the house, my nose was dripping. Despite the fact that I'd brought my pendulum, a stick of palo santo, matches, and a pocket mirror with me, I hadn't brought any Kleenex.

"Dang. Violet may be a cold-hearted, dirty bitch, but she knows how to throw a party," Mischa quipped as we reached the fountain at the center of the Simmonses' garden and looked up at the house. "It almost makes me wish we weren't enemies with her." Lights were on in every window, and we could see the silhouettes of kids dancing on the first and second floors. Hip-hop was blasting at an obnoxiously loud volume, and if the Simmons family had had any neighbors within a mile in any direction, I was sure a noise complaint already would have been filed with the police.

For a second, I thought my scalp was tingling, but I was so cold that it was hard to tell. However, I took a good look around the area where we were standing just to make sure there wasn't anything special that I was supposed to be focusing on. The only kind of strange thing about the center of the garden was that there was a bench facing the fountain, which was dry for winter. Directly behind the bench there was a much shorter row of rosebushes than all of the others in the garden. It looked as if there were five bushes around my height beneath the heavy snow, which did strike me as noteworthy, at least in how they might have related to the spell that Trey's mother had cast by planting something in the ground. Five bushes, five dead sisters. I struggled to tap my phone to activate the camera with my gloves on and snapped a quick photo with the flash off so that I could think about the significance (or lack thereof) later.

"There's the door," I said, pointing ahead to a screen door on the right side of the house. The glass panels of the sunroom were steamy, suggesting that it was a lot warmer inside the house than it was outside. My heart was pounding. I felt as if we were about to storm a castle or stage a government coup, or attempt something far more daunting than crashing a party. But as I saw the back door push open and Henry leaned outside to motion at us, I realized that it was the house that was creeping me out. I'd gotten a very bad vibe there the first time I'd visited, and now it felt as if we were forcing our way into the blackened, rotten core of the curse Violet kept casting.

I was so numb with fear by the time my frozen legs carried me the rest of the way to the back door that the relief of seeing Henry's smiling face warmed me up until I noticed a bright red lipstick stain on his cheek. A sensation close to jealousy overtook me until I reminded myself to calm down. Any girl at that party who recognized Henry might have greeted him with a kiss; the lipstick didn't mean anything. Besides which, it shouldn't have mattered to me; I was with Trey, and this volatile burst of emotion was probably just thought manipulation on the part of Violet's spirits, meant to distract me.

"You made it," he greeted us and lightly punched Mischa and me on the shoulders.

"Thanks," I said, stepping past him into the sunroom, which reeked of marijuana smoke. A cluster of about ten kids I didn't recognize looked over at us from where they stood on the other side of the sunroom. They seemed pretty disinterested in our reason for entering the party through the back door and went back to passing around an overstuffed joint.

Mischa, Cheryl, and I all stomped our boots on the jute mat just inside the door to shake off clumps of snow. My scalp was already tingling beneath my fleece hood and hat, and I was trying not to think too much of it. It hadn't tingled like that when I'd run into Violet at Hennessey's, but I assumed I was just on high alert because of what we were about to do, and the tingles were occurring to keep me vigilant. "Have you seen her yet?" Mischa asked Henry. She had to shout to be heard over the music.

"No," he said. "It's already pretty crowded, and I haven't exactly been looking for her. I didn't want to interact with her before you guys got here." His eyes fell upon Cheryl, and then he looked to me for an explanation.

"Oh," I said, realizing it was impolite to skip introductions even though we were in the most rushed and stressful of circumstances. "Henry, this is Cheryl. Cheryl, this is Henry, Olivia Richmond's older brother. I used to be in color guard with Cheryl, and she wanted to help out tonight."

Cheryl waved shyly at him. "Nice to meet you."

Over my shoulder, I peered through the open doorway into the kitchen and got my first glimpse of the party raging farther inside the house. A girl I recognized as a sophomore was running and laughing through the crowd carrying a bottle of champagne while a guy I'd never seen before chased her in his boxer shorts. Roy Needham, one of the stoner guys who Trey used to hang out with sometimes, was standing on the kitchen counter, rapping along with the music.

Shannon Liu seemed completely unaffected by the recent death of her former girlfriend, Stephani, because she was running her tongue up and down Nick Maxwell's neck as he poured vodka into a red Solo cup.

"Are we gonna do this thing or what?" Mischa asked. "My candle burned out, and if we don't get this done tonight, I'm screwed."

"Let's go," I said, pulling my knit hat down a little lower over my forehead. "Everyone stay close together."

I led the way into the crowded kitchen. If kids from school happened to recognize me and realize that I wasn't supposed to be there, I was too focused on reaching the front parlor to notice. The DJ's turntables had been set up in the house's grand front room, and over the bouncing tops of people's heads I could see what looked like enormous speakers standing on both sides of his table. Black and red light bulbs in all of the front parlor's light fixtures were making it look more like a nightclub than a mansion in a small town. Every kid I saw was holding either a bottle of beer or a cup full of booze, and the vast array of bottles in the kitchen were top-shelf: Gran Patrón Platinum, Grey Goose, Maker's Mark. Even though I'd grown up thinking of the Richmonds and the Portnoys as being wealthy because they owned big houses and luxury vehicles, the fortune that Violet had obviously dumped on this bash put her wealth on another level.

Right as we were about to push our way through the crowd into the front parlor, I felt Mischa tug on my coat. I turned to see alarm in her eyes as she pointed back into the kitchen at something. Annoyed to be slowed down, I leaned closer so that I could hear what she was shouting into my ear. "Look! The . . ." Her words were drowned out by music.

Just like that, as my eyes fell upon a silver serving tray on the kitchen counter, the tingling across my scalp burst into what felt like a blaze. There were too many people in the way for me to see exactly what was on the tray at first; Jason Arkadian and a group of girls from our class were standing in front of the tray with their fingers hovering over it as if making selections. *Stop them, stop them, stop them*, the voices in my head began chanting, and my feet began moving in that direction before I even had a chance to make sense of what I was seeing.

I squeezed in between a few twelfth-grade girls wearing tight dresses on my way closer to the counter, and then impatiently elbowed two more kids out of my way. Then I watched in a panic as Jason made his selection from the tray, and everything suddenly made horrific sense.

On the tray were rows of little paper scrolls fastened with red ribbon. A card on a little silver stand had been printed with the words, PERSONALIZED PREDICTIONS FOR NEXT YEAR.

I felt for a second as if someone had punched me in the solar plexus. All of the air rushed out of my body as the enormity of what Violet had done hit me. Mischa and Henry both saw the tray and had the same realization. Violet had thrown that party to issue as many death sentences as she possibly could with the least amount of effort, and her guests were absolutely clueless.

Even worse, if Jason's reaction was any indication, they were flattered by her attention.

Petrified, we watched as Jason unrolled the scroll with his name on it and read his prediction to the two girls standing with him for their amusement. "Jason, don't!" I shouted, but he couldn't hear me over the music, and he was laughing at whatever was printed on the paper.

Stop them, stop them, the voices continued.

I marched over to the tray and picked up the scrap of paper that Jason had discarded. On it was printed:

In the end, it will be dark and cold.

Stunning me, there was a scroll on the tray with Cheryl's name printed on it. Somehow, Violet had known all along that we'd be showing up. She'd known that Cheryl would be with us.

I tore to shreds the scrolls that remained on the tray, noticing that there were at least ten empty gaps in the rows where predictions had already been removed. Hailey West, one of the girls on pom squad with Violet who had once been friendly with Olivia, recognized me from the other side of the kitchen. I heard her yell, "Who invited McKenna Brady?" and then I felt arms pulling me away from the counter.

"Come on," I heard Henry say behind me. "We have to find her—right now."

The party turned nightmarish as we barged into the front parlor in search of Violet. Word that Mischa and I had shown up uninvited spread through the crowd like wildfire, causing heads to turn as we passed. Out of the corner of my eye, I saw people unscrolling their predictions. I spotted Chitra Bhakta, who'd been in several classes with me before I was kicked out of Willow High School, reading her scroll with a faint smile on her face and tossing the red ribbon to the floor. In a matter of seconds, I had overheated and found myself sweating beneath my heavy winter coat, hoodie, and hat.

And then we saw her. Violet. She was descending the grand staircase that led from the front parlor up to the second floor under the stern frown of Grandmother Simmons in the enormous oil portrait that hung on the wall. She was wearing a tight, strapless gold dress, nothing at all like the fashionable but conservative outfits she used to wear at the beginning of the school year. She'd always been slim, but it was plain for everyone now to see that she was in excellent shape, with a body that would make any girl our age jealous. She held hands with Pete, who walked down the stairs behind her, smiling as if she were a toy he was showing off.

Even before we spotted her, she'd seen us.

She smiled directly at me. Patiently, knowingly.

She made a hand signal to the DJ from the staircase, and the music cut out. In that instant, as the party went silent, the tables were turned. There wasn't going to be any way that we could privately coerce her into one of the house's smaller rooms to play our game, or even drag her away from her guests against her will. She had full command of the situation. Everyone who had been talking, dancing, or jumping up and down on the sofa looked around in wonderment as Violet leaned over the railing of the staircase to address us. "McKenna! Mischa! I'm so glad you could make it! And you brought Cheryl with you too. That was very kind of you."

My former classmates from Willow gathered around us and stared, some smirking as they sipped their drinks, others looking me up and down in judgment. I heard someone behind me whisper the word "crazy," which was followed by cruel giggling. Someone else said, "Cheryl Guthries," as if it was hilarious that Cheryl was at the party.

"We're here to play a game," Mischa called up to her, but I

nudged Mischa in the ribs and shook my head. Violet already knew what we were there to do. She had already put precautions in place to prevent us from getting anywhere near her.

"Cool!" Violet purred. "I love games. How about a game of keep-away? And by that, I mean you guys keep away from *me*."

Before I even had a sense of what was happening, I was lifted off my feet from behind by someone. On my left and right, Mischa and Cheryl were both raised off the ground by muscular-looking football guys wearing varsity letter jackets from St. Patrick's. They carried us toward the front door, where Hailey West smiled patronizingly at us as she held the door open. "Bye! Thanks for coming!" she teased. "Happy New Year!"

Once back out in the freezing cold on the Simmonses' front steps, I was surprised to be hurled down to the snow, landing clumsily on my back at the bottom of the cement stairs. The stairs weren't very tall, and the fall hadn't been bad, but if there hadn't been snow on the ground, I probably would have been at least bruised from the impact when I landed.

Henry whirled around, swinging at the guy who'd dragged him out of the house, but the guy was much brawnier than him and shoved him back on the shoulders with the stern warning, "This is not a fight you want to start, bro."

The Simmonses' front door closed and clicked shut. The music resumed, and we could see kids start dancing again through the front window. In silence, Mischa, Cheryl, and I sat there on the snow, trying to make sense of how our plan had fallen apart so quickly, while Henry charged at the front door and beat his fists against it. "Let me back in! I want to talk to Violet!" he roared.

I looked up at the sky, which was crystal clear. Stars shone down on us, and my eyes began watering even though my brain commanded the rest of my body not to cry. We'd failed. Not only had we blown our big plan to make Violet play the game that Jennie had recommended, we'd also totally revealed our hand. Now she knew what we were after, she knew with certainty that Cheryl and Henry were working with Mischa and me, and she'd made good on her promise to make me sorry for protecting Tracy's life.

Worst of all, Mom was driving me back up to Sheridan in nine hours. My ability to do anything to break Violet's curse was about to be taken away.

CHAPTER 13

O N THE RIDE HOME FROM VIOLET'S HOUSE IN
Mischa's car, I told the others about the little New Year's
paper scrolls and that the message in Jason's had been more or less a
death prediction.

"That bitch," Mischa hissed from behind the wheel. Our most
immediate order of business, having failed, was that Mischa's candle
had burned out. And according to Jennie, *She will always be next
until she's dead*. I didn't remind Mischa of this fact, but I was sure it
was on her mind.

"So she predicted the deaths of a bunch of kids—all tonight?"
Henry asked. "Why would she do that? Is she going to kill everyone
in one giant tragic event?"

I hadn't mentioned the way in which Violet had threatened me
at the hospital to anyone, but now it felt like I needed to fill everyone in. "She cornered me at the hospital when Cheryl and I went to
visit Tracy Hartford last week. I think she knew I was there to try to
protect Tracy from whatever she'd done to her, so she told me she was
going to make me regret trying to stop her."

"Wait a second," Cheryl piped up from the back seat. "You came to the hospital to try to *save* Tracy?"

"Of course. When you told me she had meningitis, it seemed pretty obvious that she was going to be Violet's next victim," I said.

For the rest of the drive home, Henry mused aloud about ways in which we might protect Mischa until we had a chance to formulate a new plan, but Cheryl stared out the window without joining the conversation. All of this was probably a lot for her to have to process in one night, and I didn't know how to make any of it easier to understand. I really didn't want to have to explain anything to her about how I'd been in contact with my dead twin sister for guidance on how to thwart Violet's murderous activities.

Cheryl and I made it back to her house and into her bedroom through the window over the garage before one in the morning, although neither of us could sleep.

"That's not what was supposed to happen tonight, was it?" she asked.

"No," I confirmed without elaborating. "I don't mean to leave you in the dark, but the less you know, the safer you'll be." My head was spinning long after we turned out the lights. I wondered if Violet's most recent victims had to read their predictions in order to accept their fate, or if the simple act of Violet typing them up and printing them out was enough to issue the death sentence. I was specifically worried about whether or not Cheryl was doomed now too. I hadn't told her or the others that I'd seen a scroll on the tray for her, but the fact that there'd been one freaked me out. I hadn't bothered reading the prediction that Violet had written for Cheryl when I'd had the chance in Violet's kitchen, which seemed like a hasty mistake in hindsight.

Cheryl turned off the lamp on her desk and urged me to try to get some sleep. For over an hour, I listened to my phone buzz with incoming messages, hoping that the irritating noise wasn't keeping Cheryl up. When I finally heard her lightly snoring, I got up from the cot her mom had set up for me and pulled my phone out of my bag.

The texts were, not surprisingly, coming from 000-000-0000, ID Unknown. *Olivia.* She was furious with me that I'd failed once again to stop Violet. I was furious too—that our communication was so one-sided. By now, it would have been helpful if she'd figured out more effective ways to instruct me so that I wouldn't keep messing things up. I tapped out a text reply:

I'm sorry! Just tell me what to do!

To my utter shock, when my alarm went off at seven in the morning after I'd barely gotten any sleep, I saw that Olivia had summoned the energy to respond with what I perceived to be actual instructions. My phone had already been activated, the security code already entered. My phone's map application had been opened, and my entire screen was filled with a map of a section of land topped by a blue cutout indicating water. I knew instantly what section of the country this map was showing me, and knew exactly what Olivia was implying when a red bullet appeared over Mt. Farthington as the map finished loading. It was the Lower Peninsula of Michigan, and the address of Fitzgerald's Lodge near Mt. Farthington had been entered into my phone.

Would you like to access more information about Fitzgerald's Lodge? my phone asked me.

"Sure, why not?" I muttered and tapped YES. Cheryl was already awake and using the bathroom, so at least she couldn't hear me talking to my phone as if I were totally nuts.

Michigan. Olivia wanted me to go to Michigan, which was where Violet was taking the junior class on their ski trip. I thought about Jason Arkadian's prediction describing the end for him as "dark and cold," and a chill ran down my spine. My first hunch was that Violet was going to do something on that ski trip to kill a lot of people. If I hadn't been worried about setting off all of the smoke alarms at Cheryl's house by burning a little palo santo, I would have immediately asked the pendulum about it.

The website for Fitzgerald's Lodge was everything I expected: an image gallery of a cozy ski resort that claimed to make the best hot chocolate in Michigan, roaring fireplaces, a luxury spa, and a variety of runs for beginners, intermediate skiers, and experienced ski enthusiasts. They offered snowboarding and skiing classes, had two highly rated restaurants on-site, and boasted nightly karaoke in the lodge. And, of course, they offered discounts for student groups.

Violet had been putting that ski trip together since shortly after Olivia had died. Maybe it had been a part of her big plan all along. The day Mischa, Trey, and I had confronted her out on the track at school, she'd actually made me feel kind of sorry for her. But now I had to wonder just how deeply evil she really was to have put this much strategy into organizing the party as well as the ski trip.

And since I'd botched my one shot at playing the game again with her while at home in Willow, if kids died in Michigan, some of their blood would be on my hands too.

Mom would be picking me up from Cheryl's in less than an hour to go home, fetch my bags, and hit the road for the Sheridan School for Girls. If I was going to try to strategize a way to intercept Violet on the ski trip, I had a lot of arrangements to make with Henry before my phone was taken away. I was lost in thought when Cheryl returned to her bedroom and sat down on her bed. "I'll understand if you don't want to talk about what happened at Violet's house last night," she said. "But if there's any way I can help you finish whatever it is you need to do, all you have to do is ask."

As I folded the blanket that her mom had provided to me for the night and looked over at Cheryl sitting there in her pajamas, I imagined how all of this must have seemed to her. Ever since we were little kids, I'd known Cheryl to be a profoundly good person. I'd perhaps attributed a lot of that goodness to lack of opportunity to be selfish or manipulative, because I thought it was easier for someone to be virtuous if they were ignored by boys and excluded from things like parties. But now it was easy to see how wrong I was. Cheryl was just as much of a powerhouse as Mischa, she just viewed other people and their actions through a different set of criteria. For her, accepting the reality that we were combatting a classmate who had been murdering kids in our town must have been shocking.

"I appreciate that, Cheryl, but I'll only ask as a last resort. Maybe in the fall you thought I was crazy, but now? After Olivia and Candace, and Stephani? What Violet's doing is very intentional. No one is safe," I replied. I pulled off and folded the sheets that her mom had spread out on the cot, not wanting to leave a mess behind for Mrs. Guthries to have to clean up after I left.

Cheryl nodded. "I get that now." Her voice was low and gravelly, and she hung her head as she picked at the dirt under her fingernails.

"I was upset that you didn't want to be friends anymore because you wanted to be popular. But I do understand that you've been dealing with things that are a lot more important than going to concerts and twirling flags." When our eyes met, her mouth sagged in a guilty frown, which pierced my heart because *I* was the one who'd been a lousy friend these last few months. "I'm sorry that you didn't feel like you could tell me what was going on sooner."

I set the stack of sheets I'd folded on the cot and sat down next to on her bed, wondering if this would be the last chance I'd ever have to rectify the damage I'd done to our friendship in September. "I didn't tell you because it sounds *unbelievable* that a girl at our school can make someone die just by telling them a story. You probably wouldn't have believed me, and even if you had, I wouldn't have wanted you to confront Violet. But it's all real, and if I can't figure out how to sneak away from my school and stop her within the next few weeks, Mischa will die before January twenty-fourth. Maybe other people too." I stopped short of adding, *including you.* Cheryl didn't deserve to know that Violet had placed a prediction for her on that tray.

Cheryl's eyes still looked so sad. "But I see her every day," she reminded me. "I could spy on her. I could transfer into her classes this semester and take notes on who she's talking to."

I could see that Cheryl was intent on helping, and I feared that she might go rogue and attract even more unwanted attention from Violet if I didn't allow her to believe she was aiding us in one way or another.

"Just go on the ski trip," I urged her, figuring that if Violet's prediction for Cheryl might come true even if Cheryl hadn't read it, she was already in more jeopardy than I could protect her from.

"It'll be a huge help if you can keep me informed about everything related to the trip—who's going, how you're getting there, who's rooming together . . . everything. Pretend at school like tonight never happened and be in Michigan at the end of the month with everyone else."

CHAPTER 14

"TIGHT CORNERS, LADIES. WE CAN'T HAVE wrinkles."

Guard Robinson, the staffer at Sheridan responsible for watching those of us on laundry duty, stood near the entrance of the laundry room in the basement of the Huron Building, my dorm at Sheridan. There were two large dormitories on campus, intended to keep the younger girls separated from the older girls, but in my opinion, the separation strategy would have made more sense if the extremely dangerous girls had been kept away from the less dangerous girls. There were plenty of younger girls at Sheridan who I avoided with as much caution as girls my own age, some of whom were on laundry duty with me that night.

Being assigned to laundry chores on January 22 was a significantly miserable setback in my plan to escape from my campus that night. It was almost six o'clock in the evening, and according to the haphazard plan that Henry and I had whipped up on New Year's Day, in half an hour, he, Mischa, and Trey would be waiting for me nearly half a mile away on the road that encircled my school. During the three weeks I'd been back at Sheridan, I'd been questioning my pendulum nightly about whether or not we'd be able to play Light as a Feather, Cold as Marble with Violet on the ski trip, and unfailingly it had assured me that we would. Now it was go time, and I was trapped in the custody of the toughest guard on campus.

I had butterflies in my stomach as I withdrew piping-hot gym clothes from the dryer to fold as Robinson watched us. This wasn't the way the evening was supposed to have gone down. I was supposed to have been on cafeteria duty. If I'd been there, doing predinner prep, I'd have had my winter coat with me from crossing between my dorm and the cafeteria facility. I'd have been able to slip out the back utility door of the cafeteria, where trucks dropped off big shipments of vegetables and government-issued blocks of cheese, so that I could have made my way toward the rural road that led to my school to wait for my ride.

But instead, for whatever reason, my name had been printed on the laundry list the previous day. I'd debated making some kind of appeal to Mrs. Freemantle, the disciplinary advisor in charge of assigning weekly chores to students, but had ultimately decided that it would be best to not bring attention to myself that week. I couldn't really blame that on Violet's spirits; it was just one of the infuriating aspects of attending a reform school and not having any control over my own life. Regardless of the reason why I was unexpectedly folding laundry on a Wednesday night, I was freaking out. I had only minutes to figure out how I was going to rectify this situation, and none of the possibilities I'd been entertaining for the last thirty hours or so seemed like realistic options.

I already knew from having been on laundry duty back in November that at the end of our shift, we'd pile our organized bags of students' clean laundry in carts that would be wheeled upstairs by the facilities crew for delivery to dorm rooms. The eighteen of us on duty would form two single-file lines, Robinson would count us, and we'd march up the stairs to our rooms to prepare for dinner. From there, I'd unenthusiastically greet my roommate Alecia out of social obligation, grab my coat, and we'd both stand outside our room in the hallway, dressed for the cold, at attention until Guard Carlitos, the resident assistant responsible for our floor of the dormitory until nine o'clock on weeknights, blew her whistle. All of the girls on the second floor of Huron would follow Carlitos from our dorm across the freezing-cold courtyard to the cafeteria. After our awful meal of chili and rice or chicken patty sandwiches, we'd be marched back across the courtyard to our rooms for homework and lights-out at ten.

If I didn't make my escape before returning from the laundry room to my dorm room, my chance to split unnoticed would be shot for the night. There was no way I could fall out of line while cross-ing the courtyard to the cafeteria. Any girl who spotted me would snitch. Although there was camaraderie at Sheridan, my classmates definitely did not extend it to me.

And worst of all, if I didn't connect with my friends that night, I'd have no way of getting in touch with them to let them know I was unable to get off campus. They'd be idling along the side of the high-way, having no idea what was going on. Our whole plan for the night had been very carefully constructed around the obstacle of commu-nication. Henry couldn't call me at school. He could only leave mes-sages for me in the principal's office, which was not ideal. Pretending to be Mrs. Emory, I'd called Trey's school on the prepaid phone card that Henry put money into my commissary fund for me to purchase to request a two-day leave of absence beginning Wednesday, the twenty-second. Of *course* they had asked for my pass code, and luckily, "turquoise" seemed to have worked. I had been shaking the whole time I'd been on the phone with the administrator there, all the while trying to sound convincingly like a middle-aged mom.

What stressed me out the most in the damp, overheated laundry room was that no matter what, for both me and Trey, sneaking off of our respective campuses was going to result in irreversible trouble. It was dire that we make it to Michigan without any snags, because if we weren't successful in breaking the curse this time, there wouldn't be any future opportunities. Without private phone or e-mail privileges or another way of keeping in contact with Henry, I wasn't even sure what precautions he'd taken to protect Mischa, or if she was still alive. Although I'd been in a constant state of worry since arriving back at Sheridan, asking the pendulum regularly about her health and safety, its responses weren't as reassuring as speaking to Mischa would have been. I hadn't seen her since the moment she'd dropped Cheryl and me off after Violet's party, and that had been twenty-two days ago. The next new moon was in two days.

The bus bound for Michigan would depart from Willow High School the next morning.

I carefully matched up the sleeves on the T-shirt I was folding, lost in thought. I was going to have to drop off the back of the line on the way upstairs, or figure out a way to be dismissed from laundry duty early. The dormitory building was old and complicated, and I had no idea if there were any doors in the basement near the laundry room through which I could make my way outside. But I was going to have to take that risk, even if it meant running halfway across campus in twenty-degree weather without a winter coat.

Winnie, a girl from Kenosha who had physically threatened her last foster mother, folded laundry across the table from me. Starting trouble with her (or any of my classmates) was a last resort, but if there was a way I could get Guard Robinson to send me up to the admin office early, that might be my best shot at escaping from campus before roll call upstairs.

Staring at Winnie until I caught her eye, I reached into the pocket of my uniform jumpsuit and withdrew an old tube of Blistex. It was the one small luxury from home that I'd been allowed to bring with me to Sheridan because my lips had been cracked and bleeding when Mom had dropped me off on New Year's Day (probably from having been out in the cold walking across the Simmonses' property the night before). Knowing that I had Winnie's attention, I applied the Blistex slowly, tauntingly.

"Hey," she said firmly. "Gimme some of that."

Even though it had been my intention to start an argument with her, now that I was well on my way, I was a little afraid of what she might do. "No. It's mine," I answered, and slid the Blistex back into my pocket. I returned my eyes to the pile of shirts I was folding.

"Come on. Don't make me take it from you," Winnie continued, staring me down.

Out of the corner of my eye, I stole a glimpse at Guard Robinson. Of course she'd heard Winnie and could see what was going on, but wasn't going to say a word to the girl unless she absolutely had to. Even guards were afraid of Winnie; she had shoulders like a linebacker, and I'd heard that she had a tendency to *bite*.

"It's from my doctor, for a medical condition. You can't have it," I said, trembling inside my loose jumpsuit. I wanted to be sent to the admin office to be disciplined, not to the infirmary because Winnie had bitten my ear off.

After stealing a glance over at Guard Robinson, Winnie put down the pair of socks she was bundling and walked around the end of the table to my side. She grabbed my wrist and twisted my right arm around my back.

"I told you to give me that lip balm," Winnie growled at me.

The other girls around us kept folding, none of them saying a word or even daring to look my way. My hand was pinned between my shoulder blades, and I leaned over the table in pain, praying that Guard Robinson would jump in already. I fixed my eyes straight ahead on the ugly yellow tile wall behind the row of dryers, kept my mouth pressed firmly shut, and tried to hold as still as possible because I was all too aware that Winnie was capable of snapping my arm if she felt like it. She reached into both pockets of my jumpsuit and found the stick of lip balm, and then shoved me so forcefully that I almost hit my head on the table.

"What's going on over there?" Guard Robinson finally inquired with minimal interest. She barely moved a muscle even though she must have seen that Winnie had put me in a hold. The guards at Sheridan ignored trouble, thereby fostering it. In their defense, they probably weren't paid enough to put their own lives at risk trying to keep the more violent girls subdued.

"Nothing," Winnie lied as she walked back around the table to where she'd been folding laundry. I looked down at my laundry pile and saw Guard Robinson's ugly orthopedic black shoes next to my own feet in my peripheral vision, but didn't relax just yet—at Sheridan, even interference from an authority figure didn't mean you were safe.

"Is that true?" Robinson asked me. "Did I just see her grab you, Brady, or was I imagining things?"

The moment of truth. There was a chance Robinson wasn't going to send us to the principal's office and Winnie was going to beat me to a pulp later, but I was going to have to take it. "She stole my lip balm," I answered.

"I didn't steal anything," Winnie lied. "She stole it from me, and I just took it back." She produced it from her own pocket and flashed it so that Robinson could see it. "See? Mine."

There no way Guard Robinson actually believed Winnie, but she obviously just wanted to defuse the situation without Winnie's wrath turning toward her. Guard Robinson put her hands on her hips and told me angrily, "Get on upstairs and report to Carlitos for isolation until lights-out."

Success! A solo walk to my floor was ideal.

"Bitch," Winnie muttered at me as I hung my head and passed her on my way out of the laundry room. I struggled to maintain a normal pace when all I wanted to do was burst into a run before Robinson changed her mind and assigned someone to escort me.

As soon as I slipped through the laundry room doors and into the hallway, my eyes darted around wildly. It would be at least eighteen minutes before everyone on the second floor of the dorm would line up to be led to dinner. If I were lucky, it would take them another ten minutes to figure out that I hadn't gone to Guard Carlitos's office as I'd been ordered, and realize that I'd instead made a run for it. That was almost half an hour to get out to the street to meet my friends. Before I'd left Willow, I'd emphatically stressed to Henry the importance of being on time.

Rushing, I pushed open the nearest door, which led to the boiler room. Inside, it was dark. There were water heaters and some kind of electrical control panel—but seemingly no exterior door. I tried to picture the layout of the building on the first floor and where the doors were in relation to where I stood in the basement, but it was impossible. I was way too anxious. My heart was throbbing. I stepped back out into the hall and dashed in the opposite direction of the staircase that would have taken me up to the first floor.

There was a bathroom, which I considered, but there was probably only one way in and out of that room, so it was a trap. Then I heard footsteps behind me on the stairs, echoing off of the hard cement floor and walls. As soon as whoever was descending the staircase reached the bottom, they'd see me wandering the hall alone and immediately know something was up. The next door on my right was marked STAFF ONLY, and I gently twisted the handle to see if it was locked. It opened, and without a second to spare, I slipped inside and closed the door behind me.

I dared to click on the light after I entered, unable to tolerate the thought of passing a few minutes in complete darkness. With light from a bare bulb overhead, I observed that I was in a janitorial supply storage room. Metal utility shelves held large quantities of drain openers, powdered detergent, laundry supplies, light bulbs, and floor wax. Uniforms hung on a rack in one corner, and buckets were stacked next to a row of ladders in various sizes. Like lightning striking my brain, it occurred to me that whoever was coming down the stairs was probably headed for the very storeroom in which I was hiding, so I rushed down the first row of supplies and turned right. There were four more rows of utility shelving in the small room, and past the fourth row of shelving, next to a wall painted dark gray, there was an old desktop computer on a cheap particleboard desk.

I randomly stepped into the third row of shelves, in between paint cans and a shelf holding extermination supplies, just as I heard a key being inserted into the metal doorknob. The door creaked open, and someone entered whistling. Through the spaces in between cans of paint, I watched someone in a beige one-piece uniform take a few light bulbs off the shelf in the first aisle and stack them in her arms. She then absentmindedly wandered to the end of the aisle and turned right. Needing to move before I got busted, I tiptoed down to the other side of the third row and dodged around the end of it. Hoping not to be noticed behind the circular tubs of industrial-grade rock salt, I crouched down and clung to the shelf to maintain my balance. I held my breath and then dared to look over my shoulder. The janitor was examining cans of paint. She set down all of the light bulbs she was carrying in a paint tray, added a roller to the tray, and lifted one can.

I almost passed out with relief when she turned the lights off and clicked the door shut upon her exit. After she left, I waited a few minutes, wondering if there would be any value in putting on one of the beige custodial jumpsuits either as a disguise or as outerwear. I decided against it. They were too large, too cumbersome, and would only impede my ability to run if it came to that. It would have been an amazing stroke of luck if the janitorial storage room were also where the custodial crew hung their winter coats while on their shifts, but that was not the case.

Ready to see if the coast was clear, I took a deep breath and turned the doorknob. It didn't budge.

I was locked *in*.

This cannot be happening, I thought to myself over and over again. *This is not real.*

The door must have locked from both the inside and outside. I also had no idea how long it would be before another janitor would visit the closet—although presumably not until after dinner service ended at eight o'clock. There was no way Henry would wait on the side of the road for me for an hour and a half. He'd assume something had gone wrong and change the plan.

I looked around the storage room, frantic. I went to the desk and pulled its top drawer open in search of keys. Inside was a heavy key chain, but most of the keys were labeled as having something to do with outdoor equipment—a key to the riding lawn mower, a key to the sports equipment shed. I palmed that key chain while I pawed through the other two drawers, but found nothing more exciting than some ancient, rock-hard grape bubblegum and a mess of useless office supplies.

At the door, I tried each of the keys on the key chain, but they were all too large to fit into the keyhole in the doorknob. Cursing at my predicament, I looked around. This time, I spotted a long lanyard with a bunch of keys hanging on a peg behind the rack of uniforms. I lifted it and examined the keys on its end. They were all labeled as exterior keys—the key to the front doors of Huron, the key to the front doors of the dorm for younger girls. They wouldn't help me release myself from the storage room, but watching them dangle on the lanyard suspended from my fingers, I had a terrible idea. It was a long shot.

"Pendulum, show me *yes*," I commanded in a hoarse whisper.

Unlike my own pendulum, which was hidden upstairs in my dorm room in my pillowcase, the long lanyard began swinging the keys forward and back in a linear motion. I was so happy with its response I nearly shouted for joy.

"Pendulum, am I going to make it out of this closet in time to meet Henry by the side of the road?" I asked it, terrified of the answer.

It continued swinging back and forth, back and forth. *Yes.*

Encouraged, I asked, "Pendulum, can you help me get out of here?"

The lanyard shifted the direction of the swinging keys to point to the door. I walked slowly toward the door, and the swinging grew faster. *What do I do next?* I asked myself.

I grabbed the swinging keys and inspected all of them—they all looked too big to fit in the keyhole, just like the keys on the other key chain. Just to make sure I wasn't imagining things, I held the doorknob steady with my left hand and tried to insert one of the keys with my right hand. Nope, just as I suspected, the key was way too large.

"Pendulum, can you contact my sister Jennie and ask her if she can do anything to unlock this door? Or Olivia Richmond? Or *anyone*?" And just like that, I felt the doorknob click in my left hand.

"No way," I mumbled to myself. I turned the doorknob all the way to the left, and somehow, miraculously, it was open. Maybe there *was* something to what Kirsten had insinuated about my being a medium!

"Thanks, pendulum," I said, setting it down gently on a shelf, not wanting to let go of the doorknob. I opened the door a crack and stuck my head out. I was just about to step into the hallway when I heard the booming voice of Guard Robinson down the hall in the laundry room.

"Two lines, ladies. No funny business tonight. It's turkey potpie night, and I know none of you want to miss that."

I eased back into the janitorial closet, keeping the knob turned all the way to the left so that the door wouldn't lock again. It was six fifteen already! I only had fifteen minutes to get down to the edge of the road, and there was a possibility that Henry was already there, waiting, probably making Mischa and Trey suffer through the hip-hop he loved while they waited for me to come sprinting out of my school.

It felt like it took forever for all of the thumping of footsteps up the stairwell to end. When it seemed my classmates had finally all made their way to the first floor, I stepped out of the closet. After a moment's hesitation, I took the janitors' keys on the lanyard back off the utility shelf and stuffed them into the pocket of my navy jumpsuit before letting the door shut behind me. It couldn't hurt to have a makeshift pendulum with me during the rest of my escape. At the end of the hallway, there was an unmarked door on the left side, and a door with a metallic decal with a *B* on it stood on the right side. Not really wanting any more surprises that night, I took the lanyard out of my pocket, dangled it from my index finger, and asked, "Pendulum, can I get out of the building through the door at the end of the hall?"

It swung back and forth, so I crept down the hall and entered.

The door led to another hallway. The fluorescent lights above flickered and buzzed, and I could tell I was getting closer to a door leading outside because the temperature was dropping. The hallway turned at the end, and a few feet farther down, a gray door appeared with a red EXIT sign affixed over it. It had a long push bar on it beneath a dead-bolt lock.

"Pendulum, will an alarm sound if I open that door?" I asked. The lanyard swung from left to right. *No. No alarm will sound.*

"Here goes nothing," I muttered to myself as I twisted the dead bolt open and pushed the bar to open the door outward. The door opened into an exterior stairwell, which fortunately had been recently cleared of snow. It led up to the ground level. No alarm sounded—sweet relief!

The snowy evening beckoned at the top of the stairs. *Why, oh why, of all days, did I not wear a T-shirt beneath my jumpsuit?* I reprimanded myself as I climbed up the steps, already shaking just seconds after leaving the warmth of the building.

Having no other choice but to keep going once the door closed behind me, I trotted around the back of my dorm, checked to see if anyone else was walking around outside, ran as fast as I could toward the back of one of the younger girls' dorms, and then waited. There was a parking lot behind the cafeteria with cars in it, presumably belonging to the nonstudent cafeteria staffers. All of the women in the cafeteria were much nicer than the guards and teachers at Sheridan, but I still couldn't risk one of them spotting me if they stepped outside for a cigarette break. None of them would choose aiding me over their own job security.

When I was sure no one was watching, I snaked across the parking lot in between rows of parked cars, ducking the whole way. At least the lot had been plowed, making it the only part of my unpleasant journey that didn't involve trudging through a foot and a half of snow. The sounds of clanging pots and running water coming from the kitchen heightened my sense of urgency, and when I reached the other side of the lot, I leaned up against the freezing-cold brick exterior of the building to catch my breath until I realized that the chill cut right through my jumpsuit and made my bones ache. My breath escaped my mouth in gusts of white steam. Even just standing still for five seconds made my legs feel wooden, so I sprinted back into the snow to make my way around the building that contained the gymnasium and most of our classrooms.

Beyond that were the long, sloping hill and sprinkling of pine trees that separated our campus from the stretch of highway where Henry would be waiting. Knowing that I was almost there made the burning sensation on my feet a little more tolerable, but I was already so infuriatingly cold that I promised myself that I'd run back to Huron and turn myself in if Henry wasn't waiting where we'd agreed to meet.

Three weeks had passed since we'd formulated this plan. I wasn't sure if I believed he'd actually be there, but it was too cold to stop and ask the keys for an answer.

The run down the hill was the stretch of my journey during which I'd be the visible to anyone back at Sheridan who happened to be looking out the windows on the east side of any building. I'd have to run about a quarter of a mile in distance before the trees would provide me with a little cover, and despite the fact that it was already dark out, the school property that faced the highway was well lit with floodlights. From where I stood, I could see cars flying by on the road below, and hoped none of the drivers hurrying home from their jobs in suburban Sheridan, Wisconsin, would bother to notice a girl in a navy jumpsuit running away from her boarding school against the white snow.

After counting down from five to get myself started, I jetted down that hill as fast as my legs would carry me. I lost my right shoe only a few steps in, but didn't bother to backtrack for it. My left shoe came off in the snow as I neared the edge of the pines, and I didn't waste time retrieving that, either. Instead, I kept wandering through the trees, no longer running, grateful to feel dry pine needles beneath my wet socks instead of snow. I was shaking violently from the cold, and stopped just for a second to get my bearings. Through the treetops, I saw a sliver of a moon above in the dark sky—a pesky reminder that the clock was ticking before the new moon, by which time Violet would have done everything she possibly could to catch up on sacrifices. All I could hear surrounded by trees was the whirring of cars passing by on the freeway, and the sound of my own raspy breath in the freezing night air.

I continued walking, and finally I saw a cloud of exhaust fumes pouring out of the tailpipe of Henry's truck. My heart filled with relief even though I was too cold to shout for joy. From the pine trees I burst, and as soon as Henry saw me, he threw open his driver's-side door where he was idling along the side of the freeway. My heart almost exploded with happiness that we'd both made it, we'd found each other and were on our way, and the cab of his truck would be warm as soon as I climbed into it. "You're here!" Henry exclaimed. "I can't believe it!"

He gave me a bear hug and lifted me off the ground. "What happened to your shoes?"

"I'll explain on the way. Let's just get out of here," I said, stepping past him to climb into the truck. But then I turned around, confused, to face him again. The cab of the pickup truck was empty. No Mischa, no Trey.

"Where is everyone?" I asked, feeling hot tears form in my eyes. No Mischa. It couldn't be.

"Get in," Henry urged me. "Everything's fine. We just had to modify the plan a little bit."

I climbed into the truck and scooted over to the passenger side. The truck was amazingly warm, so cozy that my legs stung and my eyelids immediately grew heavy. "But Mischa," I implored. "Is she okay? Is she alive?"

"Totally alive," Henry assured me after closing the door on his side and throwing the truck into reverse. He pulled back onto the frontage road from which we could circle the school and then return to the highway. Reaching over to the dashboard, he cranked up the heat, and I savored it as it blew on my knees through the vents. "Right after your mom drove you back up here, we reached out to that girl from Sticks & Stones for advice on what to do to keep Mischa safe until the next new moon. She suggested Mischa stay with her in Chicago until we confront Violet on this trip."

"Wait. Are you serious? Mischa has been staying with Kirsten for the last three weeks?" I asked in disbelief. "Do her parents know where she is?"

Henry raised one eyebrow, tilted his head, and made a funny face. "You don't watch the news much, do you? No one knows.

It's better for everyone that way, but the police have been looking for her."

"Geez!" I exclaimed. He was right. I didn't watch much news at Sheridan because there was only one TV in the lounge and it was no easy feat to convince the other girls to watch anything other than reruns of *Scrubs*. "What about gymnastics?" She'd been training for such a long time for the Olympic trials, I couldn't imagine that she'd willingly agreed to stop going to the gym every day.

"This is serious. Gymnastics will have to wait. Kirsten said she could put some kind of protection spell on Mischa, but it'll only work as long as she stays in one place."

I shivered and shook so violently that I could barely fasten my seat belt as I absorbed Henry's words. "Good," I managed to sputter through frozen lips. "That's good."

"I got you this," Henry said, taking his eyes off the road to hand me a red paper Starbucks cup. "It's hot chocolate. I figured you'd be freezing."

"Henry, I love you," I said, taking the cup from him. Only after I'd taken a sip of the burning-hot tasty stuff did I realize what I'd actually said. "I mean . . . You know what I mean. Thank you. That was really considerate of you."

"I was going to get food, too, but I don't know what you like, so I figured we could just hit a rest stop."

I took a few more sips of hot chocolate before I dared to ask, "What about Trey?"

"Slight change in plans there," Henry told me. "The more I thought about picking him up on my own, the less likely it seemed that the people who run his school would let him just walk out alone if his aunt was supposed to be picking him up. I mean, if I got all the way there and they wanted the aunt to go inside and sign something, we'd be busted. Sorry. I couldn't get in touch with you to tell you in advance, but that part of our plan needs some work."

"Oh," I said numbly. How could I tell Henry that there was no way I wanted to go to Mt. Farthington without Trey, without seeming incredibly childish and ungrateful for him already having driven all the way to Sheridan to get me? Although I'd had three regularly scheduled calls with Trey since returning to Sheridan, I hadn't been able to tell him about what had happened at Violet's house, or mention anything related to the ski trip. I desperately needed to discuss with Trey the spell that I'd discovered in the back of Mrs. Emory's diary. Just when I'd been convinced over the holiday break that I could trust him and he was committed to stopping Violet, I had found new evidence to make me wonder if he'd been intentionally keeping information from me that was vital to our plan. I'd been thinking about that sheet of paper I'd found the entire time I was at Sheridan; I'd even printed out the photo of it at home before driving back to school so that I could continue studying it after my phone was taken away.

"Not to worry. Mischa called the school pretending to be his aunt and told them that due to some car trouble, Trey can expect her to pick him up in the morning instead of today. She was tricky about how she phrased it because you'd said they monitor the phone conversations. Hopefully, he knows that this leave of absence you requested is our big adventure in Michigan and not a real family emergency."

"I'm sure he does," I said, instantly relieved. But then the reality of us driving all the way from Sheridan to northern Wisconsin, where Trey's school was located, hit me. "But his school is so far away!"

"It's a five-hour drive from here," Henry told me matter-of-factly, "but only two and a half hours back to Willow. So we're going to drive back to my parents' house tonight, get a good night's sleep, and then pick up Trey in the morning."

As he pulled off the freeway toward a rest stop, I said, "I don't know if it's a good idea for us to go back to Willow. People from my school are going to be looking for me in less than an hour. They're going to call my mom, you know. And she's going to suspect you."

My mom's reaction to the news that I'd disappeared from school was something I hadn't let myself imagine. She would be devastated and suspect instantly that I had betrayed her trust in favor of sneaking off with Trey. She would make incorrect assumptions about our reasons for escaping from our schools, and she'd be furious with me for making her look like an irresponsible parent, for wasting the money she'd paid our attorney to deal with my legal issues in November, and for further ruining my chances of getting into college. Allowing myself to even consider how much my actions were going to hurt her would distract me from what we needed to get done in Michigan, so as callous as it was, I tried to steer my thoughts away from her.

"I know, I know, it's not ideal," Henry admitted. "But I've factored that in too. That's part of why it's perfect that we go back to town—my parents will see that I'm home and tell your mom I couldn't have had anything to do with your disappearance. Right now they think I'm playing tennis at the indoor courts in Ortonville."

"Okay," I agreed. Our carefully laid plan seemed so immature and ridiculous now that things were in motion. It was going to be easy for anyone looking for three kids poking around in a resort area of Michigan to find us. How were we ever going to evade the cops long enough to get our hands on Violet?

"Don't think about the police," Henry said, as if reading my mind as he pulled into a rest stop parking lot. The illuminated fast-food signs hanging over the entrance made my stomach growl with hunger: McDonald's! Panda Express! Pizza Hut! "I have a feeling that they're going to stay more focused on the cute little gymnast who went missing three weeks ago than on two teen hoodlums who ran away from their reform schools."

He winked at me as he parked. His insistence on being positive about even the most depressing parts of our predicament made me even more grateful that he had taken the lead in planning this adventure to Michigan. Anything—no matter how outrageous—seemed possible in Henry's opinion. This was in sharp contrast to Trey's reluctance to believe that we might succeed, and his concern for how high the stakes would be if we failed. Although I'd continue my efforts to stop Violet no matter what the consequences were for me, Henry's steadfast optimism made me feel less like the burden of breaking the curse was mine to bear alone.

Despite his mild joking about Mischa's current whereabouts, her parents were probably freaking out. I wondered if Kirsten could get in trouble for aiding and abetting a runaway if anyone were to find out that Mischa was hiding out with her.

"Now, what'll it be, ma'am? A burger? Pizza?"

I looked down at my wet socks. "I lost my shoes in the snow," I said, as if realizing it for the first time.

"I can see that," Henry reminded me. "But you're not coming

inside, anyway. People are likely to remember a shoeless girl in a reform school uniform stumbling into a rest center with a devastatingly handsome older man."

"You're crazy, Henry Richmond," I said, grinning for the first time in the three weeks since Mom had dropped me off at Sheridan. "Pizza, if it's not too much trouble."

"One pizza for the shoeless lady, coming right up."

CHAPTER 15

EVERY HOUSE ON CABOT DRIVE LOOKED PEACEFUL and settled for the night as Henry and I drove slowly toward the Richmonds' house. Most of January's heavy snow had melted already, and sad snowmen drooped in several front yards. It was a very strange sensation to be in my own hometown and yet feel like I was trespassing. I felt paranoid enough to slide lower in my seat to avoid nonexistent passersby from seeing me in Henry's truck.

"Just wait here until I come back," Henry instructed after pulling into his driveway and shutting off the truck's engine. The windows of the Richmonds' house were illuminated—not surprisingly, since it was almost nine o'clock at night.

"What time do your parents usually go to bed?" I asked, alarmed. I didn't know Randy and Beth Richmond too well, but if they were *at all* like my mom, there was no way they were going to approve of Henry inviting a girl who he'd busted out of boarding school to spend the night in their house.

"Not until eleven, but they're probably watching TV upstairs. And sometimes my mom just hangs out in the kitchen drinking tea, so I don't want to take any chances. I'm just going to run inside and open up the back door from the laundry room. I should probably grab a pair of Olivia's old shoes, too, right?"

I looked down at my damp socks and nodded, preferring to not traipse through slush around to the back of the Richmonds' house in my socks. Henry offered me a quick smile and then slipped out of the truck, closing the door as quietly as possible behind him. He trotted up the Richmonds' front path leading to their landing, and then he unlocked the front door and disappeared into the house.

Then I was alone in the rapidly cooling cab of the pickup truck. The street was painfully silent, completely free from passing traffic. For the first time I wondered what Henry would have been doing with his life if it weren't for this ski trip shenanigan we were plotting, since there was really no reason for him not to have gone back to school that semester. I'd been so absorbed in my own plight at Sheridan and in trying to uncover as many details as possible about Violet before this ski trip, it had never once occurred to me to ask him what was going on in his own life and if he ever planned to go back to Northwestern.

More than two minutes passed, and the house showed no signs of life inside. I shivered in the front seat of the truck and wondered if Mischa knew the details of our plan, or if she was being tormented by curiosity about our progress. Surely, at that hour, both the Portnoys and my mom had been alerted by the respective authorities that we were missing. Phone calls had probably been made to my dad to inform him that I was on the run. He was probably pointing fingers at Mom and doing his best to make her feel like an inadequate parent for not having had any idea that I'd obviously been scheming my escape for quite some time.

A sickening feeling washed over me. My parents were not idiots. As soon as the administrators called them to notify them that I was missing, my mother would have called Trey's mom, assuming that the two of us had taken off together. And if Mrs. Emory had called Trey's school to ask them to keep a close eye on him, our little caper to boost him out of there for a "leave" would have been immediately revealed. If Henry and I drove to Michigan in the morning intending to pick Trey up at nine as planned, we'd be directly entering into a trap. I wouldn't have been surprised if there were Wisconsin state troopers as well as local police waiting for us, and a news crew too— that's how much of a big deal our little police car chase in Willow back in November had been.

We couldn't just pull up to the front doors of the school and expect him to come running out. Even if we had someone with us who could convincingly pretend to be his aunt Nancy and make their way inside to speak with administrators, he'd never be cleared to leave school grounds. I groaned. I was relieved that Mischa was in a presumably safer place for the time being, but changing the timeline on our plan had put the whole thing in jeopardy. We were going to have to figure out a different approach for retrieving Trey in the morning.

Finally, I saw a dark body moving around the side of the Richmonds' house, and when it reached the driveway, I saw that it was Henry, looking nervously back at his house over his shoulder. He walked around the rear of the truck and opened the passenger-side door, holding a pair of black snow boots in his hands.

"Sorry about that," he said in a low voice, as if someone nearby was eavesdropping. "My mom is awake in the kitchen. I had to create a bit of a decoy."

I slid my right foot into the right black boot.

"Does it fit?" Henry asked.

"Amazingly, yeah," I said. I hadn't been close friends long enough with Olivia to know what size shoe she wore, but I would have assumed her feet were smaller than mine. I quickly tied the laces at the tops of the boots and stepped out of the truck. "What kind of decoy?" I asked.

"Laundry," he said. "I threw some clothes in the washer. It'll cover any noise we make on our way into the house."

We scurried around the back of the house toward the cement stairs that led to the Richmonds' basement laundry room, and once we were inside the steamy, overheated room, my body shook uncontrollably as I recovered from the deep, bitter cold outside.

"Listen, Henry," I said, grateful for the mechanical sloshing noise coming from the washing machine, masking my voice. "I don't think we can just go straight to Trey's school to pick him up. If my school has figured out that I'm missing, and I'm sure they have—I mean, they'd never skip bed check before lights-out—then my mom is going to know that the first thing I'll try to do is get in contact with Trey. If we just show up at his school tomorrow, they're going to be waiting for us."

Henry bit his lower lip, considering this. "We'll have to figure out another way to get him out of there."

I sighed, leaning against the washing machine and suppressing my urge to cry. "We should have known this was going to be a disaster. What happens if Trey can't come with us? What happens if we never make it as far as Michigan?" I was worried about playing the game with Violet again before Friday, which was the twenty-fourth, for the sakes of both Mischa and Tracy, but also because I had a sickening suspicion that the predictions Violet had issued at her party meant that she had something much, much more catastrophic planned for the ski trip. The pendulum hadn't given me a clear idea of just how bad it was going to be.

If I failed this time around to get Violet to play the game, there was no telling what my punishment would be for running away from Sheridan. Violet would probably be able to keep playing her game for as long as her heart desired.

"You can't think that way, McKenna. We've already gotten this far. We're a third of the way there, if you choose to look at it that way," Henry said with hope in his voice.

I wanted to be as optimistic about our chances for the next day going smoothly as Henry was, but I wasn't good at rolling with the punches. I preferred having an ironclad plan.

"If we want to get up north right around nine or ten in the morning, we should leave here before six thirty, when my dad gets up to drive to the fitness center. If we're still here by then, it'll increase the odds that he's going to find you down here."

I raised an eyebrow at Henry. "What do you mean, down here?"

"I mean, in the basement," he said. "I brought blankets down for you to sleep on the couch."

I shuddered, remembering the last time I'd spent the night in the Richmonds' basement: the fateful night of Olivia's birthday party. "I really don't like that idea," I said. "You know how Kirsten said we should always burn sage whenever invoking the guidance of spirits? Violet played that game down here and didn't cleanse *anything*. There are probably all kinds of evil spirits and ghouls down here."

With a reassuring smile, Henry told me, "I don't think there are ghouls down here, McKenna. Dusty board games that I can't convince anyone to play with me? Yes. Substantial evidence on vinyl of my dad's horrible taste in music? Yes. But *ghouls*?"

He opened the door leading out into the main area of the basement, and thankfully the lights were already on. The large-screen television was exactly where it had been the night of Olivia's party, and Henry had set a pillow and two blankets for me on the sofa where Candace had slept. He'd also left a pair of button-down flannel pajamas, presumably Olivia's, for me to wear. I dared to examine the fireplace, where I alone had witnessed the flames surge eerily from almost completely burned-out logs during Violet's storytelling. The glass doors over it had been pulled closed, and the iron log holders were empty. The fireplace looked vacant, as if a fire hadn't been lit in months.

Yet still, the dark, gaping hole in the wall framed by brick made me uneasy. It seemed like it had served as some kind of portal through which Violet had invited her spirits to join us the night of the party.

Henry sat down on the edge of the couch and cleared his throat, signaling that he was about to ask me something of a sensitive nature. "I feel weird asking you this, and you don't have to answer if it's uncomfortable for you, but did Olivia ever give you reason to believe—when she was, like, sending you messages—that she's unhappy in the afterlife? You know, like . . ."

I knew what he was getting at without him actually asking. He was asking if she was in hell, or purgatory. "No," I told him honestly. "I didn't get that sense from Jennie, either. I don't know if those places exist, or if they're just theories humans invented to make us feel better about why good people die just like bad people do. Olivia has never given me any reason to think that she's in a lake of fire or being jabbed with a pitchfork or anything."

Completely resisting my attempt at humor, Henry hung his head and looked down at his feet. "That's good. My parents are kind of religious. It's been bothering my mom that she can't remember the last time Olivia went to church before, you know, the accident." He paused, and then continued, "It just doesn't make sense. Olivia was never anything but nice to Violet. She invited her to the party even though she barely knew her. And Violet repaid that kindness by singling her out for death?"

I sat down beside him, all too familiar with his line of thinking. "I've spent a lot of my life wondering the same things, you know? Why did Jennie have to die? Why did it take so long for the fire department to show up? Why couldn't she have been burned, but survived? I wish I could tell you that it gets easier. It gets different, but not easier."

He half laughed. "That helps a lot, McKenna," he said sarcastically.

"My dad likes to say that grief is like climbing a mountain. You never reach the top, but you get used to climbing." He remained quiet, letting that sink in. "Don't listen to me," I said, suddenly feeling like the energy between us had become a little too intense for my comfort. Henry wasn't my boyfriend. Our friendship was still so new that it felt presumptuous to consider him a *friend*, even though I genuinely liked him as a person a lot more than I ever expected I would when I still only thought of him as Olivia's hot older brother. "I'm sure I'd make a terrible therapist."

He cleared his throat again, this time perhaps to banish excess emotion from his throat. "I'm pretty sure you'll be great at whatever you decide to do." He stood up and looked around the basement again. "Are you going to be okay down here? I mean, I'd just sleep down here too, but my mom will suspect something is up if she doesn't hear me walk down the hall toward my bedroom," Henry said, sounding genuinely concerned about my welfare. "You can keep the television on mute, if that makes you feel safer."

"Yeah, I guess . . ." I trailed off, not enthusiastic about having to pass the night alone down there. "What's the plan for the morning?"

"I'm setting my alarm for five thirty, and I'll come down and get you at six. Sorry, I didn't think to bring any kind of alarm down here."

"It'll be fine," I agreed, sinking into the couch and looking around. I didn't want to tell him that the idea of borrowing an outfit from his dead sister freaked me out.

"Are you sure?" he asked, standing just a few feet away from me.

"I'm okay, I'm just . . . scared," I admitted. "I don't like sleeping alone at night. I mean, Sheridan sucks and everything, but it's kind of a good thing that I have a roommate there, even if she's kind of a bitch."

"Sorry, McKenna. I'd just sleep down here tonight, but . . . ," he said, his green eyes lingering on me. I felt a pull of magnetism between us that I knew was exactly the *wrong* thing for me to be feeling toward him in that moment, especially after the serious conversation we'd just had about grief. We would be driving to pick up my *boyfriend* in the morning. The boyfriend I *loved*. What kind of an awful jerk was I to be standing in the Richmonds' basement, not only wishing that Henry would take pity on me and sleep on the other couch for the night, but also wishing that he might just kiss me too? And yet I couldn't tear my eyes away from his face, specifically his lips—

"I think that would be a bad idea," he finished his thought, and for a second I was sure that he'd just been thinking about the same things as me. He patted me on the shoulder and then took a few steps toward the staircase. "It's just a few hours."

He rushed up the stairs to the Richmonds' kitchen, leaving me to wonder if that moment of intense attraction had been all in my head, or if Henry had felt it too. I mean, he had asked me to go to homecoming with him, but that had been months ago, before we even really knew each other. A lot had changed since that night. Did he have real feelings for me? I felt myself blushing even though there was no one around to see me. Of course, if Trey knew about his mom casting a spell on Michael Simmons and had been keeping that from me, perhaps Henry had been more deserving of my affection all along. But even thinking that made my heart ache; I needed to see Trey and ask him about his mother's diary before letting anything happen with Henry that I might regret. Almost every single night at Sheridan, I had considered asking my pendulum if Trey knew anything about the spell in the diary, and I hadn't worked up the courage to pose the question.

I sat frozen in one spot on the couch for several minutes before moving a muscle. There was nothing I could do at that hour to change the circumstances we faced in the morning, but I *could* at least use the time I had at the Richmonds' to catch up on news and get some rest. It wasn't a sure bet that I was going to get any sleep at all during our adventure in Michigan.

I wished I had a stick of palo santo or some sage with me to burn so that I could ask the keys I'd swiped from Sheridan more questions about what Violet had planned for my classmates in Michigan. Maybe now that the event was happening sooner, the pendulum would be able to provider clearer answers. My guess was that it was going to be a big event—a fire at the hotel, an open shooter, some kind of ski lift accident—to kill many people at once just so show me what she was capable of doing. But it was unrealistic to expect that the Richmonds had anything suitable for clearing energy in their basement, so posing questions to any kind of pendulum was going to have to wait.

I turned on the television and lowered the volume to barely above mute and flipped to a local network station to see if it was still broadcasting news. After watching a brief update on the case of the missing teenager from Willow, Wisconsin, during which they featured Mischa's sophomore school photo (which was really going to piss her off—goofy smile and zit on her chin), I realized I had to use the bathroom. Sleep was basically going to be impossible if I didn't empty my bladder, and the Richmonds didn't have a bathroom in their basement. There was no getting around it: I was going to have to climb up the stairs and use the bathroom in the hallway near the kitchen as discreetly as possible.

After changing into Olivia's pajamas, I ascended the staircase slowly on tiptoes, not wanting any of the boards to creak under my weight. At the top, I turned the doorknob slowly, knowing very well by now that the evil spirits protecting Violet would foil me at any possible moment. The kitchen was located at the back of the Richmonds' house, and the lights were off, but I remembered what Henry had said about his mother sitting in the kitchen when we'd first arrived. I didn't want to be unpleasantly startled by a greeting or movement in the shadows.

After listening with the door cracked open for what felt like a few minutes and convincing myself that the kitchen truly was empty, I stepped forward and was careful to close the door gently behind me so that Violet's spirits couldn't slam it while I used the bathroom. I inched down the hallway, remembering how the last time I'd taken this little journey in the night, I'd caught a glimpse of Olivia's red Prius in the driveway, waiting patiently for her to wake up in the morning.

In the bathroom, I used the toilet in the dark. But in my haste to move quickly and get back downstairs, I hadn't heard the footsteps coming down the carpeted stairs from the second floor.

When I pushed the door outward and stepped into the hallway, I gasped loudly in surprise. I found myself standing face-to-face with Mrs. Richmond, and she was as surprised to see me as I was to see her. She wore a fuzzy red robe, and her hair was limp. I couldn't recall ever having seen her without makeup before then, and her face was lined with more wrinkles than I remembered.

"Mrs. Richmond, I'm so sorry. I can explain," I began in a hushed whisper, not wanting to be heard by Mr. Richmond, who was presumably upstairs. There was a chance, especially after everything Henry's had mom been through in the last few months, that she didn't know who I was. "It's me, McKenna Brady. I'm a friend of Henry's, and I was friends with Olivia."

Mrs. Richmond blinked, and then began breathing normally again. When she dropped her hands from her mouth, she placed them over her chest, as if trying to keep her heart positioned where it belonged. "Oh my goodness. Oh, McKenna, you scared the life out of me," she said quietly. "Oh, my." After a moment of consideration, she reached for me and pulled me close in a very quick embrace. "What on earth are you doing in our house at this hour?"

Her simple question stumped me. There was no reasonable excuse for my presence in the Richmonds' house in the middle of the night, when I was supposed to be an entire state away, at a reform school, which Mrs. Richmond knew very well.

"I . . . Henry . . . ," I began, not wanting to implicate Henry in my mess, but knowing I couldn't explain how I'd gotten into the house without mentioning him.

Mrs. Richmond studied me, crossing her arms over her chest. "Come sit down. I was going to make some tea."

I sat down at the Richmonds' table in the dining room, where just four months prior, I'd sung "Happy Birthday" to Olivia as Mrs. Richmond had sliced an ice cream cake. Mrs. Richmond floated around the kitchen in the next room, placing a kettle of water on to boil. She rummaged around in the cabinets, preparing two mugs and filling two infusers with loose leaf tea. The entire time I waited for her, I convinced myself that she was going to call the police on me, and they were going to take me back to Sheridan. This was it: I was busted.

"Now, why don't you tell me what you and Henry are up to?" she asked me calmly after sitting down across from me while the water heated.

"I'm not sure how to answer that," I admitted.

Mrs. Richmond drummed her fingertips along the oak table and sat back in her chair. "McKenna, you know that my husband and I have heard the rumors from the high school. Tanya Lehrer called me shortly after Olivia's death expressing concern about this game that you girls played the night of Olivia's party."

It took me a second to realize that she was talking about Candace's mom. I always thought of Candace's mother as Mrs. Cotton, even though that hadn't been her name since she remarried.

"You know, I have to admit, when she first mentioned it to me, I was in such a state over losing Olivia, I just didn't want to hear a word of it. It sounded like childish nonsense, like that matter of chanting in the bathroom with the lights off and looking for ghosts in the mirror. But since Candace's accident in Hawaii, it's been troubling me," she said, watching me carefully. "*Distressing* me," she clarified.

"We did play a game," I said carefully, getting the sense without her directly asking me that she was hungry for details. "That new girl from Illinois—Violet—she predicted all of our deaths. Well, not mine. But Olivia's, Candace's, and Mischa's."

"And how did this game work, exactly?"

That's when I began unburdening my soul with all of it. I told Mrs. Richmond everything that had happened since Olivia's death in September. She prodded me with thoughtful questions, genuinely interested in hearing my take on things, and I realized that she was as desperate to hear what I had to say as I was to finally tell an adult the whole truth. It felt like a glorious relief to finally just share the words that had been piling up inside of me for months with someone eager to believe me, words that threatened to burst out of my mouth and ears however they could.

Never once did Mrs. Richmond shake her head at me in disbelief or question anything that I told her. She listened as if I were a perfectly rational, mature adult, and reacted as if I was providing her with an explanation for all of the suffering she'd endured since the fall. She rose from the table when the teapot whistled in the kitchen and fetched it from the stovetop, then returned to the dining room to fill both of our mugs with hot water. "Let that steep for a few minutes," she advised me.

I described Violet's total denial of having any involvement in my friends' deaths and her insistence on making predictions as often as possible throughout the fall, with as many kids from the high school as she could wheedle into participating. And then, without telling her that Henry had crashed the party with me, I told her about the fortunes Violet had distributed on New Year's.

"And what now?" she asked me. "What about Mischa?"

"I guess that's what I'm doing here," I confessed. "Mischa's next. Violet said she'd choke on something. I don't remember what, or exactly how, but we think it will happen before Friday. Henry and I want to try to stop Violet and break the curse before she . . ." I trailed off, not wanting to say the word "dies" to Mrs. Richmond.

"I knew something was going on. Henry's been very secretive lately. It's not like him to disappear for entire days like he has since Christmas Eve. I never did get a straight answer out of him about how such an enormous icicle ended up breaking the windshield of my husband's Mercedes. My husband is so worried about my state of mind, I feel like no one just *levels* with me anymore. She was my daughter. I deserve to know what happened to her," Mrs. Richmond said calmly, taking a sip of her tea. Then, taking me completely by surprise, she asked, "What can I do to help?"

At five thirty in the morning, Mrs. Richmond rubbed my arm in the Richmonds' living room and said gently, "McKenna, it's time to wake up." With her approval, I'd spent the night sleeping much more comfortably on the first floor than I ever would have down in the basement by myself. Olivia's bedroom hadn't been offered, either because it was upstairs next to Mr. and Mrs. Richmond's room, or because Mrs. Richmond had been treating it kind of like a museum since Olivia's death. I didn't know if Mrs. Richmond had ever gone to sleep, herself, that night, but she woke me up as she'd promised, right on time. She led me upstairs, where I took an indulgent hot shower and dressed in the pair of jeans and sweater that she set out for me. Although I was sure that the clothes had belonged to Olivia, I didn't recognize them.

When Henry crept down the stairs at six, dressed for the cold weather in an insulated plaid shirt and jeans, he found his mother and me sitting at the dining room table as I wolfed down a bowl of cereal.

"What's going on?" he asked, looking first at me, and then at Mrs. Richmond.

"I told your mom everything," I confessed. A mix of frustration and confusion crossed his face in reaction.

"It's all right, honey," Mrs. Richmond assured him. "But you should really eat before you guys head out. Or at least have some coffee."

Henry took a seat as if in a daze at the table, and Mrs. Richmond moved into the kitchen to fix him a cup of coffee.

"So, you guys are heading up north before driving to Michigan?"

Mrs. Richmond asked when she returned from the kitchen.

"Uh, yeah," Henry said with obvious discomfort in his voice. "We have to pick someone up at their boarding school. Although"— he hesitated, remembering that our whole plan had most likely been compromised—"that might not be the safest course of action, since people might be expecting us—or at least McKenna—to show up there. I don't want to get busted before we even cross the state line into Michigan."

As she stirred her coffee, Mrs. Richmond suggested, "You may need to create some kind of distraction. Divert everyone's attention away from him to give him a chance to slip away. They're probably keeping a close watch on him if word's spread that McKenna's escaped from her school."

Henry smiled at his mother with a strange, kind of disbelieving expression. "Mom, why are you, like, helping us? Forgive me for saying so, but this is, like . . . way too weird."

Mrs. Richmond replied, "When I was a little girl, a fortune-teller at the Wisconsin State Fair told my aunt Mary that she'd die in flight. What a ridiculous thing to say, we all thought. My aunt thought she was talking about skydiving and found it hilarious. A few years later, she won a trip to the Bahamas from a radio station. While she was there, she went on a hike along with her tour group and decided to go diving off a popular cliff. Everyone else in the group dove without a problem, but my aunt hit the water at an odd angle and broke her neck. She died as they were airlifting her to the hospital."

"That's crazy!" Henry exclaimed. "I knew your dad's sister had died in a diving accident, but I didn't know that someone had predicted it!"

"I don't often tell people that part of the story," Mrs. Richmond explained. "It sounds unbelievable. But sometimes unbelievable things happen. Not everything can be explained." She patted me on the shoulder. "If you two are serious about doing something to stop the girl who killed Olivia, how could I not be in support of that? All I ask," she said, turning to me, "is that you don't let Henry do anything risky." She placed her hand over Henry's and smiled at him. "You have to understand, he's all I have left now. If anything happens to him . . ."

From the house's second floor, I heard the familiar buzzing of an alarm clock. Henry and Mrs. Richmond exchanged worried glances. Mr. Richmond would make his way downstairs soon in his gym gear, and he probably wouldn't be as sympathetic about my presence in the house as Henry's mom was. It was time to go.

On our way out the front door, we were armed for our trip with boxes of granola bars, travel bags packed with clean clothes, and spare hats and gloves. Mrs. Richmond handed Henry her American Express card. "Just in case," she told him. "Call me if you need anything. Just call my cell, and not the house."

"Mom," Henry said, waving his hand to refuse the card, "don't worry about it. I have my credit card for school stuff."

"The credit limit on that is only a thousand dollars," Mrs. Richmond reminded him. "You're going to need a place to stay in Michigan, aren't you? Hotels aren't cheap. Just take it."

Henry stuffed his mother's credit card into his wallet, and we rushed out the door and into the pickup truck. As he started the truck's engine and let it warm up for a few seconds before we backed out of the driveway, Mrs. Richmond lingered in the front doorway, watching us.

"You know, my mom's not all, like, one hundred percent right in the head these days," Henry informed me. "How much about Violet did you tell her?"

"She asked about the game Violet had us play, and it felt good to tell someone," I confessed. "Plus, it can't hurt for us to have an adult on our side. We could realistically end up in very big trouble on this trip."

We reached the end of Cabot Drive, and Henry let his left turn signal linger as we waited for a station wagon in the distance to approach the corner and drive past us. It was still dark out, as dark as night, at a little after six thirty in the morning. "I just hope she doesn't say anything to my dad. He's really freaked out about how she's not sleeping at night, not eating. More than once, he's mentioned having her talk to someone in Ortonville and maybe getting her meds to help her through this," Henry informed me.

Having grown up with a psychiatrist as a dad, the idea of speaking to a therapist or even taking antidepressants was so normal to me that I often forgot that there were families for whom that was the strangest concept imaginable.

I didn't reply. I was pretty sure that Mrs. Richmond was going to be cool. After all, she could have called my mom or the Willow Police Department when she'd found me in her hallway, and hadn't.

The drive north was going to be long and not especially scenic. The rural roads were sloppy with melting snow, and we wouldn't be passing any large towns on our journey other than Eau Claire. Henry was pensive during the first hour of our drive before the sun began to rise, flipping nervously through talk radio stations in search of any news broadcast mentioning a missing teenage girl from a reform school in Michigan.

After we stopped at a rest station outside Eau Claire to use the bathrooms, we got down to business. Mischa still had the prepaid cell phone she'd taken with her to Chicago so that the location of her own phone couldn't be traced. Henry texted her at that number, urging her to have Kirsten get rid of the burner phone and buy a new one since Mischa had used it to call Trey's school, pretending to be his aunt.

We also had absolutely no way of getting in touch with Trey. "How are we going to let him know that we're coming, and instruct him where to go?" I wondered aloud once we were back on the road.

"Smoke signals," Henry joked.

"Your mom might be right. We're going to have to create some kind of distraction to disrupt the whole school in order to get him out of there," I said. "Don't think I'm crazy, but I think we should stop somewhere and get some herbs we can burn so that I can pose questions to this pendulum I used yesterday when I was breaking out of my school."

"Did it actually work?" he asked.

"I don't want to weird you out, but yeah. I've been practicing, and it's pretty reliable," I admitted.

Henry grinned at me. "I doubt we're going to find any witch-craft stores on the way up to Parkland in northern Wisconsin."

A quick Google search on his phone suggested that sage would work reasonably well for clearing negative energy if palo santo wasn't available. At eight in the morning, when stores in the closest town were open for business, we stopped at a supermarket, and Henry bought sage and a cigarette lighter. After an impromptu cleansing ritual in the cab of his pickup truck, I asked the keys on the lanyard if we were going to be successful in getting Trey out of his school that morning.

They told me that we would, which was encouraging. I didn't tell Henry that there was an art to asking pendulums questions, and that its answer for that particular question might change at any point if circumstances beyond our control also changed.

Northern Reserve Academy was located off of Route 53 in the very northwesternmost corner of Wisconsin, nestled in between two state parks that appeared to be identical from the rural highway on which we drove. At a few minutes before eleven in the morning, Henry and I drove in circles twice around the complex of enormous brick buildings, observing. Like the Sheridan School for Girls, Northern Reserve was set back from the street in a remote location, not close enough to any main roads or strip malls to make an escape by any student particularly easy.

The school had a large track, just like our high school in Willow, but unlike the track back in my hometown, the one at Trey's military school was enclosed by a chain-link fence seven feet high with rusty razor wire at its top. As bad as Sheridan was, Northern Reserve seemed much more like an actual prison.

We told ourselves we were staking out the territory, making a plan. But during our second pass around the building, I knew what we were really doing was panicking. My eyes scanned frosty window-panes on the school's three floors as we drove past. I allowed myself to imagine catching a lucky glimpse of Trey daydreaming out the window in one of his classrooms, but the roads that framed the school's property were simply too far away from the actual buildings to see much of anything inside.

We slowed the truck down on our third drive around the campus when we saw two single-file lines of boys crossing a courtyard briskly without jackets from one building to another. The lines were flanked in the front and back by guards wearing uniforms and heavy winter coats. My heart swelled for a split second—it would have been perfect if Trey had been in that line and had seen our truck—but out of all the boys with shaved heads marching through the snow in those two lines wearing matching gray wool coats, none of them were Trey.

"We should park somewhere and make a plan," Henry said, turning left instead of right to bring us back onto the highway rather than loop around the school a fourth time. "If a big pickup truck drives around a school building four times in a row on an otherwise empty road, someone's bound to notice."

In a McDonald's parking lot nearby, we drank coffee in silence, both of us knowing that time was slipping away. In a matter of hours, classes would be wrapping up at Willow High School, and the junior class would be boarding rented buses bound for Michigan. We couldn't afford to waste time developing some kind of master plan to spring Trey out of school, but we couldn't drive off to Michigan without him either.

"I'm not sure if creating a distraction is the best way to go," I said. "They might already be onto him because his aunt never showed up to pick him up for his leave this morning."

"Yeah," Henry agreed. "What if we just get someone to go inside and tell him we're waiting for him? Like an electrician or a deliveryman or something. Or a janitor! Janitors must work there, right?"

I agreed that sending an outsider in with a message seemed like a good idea, but it had its flaws. "We'd have to pay them. No one is going to help two kids hanging around outside a military school by delivering a message to someone on the inside for free. And then, even if we found someone to take our money, there's no way they would know which kid was Trey unless they were in the school, interacting with students, every single day. I mean, if we said he was a thin white guy, around five foot eleven, with blue eyes and a shaved head, there are probably, like, thirty guys who fit that description at that school."

Just like at Sheridan, each of the buildings appeared to have side doors, but it would have been foolish for us to think that the doors would ever be left unlocked. The worst part of the Northern Reserve setup was that the entire school was surrounded by a tall fence, and the entrance to the main parking lot had a guard station. The only part of the campus that seemed like it might be a possibility for infiltration was the track, and it was unmonitored due to the three feet of snow covering it. But the tallest fence on the school's property encircled it, and as primitive a means of security as razor wire was, it was *effective*. I sure as heck didn't have any desire to risk cutting myself up by trying to climb over it in an attempt to reach those double doors of the building, which presumably led to a gymnasium.

"You're right, you're right," Henry agreed. "Ask your magic keys!"

I dangled the keys from the lanyard and asked, "Pendulum, is it the correct course of action for us to send someone into the building to contact Trey?" The keys swung to communicate an affirmative answer. "That's a yes," I translated for Henry.

"Has Trey ever mentioned, like, times of the day when he crosses in between buildings, or gets, like, a recess or something?"

"Yeah, but that was before it got cold out," I said. If it hadn't been winter, this entire operation would have been much easier. Trey would have been allowed outside for thirty minutes after lunchtime and most likely would have walked laps around the track for an hour during his gym period. I had a terrible but awesome idea for a question to pose to the pendulum, and decided to ask it before running it past Henry. "Pendulum, will Henry be able to get inside Trey's school without being noticed?"

"Hey now," Henry cautioned. But despite Henry's protest, the keys swung back and forth, guaranteeing that he would be able to slip into Trey's school successfully. "I could get in just as much trouble for trespassing on military school property as I could for phoning in a bomb threat, McKenna."

Without acknowledging his concern, I next asked, "Pendulum, will Henry be able to get back out of Trey's school *with* Trey without either of them getting caught?"

The pendulum continued to swing back and forth without wavering or slowing down.

"Oh, come on," Henry groaned. "This sounds like an awful plan."

"The pendulum thinks it's legit," I argued. "Come on, Henry. I know it's not exactly your secret fantasy to sneak inside a boys' military school, but if we can't wait for Trey to come out, then one of us needs to go inside and *get* him, and I really don't think a girl my age is going to go unnoticed in there."

"And how do you suppose I might sneak inside?" Henry asked.

Twenty minutes later, in an aisle at Kmart, where a very bad easy-listening version of Luther Vandross's "Here and Now" was playing on the sound system, Henry flipped through a rack of white short-sleeved button-down shirts trying to find one in a size large to fit across his shoulders. He hadn't stopped grumbling or talking about how there had to be some other way, but I knew he'd follow through with what the pendulum had confirmed would work. In another aisle, he plucked a package of white V-neck undershirts from a shelf, and then I followed him toward a rack where black dress trousers were on display.

"I'll wear this, but I won't have any of those pins or anything that those guys at the school were wearing," Henry said. "I mean, I'm going to stand out like a sore thumb no matter what."

Henry's lack of a name tag to pin on his breast pocket was less concerning to me than the other very obvious difference between him and all of the other boys attending Northern Reserve Academy. Henry had thick auburn hair, as thick as Olivia's had been, but wavier, like his father's. As much as I hated to think about that beautiful hair ending up in the garbage, I had to say, "Henry, I think we might have to cut your hair."

"Oh, I know," he agreed, not sounding thrilled. "I'm not going into that school without shaving my head. I *really* don't want to go to jail, McKenna. I can't stress *enough* that starting my first year of life after high school as a freshman at Northwestern and ending it in a men's prison would *really* not be cool."

We approached the desolate checkout area carrying Henry's new outfit, an electric razor, and a family-size bag of Fudge Stripes cookies. "Don't judge," Henry warned me in reference to the cookies as the tired-looking, middle-aged cashier scanned our purchases. "If there's any chance I'm going to spend time in a jail cell today, I need cookies."

"That'll be one hundred and nineteen dollars, and fifty-nine cents," the cashier told us. Henry handed her his mother's American Express card, and I held my breath when I caught a glimpse of it as the cashier accepted it. Any cashier paying close attention would have immediately asked Henry for identification, since it was rather obvious that his name was probably not Elizabeth Richmond.

"You know," the cashier said, causing my heart to basically stop as she waited for the receipt to print out, "you look kind of like that girl."

"What girl?" I said, immediately blushing and fearing that I'd become an overnight news sensation.

"That girl on the news," the cashier said, confirming my suspicion. "The one from that school who went missing."

I giggled nervously, wishing Henry hadn't just made a joke about ending up in jail before the end of the day. "Oh yeah, *that* girl," I said. "That's awful about what happened to her."

"The police think she ran away from her school and tried to hitchhike away," the cashier said, watching Henry as he forged his mother's signature on the credit card slip. "She seemed like a real messed-up girl. Got into all kinds of trouble down near Suamico in the fall."

"Oh, I saw just a little while ago on the news that they found her body," I said, freaking myself out a little by lying about my own death. "They're investigating one of her teachers at that school."

Henry thanked the skeptical cashier with a confident smile before shooing me out to the parking lot with our purchases. "God, that was a close call," Henry said, starting the engine of his truck and evacuating the Kmart parking lot quickly. "I guess your escape from school is on the news now."

CHAPTER 16

WE RETURNED TO MCDONALD'S, AND I AGREED to stay in the truck while Henry ventured inside to use the men's room, assuming that the bathroom would have an outlet into which he could plug the electric razor. I listened to news radio nervously, paranoid that I would hear either a radio broadcast about my own disappearance or police sirens approaching. It was almost noon, and I was already tired from being in the car for so long. It would take us at least another ten hours to drive from Trey's school all the way to the ski resort where the kids from our town would be staying in Michigan, so I was growing uneasy about where we'd find ourselves at nightfall and where we'd sleep that night—*if* we even managed to break Trey out.

"Not a word," Henry commanded when he climbed back into the truck and immediately reached for his bag of cookies. Even though Henry seemed like he was in a bad mood, I could tell he wasn't genuinely angry. I wondered if he was even capable of having a truly dark moment, the kind I had seen wash over Trey so very many times.

He hadn't shaved his head completely bald, but had left a

few millimeters of auburn stubble all the way around. He'd also closely shaved the light scruff he'd had on his jaw in an attempt to look a little younger, which barely counterbalanced how much older than eighteen he appeared to be with his head shaved. Henry looked like a completely different guy—tougher, more dangerous. I smiled to myself. I, alone, was seeing a side of Henry Richmond, high school tennis star, that no one else from Willow had ever seen. The smile I was trying to suppress eventually pushed its way onto my lips. I never, ever would have thought I'd find myself on a secret mission, incognito, with Henry Richmond, hometown heartthrob.

We filled the tank of the pickup with gas at a nearby station on the way back to Trey's school. "So, how am I going to get in there?" Henry wondered aloud.

"Climb the fence?" I halfheartedly suggested, not really believing for a second that he'd ever make it over that tall fence before a guard saw him.

"No, really," Henry said. "Ask the pendulum."

The challenge in asking the pendulum was that it would only respond to questions that could be answered with "yes" or "no" without becoming confused. I ran through the list of doors on the school buildings I remembered from our drives around the campus earlier that morning. "Pendulum, will Henry be able to successfully get into the school through the back door near the cafeteria?"

The pendulum began swinging from side to side. "That's a negative," I informed Henry as he drove through the small town back in the direction of the military school campus. "Pendulum, will Henry be able to enter any of the dormitories at Northern Reserve Academy through side doors?" The pendulum continued swinging.

"Maybe I should just walk right in through the front door," Henry joked. "Like, just walk right up to that guard near the parking lot and say, *Hey, let me in. I'm not sure how I ended up outdoors, but I need to get back inside.*"

Shrugging, I said, "Pendulum, will Henry be allowed into Northern Reserve Academy if he walks up to the guard and asks to be let in?"

The pendulum went still dangling from my fingers. "I don't know what that means," I admitted.

"Maybe it wants us to keep asking it questions, because even if I can get into the school through the front door, I definitely won't be able to get out that way," Henry surmised. I thought perhaps he was giving the pendulum a little too much credit for its strategic planning skills, but what did I know? Maybe Henry was right, and the pendulum was looking out for us.

We had reached our destination, and because we still hadn't formulated our plan of action, Henry continued driving past it.

"Pendulum," I said, growing desperate, "are there any areas of that fence where someone has already cut a way to pass through?"

I held my breath as the pendulum began swinging again. "No way! Pendulum, would you be able to show us exactly where in the fence Henry will be able to get on and off campus?"

Yes.

We agreed to drive around the school once more, slowly, giving the pendulum time to point us in the right direction. On our approach, we noticed two more single-file lines of coatless boys walking from one building toward the cafeteria, which made us realize that it was lunchtime—quite possibly the most ideal time of day for a boy who wasn't really enrolled at a school to slip into the mix unnoticed.

"What's it saying?" Henry asked, trying to keep his eyes on the slushy road.

The pendulum was swinging back and forth, pointing toward the school in the direction of the track on the far end of its swing. "I think it means the track on the other side of the campus. Pendulum, is the break in the fence near the track?" The momentum of the swinging increased—*yes*.

I was beginning to feel like we were vultures hovering over the campus as we slowly made our way around to the other side. "Pendulum, can you show me where the break in the fence is?" I asked again to make sure it understood what I wanted from it. It continued its back-and-forth motion as we drove closer to the track.

"There?" I asked as Henry slowed down the truck and the pendulum swung higher and higher.

"Great," Henry muttered. "That's, like, right in plain view of anyone who happens to be looking out any window on campus." Unfortunately, this was true. If the break in the fence had been closer to the building, it would have been impossible for anyone on higher floors in other buildings to have seen someone pass through it. But if there was really a break in the fence where the pendulum was suggesting, Henry would have to cross the entire football field to reach the building, making him highly visible, especially against the bright white snow.

"Do you think I should get out and just make sure the fence is really open there?" I asked.

Henry wrinkled his brow, looking across the quiet campus

through the window on my side of the truck. "Maybe we should have gotten something to cut the fence at Kmart. We could go back."

"I think going back there and seeing that cashier again would probably be the dumbest thing we could do," I said, growing impatient.

"Maybe there's a hardware store nearby." He pulled over and searched on his phone for the nearest hardware store, but I sighed deeply, worried that he was stalling or chickening out. We had no way of knowing how long the students would remain in the cafeteria, with most of the guards' attention focused there. "I think we just have to go for it right now, Henry. We can't keep driving around all day."

"I know, I know. I just want to be sure," he said as he looked out over the snowy football field at the school. I didn't know him well enough to know how he behaved when he was frightened, but it was possible that he was genuinely scared. "If I get caught, that means you have to go to Michigan alone. And I don't like the idea of that, but you have to promise me you'll go and finish this."

"I promise," I said, meaning it in spirit but not wanting to admit how terrified I'd be to drive Henry's truck all the way to Michigan to face Violet on my own.

"Okay. I guess it's now or never." Henry sounded unconvinced. "You should probably stay here with the engine running. You know? Just in case we need to make a fast getaway, or if any cops come around."

"All right," I agreed.

"Wish me luck," Henry said with a quick smile. He wiggled out of his winter coat before he hopped out of the truck and slammed the door behind himself. I slid over to the driver's seat and watched him grow smaller in the side-view mirror as he trotted in his fake uniform toward the school's property. With my right hand, I placed the pendulum gently in the pocket of Olivia's winter coat and looked around the area through the truck's windshield. Trey's school was very close to Lake Superior, and it was bitterly cold there, even colder than it had been in Willow.

Minutes passed, and my blood began to run cold. What were we doing? The whole idea of going to Michigan, probably only to get ourselves in even *more* trouble, seemed completely asinine. Without Henry to keep me company, I started getting nervous. It had been a while since the spirits that had been trying so hard to stop us just three weeks earlier had sent us any drastic warnings. Even if Henry and Trey were to somehow sneak away from Northern Reserve (which was seeming less likely the longer I sat in the truck waiting), surely the spirits were going to pull out all the stops in trying to prevent us from reaching Michigan.

In fact, I was probably in extraordinary danger just by sitting there alone in the truck. Considering all of the potential threats to my own life made me a little wary that Henry had parked the truck not too far from a tall, old tree with snow caked on its branches. Each time the wind blew, tiny snowflakes drifted from it onto the windshield. If the tree were to fall, it would crush the cab of the truck and me inside of it.

I took the truck out of park and eased lightly on the gas to move forward by a few feet. Almost forty excruciating minutes had passed since Henry had left. There was no reason to keep the engine running other than to heat the car—I was just wasting gas—so I turned it off. It occurred to me to ask the pendulum what was going on, and if Henry and Trey were okay, and then I heard a siren in the distance.

A siren most likely meant one thing: Something had gone wrong inside the school. My pulse went into a frenzy as I tried to figure out if I should speed away or wait.

"Crap," I muttered. "Crap, crap, crap."

Then, suddenly, I saw movement in the trees on the east side of the road. I saw two white shirts emerge from the dark trees. Henry and Trey both stepped forward onto the road, rubbing their bare arms wildly and shivering. They looked both ways before rushing across the two empty lanes of the street toward the car. I was so happy to see both of them that I threw the truck into park and leapt out of the driver's seat.

Not even a month had passed since the last time I'd seen Trey, but it felt like it had been years. When we'd said good-bye in Willow, it had been complicated by Violet's party, and neither of us had been ready; this seemed more like the dramatic reunion we'd both sought back in December that we'd never truly had. Trey broke into a careful run on the icy road and threw his arms around me, pressing his open mouth to my lips before I even had a chance to say a word.

"Oh, it's totally cool to just make out right in front of me. Just pretend like I'm not here at all," I heard Henry mumble as Trey placed his freezing-cold hands on both sides of my face and continued to kiss me as if I were oxygen he needed to live.

However, Henry's voice served as a jarring reminder of the spell I'd found in the back of Trey's mom's diary. The mere thought that I still had reason to be suspicious of Trey's motivation was enough to ruin the moment.

Slowly, I became aware of the siren still wailing in the distance. "We should probably get going," Henry urged us, and we got back into the truck and started its engine, bound for Michigan to end what Violet had started at whatever the cost.

CHAPTER 17

HENRY HAD SUCCESSFULLY INVADED THE campus by slipping under the fence, strolling right into the cafeteria with slumped shoulders and a scowl, and picking up a tray in the line as if he were any other registered student at Northern Reserve Academy. The guard on duty at the front door had given him a dirty look when he'd first stumbled in from the freezing cold with snow covering his shoes, but had been too busy looking at his phone to ask how a student might have fallen almost twenty minutes behind his classmates on the way to lunch.

"So then I saw this guy sitting at a table eating macaroni and cheese, and when I sat down across from him, he didn't even look up at me." Henry chuckled, casting a glance at Trey. "I had to kick him under the table to catch his attention."

I elbowed Trey in the ribs gently to chide him, and saw a glimmer of a smile on his lips. I was sure Henry Richmond was probably the last person he expected—or hoped—to see sitting across from him in the cafeteria at Northern Reserve Academy.

"I wasn't sure what was going on," Trey admitted. "I try not to make eye contact with people, you know? So I didn't recognize him.

I thought for a second that maybe he was just a new guy looking for a buddy or something. All I knew was that the original plan had been scrapped, because I had a note in my mailbox that my leave request had been delayed until today because my aunt was having car trouble."

"I've got to say, bro," Henry said, in high spirits, "I don't know how you've suffered through the food in that joint. You'd be better off eating toilet paper and chalk."

I could sense Trey fighting the temptation to be friendly with Henry, and I was relieved that the wall between them was finally crumbling. Henry seemed to understand how dire it was to release whatever animosity existed between them, whether it was related to my relationship with Trey or the fact that Trey had been driving the car that Olivia had died in. We had stopped at a discount retail store to buy a winter coat for Trey with Mrs. Richmond's credit card, and Trey had gruffly said to Henry, "Thanks, man." That was about the maximum amount of friendliness most people could expect from Trey.

The endless miles of flat, snow-lined road that spanned the windshield from one side to the other made me sleepy. The dullness of wintry northern Wisconsin on the drive to Mt. Farthington was like a visual lullaby. I leaned back, intending just to rest my eyes for a few minutes, and drifted off into a shallow, fitful sleep. Around three in the afternoon, when Henry considered the distance we'd put between ourselves and Northern Reserve Academy to be adequately safe, we stopped at a fast-food restaurant.

I left the guys ordering at the register and took the waxy foun- tain cups that we'd been given by the guy behind the counter over to the soda machine. The restaurant was quiet at the odd hour—an older gentleman wearing a Brewers baseball cap sat in a booth alone, his jaw gently rolling in a rhythmic motion as he chewed with his eyes fixed in an upward gaze at the television mounted from the ceiling. The quiet audio drifting out of the television suggested that a late afternoon televised court show was on rather than the local news, which was a small blessing.

Henry and I took a seat in a corner booth and smiled at each other, momentarily enjoying our victory over Northern Reserve. Trey trudged to our table carrying a tray with food on it. He sat down next to me in the booth and immediately reached for my left hand under the table, reiterating what I already knew—that it was most important to him that we find a way to stay together after whatever happened in Michigan. I didn't want to be apart from him any longer, not even if it was only until July, when he turned eighteen and was released, and I hoped with all my heart that he hadn't intentionally withheld information from me about the spell his mom had cast.

"How far are we?" Trey asked after taking an enormous chomp out of his burger.

Henry pulled up his map app on his phone to show us both the blue line stretching from Wisconsin to Michigan, the path we'd take to arrive at Mt. Farthington. "See the little red thing? That's us. We've still got about eight hours of driving ahead."

Eight hours of driving. At that very moment, the junior class was probably assembled in the gym for a parting lecture from Principal Nylander about conducting themselves like ladies and gentlemen and representing Willow High School with honor while on the trip. I could just picture Matt Galanis, Mischa's boyfriend, performing his impression of Principal Nylander, his head bobbing from side to side and his mouth forming words robotically, for the entertainment of Kevin Pawelczyk and Oliver Buras. Surely Jason Arkadian's mother would be chaperoning the trip; everyone liked her because she drove a Mustang and had ombré highlights like a movie star. Hailey West and Abby Johanssen were probably sitting in the bleachers with their Coach overnight bags at their feet, rolling their eyes and whispering about how stupid and annoying everyone else was.

And just as it occurred to me that Tracy Hartford's mother was always a chaperone on field trips, I realized that I'd barely thought about Tracy Hartford since I'd left Willow to go back to the Sheridan School for Girls. Cheryl had said she'd been released from the hospital, but Tracy was in almost as much danger as Mischa if what Jennie had suggested was true—that the order in which Violet predicted deaths determined the order in which her sacrifices died.

"Henry, have you heard anything about Tracy Hartford?" I asked.

Henry's eyes turned downward, and he drummed his thumbs nervously on his cup of soda. "Yeah. God, where to begin?" His tone distressed me even before he continued. "She's back in the hospital, according to what Mischa heard from her boyfriend, and she's in *a coma*. Her doctors have already told her parents that at this point, they have to prepare themselves for the possibility that she's suffered brain damage. *If* she comes out of it. I guess she was released too early or something?"

"Is there any chance that they might take her off life support?" Trey asked in between swallowing his bite of burger and taking a long sip of soda. His words matched my exact thoughts as if he were reading them from a script in my head.

Henry's eyes offered an apology as he glanced up at me before replying, "I don't know."

"Geez," I said, perhaps a little too loudly. The old man wearing the Brewers hat looked at us over his shoulder.

I wondered if Tracy had left the stuffed toy I'd given her at the hospital when she'd been released, or if she'd put it away in a corner of her bedroom, where it was too distant from her to serve its purpose. My throat tightened with fear when I thought of poor Tracy and of Mischa, hidden away at Kirsten's apartment, having no idea as to our progress toward breaking the curse. Mischa had to know, despite whatever she was doing there to keep herself distracted, that her situation was growing more serious by the hour.

"Time to go," Henry said brusquely in a low voice, startling me out of my reverie. He lifted his tray and rose from the table, keeping his head down.

I followed Trey's eyes toward the television set, where a commercial announced the news stories that would be covered during the scheduled broadcast. "A teenage couple escapes from local boarding schools, and law enforcement officials warn they're presumed to be on the run—and potentially dangerous. The full story at five," the attractive newscaster announced in a musical delivery. The screen flashed high school pictures of both me and Trey, the very same photos that were on our current Willow High School IDs.

The vinyl of the truck's front seat was cold enough to make me shake when we slid back inside to continue our drive. It chilled me right through the pair of jeans that Mrs. Richmond had loaned me, and my teeth chattered uncontrollably. It seemed like an hour passed with heat blowing directly on us before my muscles began to thaw.

The grim winter-scape surrounding us on all sides began to wear on my nerves after another hour on the road. We talked in spurts about how we might lure Violet away from the other people from Willow to play the game, but each time one of us began talking, we arrived at the same conclusion: Planning was pointless. We were just going to have to review our options once we got to Mt. Farthington.

At four thirty, the sky was rapidly losing light. While darkness was a welcome change from the monotonous blank clouds and gray snow that had encapsulated us all day, it made me even more eager to reach our destination and get off the road. Driving in the dark on snowy roads was dangerous, and I had to remain vigilant so that Violet's spirits didn't catch us off guard. To keep myself alert, I wondered what Violet was doing at that very moment on her bus ride to Michigan.

If Tracy was in the hospital, then with whom would Violet be sharing a hotel room?

Would she attempt to predict anyone else's death on the trip?

Would the buses transporting everyone to Mt. Farthington from Willow even arrive at their destination before whatever Violet had planned for her multiple victims occurred? The waning moon in the sky was just the slimmest sliver of white.

Finally, once it was dark, there appeared to be a break in the heavy forest that surrounded both sides of Henry's truck after we'd driven through the Upper Peninsula of Michigan for a few hours. Henry had relented with his rap music and insistence on impressing us with his memorized lyrics, and had even let us switch the radio to Top 40 hits by then. It was almost seven o'clock by the time we reached the rest area in St. Ignace, Michigan, and saw ahead of us the manned tollbooths through which we'd pass to cross Mackinac Bridge, an astoundingly long suspension bridge that would carry us over the icy waters of Lake Michigan toward Michigan's Lower Peninsula, our destination.

"Man, I don't like the looks of that bridge." Henry slowed the truck down a few feet before we reached the tollbooth, frowning with consternation. Next to me on my right side, Trey tensed up.

I didn't have to ask why. We'd be vulnerable as we crossed a five-mile bridge spanning the point at which the deep waters of Lakes Huron and Michigan connected. In the dark. With the wind blowing. Perhaps Violet's spirits weren't strong enough to hurl a pickup truck off the side of a bridge, but they'd been conniving enough to distract my mom and cause her accident, which was reason enough for alarm.

"Four dollars," the tollbooth operator told Henry when he rolled down his window. The heat of the truck was immediately replaced by a bone-chilling gust from outside.

Henry fumbled with loose singles in his wallet. I let my eyes wander ahead toward the long, long bridge, the edges of its deck dotted with streetlamps flickering against the blackness of the night. I could see the first tower, well lit with golden floodlights, beckoning and reassuring, summoning us to come closer. The light from the streetlamps bounced off the surface of the calm water on both sides of the deck, generating glimmers of amber-hued texture that brought a sense of choppy dimensionality to the otherwise black scenario before us.

As we cleared the tollbooth and were about to cross the bridge, my scalp began tingling, which made me even more paranoid about the likelihood of Violet's spirits interfering with us at any second. We were the only vehicle southbound on the bridge heading toward the Lower Peninsula. Even though it was an odd hour of the evening on a bitterly cold Thursday night, the lack of traffic seemed suspicious to me.

"Henry, just wait," I said. I withdrew my keys and lanyard from my pocket.

He rolled to a stop and idled just as we were about to cross onto the body of the bridge. "There's no other way to get to Mt. Farthington at this point unless we drive all the way around the bottom of Lake Michigan. That's easily another day and a half of driving," he reminded us. He didn't have to say what another day and a half of driving probably meant. Even if we drove without stopping, which would have been impossible since Henry was already tired, we'd arrive at Mt. Farthington hours after the new moon—presumably too late to stop Violet before more people would die.

"I don't think we should cross this thing," Trey said. "If we go the other way, we'll still get to the ski place by Friday, right?"

"We'll get there too late in the day," I interjected. "The new moon starts at around four o'clock. We need to stop her as soon as possible."

Henry seemed conflicted. Surely, the tollbooth operator we had just paid was wondering what we were doing, just idling there. "Should we ask that thing of yours whether or not we should cross?" Henry asked me.

Trey told us in a softer tone, "I can already tell you what's going to happen on the bridge. I dreamed about this last night—I just didn't realize what the dream was until I saw the bridge lit up like this."

I asked, "What do you think is going to happen?" This was not an ideal time for Henry to learn about Trey's relationship to Violet or his prophetic dreams.

Before Trey could reply, Henry asked skeptically, "You dreamed about this?"

Trey nodded, keeping his eyes fixed on the bridge ahead. "The bridge is covered in ice, and a truck hasn't come through in a while to salt it."

"Ice," I repeated. Of course it was ice. Black ice, difficult to see on pavement at night.

"If we try to drive across it, we're going to slide in the middle and spin out toward one of the edges."

"Will we fall over the edge?" I asked Trey.

"Don't know," Trey admitted. "But I don't see any value in trying to cross this bridge to make it to Traverse City before the new moon if we're going to die in the process. There might not be anything we can do to save those people, anyway. And if we die, then Violet can keep doing her thing."

Henry sounded exasperated. "You guys really think we should change our entire plan and risk both Mischa and Tracy dying—and who knows how many more people—because of a bad dream?"

This was a serious matter, and because Henry didn't know that Trey had dreamed about Olivia's death right before it happened—plus I didn't completely trust that Trey wasn't intentionally trying to delay us from arriving at Mt. Farthington in time to stop Violet—I was stuck in the middle. My scalp was tingling like wild, but I was reluctant to explain what that meant to Henry. "I'm going to ask the keys, you guys. We can't leave this to chance."

Before I even had a chance to dangle the keys from my finger, Trey unbuckled his seat belt and got out of the truck. He slammed the door behind him and started walking despite the fact that it was freezing outside and he wasn't wearing a scarf or hat.

Henry reacted by rolling his eyes and grumbling, "Great."

"I'll talk to him," I said and slid over to the passenger-side door to follow Trey.

"Yeah, please do. I don't feel good about leaving anyone on a bridge at night when it's not even twenty degrees outside." He muttered something more under his breath that I didn't catch all of, but was something along the lines of "even if he watched my sister die."

Trey was walking briskly back toward the tollbooth operator's station, and I trotted to catch up with him. "Hey! Wait up!"

When he turned around to face me, he looked upset enough to punch a wall. "I'm not going over that bridge," he told me, pointing ahead toward the truck and the direction in which it had been headed. "If we end up in the water, we'll be dead within seconds."

I placed my hands on his shoulders gently. "Okay, okay. I get it. But let's talk this through. Maybe the dream you had was intended just to intimidate us out of going to Michigan."

"I don't think so." Trey shook his head. "It was pretty vivid. I don't want *you* to drive over that bridge either. They're going to try to stop us because we're getting closer."

I was terrified of crossing the bridge, but my teeth were chattering, and I was growing more anxious by the minute about getting to Mt. Farthington in time to prevent whatever big catastrophe Violet had in store for her classmates. "We don't have an option, Trey. This is literally the only way to get from here to ski lodge. If Violet's spirits are the ones that supply your dreams, then they must know that we'll never make it to Mt. Farthington in time."

Trey stared me down. He looked as if I'd slapped him. "So you don't believe me."

I glanced over my shoulder at the truck. Exhaust continued to pour from its tailpipe as Henry waited for us. "I believe you! But . . ." This was the worst possible time to bring up the diary and the spell. However, it had also become crucial that I ask Trey whether or not he knew about it so that I could determine if he was trying to prevent us from reaching Mt. Farthington. "Look. The morning your parents drove you back to Northern Reserve, I went in your basement and found your mom's diary."

I couldn't remember a time before when Trey had ever been angry with me, but now he was furious. His eyes narrowed, and his forehead wrinkled. "Are you serious? You went in my house and searched through my mom's stuff? I already told you what I found down there."

My eyes were filling with tears because there was no rewinding what I'd done or the fact that I'd confessed to him. "I'm sorry! But I had to—you don't know what it's like when I hear these voices telling me what I need to do. I thought there was something in that diary I needed to see, and there was."

Trey put his hands on his hips and glared at me. "What? What about my mom's pathetic affair with her college professor was so important that you needed to see it?"

"The spell," I managed to choke out. "The spell she cast."

He glared at me for a few seconds before shaking his head in denial. "What spell? What are you talking about?"

If he was faking ignorance, he was doing a convincing job of it.

"There was a folded piece of paper toward the back with these, like, instructions about planting something to get revenge. And it said that the revenge would grow with each cycle of the moon," I told him. "Did you see it when you went through her diary?"

"I didn't see any spell. And that doesn't seem like something my mom would do."

"I know, but it was there! Tucked in between some of the last pages. I swear. I took a picture, but it's on my phone," I explained.

Although he was listening, I could tell he didn't want to believe what I was telling him. Behind me, I heard a car door open and close. Henry had gotten out of the truck and was walking toward us. Desperate to convince Trey to get back in the truck with us before he and Henry got into an argument, I continued, "That's why I think you absolutely have to be with us when we play the game again. I think Violet having to make all these sacrifices might be connected to whatever spell your mom put on her dad. And"—I paused as Henry joined us—"I think Violet's spirits may have manipulated your dreams, because that's one of the easiest ways they have of trying to convince you not to come with us."

Henry interjected, "Look, guys. We're down to less than a quarter tank of gas. I can't keep running the engine or we're gonna need a tow. So what's it gonna be?"

I looked at Trey with pleading eyes. "Please, Trey. We can ask the pendulum anything you want if it'll make you feel safer."

He looked down at his feet dismissively as if the notion of allowing our fate to be determined by the pendulum was absurd, and for a second I was sure he was just going to tell me that he was taking off—whether it be back to Northern Reserve or Willow or wherever fortune carried him. But then he said, "Fine. Ask it if you believe I intentionally played a part in killing Olivia."

His request stunned me. At first I wondered if he wanted me to ask that of the pendulum as part of the weird adversarial thing he had going on with Henry. But then he added, "Go ahead. Ask it. I need to know whether or not you believe me." He wasn't joking around. He sensed my apprehension about what he'd been doing in Green Bay the night of the accident and having proof of my belief in his innocence was more important to him than I'd realized.

Hyperaware of Henry's presence, I didn't want to ask the pendulum anything that might result in either him or I having a reason to blame Trey for what had happened to Olivia. "I don't think that's a good idea. I don't think it can tell you what I believe."

My reluctance just served to wind Trey up more. "Right," he snapped at me. "Look, I know you think I'm holding out on you. Ever since you figured out who my dad is, you've been suspicious about me. I get it, I really do, but I don't know what more I can say or do to convince you that I don't have anything to do with the Simmons family. I'm not working with Violet!"

Henry looked from Trey over to me in confusion. "Who's his father? What are you guys talking about?" Then, inferring the obvious truth from the expressions Trey and I were trading, he balled his fists and raised his voice. "Wait—are you kidding? All this time— you didn't *tell me*?"

This was what I'd been dreading.

Henry charged forward and shoved Trey by the shoulders, knocking him backward. "What the hell, man! I *knew* it! I *knew* it was weird that Olivia was in that car with you that night."

Trying to prevent either one of them from taking a swing, I stepped in between them. "Henry, hold on. There's more you don't—"

But Henry was completely enraged. He stepped around me to shove Trey again. "She wasn't even friends with you. My parents wanted to have the cops question you, you know that? They wanted to know how she'd ended up taking a ride from some weirdo from school who she barely knew."

"Henry!"

"But I talked them out of it because it seemed like it had to be an accident. Right? Who could plan a murder around a hailstorm and make it look like a freak accident?" Henry and Trey were circling each other, both cocking their heads as if gearing up to throw a punch.

"You're wrong," Trey fired back.

"You knew all along what was supposed to happen to Olivia that night, didn't you? You went out there to make sure Violet's little story came true."

Henry had corralled Trey over to the guardrail, and I hurried toward them with my arms extended in an attempt to maintain my balance on the ice. He had grabbed Trey by the collar of his winter jacket, as if there were anywhere else for Trey to go to evade him. Trey's back was pressed against the guardrail, and icy water splashed mere feet behind him. "You guys, stop! Stop it now!" I shouted.

It was as if Henry didn't even hear me.

Trey answered, "I would never have hurt your sister, okay? You're right—we weren't friends. But that doesn't mean I was trying to *kill* her!"

The word "kill" was what finally drove Henry to raise a fist. He punched Trey square in the jaw with a right hook, and I screamed.

The impact of the blow sent Trey stumbling to the side, but fortunately it didn't knock him over the guardrail into the water. "Just stop!" I shouted again, this time throwing my full weight at Henry to prevent him from striking Trey a second time. "This is what they want, don't you get it? They want us to fight so that we never make it to Michigan."

Henry looked over at me as if hearing my voice for the first time since getting mad at Trey. His chest heaved as he breathed heavily, trying to calm himself down. Trey staggered a few more feet away while rubbing his jaw, wanting to be safely out of striking distance if Henry moved in for another punch.

"Ask that thing," Henry said hoarsely. "Ask it if we can trust him."

My blood ran cold. I was afraid of what the pendulum would reveal since I wanted to believe Trey's explanation about his dream, but I wasn't completely certain that I did. Desperately desiring someone else to be telling the truth wasn't the same thing as being positive that they were. "Is that okay with you, Trey?" I asked, not wanting him to think I was siding with Henry if I just followed a request.

Trey told me, "Ask it whatever you want."

Hating all of this, I took the pendulum out of my coat pocket, dangled it from my fingers so that both Trey and Henry could see that I wasn't influencing its movement with wrist gestures, and first said, "Pendulum, show me what *yes* looks like."

It swung back and forth.

"Now show us what *no* looks like." Side to side, just as I was expecting.

"Pendulum." My voice was shaking. The entire fate of our trip to Mt. Farthington as well as my relationship with Trey depended on how it responded. "Pendulum, did Trey drive out to Green Bay the night of Olivia's death with the intention of saving her?"

The keys hanging from the lanyard remained immobile for a few seconds, making me suspect that the pendulum was confused about what I was asking. I held my breath, paralyzed with fear about what it might do next. The three of us watched it in tense silence until it started moving on its own, wobbling in a lackadaisical circle before picking up speed and resuming its linear motion, back and forth. A solid *yes*.

"That's a yes," I informed Trey and Henry. Despite the frigid temperature and arctic wind chill, I felt the warmth of relief flooding from my heart down to my fingertips and toes. Trey had told me the truth. He'd been honest with me all along.

I looked from Trey to Henry to make sure they were both watching. "Okay?" I asked. "It's telling us that Trey is innocent, and it's never lied before." Henry's mouth tightened, and he pushed his fists deeply into his coat pockets, still too fired up to apologize.

While the three of us were standing there with the pendulum swinging through the night air, I asked, "Pendulum, if we drive across this bridge right now, will we make it to the other side safely?"

It significantly slowed down its motion as if it was less certain about our chances than it was about Trey's innocence, but it continued moving back and forth, back and forth. "It says we'll be okay," I reiterated its message for the guys.

"We should get going," Henry said. He was watching the toll-booth operator, who had a phone pressed to her ear as she watched us as if she was discussing the three crazy kids brawling outside on the bridge in the freezing cold. "We've got an audience."

"Wait," I said, stopping them both from walking back to the truck. There was one more thing I needed to ask the pendulum to confirm, because it was just my hunch, but something that I thought the boys needed to know. "Pendulum, do all three of us need to be present when we play the game with Violet to break the curse?"

The pendulum slowed its speed and then picked back up again. Whether it was because I knew I'd need help from at least two other participants in the game to lift Violet as I predicted her death, or because Trey's biological connection to Violet and Henry's spiritual connection to Olivia would be critical, I didn't know. But the pendulum reiterated my assumption. They would both have to be there in order for us to be successful.

"This can't happen again. Do you guys understand? The only chance we have of breaking this curse is if we work together. I can't do it by myself. I need both of you."

We climbed back into the truck and Henry started its engine. Driving at a safe speed of forty miles an hour over the entire five-mile length of the bridge, we arrived safely on the Lower Peninsula. Even though we'd made it across the bridge without incident, every muscle in my body remained tense. We were getting closer to Violet, and I was sure that the boys' fight on the bridge was nothing compared to what else was in store for us.

CHAPTER 18

WE STOPPED AT THE FIRST MOTEL WE CAME across outside Traverse City, and Henry went inside alone to pay for a room. Trey interrupted the uncomfortable pressure in the car first. "I'm sorry if I gave you a reason to feel like you couldn't trust me."

"You didn't," I assured him. "I've just been suspicious of everyone and everything for the last two months. I don't even trust things happening in my own head. All I want is for this to be over."

"It will be, soon," Trey told me and then asked with one eyebrow raised, "You really think my mom cast a spell on Violet's dad?"

"I think she really cast a spell. On who? I don't know. But that girl we met at the bookstore in Chicago thinks this might be a case of spell interaction. Like maybe your mom cast a spell on the Simmons family not realizing there was already one on them, and then the spells got mixed up," I explained.

Trey said, "Like if Violet's mom cast some kind of spell to help her have a baby that actually lived right around the same time as my mom cast a spell to get revenge, then . . ."

Our eyes widened in unison as Trey drifted off. The timing and sentiment of his theory were like the missing piece of a puzzle. It made perfect sense; Mrs. Simmons or anyone who knew how badly she wanted to have a healthy baby might have put a spell on her with the best of intentions, possibly without even believing that it would work. If Trey's mom's spell had interacted with it, then it was simple to see how Violet had been created with a hitch—and that hitch was that she, or someone else, had to endure the consequences of the spell every month. Her life hadn't been a gift, it had been a barter. Hence Violet's sacrifices. And if the original spell had been put on Violet's mother, then in a bizarrely logical way it made sense that she was the one who would die if Violet didn't fulfill her obligation with each passing cycle of the moon.

"That's it!" I whispered, my scalp breaking into a firestorm. I was certain that we were right. "That's the gist of it, at least." With my pulse racing, I pulled the pendulum out of my coat pocket. "Pendulum, did someone cast a spell on Violet's mother in order for her to have a healthy baby?"

The keys slowly but surely rocked back and forth. "And the spell that Trey's mom cast interfered with that original spell?"

Yes.

And finally, the clincher, "Pendulum, will Violet's mother die if Violet doesn't make a sacrifice every month?"

The pendulum slowed down as if implying that we were mostly—but not entirely—correct.

"Her mother hasn't died yet," Trey reminded me. "And as far as we know, Violet's still a month behind in her sacrifices. So maybe that's ultimately what will happen, but she's still trying to catch up."

So excited I could barely get the words out, I asked, "Pendulum, is Violet planning to make extra sacrifices right now to keep her mom safe?"

Yes.

"Holy . . ." Trey's attention had been caught by something on the passenger-side window. The windows had filled with steam from our breath while Henry had been inside the motel's front office, and we both watched in awe as an invisible finger drew stick figures of girls on the glass just inches from Trey's head.

I whispered, "That's Jennie. She's shown me these drawings before."

Again, line by line, she drew three girls, left a space, and then began drawing a fourth as Henry returned to the car. "Hey, guys," he greeted us cheerfully without any traces of his anger from an hour earlier. "I managed to get a room with two beds, but—"

"Shh." We hushed him in unison, and he instantly saw what was appearing in the condensation on the window.

"What the hell?" he murmured as he just stood there with the driver's-side door open.

"Close the door," I urged him. "Don't let the steam evaporate before we see what she's trying to show us."

Henry climbed into the truck and pulled the door shut behind him. The three of us watched as a fifth stick figure was completed, and then, unlike the first time Jennie had drawn these figures for me, a sixth girl was drawn in the gap. *Violet.* When the second of her stick legs had been drawn, completing the form of her body, a circle was drawn around all six.

"She's reminding us that the other five need to see Violet in their world in order for this to end," I explained, somehow instinctively just knowing that was what Jennie had intended.

"Right," Trey agreed. "Because maybe if Violet turns up as the sacrifice, then it breaks both spells."

"You guys have lost me," Henry said, sounding hopeless.

Still dangling the pendulum from my right index finger, I asked, "Pendulum. Has Violet made her sacrifice for this cycle of the moon yet?"

Side to side. *No.*

"Is she planning on making that sacrifice tomorrow?"

Back and forth. An irrefutable *yes.*

The motel was a typical two-story, L-shaped structure with each room overlooking the parking lot. Our room was in the corner on the second floor, and we could hear the din of TV shows through the doors of the few rooms we passed. It had two double beds covered by ugly pink-and-blue floral comforters, a painting of a seascape in a tacky frame hung in the space on the wall between the beds, and mismatched lamps. A dog-eared Bible was in the drawer of the nightstand that I opened out of curiosity, set atop a thick Yellow Pages from 2012.

Henry flipped through channels on the television, trying to find out if local news was covering the scandalous story of the teenage boy and girl who'd escaped from their reform schools to run away together. However, local stations were airing late-night talk shows at that hour, and Trey and I were definitely not big enough news to serve as the punchlines of jokes during the hosts' monologues.

Despite the fact that it was after eleven, Henry called Kirsten to check in on Mischa. She was still doing fine, but she asked to speak with me.

"You heard about Tracy, right?" she asked me. "Don't get me wrong. I don't like that girl, but I'll still feel really bad if she dies tomorrow instead of me."

I carried Henry's phone over to the window of our motel room and pulled back the dusty curtain to peer at the slim wedge of moon in the sky. It was possible that Tracy had already passed away at some point that day. The only way I could have confirmed that was if I'd called Cheryl and asked, and Cheryl was supposed to be at Fitzgerald's Lodge with the rest of the junior class at that hour, getting a good night's sleep in preparation for ski lessons the next day. "Well, we're here. And we're ready for tomorrow." This was a bit of a lie, since I still hadn't figured out what magic words I might say to convince Violet to play the game with us. But we were ready in spirit even if we lacked a tactical plan, which was all Mischa needed to know.

"Please don't mess up," Mischa begged me. "I'm sure my mom and dad are worried sick, and I have no idea what I'm going to tell them when I go home. *If* I go home. Matt, too. I wasn't allowed to tell him where I was going."

I promised her we'd do our best and said good night. It was stressful enough thinking about what we'd do when we encountered Violet in the morning. I couldn't think beyond that to how we'd start patching up the disaster I'd made of my own life by running away from school, or Trey's by convincing him to run away from his.

Although Henry had packed an overnight bag and Mrs. Richmond had sent a pair of Olivia's pajamas along with me, Trey had nothing to change into. Without any of us discussing formal sleeping arrangements, Trey kicked off his pants and pulled off his shirt before climbing into the bed closest to the door, and I crawled in beside him. I didn't want to think about what Henry inferred from our comfortability with sharing a bed. He'd probably made the incorrect assumption that Trey and I had been sleeping together since the fall, but it was not an appropriate time to clarify matters for his benefit (and I wasn't sure why I cared if he thought that).

As soon as I nestled into the blankets, my eyelids became heavy. Trey wrapped his arm around my waist and nuzzled my neck with his nose. The mattress was lumpy, but after having bounced around in the truck all day, it still felt heavenly to me. I'd just started thinking about whether it would be better for us to approach Violet at the ski lodge in the morning or out on the busy slope, where it might be more difficult for her to summon help from other people, when I fell into a deep sleep.

Bam. Bam. Bam.

I sat straight up in bed having no idea where I was, surrounded by darkness.

"Open up. Police."

Thoughts returned to my brain in jolts. I wasn't at Sheridan, and I wasn't at home. I was at Hal's Motor Lodge with Trey and Henry just outside Traverse City, Michigan. I didn't have my phone, but I glanced to the old-fashioned digital alarm clock on my nightstand and saw that it was 12:57 a.m. And the police were outside banging on the door of our room.

"What's going on?" Trey asked, his voice thick with sleep.

"Police," I whispered.

Across the room, in the other bed, Henry had stirred awake and was pushing back his blankets. "Be quiet," he urged us, motioning at us with his hands to keep our volume low. "It's probably nothing."

But considering why we were in Michigan and everything else that had happened to us, I figured there was little chance that the cops were knocking on our door arbitrarily. "We have to hide," I said.

Trey's eyes searched the dark room wildly. "Is there another way out of here?"

"Just the window in the bathroom," Henry said. "But it's a sheer drop, two stories."

"Come on, open up! Police!"

Trey gestured at me to crawl under the bed we were sharing. At warp speed, we hastily made the bed, smoothing the wrinkled sheets and pulling the comforter over the pillows.

"Just a second!" Henry called.

We shoved our winter coats and snow boots under the bed, and Trey dove under before I did. I hesitated after dropping to my knees, reluctant to follow Trey under the bed frame. The space was *very* cramped. Maybe eight, nine inches in height.

"It's dusty down here," Trey warned, which shouldn't have surprised either of us. Vacuuming regularly underneath beds was probably a huge waste of time for motel maids. But the dark space scared me. If there was dust down there, there were probably other things, like dead bugs. Junk left behind by previous guests.

Just as my fear had gotten the better of me and I was about to make a dash for the bathroom, the overhead light in our room switched on, and I wriggled under the bed next to Trey as quickly as I could. The door cracked open, and shirtless Henry greeted the police. "Hello, officers. Sorry, I was just . . . sleeping."

Under the bed, Trey and I struggled to control our breathing. The bedspread was long enough to nearly reach the floor, which obscured us but also made it impossible for us to see what was going on.

"Good evening, or rather, morning. Are you Henry Richmond?" one of the gruff-sounding cops asked.

"Yes, sir," Henry replied politely.

"You got anybody in here with you?"

"No, sir," Henry lied.

"You probably have some idea why we're here, don't ya?" the other police officer asked. "Mind if we come in?"

Before Henry replied, we heard soft footsteps on the carpeting. The bed above us sagged as someone sat down on it. Trey and I saw the springs dip toward the edge of the bed on my right side. "What brings you to Traverse City?" the seated cop asked.

"I'm meeting a friend to go skiing," Henry answered. "She's joining me tomorrow."

"Any chance this friend is named McKenna Brady?" the cop with the lower voice asked.

My heart felt as if it were beating a thousand times per minute.

"McKenna Brady? No. I barely know her. She was one of my sister's friends," Henry said coolly.

"That's interesting, since she went missing from her boarding school yesterday, and her mom told the police back in Wisconsin she suspected you might have had something to do with that, and that the two of you might be on your way here to cause some trouble on a high school ski trip. And here you are, just as Mrs. Brady thought you might be."

Ugh, my mom, I groaned inside my head.

I could see Henry's bare feet planted near the door, which he'd closed slightly but not completely to keep the cold air out. "I don't know anything about a high school ski trip," he said, and then yawned. "How did you guys even find me here? Is every cop in Michigan looking for my truck?"

"Pretty much," the cop who was standing said in a tone intended to intimidate. "Don't suppose you know that in the state of Michigan, you could be facing up to ninety days in jail for aiding and abetting a runaway?"

I became aware of the chorus of voices rising in my head and panicked. This was not a good time to be distracted, and definitely not a good time to be half focused on deciphering what they were trying to tell me. It sounded like they were hissing the name *Steven, Steven*, but that didn't make any sense. I didn't know anyone named Steven.

"I did not know that," Henry said. His nice-guy act was running out, and he was starting to sound a little sarcastic. "I'll keep that in mind if I come across any runaways."

"So," the officer sitting on the bed began, "this friend of yours who you're meeting tomorrow. Mind if we call them right now and ask them to verify that?"

"Um, sure," Henry said, sounding a little surprised. I bit my lower lip. He didn't have any friends who were planning on meeting him in Traverse City. I didn't think he even had any former classmates back in Willow who knew anything about him hanging out with us while we tried to stop Violet. He was busted, but I saw him step forward to hand his phone to the cop on the bed anyway. "Her name's Kirsten. But she might not answer. She had to work today, and she's probably sleeping."

Henry's quick thinking impressed me. I sent a swift prayer to heaven that Kirsten wouldn't answer, and if she did, that she'd quickly figure out the right answers to provide based on the questions the cop asked her.

Steven, Steven. The volume inside my head, which was really more like an increase in pressure, rose and fell. The voices demanded my attention no matter how hard I tried to subdue them. I tried to tune them out so that I could remain aware of how quietly I was breathing.

After a moment of tension, the second cop said, "Hi there, Kirsten. This is Officer Raymond Mulvaney with the Traverse City Police Department. We've got your friend Henry Richmond here, who tells us he's expecting you to join him for a ski trip in the morning. I'd appreciate it if you could give us a call back at your earliest convenience at two-three-one, five-five-five, four-seven-nine-nine."

A voice mail. I could see panic in Trey's blue eyes. I hoped that the police would be on their way, but then the one who had been sitting down on the bed stood up. The springs in the mattress squeaked with joy to be relieved of his weight. "Why don't you put on some clothes and come on down to the station with us to answer a few questions," the officer told Henry.

"I don't understand. Am I under investigation?" Henry asked.

"Not yet," the cop told him. "Let's just go downtown and get to know each other better. You've got nothing to worry about."

There was nothing Trey and I could do as Henry pulled on a pair of jeans and his plaid shirt and his coat, and followed the police officers out of the room. I held my breath as a quiet *beep beep* sounded as the door locked. I was grateful that he'd had the presence of mind to leave the light on. I would have been terrified if we'd been stuck in the darkness while he was gone out of fear that the police would linger in the parking lot for a while, keeping an eye on our room after they left. We heard footsteps descending the staircase down to the parking lot, and about a minute later, we heard a car start and pull away.

"Let's get out from underneath this thing," Trey said, and we scurried out from under the bed. The voices in my head ceased at once as if they recognized and respected that I had a bigger issue to address right then than whatever they were trying to communicate. Trey and I looked around the room helplessly. "Sounds like your mom's been worried about you."

"Yeah," I said, frustrated but also homesick. "I can't get mad at her. She's probably furious with me. Plus, it would look really bad if I went missing from Sheridan and my mom *wasn't* cooperating with the police search, you know?" Guilt filled up my stomach and made me wince with discomfort. Every minute that I stayed away from Sheridan, my future grew grimmer, and my mom had to be very aware of that.

"We should probably get out of here in case Henry cracks," Trey said.

"Someone might be watching the room outside," I reminded him. "Plus, I'm sure there's video surveillance. What if the person at the front desk sees us leave?"

Trey reasoned, "If there were video surveillance, then the person at the front desk would have told the cops they saw us enter this room. The cops wouldn't have left without searching this place top to bottom." He had a valid point.

"I really don't think Henry will crack," I said. "He wants to break the curse on Violet just as much as we do."

"Okay. But we should still probably get out of here in case they want to take another look around when they come back, and who knows when that will be?"

I was torn; I didn't want to get separated from Henry because we didn't have any way of getting in touch with him, but at the same time, there was a definite possibility that the police would return to the room either with or without him, depending on how his interrogation went. We dressed quickly and realized just as we were about to step outside that as soon as the door closed behind us, we'd be locked out, which might have turned out to be pretty inconvenient considering that it was winter.

Luckily, Henry had left a paper envelope on the dresser containing a second key card. Trey placed his hand on the doorknob and was about to twist it when he lost his nerve. "Ask your magic keys if anyone in the parking lot is casing our room."

Following protocol, I burned a bit more of the sage Henry had bought that morning, and then asked the key pendulum if it would be safe for us to leave. It assured us that we could exit the room without any problems, but it wouldn't give us an answer about whether or not Henry would be coming back. Instead, it just dangled limply from my fingers. "This isn't good," I commented.

"Probably that whole free-will thing," Trey reminded me. "Whether or not he comes back depends on how he answers their questions, and right now he's probably not thinking too clearly."

Deciding where to wait for Henry to come back was a challenge because we had no money between us and it was freezing outside.

Not only was it almost two in the morning on a Friday, but we had to be mindful that the police were looking for us.

In the end, we took our chances in the vending machine room at the hotel, which didn't seem to have any video surveillance and was warmer than it was outdoors even though it didn't seem to be heated. Although we both acknowledged that it was important to remain vigilant in case any other motel guests or the motel management stepped into the room and found us there, sleepiness got the better of us when we sat down on the floor, hidden from the doorway by the giant illuminated Coke vending machine, and huddled together for warmth. The voices in my head stirred again with the same befuddling message—*Steven, Steven*—until it seemed like they had given Steven a last name I couldn't quite catch. *Steven Sass, Steven Flash.* The repetition of their words became rhythmic, like the chorus of a song.

When I stirred awake, the sky was already bright, and I was startled by the full impact of realizing that my former classmates from Willow were probably already up and about at Fitzgerald's Lodge. I nudged Trey. "Hey. Hey, Trey, we need to get up."

His eyes opened and looked around in wonderment before he remembered that we'd fallen asleep on the floor of the vending machine room. "What time is it?"

"No idea. But after seven. It's already light outside," I replied.

We made our way toward the glass door to peer outside into the parking lot. Henry's truck was still in the spot where we'd parked it the night before, covered in a light blanket of snow that suggested it hadn't been moved. I dared to step outside and crane my neck up to the motel's second story, to our room, which didn't offer any clues from the exterior as to whether or not Henry had come back during the night.

"What should we do?" I wondered aloud after ducking back into the vending machine room.

After a moment's consideration, Trey said, "I think we should see if he's in the room, and if he's not, we'll have to figure out how we can get to Fitzgerald's without him. We can't just wait."

"But we need him," I objected. "The pendulum said he has to be there when we break the curse." I thought about asking the pendulum whether or not it was safe to make a dash up the stairs back to our room, but there was a smoke alarm in the vending room and it seemed like a bad idea to burn anything to cleanse the space.

"Okay, let's just make sure the coast is clear before we go up there," I said. We both lingered in front of the glass door, trying to confirm that the parking lot was devoid of witnesses.

After a tense moment of watching and waiting, we made a run for it. I pressed the key card to the reader on our door, and we slipped into our room. Henry's bed was still unmade, and his duffel bag was still on the floor, which we took to mean that no one had been in there since we'd left. We discussed hanging the DO NOT DISTURB sign on the door handle outside, but decided against it in case the police brought Henry back and noticed that it hadn't been there at night.

The morning began to pass, and we grew increasingly freaked out that Henry had either been arrested or was going to be held by the police for so long that we wouldn't make it to the mountain in time to stop Violet. We turned on the television and watched at the lowest possible volume, half expecting to see a local news broadcast about a tragedy at Mt. Farthington. I was so anxious about what Violet might have been up to, and about the clock counting down to the new moon, that it didn't occur to me to be hungry even though we hadn't eaten since yesterday. Henry had his phone with him, and the keys to his truck. We could neither drive over to Fitzgerald's Lodge without him nor call Mischa.

"It might not be the best idea for us to stay holed up in here," Trey told me. "If the cops get something on Henry, the motel's going to send maids in here. Or worse, the cops will swing by to pick up Henry's stuff."

But it was daytime, and there was steady foot traffic to and from the vending machine room, so we couldn't hide down there any longer until Henry surfaced.

"I *really* think we should figure out a way to get to that ski lodge on our own," Trey said.

"I told you. The pendulum says that the three of us need to work together when we play the game with Violet. You and I can't manage it alone."

Finally, at around twelve-thirty, we heard footsteps stomping up the stairs leading to our room. We both dashed into the bathroom as we heard the *beep beep* of our door unlocking from the key-card reader outside. We cowered just inside the bathroom as someone entered the room, and neither of us had the courage to lean forward and see whether it was Henry or a police officer.

"Guys? Are you here?"

It was Henry. We emerged from the bathroom with Trey griping, "Took you long enough."

Henry's eyes were bloodshot, and his voice cracked with exhaustion when he exclaimed, "You're here! Thank God! I thought you guys had gone to the lodge without me."

"You're hilarious," I teased. "We don't have any money and it's freezing outside. How would we get all the way to the lodge without you?"

Henry was jumpy with anxiety. "We need to get out of here. We were supposed to check out at eleven. If the kids from Willow were scheduled to take lessons this morning, then they'll wrap those up by lunchtime and just be taking fun runs down the hill all afternoon. It's going to be really hard to find Violet among all the other people on the mountain, because it won't just be guests from Fitzgerald's. There are four other big resorts around Mt. Farthington."

"So let's get going!" I said, not wanting to waste another second.

He shook his head as if defeated. "This is bad news, but I have a feeling everyone at the lodge where the kids from Willow are staying is going to be keeping an eye out for you guys. From what the cops were asking me, it sounds like they are definitely expecting you to turn up there today or tomorrow."

That *was* bad news. It was going to be difficult enough to get close to Violet if we were just trying to avoid being seen by kids and chaperones from Willow who would rat us out. An extra layer of security or police surveillance was a serious complication. "We'll figure it out when we get there," I decided boldly. "We just have to get over there. Are you going to be okay to drive?"

Henry stretched overhead and unleashed a mighty yawn. "Probably not, but I don't have time for a catnap. Let's do this thing."

"Should we call Kirsten and see if Mischa's still okay?" I asked.

Henry took his phone out of his pants pocket and held it in

his hand for a moment before saying, "Maybe it's better if we don't. You know? Better for us to remain focused in case something bad *did* happen."

Although I was desperately worried about Mischa, he was right. If Kirsten had bad news for us, it would debilitate me completely. Even just thinking along the lines that Mischa may have already died felt like a gut punch.

We hurried out of our motel room. Trey and I waited in the truck while Henry checked out in the hotel management office, which in hindsight seemed like a waste of ten minutes. Overhead, snow clouds blocked the sun, and as we drove toward Fitzgerald's Lodge, flakes began to fall. In the distance, over the treetops, I saw the snow-covered peak of Mt. Farthington, and my stomach turned. Within the next few hours, the course for the rest of my life would be determined, and if I failed, I'd never forgive myself.

There was no turning back. We had to conquer Violet because there was nothing left of our old lives to which we could return.

CHAPTER 19

TREY HAD THE BRILLIANT IDEA TO STOP AT A discount store we passed on the way to the ski lodge to purchase ski masks to cover our faces, which would hopefully allow us to get closer to Violet on the mountain without being identified. I was reluctant to make detours, but I realized that if we arrived unprepared at Mt. Farthington and were spotted before we found Violet, we didn't stand a chance of getting close enough to her to accomplish what we'd come so far to do. Henry ventured into the store alone and returned to the truck with a bag containing his purchases.

"We can wear these until we rent helmets and goggles," he said.

I reminded him, "We're not really going to ski." Renting full ski gear was going to slow us down even more, and we couldn't afford to waste time. The new moon was technically at 4:44 p.m.—in just over four hours.

"Well, we don't know that just yet," Henry reminded us. "You guys may get a crash course, because my guess is that we're going to have to follow her up the mountain. We'll need goggles no matter what to protect against snow blindness. It's dangerous to look at light bouncing off snow for too long."

I had never been skiing before in my whole life, so I never would have known that.

Trey pulled his ski mask over his face and then slid his sunglasses up his nose. "Do I look more like a skier or a bank robber?"

"You look like a guy who's committed about a thousand crimes in order to get his half sister to play a game where we pretend to kill her," I said grimly. The closer we got to the mountain, the tighter my chest felt.

Finally, we saw a bright green sign with shamrocks on it along the side of the road, welcoming us to Fitzgerald's Lodge. Henry turned left onto the road leading to the resort's expansive parking lot, and I took in the details of the hotel Violet had selected. It was a stunning fake Tudor complex with a peaked rooftop and turrets, a building that looked as if it had been lifted off the side of a mountain in Switzerland and plunked down in Michigan. Visible beyond the hotel's roof were several cabled chairlifts running from the base of the mountain to its top. It seemed to be a busy day during peak season, with skiers and snowboarders speckling every snowy slope.

"One twenty-nine," Henry read from the clock on his dashboard as he set his parking brake. "They're probably done with lunch by now."

We all unbuckled our seat belts and Trey asked, "So how is this going to work? Should we search the hotel for her first? Maybe find out what room she's staying in?"

Although we were tight on time, I asked the pendulum if we'd encounter Violet inside the hotel or on the mountainside. The pendulum seemed to think we'd find her outside, but that didn't mean Trey and I wouldn't have to work up the courage to pass through the hotel's lobby. Henry, the experienced skier among us, explained that if we wanted to ascend the mountain on the lift to look for Violet, we'd have to go inside with him to buy day passes, as well as rent skis and boots. "There's no other way up the mountain if it turns out she's still taking lessons," he told us. "And they're not going to let anyone on the lift without a ticket and proper gear."

With our heads hung and our ski masks clutched tightly in our fists, Trey and I followed Henry into the magnificent front lounge of the hotel. If there was any kind of increased police presence at Fitzgerald's that day, I hadn't noticed it. Henry led the way toward the concierge desk, where day passes and lift tickets could be purchased.

"The day passes are ninety-eight dollars," the curly-haired concierge informed him after he inquired about the price. "And I'm so sorry, but there's no discount for getting off to a late start. The last chairlift for the regular day pass is at four thirty, so I'm afraid you're only going to get about three and a half hours on the mountain at this point."

I stole peeks around the lounge, hoping that no one from Willow would descend the grand staircase from the upper floors and spot us. A fire crackled in an enormous brick fireplace. Leather sofas were arranged around the expansive reception area and topped by plaid pillows. A chessboard, abandoned after a game, was spread out across the top of a table next to an arrangement of pamphlets about local shopping.

Fitzgerald's Lodge was by far fancier than any hotel where I'd ever stayed with my parents, and I suppressed a pang of jealousy that I wasn't officially on the trip with my former classmates. Whatever luxuries Fitzgerald's offered beyond its rustic lobby would not be mine to enjoy.

"It's fine that it's later in the day. We were driving all morning. I'll take three passes," Henry said, pulling his mother's credit card out of his wallet.

"Great," the concierge said. She looked at the card that Henry had handed her and said, "Oh. I'm going to need some photo identification, if you don't mind."

Henry dug his driver's license out of his wallet and said, as if only just then remembering, "That's my mom's card. She knows we're using it for skiing today."

With an apologetic smile, the concierge attempted to hand the American Express card back to Henry. "I would actually need her signature to process this card. Sorry. Those are the rules."

Out of the corner of my eye, I saw Trey shift positions and sensed his growing frustration.

"Oh, sure," Henry said, trying to remain cooperative. "You could call her, and she could, like, probably e-mail you whatever you need."

Another delay. While Henry and the concierge worked out the details of how we'd pay for our passes, Trey and I drifted across the lobby to a leather couch near the fireplace. As I sank into the cushions, my muscles let me know exactly how in need of a good night's sleep I was.

"This is taking too long," he said, picking at his fingernails. "I feel like something very bad is going to happen, like, any second now. You know? Like the seconds in between when you light a firecracker and when it goes off."

"I know," I agreed, wishing I'd known more about how ski lodges operated so that I could have anticipated the holdup with the passes. Maddeningly, I wasn't hearing any voices or sensing any prickling on my scalp, so I had no sense of heightened danger if we were in it. "There's nothing we can do except wait, though."

"This is a pretty nice place," Trey observed. "I mean, I don't know much about skiing, but this seems pretty top-of-the-line."

"Did your class take a junior trip?" I asked, unable to remember much about the previous school year, when I'd been a sophomore. My life was very different when I was fifteen from how things had been at the start of junior year. As a sophomore, I'd kept quiet in classes and only answered teacher's questions when called upon so as not to draw attention to myself. I ate lunch with Cheryl, Erica, and Kelly in the band room whenever it was open so that we could avoid insults from jerky guys in the junior and senior classes.

Trey replied, "Chicago. They went for two days and saw Hull House and the Art Institute and had to write reports about it. I didn't go; I had in-school detention for doing donuts in the upper parking lot in the driver's ed car."

I rolled my eyes at him with an amused smile. He smiled back. It filled my heart with warmth to catch a glimpse of the real Trey, mischievous and confident, even if just for a second.

"Typical," I teased.

"I still had to write the report, though," he claimed. He leaned back on the sofa across from me and spread his arms wide across its back, inhaling deeply. "It would be nice to come back here one day, you know? Like on a real vacation."

I hadn't really considered it before that moment, but I wondered if Trey ever thought about the Simmonses' fortune and how, rightfully, a percentage of that family's wealth would have belonged to *him* if his mother hadn't entered into a hasty contractual agreement before he was born.

Henry crossed the lobby carrying three paper tickets and three trifold maps and handed one of each to me and Trey.

"That sucked," he complained. "The only good part of that was finding out that everyone from Willow was booked for beginners' lessons all day. So even if Violet's a more advanced skier, she's stuck on the novice runs today." I opened the map and reviewed it, surprised that there were so many different trails and runs, all color-coded by level of difficulty. It was dizzying, all of the lines and dotted lines. There were three runs designated with bright green as beginners' paths, which considerably narrowed down where we might find Violet.

"Excuse me, sir." The concierge's voice startled the three of us. My blood ran cold for a second as every terrible possibility occurred to me: *She's recognized us, the credit card's been declined, someone from Willow saw us and told her to call the police.*

"The ski shop," she said in a friendly voice, pointing down a hall. "If you didn't bring gear, they can hook you up right down there with gear for purchase or rental. We require that everyone accessing the mountain via our lift be wearing suitable pants and boots."

The entire process of renting ski gear took so infuriatingly long that I started sweating, imagining that I would hear sirens or a cataclysmic crash from the mountain at any second. I hastily pulled on ski pants, trying to find a pair that fit, and grew even more frustrated when the rental guy turned out to be a perfectionist and insisted on finding ski boots in a half size that would fit me just right.

My adrenal system was in overdrive by the time we stepped outside with our equipment and pulled our ski masks down over our heads. It was 2:55 p.m., and we still had to wait for the chairlift. We were cutting it awfully close to the new moon. My new nylon ski pants made a swishing noise when I walked, I felt ungainly in my enormous ski boots, and I was terrified of locking my boots into skis, which I'd have to do before getting on the lift. It seemed like in this mountainside setting, Violet had every advantage over me and Trey, who had also never gone skiing before. Surely, that was by design. Violet was a superb strategist.

A small group of people were waiting at the lift when we queued up and told us there would be about a ten minute wait. According to them, we had perfect weather and perfect snow conditions—a light powder—for skiing.

Aware that we had no clue what we were doing, Henry advised Trey and me to hold our ski poles in one hand as we waited our turn for the chairlift, and showed us where to stand. Fortunately, the lift allowed for three people per chair, so we were able to ride with him, or I would have been a wreck when it was time to hop off. He set the safety bar down over our laps, and I held on to it for dear life as we made our way up the mountain.

The ski lift seemed like an ideal place for the spirits to tinker with electricity and cause mayhem. As we ascended the mountain, the higher we went, the more positive I became that peril awaited us at the top. My heart was in my throat as I expected Violet's spirits to take advantage of the fact that we were as vulnerable as canaries in a cage on that lift.

I tried not to dwell on their proven ability to do exactly what I feared most as my eyes combed the mountainside. It was a busy afternoon, and there were group lessons in progress in the three beginner areas. However, from the distance we were at, I couldn't recognize anyone from Willow. Just as Henry had said there would be, there were a lot more people on the mountain that day than just students from my school.

Henry reached into his jacket and withdrew his phone. He handed it to me and said, "Maybe you should hang on to this in case we get separated."

"But it's your phone," I reminded him.

"But you'll want to call Kirsten when you're ready," he said. "The pass code is Olivia's birthday. Come on. I've got credit cards and can call my mom collect if I need to. Just take it."

I accepted the phone and tucked it into the interior pocket of my own jacket, praying that I wouldn't fall while on skis and crack the screen.

Henry coached us on how to tip our skis upward as we hopped off the chairlift at the first beginner area we reached, and I felt so victorious after managing to land without incident that I would have been happy calling it a day right then and there.

"It's so crowded," Trey marveled as we looked around. Bundled into ski jackets and ski pants, everyone on the mountain appeared to be around the same height and weight. It was hard to even distinguish the males from the females, and most of the people who weren't wearing enormous ski helmets were wearing visors that obscured their entire face. "How the hell are we ever going to find her?"

Just then, I recognized a familiar pair of winter coats in the distance standing apart from the rest of the kids in their group.

"I think that's Cheryl," I informed Trey. "Do you think I should ask her where Violet is?"

"Might as well," Henry said. "There are probably a thousand people on this mountain today. Anything to help us find her faster can't hurt."

Trey was uncommonly quiet, looking around as if he was expecting an ambush at any second.

"Cheryl!" I called out and raised my goggles. When the girl in the lime-green jacket waved back after spotting me, I breathed a sigh of sweet relief.

"You're actually here!" Cheryl was smart enough not to shout my name as we made our way over the thick snow to where she and Kelly stood. "This is totally insane!" Cheryl exclaimed once we reached her. I lowered my goggles over my face again so that no one from Willow would instantly recognize me.

Kelly, who—like Cheryl—I'd known since kindergarten, seemed uneasy about even looking at me. I could understand why. Kelly and Cheryl were good girls, the kind who always tattled at school if they thought that telling an authority figure was in the wrongdoer's best interest. Once upon a time, in the not-so-distant past, I'd been like them. I'd desperately sought out approval from everyone too, before my friends and I had gotten ourselves into trouble so deep that no one, not even well-intentioned adults, could help us.

"Yeah, we're here," I admitted, "but obviously we can't stay long. We need to find Violet. Do you know where she is?"

Cheryl and Kelly exchanged blank expressions. "I honestly don't know," Cheryl said.

But Kelly hesitated before replying and weakly said, "I don't think you should be here. You're in a lot of trouble. The police—"

"The police have it wrong," Henry interjected.

Kelly put her hands on her hips, taking a stand. Probably because she knew she would have the police and just about every parent in Willow on her side. "I saw on the news *this morning* that authorities in three states are looking for you. McKenna and Trey are presumed by local police to be *armed and dangerous*."

This made Trey smile, but it put me even more on edge. Sure, it was funny that the cops thought we were armed, but not if they actually intended to pull guns on us if we encountered them.

"Look, we don't want to get anyone in trouble," I said, trying to defuse the situation. "I just need to talk to Violet. About Tracy. That's all. Or . . ." I wondered if a different approach might be more effective. The only kids I knew who'd received personalized predictions from Violet at her New Year's party were Chitra Bhakta, Jason Arkadian, and Cheryl. Jason's had specified that his death would be "dark and cold." If tragedy was going to befall him that afternoon, it would be wise for us to figure out which spots on the mountain were the darkest and coldest. "Jason Arkadian. Do you know where he is?" I asked.

Kelly shot Cheryl a dirty look intended to keep her quiet, but Cheryl stepped forward. "He's with the snowboarders. Everyone had a choice of either skiing or snowboarding lessons, and the snowboarders took a different chairlift." She pointed farther down the mountain, where we could see a group of other students gathered around.

"Is Violet with them?" I asked, feeling my pulse quicken.

Cheryl shrugged and frowned. "I lost track of her after lunch when we split into groups. And honestly"—she hesitated—"I don't think this is the best time or place for you guys to try to talk to her. We had an assembly in the hotel restaurant at breakfast, and everyone was told to alert a chaperone if they saw either one of you."

Proving Cheryl's point, we all noticed that Kelly had already stalked off on her skis toward the larger group. "Great," Cheryl mumbled. "She's probably telling Miss Kirkovic."

I turned to Henry and asked, "How can we get down there?"

He opened up one of the trifold brochures I'd tucked into my pocket and examined it. "We'd have to go all the way back down to the base of the mountain and then take this other lift up to Stevens' Pass."

Stevens' Pass. That was what the voices had been saying to me the night before, when I hadn't been able to make out the second word! Whether Violet's big event was going to happen on Stevens' Pass or there was simply something at that location I needed to see, it felt important that we get down there—and quickly.

"Is there any other way to get there faster?" I asked.

"Hey, guys," Trey interjected. His head was turned in the direction of the larger group, where Kelly had gotten Miss Kirkovic's attention, just as Cheryl had assumed she would. Kelly was pointing directly at us, and Miss Kirkovic unzipped her ski jacket halfway, reached inside, and withdrew her cell phone from one of the jacket's interior pockets. "We should really get out of here."

Henry ran his fingers over the lines on the map in the brochure. "The only other way is for us to ski down this path over to the pass. But it's not really a novice run. It's safer to take the lift."

Miss Kirkovic was marching toward us with her phone pressed

to her ear, and a much larger guy on skis, perhaps one of the instructors, was accompanying her.

"No time for the lift," Trey said. "I think we need a crash course in skiing."

Henry glanced down the slope to where the snowboarders were gathered for their lesson. Skiing down the mountain and veering off in that direction would require us to dodge all of the other skiers headed straight down the hill. We'd also have to navigate our way down a particularly steep part of the hill through a patch of trees. Mrs. Kirkovic was only about fifty feet away. We were going to have to get moving and hope that she wasn't a skilled skier.

"Okay," he said, sounding unconfident. "Don't point your skis directly downhill. Angle them like this." He demonstrated by pointing the fronts of his skis toward each other, in a V shape. "To turn, push your weight onto the leg opposite of the direction you want to go in, got it? Lean on your left leg to turn right. And to stop, try to keep your skis parallel as you swerve them to one side, like this." He slid forward by a few feet and then turned both of his skis to the right and came to a stop.

"Got it?" he asked.

And with that, he took off down the hill, weaving in between two kids from Willow who had just clumsily started their descent. Despite telling us to angle our skis seconds earlier, Henry made his skis parallel and not fixed in a V shape.

"McKenna!" Miss Kirkovic called out my name, and the heads of several kids participating in the group lesson turned in my direction. I couldn't wait another second, even if I felt unsteady on my skis and was terrified to pick up speed. Ditching Miss Kirkovic like that was lousy of me; she taught art at Willow High and had been one of my favorite teachers. But I angled my skis the way that Henry had shown me and used my poles to push myself down the hill, following after him.

"Here goes nothing," I heard Trey mutter as he, too, launched himself into motion.

Wind whipped against my body as I picked up more speed than I wanted. I constantly shifted my view from straight ahead to my right, to make sure that any skiers headed my way were doing their best to avoid hitting me. "What the hell?" a girl yelled as she narrowly avoided crashing into me. It was very possible that she was a classmate from Willow.

Ahead of me, I saw Henry disappear into the trees. He was a fantastic skier, even at a high speed, and nimbly dodged in between two tall pines. As I approached the trees and tried to slow down, my heart beating wildly out of control in my chest, I looked over my shoulder and saw that Trey had collided with someone on skis. Cheryl was slowing to a stop to help him back up to his feet, and behind them, Miss Kirkovic and the instructor were hot on our trail. I had to trust that Trey would recover because I couldn't have slowed down to wait for him even if I'd wanted to.

Avoiding the trees was much more challenging than navigating my way through skiers. I moved through the sparsely wooded area with my arms outstretched in front of me, trying my best to remember Henry's advice about turning to shift my weight from one leg to the other. Still gaining speed as I descended the mountain, I knocked into one tree with my shoulder and spun around, ending up skiing backward until I fell over on my side and climbed back up on my feet. I could see Trey and Cheryl catching up to me, which encouraged me to use my poles to launch back into motion.

Having finally made my way through the trees, I found myself on the steepest part of the incline I'd experienced yet. Ahead, Henry had made his way all the way down to where the snowboarding lesson was taking place, at which point the slope evened out to more of a landing. It was all I could do to remain upright as my skis moved faster than the rest of my body, making me feel the entire way down the slope as if I was going to fall backward and seriously hurt myself.

And then I saw her.

Violet, in a shiny lavender ski jacket with matching pants and an electric purple helmet. I knew even from a distance that it was her from the shock of dark hair spilling out from beneath her helmet and the poise with which she carried herself. She was standing next to someone taller than her, a guy in a black ski jacket—Pete Nicholson, presumably. She threw her head back and laughed.

Her carefree nature infuriated me.

I was so irate as I reached the area where the snowboarding lesson was taking place that I didn't turn my skis to the side in unison to stop the way Henry had shown me, and I bumped into someone, nearly knocking them over on their snowboard. The person who turned around to glare at me was Jeff Harrison, one of Pete's friends from the basketball team with whom I'd been driving to the football game in Kenosha the night that Olivia had died.

"Sorry," I apologized, grateful that he'd prevented me from cruising right on down to the next steep slope.

"It's all good," he said, obviously not recognizing me.

I spotted Henry and half skied/half walked over to him. "She's there, in the purple," I informed him, so nervous that I felt like my heart was going to pop out of my mouth.

Trey and Cheryl slid up to us at that exact moment, and Trey asked, "Are we doing this?"

Together, we walked up to Violet. I hadn't prepared anything special to say for this confrontation; I'd trusted that the words would come naturally. I lifted the helmet off my head just as she turned around and smiled at me with her perfectly lush lips.

"Hello, Violet," I said. "What a lovely ski trip you planned."

"So nice to see you here," Violet greeted us with false sweetness. "It's a shame that you came all this way only to be thrown in the back of a police car."

During all the weeks I'd had to prepare for this moment since the night of her New Year's Party, I'd thought I'd be furious the next time I saw her. I thought I'd barely be able to control my rage, and lunge at her with the intention of tearing her head off. But now I pitied her, in a way. The pendulum had confirmed that she had been sacrificing victims to keep her mother alive. Perhaps she was a cunning killer, but I could sympathize with her reason for fulfilling the requirements of the curse. She may have even resorted to complete denial in avoidance of facing the reality that she was taking away people's lives.

Unless she was truly evil and relished her ability to issue death sentences. There was still that possibility.

"We figured out a way to end this thing, Violet. It's easy. You just have to trust us."

Pete stepped in front of Violet as if to protect her from us. "You guys are not supposed to come anywhere near her."

Henry took off his helmet and shook his head in disgust. "You're a real piece of trash, Nicholson. How long did you wait after Olivia died before you hooked up with Violet?"

I'd kind of forgotten that Henry and Pete went way back. It must have been really bothering him that Pete had started dating Violet so seriously, so soon after Olivia's accident.

We were too late. Miss Kirkovic and the ski instructor had reached us and Miss Kirkovic tore her helmet and goggles off, extending an arm toward us as if urging us to put down guns we weren't carrying. "Everyone just *stay calm*!" she shouted. "The police are on their way."

Trying not to be rattled by the imminent arrival of police, I stared Violet down and removed all sarcasm from my voice. "If you come with us now, we can end this together. You'll never have to predict another death. But if you let the police take us away, then I think you already know that this will go on forever."

Violet blinked twice, her mouth tightened into a pout. She was listening. She was curious.

Next to me, Trey chimed in, "You don't want this to be the story of your life, do you? What happens when you get married? When you have kids? How long can you keep hiding what you do?"

He'd struck a nerve. Her face softened, her eyes downturned slightly, and I knew we'd tempted her. She must have been wondering for quite a while about the very same questions Trey had just posed. I didn't see the slightest hint of scorn on her face, and she was waiting for one of us to continue.

"Shut up, Emory," Pete snapped. "You freak. You guys sound *crazy*, you know that? You should be locked up."

Violet was staring at me with a serious expression on her face.

"Just wait, Pete," she said as if trying to decide whether or not she wanted to hear what we were there to tell her.

Kids from Willow had formed a group around us, and I heard our names in whispers:

"McKenna Brady."

"Trey Emory."

At that point, even if Henry, Trey, and I had wanted to make a run for it, there would have been nowhere for us to go without having to push our way through a wall of people. I felt Henry's phone inside my jacket buzzing with an incoming call. It was probably Kirsten, calling at the worst possible time.

Violet whispered, "You really have no idea what you're talking about. There *is* no way to end it. I've tried everything, and no matter what, it always ends the same way."

Despite every answer the pendulum had provided, for the first time since Jennie had instructed me on how to break the curse, the tiniest glimmer of hope sparked in my chest that Violet might actually cooperate with us. Never had I imagined that she would admit to unsuccessfully having tried to rid herself of the curse. Confessing to me that she'd tried to break the curse previously and failed meant that she *wasn't* evil. She was, in a way, just as much of a victim of this curse as her sacrifices were.

All of us heard the helicopter overhead in unison and looked up.

"Drop your weapons," a police officer was shouting at us over a loudspeaker from the helicopter as it dropped a little lower toward us.

Out of the corner of my eye I noticed tall, slender Jason Arkadian in the group, watching our confrontation unfold with interest. Behind us, higher up on the mountain, I heard the engines of snowmobiles approaching. That suggested more police were on their way, reaching us as quickly as possible over the difficult landscape. "Oh my God," I heard a female voice say, and I turned to see Chitra Bhakta a few feet behind me.

And suddenly, my scalp was on fire. My blood felt as if it were freezing in my veins. I knew exactly what was going to happen—and worst of all, our actions had been the catalyst for it.

Henry said to Miss Kirkovic, "We don't have any weapons. Tell them we're not armed!"

Miss Kirkovic waved her arms and shouted up at the helicopter, "They're not armed!"

I charged toward Violet, reaching for her in a panic. "It's going to happen now! We have to play the game *right now* or we're all going to die!"

She stumbled backward, and Pete tried to pry me off of her. Above us, from the helicopter, a single gunshot punctuated the snowy afternoon. It cracked against the sky and echoed around us.

Henry and Trey pulled me away from Violet by the arms, and Violet fell against Pete. It took a second before all of us on that snowy slope heard the deep, monstrous rumble growing around us. "What is that?" Trey asked. All of us looked around wildly, but I already knew what was coming our way.

"Avalanche!" I shouted.

The snow from above us on the slope seemed to slide directly down toward us as if someone had cut a slice of it off the mountainside. It descended upon us faster than I could even consider the best action to take to protect myself. Some kids facing the snow just stood there, paralyzed with fear. Others tried to get out of the way, but the snow was just too fast. It crashed toward us with a deafening roar, uprooting trees and carrying them down toward us. The last thing I saw before being knocked off my feet by snow was Trey, who extended his arms toward me, fingers outstretched, reaching.

But he was just a second too late. The snow tore us apart, and in a flash of white, he was gone.

Tumbling, crashing. For what felt like a lifetime I was thrown in every direction, upside down, skidding, and rolling on my side. I squeezed my eyes shut, but snow filled my mouth and ears, and my gloves came off. It occurred to me to try to curl my body into a ball to prevent my arms and legs from being pulled every which way, but I was moving so fast that I couldn't even make my extremities accept commands from my brain.

And then finally, it stopped. I couldn't breathe; there was no air in my lungs at all, and they felt as if they were ablaze. Everything around me was dark, and I tried to move my arms as if I were swimming through the snow, doing everything I could to push them over my head. Back in the days when Olivia had first haunted my bedroom, I thought I'd known what terror was. But this was a different kind of terror, not even knowing if I was right side up or upside down, clawing my way through snow, unaware of whether I was making my way toward the surface or digging myself further toward my death.

I knew I needed to calm down and think rationally, but fighting the nature of the human body as it shuts down is impossible. My thoughts slowed down and turned to Jennie. Had the final moments of her life been like this—dark and charged with panic? Had she suffocated on smoke the same way in which I was suffocating on snow? I wondered if she'd appear to me as my neurons stopped firing to accompany me into the spirit world . . . if what I was experiencing was physical death. And I was pretty sure it was.

I found myself hoping that would be the case. I longed to see my sister again, and any thoughts I had about how my parents would grieve me after my body was found seemed unimportant and distant. All of the details of my life blurred together into a mist; Sheridan, Violet, even Trey. A blur of images without details. This must have been what people meant when they talked about your life flashing before your eyes. I thought of a thousand arbitrary things at once: elementary school pencil cases, the smell of freshly cut grass, the velvety texture of my favorite chenille blanket, Trey's boyish laugh when we were kids and would climb trees together.

Then, suddenly, I became aware that I could move my left foot, and that awareness blossomed into a realization that my left ski was still attached to my boot and it felt as if part of the ski was sticking out of the snow. Adrenaline flooded through me, reviving me with one last gust of energy to fight for my life. I wildly kicked my left leg, afraid that I might trigger the snow to begin siding again, but desperately needing oxygen. Contorting my body, I kicked my right leg and clawed with my hands until somehow, miraculously, I saw a speck of light.

I broke through the snow and inhaled so deeply it sounded as if I were screaming. My breathing remained a howl as I gulped down oxygen, unable to even assess my whereabouts or the aftermath of the avalanche until the fire in my brain and lungs had been extinguished.

And then I looked around and realized that I had no idea where I was. The helicopter that had been circling overhead when we'd confronted Violet was so far away that I could barely hear its blades chopping at the sky. My goggles had been knocked off, and I peered up the mountain, realizing that the snow must have carried me through trees. At first, I thought I was completely alone because all I heard around me was silence. And then—twenty, thirty feet above me on the slope—I saw skis sticking out of the snow.

I couldn't tell if they were still attached to anyone's feet.

Slowly, feeling as if every bone in my body had been bruised, I climbed out of the deep snow, crawling out onto the surface with extra caution to avoid triggering another slide.

Requiring every ounce of willpower I could summon, I stood up and assessed the damage to my body. My nose was bleeding, probably from when the goggles had been knocked off. I'd lost my right ski and my helmet, too. The skin on my hands was bright red and raw from being exposed to snow for so long.

I was alive, and as far as I could tell, I wasn't seriously injured. Once I realized that, I felt as if I'd been stabbed in the gut. Because as I looked around, I had no idea where Henry, Trey, or Cheryl were.

Violet's prediction had come true. But this time she might have been one of her own victims.

CHAPTER 20

THE LOGICAL COURSE OF ACTION WOULD HAVE been to use Henry's phone to call the police and alert them to my location. But I couldn't make that call and attempt to express coherent thoughts until I knew where Henry and Trey were. So instead of reaching into my jacket for the phone, I wandered around, stunned, through the trees. There had to have been around thirty people on the landing at Stevens' Pass when I'd arrived with my friends to confront Violet, but when I dug around the skis I saw poking out of the snow a little higher up on the mountain from where I'd landed, I was relieved but still distressed because they weren't attached to any boots. The force of the sliding snow must have torn them off of the feet of whoever had been wearing them.

Ahead of me, I thought I saw a flash of lime green in between two trees, and I took a few more steps in that direction until I was sure that my eyes weren't deceiving me. It was Cheryl. She was sitting upright, and she was stunned—but alive.

"Cheryl!" I cried and broke into a run. She stood up, and we threw our arms around each other, collapsing into sobs.

"I thought I was dead!" she sobbed into my hair.

328

"You're not dead. We're here. We're okay," I assured her.

I wiped tears from my eyes and looked around, wondering just how massive the avalanche had been to have thrown us so far apart from each other. "We have to find Henry and Trey," I told her.

"They could be anywhere," she replied, sounding overwhelmed. Looking upward in the direction of the top of the mountain, it was impossible to distinguish natural debris from anything that might have been part of a human body. Overhead, we heard the helicopter growing closer, but I hoped that it would keep its distance so as to not loosen any more shelves of snow.

I unfastened my one remaining ski and ditched it to be more nimble. We wandered around on wobbly legs until I saw what looked like a hole in the snow that someone had crawled out of. "It looks like someone pulled themselves out of there!" I exclaimed. There were footsteps in the snow leading out of that hole and up the mountain farther, into a thicker wooded area, and we hurried along to see where they led.

This area of the mountainside was so dense with trees that there wasn't even much snow on the ground; it had instead collected on the branches of the pine trees around us. It was odd, after having been surrounded by snow from every angle all afternoon, to suddenly find ourselves walking on dry pine needles in a stretch of terrain that felt completely disconnected from the activity of the bustling resort.

Then I saw something that made me cry out in joy. Both Trey and Henry were kneeling on the ground, fully focused on arranging something. "Trey!" I called. My voice broke, and I started crying uncontrollably, pretty sure I'd never been happier in my whole life than right then. When he turned and saw me, he got up on his feet and ran toward me.

"Oh my God. You're alive!" he exclaimed, smothering me with kisses. He lifted me off the ground and spun me around.

"And *you're* alive!" I cradled his face in my hands and stared into his eyes, never wanting to look away.

But Cheryl cleared her throat to catch my attention. "Ahem," she said, and nodded to where, thirty feet away, Henry was positioning an unmoving body on the ground.

The body wore a shiny lavender ski jacket and matching pants.

My jaw dropped. "Is she . . . ," I asked Trey.

"She has a pulse," Trey informed us. "Henry and I were looking for you when we found her."

I reached inside my coat for Henry's phone to check the time, and discovered that the screen had cracked. It was 3:47 p.m. I estimated that Cheryl and I hadn't walked around looking for others for more than ten minutes. But I couldn't guess how long Violet had gone without oxygen. The responsible course of action would have been to call 911 immediately to request medical attention for her. . . .

And yet, this *was* all her fault.

Her spirits must have told her to predict this avalanche and issue deaths for Jason, Chitra, Cheryl, and who knew how many others. However, Cheryl was standing next to me, perfectly fine except for a limp and probably a future case of PTSD.

So far.

Violet had predicted a death for Cheryl, and there was just less than an hour remaining before the new moon occurred. The curse was not yet broken.

"Is she okay?" I asked, walking toward Henry. Trey and Cheryl followed me, and when we got closer I saw that Violet's enormous blue eyes were open.

"Don't try to move," Henry was instructing her. But he wasn't telling her to hold still because he wanted to keep her immobile until we had a chance to play the game. Her right leg was bent below the knee at a gnarly angle, surely broken. He looked up at us, concerned. "She's hurt pretty bad."

Upon noticing us, Violet began crying. "You're going to kill me, aren't you?"

I was surprised—and offended—that she really believed Trey and I were capable of murder. Then it dawned on me that she must have concluded that the way I intended to break the curse was to actually *end her life*. "We're not going to kill you, Violet," I assured her, trying to sound comforting. "We just have to play the game with you. That's it. No one has to die." However, even as I explained this to her, panic was building in my chest that she might go into shock at any moment. The game might not work if she was incapacitated. And it was unimaginable what would happen to Trey, Henry, and me if she were to die out there on the side of the mountain while we watched.

I noticed on Henry's phone that Kirsten had left a voice mail twenty-two minutes earlier, which must have been when I'd felt the vibration of the phone ringing. With a flash of pain in my gut, I hoped that Kirsten hadn't been calling with bad news about Mischa.

"She really needs medical attention," Cheryl murmured.

It was sickeningly callous and inhumane of me, but we wouldn't get another chance to play the game before we ran out of time. I glanced at the phone again to check the time. It was 3:49 p.m. We had fifty-five minutes, and it probably wouldn't take rescuers that long to find us. So I knelt down alongside Violet and informed her, "All we have to do is play a game like Light as a Feather, and I'll tell a story for you. Then the curse will be broken, and you won't have to protect your mom anymore. Do you think you can hang on just for, like, five minutes?"

With glazed eyes, she struggled to prop herself up on her elbows. "It really hurts," she sputtered.

"I know. I'm sorry," I said, feeling truly awful that I hadn't already called for help. "But just five minutes, Violet. That's all it'll take."

She looked around at all of our faces. I couldn't wager a guess what she was thinking, but I was sure that her physical pain was probably outweighing her inclination to make the logical choice, which was to break the curse once and for all while we were all assembled before the new moon. Finally, with a trembling lower lip, she said, "Just make it fast." She set her head back down on the ground, ready for me to initiate the game.

Since I was the only one among us who had played the game before, I directed my friends to take positions kneeling on the ground around Violet's body as she blinked up at the sky. Cheryl and Trey placed outstretched fingers beneath Violet's hips on both sides, and Henry placed them under her feet. We debated whether or not to remove her ski boots, but decided against it for fear of messing up her broken leg even more. I explained to my friends how, after I predicted Violet's death, they would have to chant, *light as a feather, cold as marble*, and attempt to raise Violet's body off the ground.

I placed my fingers on her temples, remembering that Jennie

had told me she'd show me Violet's death. "It's not going to work for you," Violet mumbled. "Not the way it works for me. They're going to be so . . . angry."

Suddenly afraid of what it might mean for my own conscience if ending the curse actually resulted in Violet's mom dying, I unzipped my coat pocket and was very happy to find that my makeshift pendulum and the cigarette lighter were still in there. "Hand me some of those pine needles, Cheryl," I instructed her. She twisted around to grab a handful of golden needles off the ground and passed them to me. At that point in the winter, there were no leaves to be found on trees, and I believed it would be better to burn what was available than to burn nothing at all.

Carefully holding the pine needles off to the side so that embers wouldn't fall on Violet's face, I lit a few of them and waved them around so that wisps of smoke swirled around all four of us and across Violet's body. Then I dangled the lanyard from my index finger and asked, "Pendulum. If we play Light as a Feather, Cold as Marble with Violet, will we be putting her mother's life in jeopardy?"

Side to side. *No.* Violet's mother would survive if we broke the curse.

Cheryl looked utterly horrified. "What the hell are you doing?" she asked.

"Just . . . trust her," Henry said.

"I'll explain later," I promised Cheryl. "Pendulum, is Jennie here with us?" The pendulum slowed to a stop, dangled motionlessly, and then reversed its direction to move back and forth. *Yes.*

"Is she listening?" I asked. The pendulum swung back and forth.

"Jennie, if we play Light as a Feather, Cold as Marble, will you show me Violet's death?"

Yes.

I still wasn't sure how she was going to actually *do* that, though. When we'd cast a spell with Kirsten at the bookstore, she'd used mirrors as a method of allowing spirits to visually show us things. But we were on the side of the mountain in the aftermath of a natural disaster. There was no chance we had a cosmetic mirror among us. "I need something reflective," I announced.

Trey hopped up and dashed over to a nearby tree. He returned to us carrying the ski goggles that Henry had bought for him earlier that afternoon. They had a hot orange tint to them but were, indeed, reflective. "Will that work?"

The image of my face was slightly distorted in the goggles, but they were the best option I had. "It'll work," I told him. "Could you hold it, just like that?"

He slipped the index finger of his right hand beneath Violet's hip again and held the goggles toward me with his left hand.

I knelt behind Violet's head, my knees just barely touching the top of her hair. She closed her eyes, knowing what her role was in this routine.

I pressed the tips of the fingers on my left hand to Violet's temple and continued to hold the lanyard in my right hand. "Pendulum," I asked, my voice anxiously fluttering as I looked at my reflection in the goggles. I placed my left hand firmly on top of Violet's head, tightly gripping her skull. "Can you show me Violet's future death?"

Violet flinched beneath my fingertips. She winced but did not open her eyes. The pendulum began moving in a clockwise circular pattern and swung faster as the diameter of the circle in which it spun widened.

"What . . . is . . . happening?" Trey asked.

I kept my eyes focused on the goggles, ignoring Cheryl's comment of "Oh my God," but all I saw were my own expectant dark eyes with pine trees behind me in the distance and snow clouds overhead.

"Can you see anything?" Henry asked.

"I don't know," I admitted, confused and a little disappointed. "I really thought this would work." Panic rose in my throat. If we'd come this far—escaped from our respective schools, lied to our parents and destroyed their trust in us, thrown away our plans for college, managed to get Violet away from everyone else to play the game—and I couldn't visualize her death, I didn't know what else I could do. It would be a failure of epic proportions.

And just then, I realized that I wasn't looking at my own reflection in the goggles. I was looking at Jennie as if she were my age—sixteen—and not eight, as she was when I'd last seen her alive. She blinked when I didn't, and she mouthed, *Watch.* "Wait, wait, something's happening," I mumbled distractedly just to ensure that Trey wouldn't move the goggles.

The goggles clouded over, and a scene slowly took shape. It appeared to be a doctor's office. It was the middle of the afternoon, with sunlight streaming in through horizontal blinds, casting stripes of sunlight on the far wall, bouncing off of yellowed medical school diplomas framed behind glass. A male doctor with a white beard was seated at the desk, and he folded his hands on the desktop, fighting the urge to open the file before him. He was speaking with a woman who was seated across from him on the other side of the desk, a woman with short gray hair who was listening attentively. Although I couldn't hear anything with my ears related to what I saw happening, I sensed pulses of energy in my head similar to the voices I often heard that explained to me well enough what was going on. I began narrating out of fear that I'd not describe the story being shown to me well enough for the game to work if I waited too long and forgot details.

"It was the middle of the afternoon in a doctor's office. A doctor with a white beard was informing Violet about some test results that had come back."

The scene playing out in the goggles switched angles to show me Violet's reaction. I was startled by her appearance; it was definitely her, although she appeared to be much, much older. Perhaps as old as seventy or eighty, with fine wrinkles in her heavily powdered skin. She was still pretty, her eyes still framed with long lashes. Heavy pearl earrings stretched out her earlobes, and she was tastefully dressed in a stylish cashmere sweater. She always had favored sweaters. She seemed to be listening to the doctor attentively, and I was able to distinguish the word "cancer" as his mouth formed it.

"She'd been feeling ill for weeks, exhausted. Weak. No matter how much sleep she got, she felt unrested. The doctor confirmed her worst fear: that she had inoperable cancer. It had begun in her colon and had rapidly spread to her lymph nodes, significantly decreasing her chances for survival."

The goggles continued, advancing a little further into the future. A group of middle-aged men and women had gathered in the parlor of a grand house—possibly but not definitely the Simmons mansion—and they all sat patiently on a sofa. Violet was breaking the news to these people, who I suspected were her children and their spouses.

"Violet was told she had less than a year to live. Because her husband had already passed away, she decided right there and then in the doctor's office that she wouldn't seek treatment. If her time had come, she wanted to face it, and not spend the last months of her life ill from chemotherapy. She knew that, because of terrible things she'd done as a girl, she would welcome the death meant for her with open arms. She gathered her sons and their wives, her daughter and her husband, and all of her grandchildren together—"

I choked, becoming overwhelmed by the sadness of it all despite my strong dislike for Violet. She remained completely still beneath my fingertips, not reacting to the story I was telling about her future death in any way.

"—and told them that it was her wish to enjoy her last few months spending as much time with her grandchildren as possible, and to die at home rather than in a sterile, impersonal hospital. So she grew thinner and frailer, passing each morning in the garden that reminded her of the one which had been planted by her grandmother in Willow."

The scene being revealed to me in the goggles was so vivid that it was like watching a movie, and I wondered if Violet's spirits had shown her my friends' deaths in such precise detail. "Violet awakened in the middle of the night, and sensed that her visiting nurse was in the room, snoring gently in the nearby rocking chair. She knew that her time had come. She kept her eyes closed and focused on breathing until at last her lungs would not take in any more air.

In the morning, the nurse found Violet's lifeless body in her bed."

Next, the goggles showed me a memorial service at Gundarsson's, and I understood this to mean that Violet would live out the rest of her life in our hometown. "Two days later, Violet lay in her coffin. . . ." I took a deep breath, praying to heaven with all my might that what I was about to do would work and spare Mischa and Tracy from the same fate met by Olivia and Candace, if they were still alive.

"Light as a feather, cold as marble."

I felt Violet's body jerk beneath my hand, and looked up to see Henry, Trey, and Cheryl all looking as bewildered as I was. "Light as a feather, cold as marble," I repeated.

They joined in my chant, "Light as a feather, cold as marble. Light as a feather, cold as marble." We began to raise her off the ground slowly, and she was as weightless as I remembered Olivia and Candace's bodies being when we'd first played the game.

Beneath the palm of my hand and through Violet's thick dark hair, I felt the temperature of her head dropping. It became cold quickly. Inhumanly cold, like a block of ice, so much that the bones of my left hand ached as the chill seeped through the skin on my fingertips. I heard Henry gasp, and we observed the skin on Violet's forehead and cheeks turning a pale shade of periwinkle blue, marbling over like stone. Her chest had ceased rising and falling, and a fuzzy white film of frost had accumulated on her lower lip. By all appearances, she was dead, frozen solid.

Cold as marble.

"She's freezing!" Cheryl whispered hysterically.

"Don't let go of her," I commanded. "Light as a feather, cold as marble."

"Holy shit," Trey mumbled.

"Light as a feather, cold as marble," Henry managed to chant.

Jennie wasn't finished showing me details in the goggles. I saw Violet's family gathered at the cemetery behind St. Monica's church, a sight all too familiar to me from my many visits to Jennie's grave. They all wore black, and a young priest I didn't recognize led them in prayer as Violet's coffin was lowered into the ground. It was a magnificent spring day, with not a cloud in the sky, and birds chirped high above in the tree branches. As the family began to disperse, wrapping arms around one another and blotting away tears with handkerchiefs, Jennie panned my view to show me a headstone a few feet away from the grave into which Violet's coffin had been placed. On it was engraved the name TREY EMORY.

It was all I could do to not cry out in objection.

But there wasn't time to dwell on whatever Jennie was trying to communicate about the importance of Trey being buried near Violet. The tip of Violet's nose was turning blue, and the color was spreading across her face. Her head was so cold beneath the fingers of my left hand that it seemed like if someone were to tap her body with a hammer, she'd shatter like a ceramic vase. In the second that I turned my attention away from the goggles and dared to look at her, the scene I'd been watching unfold in the reflection vanished and was replaced with something terrifying.

I saw myself, my own reflection, right at that very moment, with the trees towering behind me. And then I saw three forms take shape to the left of me as if people were standing behind me, and two more appeared over my right shoulder. I shuddered, and the breath that I exhaled was frigid with horror. I squinted at the reflection in the goggles in an attempt to see more detail, but the five forms looked like faceless girls my age with long dark hair. They were Violet's five sisters, I was sure of it, and I struggled to maintain my composure as it seemed in the reflection like they were leaning over my shoulders to get closer to Violet.

And then I saw in the gap between the first three forms and the last two that another shape had appeared. This one, it seemed, was Violet. The features of her face were blurred, but the contours of her head were recognizable.

She was there with them, in their realm. Their forms turned to acknowledge her.

We'd done what Jennie had advised us to do.

"McKenna! We have to stop! We're killing her!" Henry said.

I would have thought that if Violet were still breathing, her breath would have poured out of her frozen nostrils and through her parted, frosty lips as steam. But she appeared to be as solid as a block of ice. Unbreathing.

We'd perhaps gone too far. If her body was truly frozen, her internal organs were frozen too, and her life functions had stopped. She had truly joined her sisters in their realm.

"Pendulum, are we done? Did we break the curse?" I asked in a hoarse whisper, afraid that we had murdered Violet.

It swung back and forth. *Yes.*

"Set her down and stop touching her!" I commanded my friends in a shrill voice, and they lowered her the few inches she'd been raised back down to the forest floor.

Color quickly returned to Violet's cheeks. The frost on her lips melted into drops of liquid reminiscent of dew. None of us dared to move or speak until she finally wiggled her fingers and then mashed her lips together. Before even opening her eyes, she managed to croak, "It's cold."

Groaning in pain, she propped herself up on one elbow and then coughed into her fist. The four of us all eased back, in awe of what we'd done.

"Is it over for good?" Trey asked eagerly, nodding at the pendulum. "Ask it."

I asked the makeshift pendulum, "Is it over for good?"

It stopped swinging abruptly, which I interpreted as its refusal to respond one way or another. This was obviously not the answer that I wanted, but Violet's eyes popped open as she continued coughing, becoming aware of what we'd just done.

"Ask it if it's over for evil," Trey joked.

"Are they done with me?" she asked when she was finally able to get words out.

"I think so," I informed her.

"What about the snow? How did I get here? Where's Pete?" It seemed like perhaps either the game or the excruciating pain she was in had stunted her memory.

I calmly described the avalanche to her, and that everyone who had been standing with us at Stevens' Pass had been carried farther down the mountain with the sliding snow. "I don't know who, other than the five of us, survived," I admitted. "When we get out of here, we have to be prepared for some very bad news."

"That can't be right," she whimpered. "I didn't tell a story for him. I wouldn't do that." Violet processed what it meant that we'd played the game and I'd predicted her death while she'd been frozen.

"You have to let me call my mother," she said, her huge blue eyes round with worry. "I need to know she's okay."

Suddenly, since having seen Violet's future death, I didn't view the girl in front of me as such an evil threat anymore. I'd spent months despising her, fearing her, and wishing I'd never crossed paths with her, but now she sat before us, defenseless. She was more worried about her mother's life than about her own broken leg. If everything she'd previously told us about how the curse functioned was true, I couldn't feel anything but pity for her. I knew in my heart that if I'd been in her position, I would have done *anything* to save my own mother, such was my fierce love for her. Maybe Violet wasn't such a heartless monster, after all. It had probably been pretty awful for her, having to do such terrible things and not being able to confide in anyone about it.

"We should call for help first," I told her. Truthfully, I didn't trust her. There was no telling what kind of lies she might tell her mother about what we'd done to her on the mountain that day if I let her use the phone before I reached out for help. I wouldn't put it past her to tell her mother that we were holding her hostage. I dialed 911, and emergency operator told me that she would pinpoint our location from the cell phone's position and send a rescue team on snowmobiles. "One of the people with us is injured," I told her. "She has a broken leg."

Once help was on the way, I decided it might be best to use the remaining time we had with Violet to our advantage. "You should tell us everything you know about how and why you predicted deaths. We deserve the truth, Violet. Especially Henry. Olivia didn't do anything to hurt anyone."

She looked around at all of us with saucer eyes that no longer danced with sarcasm and contempt. "They told me," she sputtered, "that if I didn't go out and get who they wanted, they'd kill my mom." Every time I said no, they threatened me. They showed me how they'd do it. They told me that my life was a gift to her, and that if I didn't serve them, they'd take *her* life away as a punishment."

"Who, Violet?" I asked. "Who said they'd punish your mom?"

"I don't know *what* they are. Ghosts, maybe? There are five of them. My mom had three stillborn daughters before I was born, and then another and a miscarriage when I was little. I don't know if they're the spirits of my real sisters, or something else just pretending to be my sisters. They died so that I could live, or at least that's what . . . they say. It doesn't make any sense to me, but that's the reason they always give me for why they make me do things."

She nodded in Trey's direction and told us all, "He knows. They told me he knows too."

Trey shrugged innocently. "I've seen them in dreams, but they've never asked me to do anything to another person."

Violet's magnificent blue eyes filled with tears. "Every time I've told them that I won't do what they want, they make my mom get sick, and then they get greedy. They usually only want me to get them one person every month, but when they're angry, they want more."

"I think we ended it," I told her. "I really and truly do. I don't think they're ever going to ask you to do anything for them again."

Violet disagreed vehemently. "There's no way to break it without my mom dying. Believe me. I've read books. I've Googled. Maybe you don't care about *me*. That's fine. I guess I couldn't expect anything more. But my mom didn't do anything wrong. She doesn't deserve what they'll do to her."

"Olivia didn't deserve to die," I reminded her. "Neither did Candace, or Rebecca, or any of the people you killed in Lake Forest before you moved to our town."

She squeezed her eyes shut, refusing to look at me. "I didn't ask for this to happen to me, okay? I never wanted to kill anyone, and I don't care if you believe me. You don't know what it's been like," she shouted at me.

There was no consoling Violet at that point, so I did what any normal person would do now that help was on the way, and I gave her Henry's phone. Tapping the shattered glass of the screen, she entered in the numbers of her family's landline and waited. When her mother answered at the other end of the line, she burst into tears and yelped, "Mom?"

Violet's mother was alive. She'd heard about the tragedy on Mt. Farthington, and she and her husband had been on pins and needles waiting for authorities in Traverse City to contact them about Violet's status. The sun was starting to get low in the sky, and we were alone on a cold mountainside. The temperature was rapidly dropping, and I wished our rescuers would hurry up and arrive even if salvation meant we had to face the death toll of the avalanche.

Finally, at long last, we heard snowmobiles in the distance.

Henry and Trey stood and began shouting to catch their attention, but I remained kneeling next to Violet until two EMTs located us and examined her leg. Even though one of the rescuers insisted that I ride down to the base of the mountain to be examined by doctors, I waited until Violet was stabilized to be transported before

I agreed to leave. Although I wouldn't say that I felt any sympathy for her, I felt an odd connection to her that I hadn't sensed before playing the game. Perhaps watching her future death had bound me to her. I wondered as I watched the EMTs position her on the back of one of the snowmobiles if she'd felt a similar tie to her victims before they'd died.

It was starting to get dark by the time I rode on the back of a snowmobile out from underneath the branches of the pine trees that had hidden us from helicopters while we played the game that ended the curse. That night there would be no moonlight in the sky. It was the start of a new lunar cycle, and the start of a new beginning for all of us. Despite the questions I knew that I'd be asked by police, school officials, and my parents, and despite the fact that I had no idea what kind of punishment Trey and I would be facing for running away from our respective boarding schools, my heart felt light and bouncy. Tiny flurries flitted around me as I cruised down the mountain over snowdrifts, almost as if celebrating our victory.

We'd done it. We'd ended the curse.

CHAPTER 21

TO OUR SURPRISE, OUR RESCUERS TOLD US when we reached the base of the mountain that they'd been searching for us for over an hour. They'd been just about to bring in dogs to aid in the search before nightfall when I'd called for help.

Trey, Henry, and I were lucky that the rescuers had been told to prioritize our health and safety over enforcing criminal justice. Just like Violet and Cheryl, we were seen immediately by physicians from local hospitals who'd been brought to Mt. Farthington after the avalanche.

The scene around us was chaotic; there were police cars and news vans and news crews shooting live footage of us sitting in the backs of ambulances having our vitals taken. Even though at that point I didn't want to be poked and prodded by doctors—I just wanted to go home to Willow and see my mom—the doctors on the scene explained that we would all need to be examined in the emergency room. Everyone else who'd been rescued that afternoon had also been taken to the hospital, so we didn't have much of a choice.

The EMTs split us up to transport us in three different ambulances. Trey and I insisted on riding together. We sat together on the gurney in the back of the ambulance and politely ignored the red-headed EMT who rode back there with us. Trey put his arm around my shoulders, and I eased into his embrace. Although the ride to the hospital was hardly private or romantic, I wondered if we would have another moment like that together before we were shipped back to Northern Reserve and Sheridan.

"You are amazing, do you know that?" he whispered into my ear, his breath tickling my skin. "I always thought you were special, but I just didn't know *how* special."

I thought he was referring to the way in which I had handled the pendulum and been able to watch what Jennie had shown me in the goggles. "It's a gift. It doesn't make me amazing, really. It just means that half of my soul is in the spirit world, you know? The connection between me and Jennie was never really broken when she died. But it took eight years for us to get back in touch."

Trey pulled me closer so that he could kiss the top of my head. "Sure. All that may be true. But you're still the most fearless, badass person I've ever met. I don't know anyone else who would have found a way to get all of us here and still have the presence of mind after being involved in *an avalanche* to do what you did today."

"I couldn't have done it without you," I reminded him. And Henry, too, but I didn't want to say Henry's name during such a tender moment.

"I think you could have," Trey argued. "I think you're capable of a lot more than you know."

I smiled weakly at the EMT who sat facing us, wishing he weren't there. Even though he could still hear me because he was only about two feet away from us in the cramped space, I dropped my voice to a whisper. "I can't stand being away from you anymore," I told Trey. "We have to find a way to be together after you're released from Northern Reserve."

"We will," he told me. "What else am I gonna do with my life except love you? That's what I've always done, and what I'll always do."

When we arrived at the Munson Medical Center, local police were waiting there to speak with Trey and me, but the EMTs pushed them aside and told them they'd have to wait until after we were examined. Henry hopped out of the ambulance in which he'd ridden with Cheryl and told me that he'd been able to reach Kirsten. Mischa was just fine, although getting very irritable about missing gym time. Henry told me that Kirsten said she needed to speak with me, but that it could wait until after we were released from the hospital. Evidently, the avalanche at Mt. Farthington had been a big enough news story that it had even been featured on the evening news in Chicago. Kirsten had seen it and instantly known that we must have been involved, and she'd feared for the worst—that Violet had found a way to kill all of us in a natural disaster.

We were all led into the busy emergency room and told to change into hospital gowns. Several people from Willow were already there, receiving medical attention on beds that were separated by curtains. I caught a glimpse of Miss Kirkovic when a nurse left her little area across from my bed. She was hooked up to IVs and appeared to be either sleeping or unconscious. Cheryl and I had been placed in beds next to each other, and chose to keep the curtain partition open so that we could talk. Cheryl called her mother to let her know that she was all right and asked about Tracy's condition. She gave me the thumbs-up to indicate that Tracy was still alive.

I held off on calling my mom when Cheryl ended her call. Perhaps I'd had the courage to confront Violet's evil spirits, but I hadn't worked up enough of it yet to find out just how angry my mom was for my having run away from Sheridan.

Nurses came along and took my temperature and blood pressure. They brought us compression socks, orange juice, and crackers, which made me realize I was absolutely ravenous. Henry, Trey, and I hadn't eaten all day, and when I informed the nurse of that, she had dinner trays brought over for us from the cafeteria.

We'd find out later that all ten people from Willow who had been standing at Stevens' Pass at the moment of the avalanche had not been as lucky as we were. Jason Arkadian had broken two ribs and his leg. He had already been brought upstairs at the hospital to be prepared for surgery by the time we'd arrived. Chitra Bhakta had suffered hypothermia and would have to be hospitalized overnight. Two of Miss Kirkovic's teeth had been knocked out, and she'd sprained an ankle and a wrist. Pete Nicholson had broken his collarbone and suffered a concussion. The three instructors from Fitzgerald's who had also been caught in the sliding snow had walked away without a scratch.

But no one had died.

As EMTs attended to Violet in the emergency room, she smiled at me from her bed, which was across from mine. The new moon had risen, not a single one of Violet's sacrifices had died, and her mother was fine. After living under the constraints of such a hideous curse for so long, it was going to take a while for Violet to believe that it was actually over. But it seemed that night that she was at least willing to believe that it was.

Trey and I were both interrogated by Traverse City police for over an hour, and then we were separated to wait for our parents to arrive. It seemed like the cops weren't sure what kind of tone was appropriate to use with us, because although we were still the same kids who'd escaped from our reform schools earlier in the week, Violet had told them that Henry and Trey had pulled her out of the snow and I'd been the one to save her life by calling for help. They weren't sure whether to treat us like villains or heroes, and the local news announcing that it was a miracle no one had been killed in the avalanche worked in our favor. The police didn't want to spoil such a heartwarming story by taking us into custody at the hospital, and their focus on us faded as the night wore on, until it became clear that they were going to let the authorities in Wisconsin deal with us.

My mom drove up to Michigan to fetch me that night, arriving after midnight. Her fury with me for leaving Sheridan was outmatched by her relief that I'd survived the avalanche without sustaining any injuries. I was allowed to say good-bye to Trey and Henry when I was released from the hospital, but out of respect for my mom, I didn't go overboard with emotion. Henry's mom and dad were both on their way over from Willow. Trey's parents were driving up too, even though it was kind of funny that they hadn't carpooled with my mom considering that they were making identical seven-hour journeys from practically the same starting point.

Since the boys were in beds on opposite sides of the emergency room, I pulled back the curtain of Henry's private area after saying good-bye to Trey. The sight of him in his hospital gown made me uncomfortable; it felt more intrusive than even having seen him shirtless in our motel room the night before.

"Henry, saying 'thank you' doesn't even start to express my gratitude," I said quietly so that my mom, waiting outside his curtained area, wouldn't overhear. "I don't think there's anything I'll ever be able to do to show you how much having you on my side has meant to me."

He looked up quickly at me, barely making eye contact, and shrugged. "You did all the hard stuff. I just drove, which is what I like to do anyway."

I leaned forward and pecked him on the cheek. "You did a lot more than drive, Henry Richmond."

Just as I was about to pull the curtain back again to rejoin my mom, he reached for my hand. The touch of his skin surprised me, and we held hands for a long moment while I stood there next to his bed before he said, "Everything I want to say to you right now is probably super inappropriate. So I'll just say this: I hope one day I'll have a chance to tell you everything that's in my heart. And until then, just know that if you ever need anything—anything at all—all you have to do is ask."

He wouldn't look me in the eye again. I whispered, "Okay," knowing that sometimes things are better left unsaid.

I slept for most of the drive home from Traverse City, waking up sporadically confused and almost hysterical, believing that I was surrounded by snow again.

Mom and her attorney spent the weekend jumping through

hoops, trying to figure out how to keep me from having to go directly back to Sheridan. The attorney seemed to think we might be able to ask for an exception to be made on my behalf because of the psychological trauma I was going to face after the avalanche. He thought we stood a good chance of asking that the rest of my sentence for the antics in the fall be altered to require me to transfer to the high school in Tampa where my dad lived, and for Dad to be granted temporary custody of me.

When Mom ran this prospect past Dad over the phone, he was all for it, which seemed to make her angry instead of happy. Even though she didn't want me going back to Sheridan, she also didn't want to surrender custody of me to the man who'd ditched her for a bohemian lifestyle with a younger wife. I kept my opinion to myself, which was that I didn't care what became of me for the next five months as long as I was reunited with Trey in July.

Mischa appeared on the doorstep of her house on Saturday morning without a single scratch on her or any memory whatso-ever of where she'd spent the entire month of January. The local news anchors had a field day with the story, baffled that she'd been returned home safe and sound with complete amnesia. I watched the coverage on the news with amusement, impressed with Mischa's acting abilities as she told the cameras that she didn't know where she'd been and couldn't remember anything after stepping outside the front door of her house the day she disappeared, other than that the place where she'd been held smelled strongly of incense. The police had also found abundant cat fur on her clothes, which was fortunately a vague enough clue, since they couldn't exactly consider every cat owner in the Midwest a suspect in Mischa's kidnapping.

Naturally, I was dying to reconnect with Trey about all of this, but although he was at home in the house next door, both of us knew we were in way too much trouble to risk seeing each other.

It was hard for me to get even five minutes of privacy that weekend to touch base with Kirsten about how she and Mischa had decided to deal with the matter of criminality in Mischa's extended disappearance, but I started to suspect witchcraft when Mischa called me on Sunday morning. "Do *you* know where I've been all this time?" she asked, sounding as if she truly had no idea. "Did Violet do something to me?"

Up until that point, I thought she'd been going along with a cover story that she and Kirsten had cooked up, but it seemed like her confusion was real.

"I don't know," I lied, not wanting to tell her the truth until I'd had a chance to check in with Kirsten. "I really don't. I was at Sheridan the whole time up until I met up with the kids from school on the ski trip. I mean, obviously Trey and I planned that. You knew about it too, but you might not remember us talking about it over the holidays."

"I wonder if I was practicing my floor routine while I was away," she mused. "I've been kind of rusty at the gym. It's going to take a few weeks for me to get back in shape."

In a very surprising twist, Michael and Vanessa Simmons, Violet's parents, made an appeal to Judge Roberts in Suamico about my case first thing on Monday morning, asking for leniency because they believed I'd saved Violet's life in the aftermath of the avalanche. They had not, however, said anything on behalf of Trey, even though he and Henry were technically the ones who had plucked Violet out of the snow.

I had been shocked that Trey had been allowed to return home to Willow on Saturday with his parents; I had assumed that they would have taken him directly back to Northern Reserve. It turned out that he, too, had to revisit the judge in Suamico, since we'd both violated the terms of our original punishments.

After receiving a call from the court administrator on Monday morning, Mom left me alone to meet with her attorney for lunch in Green Bay. He was under the impression that they might be able to negotiate more on my behalf while I was in good favor with the Simmons family, but wanted to talk to her without me present (probably so that he could speak freely about what a loose cannon I was). Not long after Mom left the house, the doorbell rang, and I found Violet Simmons standing on my doorstep. Although she usually looked flawless, her skin was peeling and red as if she'd had an allergic reaction to something.

"Can I come in?" she asked.

"I don't think that's a good idea," I replied, not wanting to jeopardize whatever deal my mom was putting together to try to salvage my future at that very moment.

She wrinkled her nose nervously and adjusted the strap of her bag on her shoulder. "I just wanted to say thank you, I guess. And give you a little bit more background about how all of this started so that you know it wasn't my fault."

I was about to tell her that I honestly didn't care whose fault it was when she continued, "I'm not a bad person, McKenna. It bothers me that you probably think I am, especially because . . ." She trailed off and then completed the thought. "You're awesome. I don't think I ever could have done what you did."

Against my better judgment, I let her step inside and take a seat in our living room. "I know my skin looks really bad," she admitted self-consciously. "The doctors think it's because I was in the snow for so long."

I was willing to bet that her skin had been damaged when I'd frozen her entire body during the game of Light as a Feather, Cold as Marble, but it was probably best that she didn't know that.

"I don't even know where to begin. This routine has been my life for over a year. It used to be all I would ever think about—*who* they wanted me to claim and *how* I'd get that person to agree to let me predict their death, and then eventually how horrible I felt after they died. I'd hoped that things would get better when we moved to Willow. But . . . it wasn't long before it was just the same old routine. And the people that they specifically requested for me to get them were the last people I wanted to die. You have to believe me about that."

I wasn't sure that I was ever going to completely believe Violet about anything, but I was willing to listen. "So how did it start?"

Violet leaned back on the couch and crossed her legs, settling in to tell me the whole story. She took a deep breath as if it scared her to simply remember back to how everything began, and picked at the skin around her fingernails as she spoke. "The first time I ever saw them was the night after my grandmother died. I was at home, in my bedroom in Lake Forest last fall. I thought I was having a bad dream, the kind of vivid bad dream where you *know* you're dreaming but your heart is racing and you wake up sweating and moving your arms and legs and it takes you a while to calm down even after you realize you're awake."

I'd had those sorts of dreams myself. The image of a house on fire and my sister's silhouette in the front window waving farewell to me flashed behind my eyes.

"But this wasn't a dream," Violet continued, her voice dropping to a lower key. "They appeared as kind of . . . blue lights. I saw them in my bedroom mirror first, as if they were reflections, but then I realized they were just orbs of light floating in my room; they weren't a reflection of anything in the mirror at all.

"There were five of them, and that first time they appeared, I didn't know what they were. They didn't exactly *talk* to me, like, using words, so I'm not sure how to explain this, but they made it clear that they wanted me to get *one*. One what? I wondered. They lifted one of my stuffed animals right off of my bed and made it levitate over me. Just *one*.

"Obviously, I was freaked out about the whole thing, but I convinced myself it had just been a hallucination. I didn't tell my parents. My grandmother had just died, and my father was super busy making funeral arrangements. My mom was already pitching a fit about his suggestion that we might have to move to Willow while my parents settled my grandmother's estate. My mom had just been made a partner at the law firm where she'd been working since before I was born, so she didn't want to just move to some tiny town in Wisconsin. They didn't need the stress of having a daughter who was losing her mind, so I didn't say anything.

"Basically, by the time we'd buried my grandmother and I went back to school, I forgot about the lights and the floating stuffed animal. Then, one day in study hall two or three weeks later, this kid named Michael had a deck of cards. He wanted to play War, but as he broke up the deck of cards into stacks for all of us, I started getting this weird feeling. Like my scalp was tingling, in a cool way, like when someone's braiding your hair. Or like the feeling I would get on Christmas Eve when I was a little kid, knowing that Santa was on his way. Just looking at the cards made me feel like I should pick them up, so I reached out and held them. And I said, *Do you guys want to see something cool?*"

I listened intently, completely caught up in the tale Violet was telling.

She hesitated and frowned, seeming sad about whatever followed in the story. "I didn't know what was going to happen; I honestly didn't. I just had this weird impulse and suspicion that if I kept going, something important would happen. When I fanned the cards out in front of me, it was like . . . like the cards didn't look like cards anymore. I could see stories on each of them, almost like little frames from a movie from each of my friends' lives. There was one of Mike Goldsmith on his bicycle, riding in the dark. There was one of my best friend, Rebecca, coughing up blood in the back of an ambulance. There was one of this other girl, Brianna, who I didn't even know that well—she always picked at her skin with a sewing needle during class. And one of . . ." She trailed off for a second, seemingly lost in the memory, before continuing. "My boyfriend—I guess you could call him that—on a basketball court.

"I asked my friends if any of them wanted to pick a card. I shuffled the deck and held the cards out so that they could choose. That first time, the lights hadn't specified who they wanted me to get. It could have been anyone. But Rebecca was the one who took a card. I wasn't sure what I was supposed to do next, so I told her to put it back in the deck. I shuffled the cards again, and then nothing happened. Everyone started joking around then, like, *Wow, cool trick, Violet.*

"But I still had this weird feeling like something was *supposed* to happen, so I just put the stack of cards on the table and watched it. Then a single card rose right out of the middle of the deck. It was"—she squeezed her eyes shut and shook her head as if even the memory of that day still bothered her—"just . . . crazy. I knew without even seeing it that it was the card that Rebecca had chosen, and it was. Everyone freaked out. They thought it was so awesome. I mean, it was, like, the eight of hearts or something. No one but me knew that the card had something to do with Rebecca dying in an ambulance.

"When I hung out with Rebecca that weekend, it didn't seem like the card trick had mattered. But then the following Monday, she didn't show up for school. I found out she'd been walking home from babysitting late on Saturday night in her subdivision and had been hit by a car that just . . . drove away. I didn't know it was really going to happen. Honestly. I didn't."

"Geez," I commented. Violet's eyes were puffing up as she began getting emotional. I didn't tell her that I'd seen Rebecca in Kirsten's mirror at the bookstore.

Violet shifted positions uncomfortably and sniffed. "So, yeah," she said. "That was just the beginning. After Rebecca died, the lights came back again. They wanted me to get someone else, and this time they opened my yearbook and showed me that they wanted this girl Brianna, who was in a few classes with me. We weren't even friends. I mean, she was big-time into video games and mostly hung out with kids who spent all their time on Twitch. But still I knew they wanted me to tell her how she was going to die. I told them I wouldn't do it. I mean, you probably don't believe me, but Rebecca was my *friend*. They *tricked* me. They made me feel like I had some kind of cool magic power, and I didn't realize . . ."

She trailed off, but I wanted her to keep going, so I asked, "What happened when you told them you wouldn't do it?"

Bitterness crept into her voice. "About two weeks later? My mom had this accident out of the blue. Somehow her blow-dryer electrocuted her when she was getting ready for work in the morning. I was the one who found her on the bathroom floor, and the whole time I was on the phone with the ambulance, I could hear them in my head saying Brianna's name over and over again. My mom's doctors said it was a miracle that she didn't have any kind of brain damage."

"This is the part I don't understand," I interjected. "Why would they hurt your mom and not you? If they're really the spirits of your sisters, then she's their mom too."

"I really don't know," Violet admitted. "My mom had a lot of fertility problems before I was born. Before she died, my grandmother told me that she had started to worry about my mom's state of mind by the time she lost the third baby. I mean, giving birth to three dead babies in a row. That's . . . you know. I can't even imagine."

Inspired, because this was the part of the story that overlapped with Trey's mom's history with the Simmons family, I asked, "Is there any chance that someone might have done something to help your mom through the pregnancy when she was expecting you? Like saying a special prayer, or . . . casting a spell?"

Violet shrugged. "I don't know. Probably lots of people were praying for her, or at least said they were." She hesitated and then brightened. "My grandmother, the paternal one, the one who lived here in Willow, was really into herbs and tarot cards and stuff like that. She used to keep small sachets of dried parsley around the house for good luck. In fact, she planted a rosebush in her garden for each of the stillborn babies my mom had as some kind of new age–y way of honoring each of their spirits."

The five rosebushes. The night of Violet's New Year's party, my scalp had tingled so strongly when I'd walked past them; I should have guessed that they were part of whatever spell had been cast on Violet's mom.

"And right around this time, your dad was teaching in Chicago," I said, not wanting to raise a sore topic but yearning to know how much she knew about Trey's background.

Violet rolled her eyes and wiped away a tear. "Yeah, well. Parents aren't perfect people, you know. Women throw themselves at my dad everywhere he goes. It's embarrassing, honestly. Waitresses flirt with him, like, right in front of me. I didn't know anything about Trey until my grandmother died and we moved here. Then my dad figured he'd better tell me before I heard rumors and figured it out for myself. I guess they met on campus and had a connection because they'd both grown up in this town."

"Why *did* you move here?" I asked. It seemed to me that Michael Simmons would have wanted to keep his wife and daughter as far away from Willow, Mary Jane Svensson, and his illegitimate son as possible.

She looked at me in confusion and replied, "My grandmother left everything to me. The house, the land, all of it. My father's brother took us to court to try to get some of the inheritance for his kids. I really didn't want all of it, you know? It's weird to have your cousins hate you. But my dad's attorneys recommended that we move here and occupy the house because residency would strengthen my claim."

All of that seemed very odd to me. Who would leave an estate and a fortune to a sixteen-year-old girl? "Why do you think your grandmother left everything to you?"

Violet fell silent and stared down at her hands in her lap for a long time before saying, "I think she felt sorry for me. Because all of this." She waved her hand around. "Having to predict someone's death every month? Before she died, my grandmother was the one getting sacrifices for them. She wrote me a letter explaining how all of it worked and what would be expected of me. And she apologized, like, fifty times in it. But the letter was tied up with the rest of her legal affairs, so her attorney didn't give it to me until about six months after she'd died. I'd already figured out what was expected of me by then, I just didn't know why I was being ordered to kill people. The letter explained that the obligation was part of my inheritance."

She choked back a sob in reaction to her admission that she'd *killed* people. Back in the fall when we'd confronted her on the track at school, she had vehemently denied ever having killed anyone, but now she was owning up to the severity of her actions. If we'd prevented her from killing anyone during the last lunar cycle, that was still fourteen sacrifices.

"My grandmother was smarter about all of it than I've been. She told me in the letter that she volunteered at nursing homes and the children's hospital so that she could bargain with the lights and make suggestions about who to sacrifice. She only told stories for people who had terminal illnesses and were going to die anyway. But they've never let me choose who I take. They always tell me instead who they want."

"Wow," I said. The grandmother. If I had to guess (and I did), it must have been Violet's grandmother who had put the original spell on Violet's mother.

"You can't tell my mom any of this, okay?" Violet said, wiping her cheeks dry with the backs of her hands. "She doesn't know any of it—not about Trey. It would kill her if she found out about him."

I found that very hard to believe. Mrs. Simmons had sat in the courtroom back in November. Surely, she must have noticed the strong resemblance between Trey and her husband.

Even though she had just shared more with me than I ever would have expected about the origin of the curse that had killed my friends, I still didn't trust her enough to tell her all I knew about the contractual arrangements between her father and Trey's mother. I still didn't know exactly what Trey's mom had agreed to do, and how she'd violated that agreement, and I had to accept the fact that there was a chance I'd never know. "It would mean a lot to me if you could talk to your dad and have the judge in Suamico ease up on his sentence. Or at least make sure he gets released on his birthday in July. I mean, if you're truly sorry about everything you've done, that's one small way you could make things right."

She thought this over, and her lower lip wrinkled as if she was going to start crying again. "I'll talk to him. I swear. I can't promise he'll do anything, but I'll ask."

"Violet," I began, wishing the history between us were different so that I could really put faith in her answer. "Do you think the spell is broken? Does anything feel different to you?"

"Pretty sure it's broken," she replied. "Did you look at the sky last night? Crescent moon. That means a full cycle of the moon passed and no one died."

She lingered in my doorway after telling me she had to get back home because she was supposed to be resting and said, "I really don't know how to thank you, McKenna. I know you probably would never consider me a friend at this point, and that's . . . beyond understandable. But I never thought I'd be free of this thing, and you even found a way to end it and still protect my mom. So thank you. It's the most anyone has ever done for me."

Although her gratitude seemed authentic, my heart remained hardened. My dad had always told me that carrying a grudge and refusing forgiveness was the most powerful form of stress a person could hang on to, but I didn't think I could ever bring myself to forgive Violet for the way in which she had so cheerfully suggested we play a game of Light as a Feather, Stiff as a Board at Olivia's birthday party. Memories of that night were going to haunt my dreams for the rest of my life. I felt justified in clinging to at least part of my hatred for her, even if I pitied her for the terrible inheritance she'd been given by her grandmother.

Not long after Violet left, Kirsten finally returned my call. "Sorry it's taken me so long to call," she apologized. "Is your phone cool? Any chance the cops bugged it?"

"It's been here in Willow for the entire month of January, so I don't think anyone's done anything to it," I said. My mom had given it back to me when I'd gotten home on Saturday, and as far as I could tell, it had been in a drawer in the kitchen since I'd left for Sheridan on New Year's Day. "What in the world did you do to Mischa?"

Kirsten chuckled. "It was actually *her* idea. We couldn't come up with any story to explain where she'd been for the past month that wouldn't lead the police directly to my apartment, and honestly, between student loan collectors and my ex-boyfriend, I don't need that kind of drama in my life. Mischa said she had the biggest mouth on earth, so she suggested that I put some kind of spell on her to just wipe her memory completely clean."

"You must have mad skills," I complimented her. "I'm impressed."

"I can't take all the credit. My boss helped. That kind of spell casting is next level. Way over my head," Kirsten explained. "You guys didn't pick up on Friday when I called!"

"Yeah, it was kind of a bad time," I said. I'd been hearing the rumble of the avalanche in my dreams at night, and even though conquering Violet had been nerve-wracking, completely recovering from the horror of being buried alive in snow was a new source of nightmares. "Sorry about that."

"Listen. Remember when we last spoke, you were asking me if there was a way I could find out all of the different spells that had been cast on that girl Violet? Like to try to peel them back and figure out what had been mixed together?"

"Yes," I said. "I think we figured out most of it. Violet's grandmother cast a fertility spell on her mom, and then whatever Trey's mom did out of spite probably subverted it."

"You're on the right track," Kirsten said excitedly. "I had to do a ton of research to figure out how to do this because it's pretty out of the ordinary. But I put a spell on a pair of glasses and asked them to show me all of the magic involved. And here's what I got. The grand-mother cast a very basic spell asking the souls of the three daughters who had died before Violet was born to safeguard her life. To honor those souls, she planted three things—"

"Rosebushes," I clarified.

"Yes, that makes sense," Kirsten said. "I couldn't make out what they were, but that sounds right. So check this out. When the interacting spell was cast, presumably the one that your boy-friend's mom put together, those three rosebushes were turned into, like, *portals*. So it wasn't the souls of the daughters who were demanding sacrifices. It was whatever evil thing had passed through the portal, all of which was made possible because your boyfriend's mom dabbled in witchcraft while she was angry, which is a big no-no."

"But . . ." I tried to wrap my mind around all of this. "There were five of those things, whatever they were. I saw them."

"Sure. The grandmother planted two more at some point. Spells aren't just a thing that you say once and then they're over. A spell can be like a living entity if it doesn't have a defined end point. Once it's put into play, it just keeps growing however it was designed to grow. So probably if you planted another rosebush in the same place as the other five, then you'd have *six* of those things demanding a sacrifice every month. It would have been different if it had been a love spell or something, where the person falls in love and then the desired out-come has been achieved and then it's over. The spell your boyfriend's mom cast was pretty open-ended."

I shuddered at the memory of seeing those five otherworldly *things* in the reflection of Trey's ski goggles. "Well, luckily, we ended it. Violet was just at my house, and we were talking about it. The new moon passed and no one died, so it's over."

Kirsten was quiet for a moment, long enough to stress me out. "That's why I called you on Friday. God, I wish you'd picked up. If those rosebushes are still in the ground, growing and receiving moonlight every night, then the spell may have changed, but I don't think it's over."

I refused to believe that after the lengths I'd gone to, the spell still wasn't broken. "Impossible. We saved everyone Violet predicted deaths for, her mom's still alive, and *she's* still alive. It's over," I insisted, even though my fingers were going numb with fear.

"I really think you guys need to uproot those bushes. At a minimum," Kirsten insisted. "And even *that* might not be enough. Spells cast with serious intention are *durable*. I know this isn't exactly good news, but you're just gonna have to be kind of vigilant for a while. Keep your eyes open and your ears peeled for weirdness, because if I'm right, that magic is going to continue to thrive one way or another."

I thanked her for taking such good care of Mischa and sat down on the edge of my bed with a heavy heart. I called Violet, and she didn't answer, so I left a garbled and rambling voice mail asking her to have her landscapers uproot the rosebushes in her garden. When Mom arrived home from Green Bay with the great news that she'd landed a meeting with the judge the next morning, it was hard to pretend I was excited.

Violet texted me later in the day and promised that she'd deal with the rosebushes. Even though I believed her, I tossed and turned that night because of Kirsten's suggestion that that still might not be enough. I couldn't bring myself to share this development with

Henry, Trey, or Mischa. I hoped I wasn't being reckless or selfish by deciding to wait and see if there were signs that the curse wasn't yet completely broken.

It just seemed too cruel to inform them that there was a chance we still weren't done.

EPILOGUE

THE COURT HAS JUST ABOUT HAD ENOUGH OF your outlandish antics, young lady," the judge told me on Tuesday morning. I kept my eyes focused on my hands folded in my lap, too tired and grateful to have gotten to spend the weekend at home at my house to challenge him. "This latest little escapade caused by you and your lover boy has cost the state of Michigan quite a pretty penny, and authorities there would be delighted to have me lock you up as an adult and throw away the key for a few years."

Mr. Whaley, the attorney that my mother had hired, a balding, potbellied guy she'd found in Suamico, cleared his throat to speak. We were in the judge's private chambers instead of in the courtroom, negotiating the next phase of my punishment in private. "Your honor, we would like to propose that Miss Brady be entrusted to the care of her father in Tampa, Florida, until her eighteenth birthday."

The judge reviewed the proposal that Mr. Whaley had put together with input from my mother while I sat in respectful silence. He clucked his tongue and stroked his chin, considering my fate. My mom's boyfriend, Glenn, had insisted on coming with us, and he squeezed my mom's hand tightly. I was happy that she'd found someone to support her throughout the chaos I'd inflicted on her life. I didn't believe for a second that the judge was going to go for the Florida proposal, and was prepared to be delivered back to my dank room at Sheridan the next day. Whether I spent the next few months at a reform school or in Florida didn't matter much; both would feel like prisons because I wouldn't be able to see Trey. If we were separated, geographic distance between us wouldn't matter. If he was going to be in northern Wisconsin, I might as well be sent to Charon, the largest moon of Pluto.

"We'll give this a limited trial," the judge finally said, not sounding convinced that he thought it was a good idea. Mr. Whaley had communicated to me and my mother that Sheridan wasn't particularly interested in taking me back, which surely had to have been a factor in Judge Roberts's ruling. The judge turned to me and continued, "You've got until the end of the school year to prove that you can conduct yourself in a responsible fashion and uphold decent grades living in your father's community."

A sob of joy escaped from my mother. She smiled at me and exclaimed, "That's great news, isn't it, honey?" I nodded, overwhelmed by the idea of being a new kid at a new school in a new state within a matter of days. It would be temporary, I reminded myself. I was still putting a lot of hope into the idea that we'd broken the curse and Mischa was back in school at St. Patrick's, so whatever I'd have to endure for the next few months would be worth it.

The judge ran us through the details of his decision. My mother would have to sign paperwork that afternoon granting my father temporary full parental custody of me. I would have to fly to Tampa before Friday and get the heck out of Wisconsin; no dillydallying around Willow would be tolerated. My father would have to meet me at the airport and sign for my release from the airline staff, Mom would have to register my enrollment at the local high school in Tampa with the court in Shawano County, and my new high school in Tampa would have to be made fully aware of my history. The court was retaining the right to check in with the administrators at my new high school at their discretion, and could request to see my performance and behavioral records whenever they wanted.

"You'd better be planning on maintaining perfect attendance," Judge Roberts warned me as I stood up from my chair. "Don't give me any reason whatsoever to suspect that you're up to no good down there."

My mother was bubbling with excitement as we left the judge's private office. Although she was still furious with me, the statement that Violet had written and presented to the judge in defense of Trey and me seemed to have convinced my mom that maybe there *was* a good—if perhaps kind of incredible—reason for our high-stakes adventures over the last three months. Since Judge Roberts had announced that he'd reviewed a statement written by Violet Simmons, I'd wondered just exactly what that girl had put in her letter. It was crazy to think I'd ever be allowed to read it, or that I'd see her anytime soon enough to ask her, myself.

As we stepped into the cool hallway of the courthouse, my breath caught in my throat when my eyes landed on Trey. I hadn't known he was going to be there that day, presumably also meeting with Judge Roberts about revising the punishment he'd been issued back in November. Miserable, he sat in between his mother and Walter.

When he looked up and saw me, I fell into the aquamarine pools of his eyes, and the rest of the world dropped away.

"Hey," he said, rising to his feet.

"Trey," his mother warned, urging him to sit back down.

"Hey," I said back shyly, ignoring his mother. "You saw Mischa on TV, right?"

He glanced over his shoulder in the direction of his parents. "I haven't been allowed to watch."

"She's safe," I said as tears formed in my eyes. I placed my hands on his forearms just to touch him, to feel connected to him. "She's alive and back at home."

A slow smile formed on Trey's lips, and he nodded in approval. "Are they sending you back to Sheridan?" he asked. He was wearing his one and only suit, the same one he'd worn to Olivia's and Candace's wakes, as well as to our previous fun encounters with Judge Roberts back in the fall. It still looked as absurd on him as if he were wearing a space suit or a Halloween costume.

"Florida," I told him. "My dad's house."

Just then, a uniformed security guard opened one of the double doors of the courtroom and announced, "Emory," summoning Trey and his parents for their hearing with the judge.

Trey wrapped his arms around me and whispered in my ear, "Wait for me," before his mother yanked him into the courtroom to learn his fate. I didn't know whether or not Violet had kept her word about speaking with her father on Trey's behalf. She'd texted me a photo of her garden after the rosebushes had been dug up early that morning, so at least she had taken to heart my request to deal with that and hadn't wasted any time. But she hadn't included any sort of message, which was fine with me. Although we had sort of reconciled, I didn't have any desire to keep in touch with her on friendly terms.

I more or less got my answer about whether or not Trey would be returning to Northern Reserve when I saw Walter Emory's Hyundai pull out of the driveway next door the next morning with Trey buckled into the front passenger seat. I knew from experience that we wouldn't be allowed to talk on the phone during the first full week of his readmission there, so it would be a long, painful wait until I could hear from him firsthand whether or not his sentence had been changed.

Even though I cried like a baby on my flight to Tampa at the thought of not seeing Trey again until July, when he turned eighteen, Florida turned out not to be so bad. By the time I arrived, Rhonda and Dad had already gotten my room ready for me, and Dad had taken the liberty of buying me a new laptop for school. They were in full-tilt super-parent overdrive, asking me tons of questions and making all kinds of promises of weekend road trips we'd take together to keep me in positive spirits about my new surroundings. It was weird to sleep in a perfectly normal, not-haunted bedroom.

I tried to seem as appreciative and positive as possible for Dad and Rhonda's benefit and grinned at every suggestion they made of airboat rides and visits to crocodile farms. When I was finally told by one of the administrators at Northern Reserve that Trey's phone privileges were being resumed two weeks after he arrived back on campus, I couldn't wait until that Wednesday evening, when he would be allowed to call me.

"July," he informed me proudly. "If I'm a good little soldier and don't mess anything up, I'll be free to walk out of here on my birthday."

I knew in my heart that as soon as Trey was permitted to leave his school, he'd make his way to Florida to be with me. Playing by the rules in Florida was my plan, no matter how much I missed home and regretted everything that had happened so far that year.

At my new school, it seemed like all of my new classmates had some kind of strange intuition that I was suddenly among them due to suspicious circumstances (even though Dad had assured me that I was not nearly as much of a nightly news star in Florida as I was in the Midwest). Life in Florida was still unfamiliar and new, but I chatted with Henry frequently on WhatsApp, although we were both careful not to discuss details of what we'd done in Michigan. The story he'd told the police in Michigan was that he'd just happened to be skiing down the slope at Stevens' Pass when the avalanche occurred. He insisted he'd been totally oblivious that kids from his hometown, including Trey and me, had been on that part of the mountain that afternoon.

Knowing that he was lucky to have gotten out of Michigan without being punished for aiding and abetting runaways, he made fast plans to get himself out of the Midwest. Confident that he'd avenged Olivia's death, he signed up to teach tennis at a fancy resort in the South of France. He jetted off for what he hoped would be the adventure of a lifetime, with every intention of continuing his college studies at Northwestern in the fall. I didn't mention anything to him about my last conversation with Kirsten, and prayed that she didn't reach out to him directly. I considered it a small mercy instead of an act of deceit to let him enjoy his time in France without burdening him with the knowledge that Kirsten suspected the curse was still active in one way or another.

Strangely enough, surviving the avalanche together and participating in the game of Light as a Feather, Cold as Marble made Cheryl and me closer friends than ever before. Using carefully chosen words in text messages, we both shared our experiences of bad dreams about being buried in snow. Of course, Cheryl was sensitive enough not to ask me about the pendulum I'd used during the game we'd played with Violet (I was still a little paranoid about my parents spying on my private communication). There were a lot of things I'd done back in the fall that I regretted, but mistreating Cheryl and not valuing her as a friend was right up there alongside agreeing to play Light as a Feather, Stiff as a Board at Olivia's birthday party when Violet had suggested it. Cheryl was the best kind of friend anyone could ever hope to have, and I knew I wouldn't soon forget that.

Mischa didn't hold back at all once she finally realized that I had unrestricted use of my phone in Florida. I'd waited for her to contact me rather than reaching out to her first, not wanting to accidentally say something that broke the memory spell that Kirsten had put on her to make her forget her time in hiding. It would have been understandable if she'd wanted to put the entire experience with Violet behind her, and never again dwell on the horrible weeks she'd spent believing that she could die at any moment. But as soon as I posted to Instagram from Tampa for the first time, she sent me an uncharacteristically long message.

> OMG, McKenna! I've been trying to figure out
> what happened to you guys, but the news of your
> sentences was only revealed for the first time in
> the Willow Gazette today! Florida? I am so jelly!

How is getting a tan and drinking coconut water considered a punishment? So not fair!

Anyway, it's weird to be back at school. Everyone treats me strangely now because of the amnesia, and my trauma counselor constantly asks me weird stuff to try to trigger memories. She believes that I endured horrible things while I was missing that I've blocked out. I can't explain it, but I really don't think anything bad happened to me while I was gone. I still have no idea where I was all that time, but a couple weird things have happened in the last few weeks that make me wonder exactly what I was doing and who I was with!

One of the weird things is that there's this girl in my lunch period who always has a deck of tarot cards with her, and the first time she did a spread for me I somehow knew what all the meanings of the cards were. How is that even possible? Where would I have learned all that? The girl at my school said that everyone has a tarot card that aligns to their personality and it has special meaning when it comes up in their spreads.

She had everyone who sits at our table try to find their special card by pulling one from the deck. Sometimes people didn't like the first card they chose and tried again to get another one. But I pulled the same card every single time! It's the Tower. When it appears in a spread upright, it's supposed to mean broken pride, or disaster. When it shows up upside down, that's called a reversal, and it means delayed disaster or fear of suffering. Funny that it should keep popping up for me as my personal card, right?

Anyway, this girl is going to teach me how to do readings because she thinks it's cool that I can always pick the Tower out of the deck no matter how she shuffles the stack. Next time I see you, I'll read your cards for you!

My heart was beating so hard as I tapped my phone to call Mischa that I believed there was a good chance I'd go into cardiac arrest before she answered. Very annoyingly, my call went straight to her voice mail.

Mischa's message was shockingly similar to the story Violet had told me about how she'd discovered the powers she'd acquired through the curse by playing with cards at school. I should have known—*we* should have known—that Violet's spirits would outsmart us. Just as Kirsten had told me, we hadn't broken the curse, we'd just changed the spell. Because we'd tricked the spell into bypassing Mischa, she'd inherited it. *She will always be next*, Jennie had told me.

And just like the spirits had tricked Violet into believing at first that her evil power was a fun new talent, they were doing the same thing to Mischa. She was probably unknowingly assigning deaths to everyone around her, and she had to be stopped.

★ GOOD BYE ★

ACKNOWLEDGMENTS

The original draft of this sequel was written online for my Wattpad readers who had been asking about Mischa's destiny and whether or not McKenna would restore her friendship with Cheryl. It delighted me that everyone was just as interested in the strength of my characters' friendships as they were in McKenna's romantic relationship with Trey because this story is, at its heart, about a girl doing whatever it takes to save her friend's life.

Although this version of the sequel is different—and I think better—than the online version, my readers' investment in these characters was my inspiration to keep writing. So, many thanks to @TatianaCanFly and @Schlag_girl for their beautiful fan art, @MissNoor, @DeaAspasia, @Katieisapenguin, @insha921 and so many more for your gorgeous book covers. Thank you to @TasonyaGray, @LGBTfantasy, @kaykay_is_vogue, @TaylorManton1, @SomeLikeitMalik, @tiffanygy, @edenae22, @mandyoysmoysoy, @Missbookaholic_4ever, @ash_lynn_18, @immakiller, @GeminiQueenRocks, @SGMitchell, @Starquinski, @sushinegirl29c, @BMadden18 and hundreds more of you who were my frequent commenters!

Special thanks to the team at Simon Pulse who helped me reimagine this next installment of McKenna's quest to make it more exciting and provide readers with a better understanding of how Violet came into her deadly powers. Jessi Smith's direction heightened the stakes for breaking the curse and shaped Henry Richmond into a stronger love interest for McKenna. I am so very grateful for Rebecca Vitkus's sharp eye as well as her familiarity with Wisconsin and the real towns on which Willow was based. And as always, I'd like to thank and acknowledge my high school English teacher, the late Sonia Kallick, and my French teacher, Kelly Ercoli, for encouraging me to dream beyond the edges of my small hometown.